THE DROWNED

A Novel by
Moniro Ravanipour

Translated from the Persian by
M. R. Ghanoonparvar

The Drowned

A Novel by **Moniro Ravanipour**

Translated from the Persian by **M. R. Ghanoonparvar**

© Moniro Ravanipour 2019

Moniro Ravanipour is hereby identified as author of this work in accordance with Section 77 of the Copyright, Design and Patents Act 1988

Cover and Layout: Kourosh Beigpour | ISBN: 9781081589165

Contents

TRANSLATOR'S FOREWORD

The Drowned is the translation of Moniro Ravanipour's first novel, *Ahl-e Gharq* (1989), which brought her overnight nationwide recognition in Iran a decade after the tumultuous Islamic Revolution and a year after the devastating Iran-Iraq War. In general, in this novel, Ravanipour taps the rich culture of southwestern Iran, the region most affected by the destruction of the war, and more specifically, that of Jofreh, the village of her birth, and its inhabitants' lives, customs, beliefs, superstitions, and struggles for survival.

Many critics have described *The Drowned* as a novel in the mode of magic realism, and it may in some respects qualify as such.[1] More importantly, however, is that this novel is a story of the author's village of birth and the people of that village, which was established sometime in the late nineteenth or early twentieth century by a small group of people who migrated from another part of Iran and lived for several decades in relative isolation until the second half of the twentieth century. Finally, the onslaught of modernization and industrialization as well as political events and developments not

---

1- For an enlightening and insightful assessment of this novel in English, see: Nasrin Rahimieh, "Magical Realism in Moniru Ravanipur's *Ahl-e Gharq*," *Iranian Studies* 23, no. 1/4 (1990): 61-75.

only forced the people of the village out of isolation, but devoured the village and changed Jofreh into a neighborhood of the nearby city of Bushehr.

While magic realism may describe many aspects of this novel, from a broader perspective, with its central hero, *The Drowned* is a modern epic in which Ravanipour records not only the short life of the village but also its mythology and history. In a sense, the book immortalizes the place and the people of her birth and childhood which, for all intents and purposes, no longer exist.

Jofreh is also featured in a number of stories in Ravanipour's *Kanizu* (1988) and *Sangha-ye Sheytan* (1991), the latter translated into English as *Satan's Stones*.[2] In her third collection of short stories, *Siriya, Siriya* (1993), she explores the mythology of other small communities in Iran, such as the northern island of Ashradeh and the Persian Gulf islands of Hengam and Qeshm. *The Drowned* is the fourth volume of Ravanipour's work translated into English. After the success of *The Drowned*, Ravanipour published two other novels, *Del-e Fulad* [Heart of Steel] in 1990 and *Kowli Kenar-e Atash* [Gypsy by the Fire] in 1999, in Iran.[3]

Since 2007, when she was invited to serve as an International Writers Project fellow at Brown University, Ravanipour has been living in the United States. She was also a writer in residence at the Black Mountain Institute's City of Asylum, University of Nevada, Las Vegas, for three years. Despite her work being banned in Iran since 2006, not only has her national status in Iran not diminished, but also, she now enjoys an international reputation, her work having been translated and published in many different languages, including Arabic, Chinese, French, German, Kurdish, Swedish, and Turkish.

2- For an English translation of *Kanizu*, see: Moniro Ravanipour, *Kanizu* (Costa Mesa, CA: Mazda Publishers, 2004), edited by M. R. Ghanoonparvar; and for an English translation of *Sangha-ye Sheytan*, see: Moniro Ravanipour, *Satan's Stones* (Austin: University of Texas Press, 1996), edited by M. R. Ghanoonparvar.

3- *Del-e Fulad* was retitled and translated into English as *Afsaneh* by Rebecca Joubin in 2014 (Bethesda, MD: Ibex Publishers).

A list of the main characters of the village of Jofreh and their connection to one another in this novel has been provided at the end of the volume.

I am most grateful to Ms. Ravanipour for clarifying some of the local Bushehri terms and expressions with which not all speakers of the Persian language are familiar. I would also like to thank Matthew O'Brien for his assistance in copyediting and Bita Gholamali for checking the English text against the original. As always, I am most indebted to my wife Diane for her critical insight and painstaking editing of this translation.

THE DROWNED

With gratitude to my cousins:
Khadar Rahnema, an elementary teacher in Gonaveh, and
Naser Gharibzadeh, a fisherman in the Jofreh Sea

The old man writhed in pain and looked confused and lost. I wanted to know to what extent the illness that was plundering his life was toying with his mind and memory. I said: "Papa, recite a poem, so you can go back to sleep." With a tongue that had become heavy, he recited:

I'd give my all for the color of your face
And give my all for your blue dress

I hear you cannot sleep without me
I'd give my all for your eyes, and for your sleeplessness

My mother, a sixty-two year old woman, was standing there. She was wearing a blue dress, and she had stayed awake all night until morning beside my father. My father wept, and with the same heavy tongue said: "I recite it for your mother."

This book is a gift to the lovers in this world

❖ 1 ❖

The first person to see the mermaid did not dare let herself be seen. Bubuni was standing behind the window facing the village road. When she heard the sound, thinking that it was Captain Ali coming back from Mama Mansur's house, she picked up the lantern and put it in the window. The road was empty, empty and quiet. Bubuni turned, looked toward the sea, and froze. It was her, the mermaid! On the sea, tambourine in hand, she was jingling and jingling it and dancing, her long blue hair spilling across the gentle waves of the sea. Bubuni closed her eyes, said a prayer under her breath, and looked again. When she heard the jingling sound even louder than before, and as she saw the seagulls twist and arc in the sky over Jofreh, she knew she was not mistaken.

It was getting dark. The moon, dusty and despondent, sat in the sky. The sea was filled with inhabitants, blue denizens of the waters. They were dancing. Sea lanterns hung on the masts of ships that had dropped anchor in the cove. Sometimes, one of the little blue mermaids would go to a lantern and turn its wick up higher. The jingling sound of the mermaids' tambourines fluttered in the sky over Jofreh, and Bubuni feared that Captain Ali might be stuck on the road, and that the blue ones would whisk him away and take him to the bottom of the sea. The doors and windows of the houses were all shut. Not even a drop of light could be seen through the layers of the palm-branch huts. It was as though no human being lived in the village of Jofreh. Bubuni knew that by then, the whole village had seen them. The mermaids, lanterns in hand, were coming toward the shore. Bubuni thought, "Oh protector saint of lonely strangers! I hope they aren't going to take Jofreh to the bottom of the sea."

And then came the sound of religious salutations to the Prophet and his family. Bubuni took out her talismans and, like all the women of Jofreh, hung them in the window, threw a handful of salt in the charcoal brazier, and the mermaids disappeared.

At night, on the doors of the huts and on the deer antlers hanging over the houses, small and large lanterns were lit. The villagers gathered in the house of Zayer[4] Ahmad Hakim. The village was jubilant. Busalmeh, the ugly-faced denizen of the seas, was wedding one of the mermaids, and he was placing the largest pearl of the sea into the mouth of a tiny fish, so that the denizens of the land, who would send their most handsome young man to play the reed flute to wish him a happy wedding, would find that pearl and forever be freed from the daily struggle for bread.

The village was jubilant. The women put on their most beautiful petticoats, all eyes sparkled, and no one but Madineh, the wife of Zayer Ahmad, thought about the moon that sat dusty and despondent in the sky.

Zayer Ahmad's stucco house was beside the sea, with two doors, a big one that looked south toward Mecca and a small one that faced the sea. On winter nights, when the sea was restless and Busalmeh was wrathful, the waves would roll over the water cistern,[5] which was quite a ways from the small door. It was a big water cistern, and its belly held enough water for the entire year.

4- Or Za'er, literally "pilgrim," is an honorific used in southern Iran for males who have made a pilgrimage to one of the Shi'ite holy shrines.
5- In Persian, *abanbar*, a traditional water reservoir, generally made of bricks or stones with an aboveground structure leading to the underground storage area, found in many neighborhoods of most cities and many villages.

The men, old and young, were sitting all around Zayer Ahmad Hakim on the top of the water cistern. He was the *hakim*, the medicine man. Zayer Ahmad had pushed back his skullcap, and sat thinking on a soft, white straw mat.

Captain Ali sat next to Mansur, facing Zayer Ahmad, his eyes sparkling. He was restless; he wanted to speak, to say something. Zayer Ahmad's silence was tormenting him.

"Tomorrow is the full moon, Zayer..."

Zayer Ahmad looked at him. A gleeful smile welled up in his amber eyes. He knew that the village men were waiting. Sooner or later, Jofreh would take on a different hue. A new life was beginning; there would be no sign of poverty and sickness. Busalmeh would take care of the village. Busalmeh—who always sank the most handsome and daring young fishermen down into the sea, who was always irate over the affection the mermaids held for the young fishermen—from now on would leave the village alone. Darkness is defeated in the face of kindness and love. It is quite possible that a mermaid would be able to tame Busalmeh to the end of the earth, to the time when the land is submersed in water, to heal his black heart and wash away the rust of his wrath. It could really happen that Busalmeh would take on a human character and temperament, learn the ways of love, and make life easy for the fishermen of Jofreh.

Impatient with Zayer Ahmad's silence, Mansur sighed:

"What a pity. How could she consent to marry Busalmeh?"

Zayer Ahmad frowned. Quickly and sharply, he stared into Mansur's eyes. All those who heard him looked at him, stunned and dumbfounded. Mansur was taken aback; he was terrified, and hiding behind Captain Ali, he diverted his eyes.

Any word that angered Busalmeh or made the mermaid change her mind would end in the obliteration of Jofreh. Anyone who had any opinion was not supposed to state it out loud. The denizens of the seas were not supposed to hear the young men's complaints about this union.

Mansur knew all this. He was young, and the only one left out of seven sons. The others had been swallowed up by the sea two years earlier.

Mansur bit his lip because of the few words that had suddenly slipped from his mouth! He called on the earth and sky and seagulls as witnesses that he had never been in love, nor pawned his heart for the love of any mermaid. Mansur repented; a thousand times he repented. He feared that Busalmeh had heard his voice. He feared that he would mark him, and on a voyage to the sea, he would take him down into the depths of the gray waters. But Busalmeh was listening to the sound of human hearts, and he knew that Mansur had never been in love.

Large beads of sweat covered Mansur's forehead. Slender-waist tea glasses were being emptied and filled. The women waited in the courtyard and on the stairs to the water cistern. There was not a sound but the pleasant sound of the bubbling of the hookahs.

All the villagers knew they must not show their happiness. They all knew that the mermaids had submitted to this union by force, that the mermaids would become angry at the happiness of the village, that their blue hearts would turn red, and that when the mermaids turned red, they sank the ships.

Among the women, Madineh was the only one who knew why the moon was dusty and despondent, and why the sea waters were slowly rising. For sure, somewhere among the coral in the depths of the green waters, that little blue mermaid was weeping, moaning, hidden from Busalmeh's eyes. Smoking the hookah, Madineh turned her face away so that the other women wouldn't see the grief in her eyes.

Zayer Ahmad coughed. The village men were familiar with that signal. Everyone held his breath. They could hear the fluttering of the seagulls. The sea was calm, and the sky near.

"After seventy years, once again a page is turning in this world. Seventy years ago, one of the mermaids died on the occasion of her wedding. Not here, but in the Fekseno Sea. The sea fairy died because no young man agreed to play the reed flute for her. No one went to her wedding. But this time, I am sure there will be someone who will go to the threshold, to the sea."

Zayer Gholam, an old man who wore a loincloth tied at his waist and whose upper body was bare, hesitantly puffed on his hookah, cleared his chest, and in a raspy and fearful voice, said:

"Zayer Ahmad, we must go north, near Jinn-Haunted Cove. That's where Busalmeh's wedding will be."

"What an awful thought, such a place for..."

It was Mansur. He swallowed the rest of his sentence. It was unclear what creature had gotten under Mansur's skin and was talking so abruptly through his mouth.

Was there anyone who did not know where Jinn-Haunted Cove was? Time and time again, in the dark nights and cold winters of the village, he had heard the drums and pipes of the jinn coming from Jinn-Haunted Cove. No fisherman steered his boat near Jinn-Haunted Cove. No man was brave enough to get close to Jinn-Haunted Cove. Only once, years ago, when the Jofreh Sea was still unknown to the villagers, had Zayer Gholam steered his boat there. Later on, when he finally was able to talk in the village men's gathering, he told Zayer Ahmad:

"I heard the voice of a woman singing. I thought maybe one of the village women had gone crazy around sunset and had gone to the sea. When I got closer, the voice got quieter. It wasn't clear what she was saying, but her voice sounded sad. It was as if her hands and feet were chained at the bottom of the sea. I looked and looked, but saw no one. But when I dropped anchor, the voice said, 'Young man, leave this place!' It was her voice. I laughed and said, 'Is now the time to leave?' The words were still in my mouth when a woman emerged from under the water. Her two eyes were like blazing fire. She kept staring at me, and then slapped me so hard I was knocked unconscious."

Mansur suddenly felt a chill. He curled up and hid even more behind Captain Ali. Zayer Gholam was looking at him reproachfully, and Mansur did not want to get into an argument with Zayer Gholam.

The villagers knew what Zayer Gholam was like. He was Jofreh's chanter of religious songs. Sometimes, he would open the flap of his loincloth in front of the children, and the children would run away. When he sang, his testicles would swell up. On such occasions, Jofreh's nosy children would sit facing him to watch the swelling of his testicles from a distance. The women of the village would not make a peep in front of him. Zayer Gholam was ready at any moment to open his loincloth in front of the men and women and send them all running.

Before Zayer Gholam had gone to Jinn-Haunted Cove, he had been a calm and quiet man. Like all the village men, he fished, and he lived with his wife and his only daughter, Nabati, in a palm-branch hut. But after the aquatic jinn Yal had lured him to Jinn-Haunted Cove with her voice, he completely changed. He began to sing. He tossed off his clothing and only wore a loincloth. Hoping to appease Yal, he stopped going to the sea for a long time. He hung around the village women. Associating with the women made him a jokester, and a year later, when his wife died in childbirth and Zayer Gholam saw that Yal had taken his wife's liver at night and was washing it in the sea, he breathed a sigh of relief. Yal would no longer bother him.

Mansur was afraid, afraid of Zayer Gholam, and of Yal; as soon as someone would approach Jinn-Haunted Cove, Yal would come to the village at night in the alleyways to sniff out the liver of a pregnant woman. Was there anyone in the village who didn't know that Yal gave women's livers to Busalmeh, for him to put at the bottom of the sea for himself and sing in Jinn-Haunted Cove?

Captain Ali understood how Mansur felt. He could read the men's minds; he knew what they were thinking. He, too, was afraid of Jinn-Haunted Cove, even though for many years Bubuni had been living in his house without bearing a child. So, to break the string of fear in the village men's minds, he said:

"So now, who will play the reed flute?"

Zayer Ahmad looked toward the corner of the water cistern. Mahjamal smiled upon his glance, as though he had been waiting for, as though he had been anticipating, that very gesture.

Mahjamal was tall and broad-shouldered. No one really knew about his origins and his lineage. He was twenty years old. He had a darkish face and two strange blue eyes. The women of Jofreh, who were used to making up stories about every little thing, in their chitter-chatter attributed his parentage to a gypsy woman who one day at sunset, dead tired, separated from her tribe without saying a word to come to the sea and lay down her burden on the tiny waves of the beach and the damp sand, and leave without anyone seeing her.

And now, the men of the village, the young girls, and the women who had grown old with their memories looked at Mahjamal and waited with bated breath.

Everything was already both clear and unclear. Mahjamal had to go. Had to. It was what the village expected of Mahjamal, the command that was screaming in everyone's mind. But what if he would not agree to go? What if he disregarded the "had to"? What if he decided to disobey? Doubt and suspicion were nesting in their hearts, and everything, similar to Mahjamal's presence, his twenty-year presence in the village, was uncertain and up in the air. For twenty years, he both was and was not in the village. He had no roots here; and he himself had not wanted to surrender his heart to the soil of the village, as though he were not of the land.

"Aha! Mahjamal!"

Zayer Ahmad's voice relieved the young village men. They suddenly let go of their breaths, and a faint smile appeared on their faces. Mahjamal lifted his head, his eyes gazing into Zayer Ahmad's.

"When are we leaving?"

Mahjamal and his same old ways! It was always like this; with a single utterance, he would end the story.

The sound of the women's ululations echoed far and wide. The men slapped Mahjamal's shoulders in gratitude. Mahjamal stood up, walked over to Zayer Ahmad, kissed his hand, and prostrated himself toward Mecca. Mansur suddenly felt depressed. He liked Mahjamal; he had gotten used to him.

"Now, what if Mahjamal doesn't come back?"

Zayer Gholam's scowl silenced him. In the hearts of the village men, there was a secret that even the women, with all their gossip, would never talk about openly. And perhaps Mahjamal did not know this secret. Joy and excitement do not nest in the eyes of a person who is conscious of his own impending death. He would not return.

Busalmeh, the ugly-faced denizen of the seas, would never allow the most handsome denizen of the land to see his bride and then return to the land. Mermaids had frequently fallen in love with young fishermen, but never had they easily given their hearts to a union with Busalmeh; and now Mahjamal was going to go, so that the village would gain its largest pearl, and Busalmeh, his old wish.

The villagers stayed in Zayer Ahmad Hakim's house into the late hours of the night. When the moon, high and dusty, sat behind the palm trees, the people left one by one, to enjoy dreaming about their pearl. Mahjamal stayed in Zayer Ahmad's house.

It had taken Zayer Ahmad a long time to accept Mahjamal's presence in the village. In contrast, Madineh respected him. Madineh, who in the first days of their migration to and settling in Jofreh had lost all her consciousness and senses of the land, seemed to recognize the scent of Mahjamal. The story went back to many years earlier, before anyone yet knew about the Jofreh Sea. Madineh, the lonely girl from Fekseno whose feet had blistered from the journey and their migration, one day sat looking at the sea, entrusting her blistered feet to the cool seawater; and free from all that had passed, she listened to the ripples of the sea. The wind that blew in from the sea toyed with her youthful black hair. For a moment, Madineh closed her tired hazel eyes and abandoned her fair-like-the-moon round face to the sea breeze, when suddenly she was startled by the sound of a pair of hands splitting the surface of the water and moving toward her. She opened her eyes. A little blue mermaid rose out of the sea. Smiling, the mermaid got herself to the edge of the sea. The silly little mermaid, who had seen some hustle and bustle on the shore, in order to figure out the ways of the world, accompanied Madineh to the village, which was not yet a village. Madineh took her to the little palm hut that the village men had built for her; and in order to forget the pain of being away from home and to have the mermaid get used to staying with her, she closed the door of the hut on the mermaid, without remembering that if mermaids stay on dry land for too long, their fish halves dry up, their little hearts stop beating, and with a sigh toward the sea, they die. A month later, Zayer Ahmad Hakim, then fifteen years old, and his maternal uncle brought out the little mermaid that had been kept away from the sea, and returned it to the sea. From then on, Madineh, who had lost all her consciousness and senses of the land, told the village women tales from the sea that the little mermaid had told her over the course her month-long stay, hoping that she might put Madineh to sleep for a moment and thus flee from her hands of the land.

Now, distraught by the sea and the mermaids, Madineh could smell the salty scent of the sea, even from the other side of the world. She regarded Mahjamal as a sign from the sea, a man who had risen out of the sea and had no connection with the gypsies of the land.

But eventually, Zayer Ahmad's mind succumbed to the women's stories. Six years had passed since the day they had found Mahjamal by the sea, in the year of the famine, when Mahjamal came running to Zayer Ahmad and said that Zayer's boat was going to catch fire before it reached the offing of the sea. It was a newly-built boat that was due to embark on its first sea voyage a week later. When the boat caught fire—a boat that was viewed by the villagers as the source of their daily bread and sustenance and which was supposed to travel to faraway lands—when all the worldly possessions of the people of Jofreh turned into ashes, Zayer Ahmad Hakim, who was always frustrated by the women's chatter, believed that Mahjamal was a gypsy and fortuneteller through and through.

From then on, from the moment the image of the burning boat was imprinted on the minds of the village men, the fishermen, who never put their hearts into their work out of fear of Busalmeh, would head out to sea upon a single word uttered from Mahjamal's mouth; and Mahjamal grew up, growing taller and taller, on the sand and in the corners of the huts, or under the trees of the pomegranate orchard behind Zayer Ahmad's house, or in the palm grove.

No one bothered about him; not even now that he was becoming a man and his golden mustache was covering up his strange smile did anyone bother about setting him up with a life and a living, and, in exchange for his many years of service to the village, building a shelter for him.

Also, Mahjamal never set his heart in one place. Every night in a different place and every moment in a different mood, he was looking for something, or searching for something, and what that was, he himself did not know. Perhaps if Madineh had not been there—Madineh who struggled to figure him out, to make this fifteen-year-old young man a denizen of the land like herself—he would have remained a wanderer forever.

Madineh, in search of a sea companion, opened her heart to Mahjamal with hints and disjointed words... She would tell him about the little blue mermaid, and about the land that ties everyone down. She would tell him about the depths of the blue and green waters, and Mahjamal would remain silent, paying no attention to her, as though he did not understand Madineh's words. But Zayer Ahmad's wife would not give up. The scent of the sea and the scent of Mahjamal were one and the same.

In the end, Madineh ignited a fire in Mahjamal's heart, the heart of a young man who had never thought of anything but premonitions of the wind and rains that would bring turbulence to the Jofreh Sea, or thoughts and dreams of children not yet born whose names he already knew.

One day, on the top of that same water cistern, when the women had surrounded Mahjamal and were giggling, Madineh said:

"So, what is your fortune? What is written on your palm?"

And it was there that he looked at the palm of his hand, his eyes lit up, and he burst out laughing in disbelief. Five years had passed since that day. All that Mahjamal could think about and feel was the sea.

At twilight, Zayer Ahmad handed Mahjamal the reed flute and said:

"Don't play Fayez[6] songs, lest they become sorrowful and anger should overtake them. Do not go near the blue mermaids, and do not touch them... Busalmeh will blind the sea, and the gray waters of the sea will roll over the village."

In the morning, the village was awake at dawn. Bubuni was sitting on the ground with her oiled hair, wearing her lace-trimmed petticoat, milking a goat. Flour was being kneaded into dough in Mama Mansur's strong hands. The dough was rising. Kheyju, the eighteen-year-old daughter of Zayer Ahmad, was lighting the clay bread oven. The young village girls by the clay bread oven were poking at the flames of the fire restlessly, with their eyes on the sun, waiting for it to set. Below stood a row of round wooden bread pans waiting their turn, and Zayer Gholam's daughter, Nabati, in her perpetual silence, sat beside Kheyju on the stone seat by the bread oven. Kheyju, whose face was red from the flames, poked the fire in the bread oven and said, "He's leaving, Nabati."

"I know."

"Well, tell him. Do you think there's going to be bloodshed?"

"It's no use. He doesn't even know I exist."

"Then, who is he thinking about?"

"Nobody."

"Wouldn't it be better if you said something?"

6- Also known as Fa'ez, Dashti, or Dashtestani, was a 19th- and early 20th-century poet of southern Iran, whose lyrical love quatrains are extremely melancholic.

"My Papa will find out."

"What's he going to do, kill you?"

"Yeah. Mahjamal's a gypsy vagabond!"

"When it comes to matters of the heart, things like that don't make any difference."

Nabati fell silent. Madineh and Mama Mansur arrived with their bread pans. The girls got down, and Mama Mansur and Madineh sat on the platform beside the oven.

Mama Mansur was fat and fleshy, with a round face. Many years earlier, she had lost her man to the sea. The sea had also swallowed six of her seven sons; and for two years now, she could not bear to look at the sea. Every time she went along the village road that passed by the edge of the sea, she pulled her black headscarf over her face. She had broken up with the sea, with all the denizens of the sea, who had taken from her everything she had.

Mama Mansur placed the first chunk of dough on the back of the pan. Her hands beating the dough made a pleasant sound. Back when she was fourteen, she had captivated her man with the same pleasant-sounding beating of her hands. But now, every blow of her hands was a bitter reminder that stung her soul.

The chunk of dough was made into a round shape that was flattened into a bigger loaf. As she watched Mama Mansur's hands, Madineh placed her own hand into the pocket of the thick pad used for sticking the loaves to the inside wall of the oven. It was a good pretext to keep Mama Mansur from seeing the mist in her eyes, a melancholy mist that had found its way into her eyes since the night before. Madineh had lain awake all night until dawn. The distant sound of a mermaid that was weeping quietly had not let sleep come to her eyes.

When the chunk of dough was flattened to the size of a round loaf of flatbread, Madineh took it. She spread it on the bread pad and beat it with her palm to flatten it out even more; then, leaning over the oven, she stuck it to the oven wall. Mama Mansur was busy with another chunk of dough.

"When are they leaving, Madineh?"

"When it gets dark."

"Wouldn't it be better for them to set out at sundown?"

Madineh sighed. With her sleeve, she wiped her eyes, which were burning from the flames.

"I don't know... The blue ones aren't happy with this wedding. The red ones might raise some hell."

"With Busalmeh?"

"Yep. It isn't unlikely."

"I wish my Mansur wasn't going."

"I wish no one was going."

"The sea, the man-eating sea," Mama Mansur groaned under her breath, as she handed the rounded dough to Madineh. Madineh spread it out on the bread pad.

"Humans are prisoners, prisoners of their own breath."

At sundown, everything was ready. The men had lifted their anchors from the water. Zayer Ahmad's courtyard was filled with people. Kheyju was restlessly sitting beside Nabati on the stairs of the water cistern. Her voice trembled. She spoke in broken sentences. Like someone who is losing the moments as fast as the wind, like someone whose very being was fleeing her, fleeing toward the black sea.

"What do we want the pearl for? Go, go tell him."

"I can't! I just can't do it! Do you want the whole village to come crashing down on my head?"

"Then you must not really love him. Nothing is going on at the bottom of your heart."

"What do you mean, nothing? I thought you understood."

"No. I don't understand. If it was me, I'd drive the whole village off with a club, take Mahjamal by the hand, and just go away."

"Go where?"

"God's earth is big."

Bubuni, who was cracking and eating roasted melon seeds and was hanging around in the middle of the crowd, saw the two of them and came over laughing.

"Are you pouring your hearts out to each other, or talking behind other people's backs?"

"Neither; just about what's in our hearts," said Kheyju.

"Whose heart? Yours, or Nabati's?"

Nabati turned pale and her hands trembled. Kheyju looked at her and said:

"My heart."

"Who's the object?"

"What's it to you? Are you an interrogator or something?"

Bubuni laughed, and poured a handful of roasted melon seeds into their hands.

"Captain Ali is also going. I'm afraid."

"Tonight, they won't bother with humans."

"Poor Mahjamal. What a fate!"

Carrying a charcoal brazier filled with fire from which smoke of alum and wild rue was rising, Mama Mansur was circling around Mansur and crying. On the other side was Setareh and the other women, pouring kerosene into lanterns. Captain Ali at the corner of the water cistern, near the women, took the lantern from Setareh and lit it.

When she saw Captain Ali, Bubuni made her way through the

crowd, and put her hand on the edge of the water cistern. Bubuni was fuming. Captain Ali always hung around the women, and now he had come near them and in his own mind was doing something. Bubuni was furious:

"This is the first and last time I'm letting you go out to sea."

Captain Ali laughed:

"Tonight, the mermaids won't fall in love with any human. Rest assured."

"Now, who do you think you are for the mermaids to chase after you? Even on land, nobody pays any more attention to you than to a dog."

"But you do."

"The hell I do."

"Stop pestering me, woman! What if I don't come back?"

Bubuni, who was in the habit of sweeping all around the outside of her house every afternoon and sprinkling salt so the mermaids would not come close to her house or steal Captain Ali's wits away, swallowed her anger and said nothing. She was afraid Captain Ali would take her words to heart, afraid the mermaids would hear her quarrelling with Captain Ali, and, who knows, one of them might entrap him.

It was getting dark when the women took up their lit lanterns. Madineh swallowed her tears and raised her lantern high. The women ululated. Mahjamal, together with Zayer Ahmad, came out of the room with five sash windows. His eyes sparkled, as if he were not in the village. As if he couldn't see anyone. Someone shouted:

"Salutations to the Prophet and his family!"

The sound of loud salutations resonated throughout the village. The women made a pathway, holding their lanterns. Mahjamal had to pass through it. Kheyju was standing beside Nabati, lantern in hand.

"Nabati! When he passes in front of you, tell him he won't come back."

Nabati was silent, her lips trembling. Mahjamal was approaching, getting closer. It was as though the women of the village were seeing him for the first time. How quickly he had grown tall. What a short time he had stayed in the village. Had Mahjamal really lived among them? They had never seen a man of such grace and comeliness.

Bubuni sighed. She sighed all the while that Mahjamal was coming. She sighed for his youthfulness. How handsome Mahjamal was, what clear blue eyes he had, as if a thousand mermaids nested in them.

Setareh wiped her eyes; the sea had swallowed her husband, and in her mourning for her man, she had lamented so much that she had never been able to see Mahjamal.

The women's lips were quietly moving. Nabati was crying, her face covered with tears, as she was melting in her helplessness. Hesitation settled in the hearts. What a pity that tonight a man like Mahjamal would be enslaved at the hands of Busalmeh; what a pity for the village to be left without Mahjamal, without his forlorn presence.

But ultimately, necessity blocks the path of the human's temperament. Bread entraps him in its coils. The thought of that large pearl, the thought of life without Busalmeh's wrath and without pain or suffering, tied the tongues, even the tongue of Madineh, who cried all night until dawn remembering the mermaid.

Who ever wanted to be enslaved at the hands of Busalmeh until the end of his life? Enslaved to poverty and misery? Mahjamal was a vagabond gypsy; he did not have family or kinfolk, and most likely, he could not make head nor tail of such thoughts and concerns.

Nabati did not break her silence, and when Mahjamal reached the pair, Kheyju, with her face flushed and her large eyes restless, stood face-to-face with him and shouted:

"Mahjamal! You're not coming back, do you understand?

Busalmeh will kill you."

A hand from behind covered her mouth and took her away. The crowd became introspective, and Mahjamal laughed; he laughed without pain or suffering, a laugher that was not the laugher of a person who was heading to the place of his slaughter. He was unconcerned. He laughed unlike any human being.

Zayer Gholam yelled:

"Salutations to the Prophet and his family..."

The crowd's salutations grew even louder than before. The women handed the lanterns to the village men. Kheyju's lantern flickered inside her house.

The men hit the water. They held the lanterns high as they left. The women remained on the shore until late, until the men climbed into their boats, hoisted the anchors, and began rowing toward Jinn-Haunted Cove.

2

The moon had risen, and it was so bright that everything, even far away, was visible. Zayer Ahmad's boat was in the lead, and the others followed close behind.

Their eyes were watchful for the slightest swelling of the waves. The men rowed quietly, taking turns so that they could save their lives in the area where the red ones were likely to be present. The oars sank into the water quietly and slowly, and were raised out even more quietly. The moon, like a large golden tray, sat in the sky; there was no trace of the previous night's dust on its face, as though pretending to be happy out of fear of Busalmeh.

Occasionally, the sound of a sleepy bird came from afar. Nothing in the village was visible. It was as though on that side of the sea, a village called Jofreh had never existed, as though from the beginning, everything and everywhere was only water and more water.

They were approaching Jinn-Haunted Cove. The fluttering of seagulls' wings could be heard. On the other side, white birds were flying near the cove.

In Zayer Ahmad's boat, Mahjamal and Mansur took turns rowing. Zayer Ahmad sat on top of the hold. He was wearing a white *dishdasha.*[7] No woman's voice could be heard, no woman with her hands and feet in chains in the depths of Jinn-Haunted Cove. Perhaps Busalmeh had set her free. Perhaps Busalmeh had returned to her the joy of her heart.

Zayer Ahmad sat thinking. He feared that the sound of the reed flute would suddenly turn into weeping and wailing.

"Don't play sad Fayez songs, Mahjamal!"

"No..."

Mahjamal's voice was happy. Excitement rippled in his words, and Zayer Ahmad remembered that no one in the village had ever seen him sad. When you are without kith and kin, when you are not solidly rooted on the land with a father and mother and offspring, why would you be sad? Mahjamal was like a breeze that blew into the village, rustled the palm trees in the sweltering heat, and became the cool air in people's lives, without being seen or having a permanent place.

Now, as Zayer Ahmad thought of Mahjamal's twenty-year presence in Jofreh, he had doubts about him. He had never seen him cry or complain, get sick, or sigh, yearning for things he wanted to have. It was as though he was not a denizen of the land. As though he did not know human needs.

They were moving away from the offing of the sea. Far off, they saw the flock of white birds sitting on the calm surface of the water, and sometimes with a rapid movement of their red beaks, they welcomed a ripple that came from somewhere, though unclear from where.

Mansur was holding the oars in his cupped hands. He was frightened. No fisherman dared come to this place at night. Even during the day, if a fisherman's course happened to pass by this place, this place which was full of the denizens of the water, he would

---

7- A long robe traditionally worn by men in various parts of the Middle East, including parts of southern Iran.

change his course so as not to be caught up in a strange whirlpool, the velocity of which increased with the voice of a woman pulling the boats toward it, and suddenly swallowing them. Even Mahjamal, for whom hardship and comfort were no different, had never come to this place. But who was this Mahjamal?

Mansur turned his head and looked at him. Oblivious to the world, Mahjamal was rowing, a faint smile on his lips. Many nights Mansur had sat with him, with Mahjamal and other young people, on the dirt mounds along the side of the road, and each talked about his life and hopes and dreams. But now that Mansur thought of those nights, he realized that Mahjamal had always listened, and apparently never said a word... What a pity! How could it be that not even one of the village girls was able to stir something in his heart, to want him and capture him? How unlucky was Mahjamal, or perhaps that was exactly his predestined fate, that he should suddenly rise out of the sea in the year of the famine and hang around the village like a shadow for twenty years, and then, that Busalmeh should suddenly seal his fate.

Mansur sighed sorrowfully. He knew that he respected Mahjamal, that he liked this shadow, this perpetual phantom of the village. But who would be able to keep a shadow for himself forever, even if that shadow were his own? It was as though Mahjamal himself had never given his heart to others, to be etched in anyone's mind. As though in his lonesome self, he saw his lack of fulfilment and his failures. Wasn't he a fortuneteller and palm reader? Did this mean that he had accepted his own fate? That he had looked ahead of himself stunned and dazed?

Mansur was distressed. Sweat covered his forehead, and he thought: "This weather is so gloomy, perfect for a Fayez song."

As if reading his mind, Mahjamal turned and looked at him. His smile was strange. Mansur thought he seemed to be admonishing him. He turned his face so that Mahjamal could not see his distress and regret. Zayer Ahmad got up from the top of the hold. His chin was trembling, and with his index finger, he pointed to the port side of the boat. Something was moving on the surface of the water. It had rendered Zayer Ahmad speechless.

"She's here. It's her. Don't move... They're right now all around the boat; they're everywhere."

Zayer Ahmad gestured to Mahjamal. Mahjamal got up and sat down next to him. He bent over the side of the boat and looked down. Just below the clear surface of the water, mermaids with their human halves and their long, smooth hair were moving alongside the boat. Mansur tossed his oar into the boat. The boat was now standing still. The other boats stopped close to one another. Mansur looked at them like a young child. Never in his life had he seen a mermaid, and now he was seeing all of them in one place, only a few steps away, so close that by jumping into the water, he could grab their hair or squeeze their long blue fingers. But, what a pity... those fish-like halves of theirs killed all desire in the hearts of men. Suddenly, you remembered that she is not human. Suddenly, the sound of the village girls' anklets resonated in your ears, resonated and would not let you go.

Mahjamal stood waiting beside Zayer Ahmad, looking at the blue water of the sea, which was now stirring. A moment later, a woman rose out of the water, as high as her human half, and shook the little jingling tambourine she held in her hand. The soft sound of the tambourine echoed far and wide, and Mahjamal turned and kissed Mansur, who had come to stand beside him, the color having drained from his face. Zayer Ahmad struck Mahjamal hard on the back. Slowly, as though the soles of her feet were on dry land, the mermaid came toward Mahjamal with her human half, took his hand, which was curled around the edge of the boat, and they both disappeared into the sea.

3

Mahjamal and the mermaid passed among coral and starfish, through colorful seaweed and aquatic flowers, which, upon seeing them, would suddenly bend down and scatter petals at their feet.

Everything seemed familiar. He didn't know when or where he had seen all this, in a dream or wakefulness. Perhaps many years earlier, when on the top of Zayer Ahmad's water cistern, when he had looked at his own palm to read his fortune, he had seen them; and the name of Zayer Ahmad was so strange and distant in this place, in the depths of the green waters. It was as if on the other side of time, something was whirling in his mind. As if he had seen Zayer Ahmad and the village in a dream, and now he was awestruck in the midst of clear reality.

He was pondering. He argued with himself, and he was struggling to preserve his memory, his memory of Zayer Ahmad and Mansur and Captain Ali, and that woman... Who was that woman who wanted to alert him to Busalmeh's wrath?

He was ruminating and passing by wrecked boats and crates that had turned the color of seaweed.

As he was passing by one of the wrecked boats, he stopped. He recognized that boat. He went closer and saw the sons of Mama

Mansur, who were still at the bottom of the sea in the depths of the green waters, still struggling to repair the boat to get back to the village. Hope, that aspect that is particular to the denizens of the land, was still, after two years, setting their hands in motion. Hope and memories, hope of returning to their memories, to the village where their lives had been shaped. The same things that with lesser appeal forced Mahjamal to accept everything tonight, to find lost memories.

And those who die at sea believe very late that there is no return, and that when a dead man is sentenced to his own death, or begins to understand this secret, his face changes. Traces of the passage of time, hope and hopelessness, always remain on the faces of humans, even if they have died.

Such pain had dazed the faces of the six sons, and their eyes were so sad and sorrowful that for the first time in his twenty-year life, Mahjamal's heart shuddered. Never had any human on the land, in the village, been able to look at him with such regret and pain. And the land, what a strange trickster! Somewhere, it grabs you by the collar, somewhere you want to forget.

Never had he imagined that that little village he was away from—that place in which, waiting for years for tonight and to find himself, he had emptied out the beads of night and day—could capture such a human offspring in the coils of pain and suffering.

Mahjamal was not supposed to be hesitant. He was not supposed to be woeful. He was not supposed to make the mermaids wait. In the depths of the green waters some distance from the boat, the mermaid was standing in restless expectation, a faint smile on her lips. Mahjamal came to realize that the six sons had not given their hearts to the mermaids. He saw the six sons, who tried to avoid looking at the mermaid's fish half. The sound of the anklets of the village women seemed to echo in their ears. Their glances, the movement of their heads and necks, were in the direction of that sound. The sound of anklets, in the direction of the village! Now he understood the meaning of the mermaid's faint smile, a smile of complaint and defeat, a smile of the rebellion of the offspring of

Adam, the captives of the land.

The mermaid approached Mahjamal as though he were an old friend returning from a voyage. She took him by the arm and began to move. Mahjamal was dragged behind the mermaid, the water moving by so rapidly that it made him dizzy, and he closed his eyes.

He was in the depths of the blue waters. When he opened his eyes, he saw a huge area of sea corals and large and small mermaids, who looked at him with familiar smiles. The smile of one of the mermaids, who was standing in front of the rest and looking at him, was untangling his mental knots one by one, as he was recognizing who she was. He had found his mother, a mother with long blue hair, eyes the color of blue water, and her fish half.

Now, he would be able to forget that gypsy woman, the gypsy woman who, with his coming up from the sea, had evolved in the minds of the women of Jofreh and had followed him like a shadow for twenty years.

At the name that he was being called, Mahjamal saw the other one. The voice was so familiar and friendly that without even having to think about it, he recognized his father. A man who had been shipwrecked in a storm twenty years and nine months and nine days earlier, and was brought by one of the mermaids to the depths of the blue waters who that same night had mated with him.

You must be so angry with the earth and all that has happened to you that you would seek warmth, at the very moment you sink into the blue waters, in the embrace of a mermaid; and Mahjamal's father, whoever he was and wherever he had come from, had put to sleep his earthly pain and suffering in the embrace of a mermaid.

Mahjamal could still hear his father's breathing as he was mating with the mermaid, and he knew who he was, why he was restless on the land, and why during these last five years his eyes were drawn to the sea.

Like the six brothers of Mansur, the man had not become accustomed to his own death. Mahjamal could gather this from the strange sorrow that welled in his eyes.

Twenty years is not a short time in which to forget; but the footprints of life are not so easily erased. The man's voice seemed to come from strange twisting and turning tunnels.

"Mahjamal, play something so we can cry."

This is a familiar voice, the voice of a human accustomed to sorrow, a voice that wants to unleash a twenty-year-old lump from his throat with the wailing of Fayez's poetry.

When the denizens of the land arrive in the depths of the blue waters, aquatic love takes them into its shelter. They forget the sound of the anklets of the daughters of the land. They sleep with the mermaids. And afterwards, they sigh with regret for the warmth they have lost. They long for weeping. And awaiting a reed flute player, they stare at the far-away surface of the water.

Thus, no matter where you go, it is all the same; the land does not let you go, the land and all that passes upon it, its sorrows and its joys.

Something unfamiliar was clawing at Mahjamal's heart and crushing it with sadness. He had come in search of his lost memories with such excitement, and now this man, his father, was homesick for the land.

Under the gaze of the blue ones, he was curling up and looking at the man who, before he had left his seed in the womb of a mermaid, had been tall and broad-shouldered, but was now gaunt and scrawny, with the white skin of the dead.

The water rippled sometimes, and his father's face was lost in the ripples. A little further back, behind his father, there were other men with the same sorrow-struck, tearless eyes, standing like dazed white statues, as though they were trying to find him in their drowned memories.

Mahjamal moved toward the man. In the manner of the denizens of the land, he wished to embrace him and feel the warmth of the love that he had never known. Here in the depths of the cold waters, he knew the meaning of having no one, a feeling that the warmth of the human presence in the village had not allowed him to contemplate. There was a warm smile on the man's lips. When he reached the man, he held his slim, tall body, which living in the water had made gaunt and cold, in his arms; but everything was different, cold and frozen. Other drowned ones, dazed white statues, came and gathered around him and his father in a circle. Sometimes they looked at the two with a smile that was the result of recalling distant memories, and at times they looked at Mahjamal with their doleful, strange eyes and wanted him to tell them about the village, about the denizens of the land; and Mahjamal told them the news of things that he had previously passed by unheedingly: the sound of a shepherd's reed flute, the bleating of goats, the rising and setting of the sun, winter nights and sitting by the charcoal brazier, singing sad songs, the smell of freshly-baked bread...

Indeed, how dear yet distant were all these. Mahjamal's heart felt saddened, so saddened that it seemed to him that the big pearl that Busalmeh had promised, and that would save the village from poverty, was the most worthless thing in the world, and it could not make anyone happy, not even as much as a goat dropping.

When the sound of the mermaids' tambourines arose, the drowned men, with sad eyes and stooped shoulders, dispersed, and Mahjamal heard the dejected voice of the man:

"Play a Fayez song, play a Fayez song so we can cry."

Mahjamal took the reed flute and played. Little by little, the music slowly climaxed. It was a groaning sound that rose from the hearts of people who had lived for many long years away from the land and its customs, at the bottom of the sea among the coral and starfish. The sound was of those who had not yet become accustomed to living in the sea. They were living among the denizens of the sea who did not know the meaning of human pain and suffering. Mahjamal came to understand that what he had inherited from his father was greater. He did not want to remain in the seas, wandering and lonesome.

The sound was climaxing. It was passing through the seaweed and coral and bouncing against the skin of the blue ones; and as though causing a tremor in their bodies, it changed their color, and before his eyes, repeated images of Zayer Ahmad appeared, cautioning him.

Mahjamal closed his eyes so he would not see Zayer Ahmad. Mahjamal did not see that the blue ones were gradually turning red.

A painful moaning sound made Mahjamal open his eyes. He saw a little blue mermaid sitting in the corner on the corals, weeping. She moaned so sadly that without resorting to his clairvoyance, Mahjamal recognized her. She was Busalmeh's bride. She had submitted to this union by force. When thousands of young, handsome fishermen lived in villages near and far, what mermaid of the sea would willingly agree to union with Busalmeh, the ugly-faced demon of the seas and the enemy of all the young, handsome fishermen?

The mermaid was sobbing. Never had any woman in the village moaned so intensely, so distressed and so lost... The mermaid was coming toward him with her fish half, in search of a refuge of love, so that she could endure the wrath of Busalmeh... Mahjamal was fearful. What if the mermaid fell in love with him and took him captive? What if he would not go back to the village and would not breathe in the scent of the soil with his whole being? No! He would not stay in the blue waters of the sea, even if he took the hand of the mermaid that was now stretched toward him, and went with her...

The color of the water was changing. Everything was becoming compressed and chaotic, spinning around his head, and Mahjamal saw that the sea had suddenly turned black. The drowned men descended into darkness and the mermaid's hand took his firmly, and in the black-colored water and the strange ensuing uproar, she led him upward.

A storm had risen. The sound of crashing waves was deafening. Busalmeh was roaring. Frightened and horrified, the fish of the sea fled from within the dense waters. The seaweed was being uprooted, and the mermaid was taking him along.

They seemed to have lost their way, when he heard the blue one's voice:

"Shut them, shut your eyes."

But Mahjamal had inherited curiosity from humans. He looked. They were in the depths of the gray waters, and woe to you if you disturbed the sleep of the dead of the gray waters. Mahjamal saw them; slow and free of time, they lifted their heads from the sleep of death, and glued their vindictive glares on him, cold, icy glares that demanded the sleep of death. The denizen of the land, Mahjamal, trembled. Terrified, he closed his eyes to never see the dead of the gray waters any longer.

When they reached the surface of the water, screaming high waves blocked his view. The sea was black and frothy. Nothing was visible. Busalmeh had captured the moonlight and put it in chains.

Mahjamal was tired. The mermaid zig-zagged through the water, taking him this way and that, and Mahjamal did not want to stay in the sea. He did not want to become a wanderer. He had seen everything up close; he wanted to return to the land. He should not have gotten close to the mermaid, but he was so tired that he lay his head on her shoulders and fell unconscious.

* * *

He came to with a splashing of water on his face. He was on the hold of the boat. Zayer Ahmad and Mansur were by his side. High waves crashed over the boat. The sky was black and a strange hubbub resonated in the sea. The wind howled; the corpses of seagulls fell from the sky onto the boat.

The crying sound of fishermen pleading with Busalmeh whirled around his head, and Zayer Ahmad and Mansur's faces came and went within a circle.

A high wave tilted Zayer Ahmad's big boat. Zayer Ahmad was thrown and hit his head on the edge of the boat. He cried out in pain. Mahjamal tried to get up. Mansur struggled with the mast, and nobody could tell whether it was day or night. He heard a distant voice:

"They are mourning in the village right now."

$\diamondsuit$ **4** $\diamondsuit$

The village was in mourning. The sea had been roaring for an entire week. The wind howled. High waves crashed over the village and rolled over the walls. The huts were flooded, and fearing the waves, the people had been forced to remain on the roofs of those houses made of stucco. Water came up to one's knees in Jofreh. The sea was relentless. Busalmeh showed no mercy. The fish were scattered in the air by the sea waves and tossed on the doors and walls and rooftops. Colorful ear-shells with their lime shells climbed the walls; and sometimes the hand of a child who did not yet understand fear would pull them off the walls, and away from the watchful eyes of others, the child would sit and play with them.

The sound of the women's wailing and screaming could be heard from the rooftops night and day, and no one listened to Madineh, whose mind was now at ease regarding the mermaids and who knew that the wedding of the mermaid and Busalmeh had been disrupted, as she called on the women to have patience and self-control. Despite all this, the village remained hesitant.

In the morning of the eighth day, Mama Mansur came down from the rooftop and went up to her waist in water to Zayer Ahmad's house, the rooms of which were above ground level, and the sea water only reached its top step. Her face scratched and her scarf in shreds, Mama Mansur moaned. When they saw her, the other women held up their petticoats and came to Zayer Ahmad's house. They all gathered in the room with five sashed windows. Wailing and screaming, the women hit themselves on their heads and faces. Bubuni was chewing her gum rapidly, soaking wet, and her eyes were twitching. Without Captain Ali, the village seemed empty to her. If the waves would give her a chance, if she could get anywhere, she would throw herself into the sea and go to the depths of the green waters, grab the mermaids by the hair, wrap it around her hand, and hit their heads with sea rocks so much that they would tell her where they had hidden her Captain. Bubuni chewed her gum harder than ever. Her jaws were aching, and her heart was bursting from grief. She could envision Captain Ali, away from her watchful eyes, laughing and chatting hand-in-hand with a mermaid. She was afraid, afraid of Captain Ali wedding one of the mermaids, making children of all sizes and shapes with her, and for years and years, talking about a wife he had in the village who couldn't bear children. Her baby-making oven was cold, and no talisman could help her. The sound of the mermaid's boisterous laughter resonated in her ears. There was nothing she could do about it. She wanted to put her head on Mama Mansur's shoulder and cry her heart out.

Mama Mansur moaned: "I am grieving, my tall handsome one, grieving..."

She moaned, soaking wet, and rocked back and forth like an ownerless boat abandoned at sea. More silent than ever, Nabati sat beside Kheyju, whose eyes were brimming with anger. Others were wailing and screaming, while Madineh silently pressed her lips together to conceal her happiness from others.

Kheyju knew that it was time to bring out the black mourning banners. Eight days had passed, and if anyone had remained alive, he would have shown up by the day before. Now, all the women were aware that with this storm and Busalmeh's wrath, no one would escape with his life; but Kheyju, the sole daughter of Zayer Ahmad, did not know how the wedding of the mermaid and Busalmeh had been disrupted. Had the mermaid taken Mahjamal with her? No one, even if she is a denizen, even if she lives in the depths of the blue waters, would allow a human like Mahjamal to just leave. It is only the defective reasoning of humans that ties the tongue of the human heart, that lets you stand there, like Nabati, with a lantern in hand, and watch him leave. If she were like Nabati and loved Mahjamal, she would not have let him set out for Jinn-Haunted Cove. Had it been her, if she had been in Nabati's shoes, she would have taken Mahjamal by the hand a long time ago, left for other lands, and lived with him with a morsel of bread on God's earth, with him whom she loved. But why did Nabati not say a word? Why did she not do anything? Something bitter and biting choked her, and she could see Nabati looking silently and with frightened eyes at the women.

Nabati was indeed afraid, afraid that he might die, afraid that the village would be destroyed, that her father, Zayer Gholam, would not return from the sea, and that she would be all alone forever. Who in the world would take care of her? How could she spend her nights all alone? At whose supper cloth could she dine for all eternity? Although Kheyju, the sole daughter of Zayer Ahmad, always watched over her, and during the year of the famine, like all other people, they went to Zayer Ahmad's house and sat at the supper cloth that was spread for everyone, now Zayer Ahmad, too, was not there... No man was there, and a world without men was an unprotected world that could be plundered by any jinn or jinn offspring.

A stifled voice in the midst of sobbing said:

"What are we to do? Oh God, what are we to do? I hope to God their lineage is cut off forever."

Human destiny is to lose. The village, whether secretly or openly, was cursing. When the water was over your head, being considerate regarding Busalmeh was meaningless.

Kheyju stood up and walked through a small door on which a curtain with faded colors hung, separating the room with five sashed windows from the smaller room. She entered the small room. Several ear-shells were climbing the wall, and the smell of dampness made breathing difficult. She opened the black coffer, took out the black mourning banners, and went back to the room with five sashed windows. Upon seeing the banners, the women wailed. Kheyju placed the biggest banner in the middle of the room. The women sang and danced around it. Mama Mansur said:

"Let's wail, let's wail for our young ones."

And Kheyju took off her scarf, held the two ends in her hands, stood in the middle of the circle the women had formed, and chanted:

"Woe to us, beat the drums of mourning,
The men of Jofreh will come back no more."

Mahjamal's face would not disappear before her eyes. His blue eyes and his last smile. Kheyju seemed to be moaning for her own heart; her voice was raspy, her face scratched and flushed. A strange yearning flared up in her heart. For so many years, year after year, the presence of Nabati next to her, her silence and broken sentences, had not given her the chance to hear the voice of her own heart, and now everything was on fire. Her heart was burning, and Mahjamal would not disappear before her eyes. How had he passed by her without her even noticing? All those long years, he would come and sit in this very corner of the room with five sashed windows, at dinnertime and lunchtime, so that Madineh would give him something to eat, a plateful of rice and fried fish. Oh... His scent was in the room.

Kheyju wept. She had been born four years after the year of the famine when Mahjamal had risen out of the sea, and little Mahjamal always, whenever Madineh was busy, would go to the well or milk the goat, pick her up and sing a lullaby for her, and wipe her tears with his hands.

Like all the people of the village, Mahjamal held the daughter of Zayer Ahmad in respect; but now, Kheyju no longer boasted of this respect and endearment. Lost memories and plundered moments sprung to life in her heart. Distressed and stricken by regret, she moaned:

"Come back... Come back... All of you, come back."

The daughter of Zayer Ahmad wailed. The women hit their faces; they ululated in reverse: the happy, joyful sound of ululation rose, and then ended in the sorrowful howling of women who had forever lost their men. Their faces were flushed. Their voices were lost in the hubbub of the sea waves that crashed madly over the village. They all danced, mournfully and in distress.

When the lamentation and mourning stopped, the women, each carrying a black banner, came out of the room with five sashed windows and stepped into the water, which reached up to their knees. As they passed through the large door facing Mecca, they saw the silk tassel acacia tree, the trunk of which was covered with moss from the water. Small and large ear-shells with lime shells were climbing the trunk of the silk tassel acacia tree, and seagulls were flying around screeching. Broken coral branches were settling down at the bottom of the water. Zayer Ahmad's old boat, which had been in disrepair for a long while and had been abandoned under the silk tassel acacia tree in front of his house, was rocking back and forth on the water. The decomposing smell of the walls mingled with the smell of drainage. Sometimes the wind whipped the women's bodies with water, and they grabbed onto one another and bent back and forth.

The end of the world had arrived. Stifled sounds of crying could be heard here and there. Mama Mansur, who could hardly move forward, shook a black banner and said:

"Salutations to the Prophet and his family!"

Desperate, hopeless voices uttered salutations. Mama Mansur cut her way through the water to Setareh's hut, little of which remained. She placed the banner among the dried palm branches and tied it firmly. The wind was flapping the black cloth. Setareh shrieked loudly. Kheyju held her to prevent her from falling.

By sunset, they had put up all the banners. As if someone were whipping the body of the village, wind blew through the banners and made a thrashing sound. Among all the houses, only Bubuni's did not have a banner.

Bubuni said, "He might come back," and she did not let anyone place a banner between the two deer antlers over the door of her house.

At twilight, the women put on their black clothes, which were soaking wet and had the salty smell of the sea. As she was putting on her mourning clothes, Kheyju thought:

"He was the only one who did not have a house to need a banner. Oh God, is there any difference between You and Busalmeh?"

5

The sea had been crashing over the boats for nine days. During the daytime, a dusty white circle could be seen in the darkness far away in the sky, and at nighttime, everything was as black as tar. Their food had run out. There was no time for making a fire, and the exhausted fishermen had tossed all their gear and supplies into the sea. Their lips were parched and blistered. Their water had run out. The boats had lost sight of one another, each struggling with the waves in some spot or other.

On Zayer Ahmad's boat, everyone was out of breath. Exhausted and soaking wet, Mansur was bailing out the water with a can. From the other side, a wave would crash over the boat, and once again the boat would fill with water.

Zayer Ahmad was frustrated. He missed the silence, and he no longer knew the hue and scent of the tumult-free world of the sea. Neither thirst nor hunger could bring Zayer Ahmad to his knees. He had boundless energy and endurance. What was diminishing his abilities now was the tumult of the waves and the crashing sound of the storm at sea.

He was dazed and confused. Noises from every direction, and high black waves as far as the eye could see. It was as though someone had stuffed date pits into his ears. It was as though something was pounding in his head. He could not collect his thoughts, as though Busalmeh was intentionally breaking the thread of his thoughts. Everything was broken asunder in his mind, like the boats adrift— where, he did not know, nor on which shore their skeletons had surfaced, nor on which wave they remained.

Worn out, Mansur tossed the can to some corner. He gave up on his futile task. Mahjamal picked up the can and resumed that doomed effort.

Staggering and dazed from the salty rebellious sea, in the midst of the sound of the squall and the crashing of water, Mansur staggered closer to Zayer Ahmad in order for Zayer Ahmad to hear his voice, and also for Mahjamal to know what he intended to do. He yelled from the bottom of his throat:

"How long is it going to be like this, Zayer? Is there some remedy?"

He knew himself that there had to be a remedy, but he had not said anything so far, for the sake of Mahjamal. Now, soaking wet and exhausted, he had lost his stamina.

Helplessly, Zayer Ahmad looked at Mahjamal. He felt angry. He wanted to hit Mahjamal on the head with the pain and suffering of those nine days of futile quarreling with Busalmeh. He wanted to see Mahjamal beg and plead.

During those nine days, as though observing the most natural events in the world, Mahjamal had put up with them, and he had not even once pleaded with Busalmeh to let him be. It was as though he was not remorseful at all, remorseful that he had brought misery and mourning to the village, that he had caused Busalmeh's wrath to dominate Jofreh forever, and had taken away the pearl from them.

Zayer Ahmad yelled, "The remedy is blood! Blood!" He shouted so angrily that Mahjamal dropped the can, and as though he had been waiting these nine days for that word from Zayer Ahmad, he said:

"I'm ready, Zayer."

Zayer Ahmad was taken aback; he became hesitant. From now on, Mahjamal would be a symbol of misfortune and anger. They needed to get rid of him. He needed to be sacrificed before they reached dry land. One person to be sacrificed for all, or all to be sacrificed for one? No, he did not want Busalmeh to level the village in black dirt. He was prepared to do anything it took; but Mahjamal's answer embarrassed him. It was as though no trick or plan would work in facing Mahjamal. He was simple and willing to do anything he could. Perhaps he, Mahjamal, had also in his nine days of silence thought about the eternal wrath of Busalmeh and the fishermen. Perhaps he, too, was worried about the village.

With difficulty, Zayer Ahmad pulled out from the hold the knife that was for cutting off the tails of sharks. Mansur's lips trembled. His face was drained of all color. He wished he had never complained. He wished he had taken the misfortune of Busalmeh's wrath upon his own head and had not called on Zayer Ahmad to engage in such a heinous, black deed.

Mahjamal came forward, sat at the side of the boat, and placed his neck on the edge of the boat in order for Zayer Ahmad to sever his head from his body, and by spilling his blood into the sea, to calm the storm. But the knife was shaking in Zayer Ahmad's hand, and Mahjamal was looking at him like a sacrificial lamb.

Zayer Ahmad's hesitation, and those eyes, Mahjamal's eyes, the way Mahjamal acted, his simplicity and innocence, reminded Zayer of someone, a man, a stranger with whom many years earlier in Fekseno his fourteen-year-old sister, Fanus, had fallen in love.

No! Zayer Ahmad could not destroy a human being for the sake of Busalmeh. Is kinship only through blood, Zayer? He has grown up in the village. He has walked on God's earth. Mahjamal is like the soil of the village, like the silk tassel acacia tree in front of your house. You need a solution, Zayer, another solution, a kinder, more humane one. What does Zayer need to do to calm vengeful Busalmeh, to free the tired men from their nine-day battle with the sea, to allow the fishermen to breathe a sigh of relief?

Perhaps he could stab some part of Mahjamal's body, spill some of his blood into the sea, and deceive Busalmeh. Human beings live by their intellect. Even Satan is annihilated in the face of human intellect. Intellect and the efforts of the white wings of the bird of life... Do something, think of something, Zayer...

A high, begrudging wave rolled over the boat. Zayer Ahmad grabbed Mahjamal's back and pulled him toward himself. They both stretched out in the middle of the boat. To prevent Mahjamal from falling into the water, Mansur placed himself between Mahjamal and the sea. If Mahjamal were to fall into the sea alive, the dead of the gray waters would come up, devour the fishermen throughout the world, and the loud laughter of the red mermaids would split the ceiling of the sky. Angels would fall out of the sky and the world would be annihilated, annihilated.

Struggling to get up from the bottom of the boat, quietly, Zayer Ahmad whispered in Mahjamal's ear:

"He wants blood. I will cut your finger. You cry out and say, 'Don't kill me.'"

A strange smile appeared on Mahjamal's face. Excitement welled under his skin, and he looked at his index finger. Then he whispered in Zayer Ahmad's ear:

"Stab me in the arm...not my finger."

Zayer Ahmad was at a loss momentarily. Why did Mahjamal want to keep his index finger? Aha! Youth and ardent aspirations! So, this vagabond Mahjamal wants to save himself like other young men in the village, hoping for the hands of a woman or the long tresses of a girl?

Mahjamal rolled over toward the edge of the boat and sat with his back to the sea, and Zayer Ahmad sat up on his knees. Finger, shoulder, or foot, it made no difference to Zayer Ahmad. The only thing was that Mahjamal needed to feel pain and cry out from pain in order for Busalmeh to think that he had left this world in pain and suffering, and that he had not been in love with any mermaid, and that no mermaid could ever again fall in love with him.

Mansur stood there, worried. The knife was in Zayer Ahmad's hand, the knife with which he had many times ripped the bellies and cut off the tails of sharks. Zayer Ahmad bent down toward Mahjamal, Mansur turned his face away, and Mahjamal screamed:

"Don't kill me!"

Zayer Ahmad made a deep gash in Mahjamal's arm and placed his arm on the edge of the boat in such a way that the sea would become bloody.

As Mansur turned around and looked, Mahjamal collapsed on the hold, unconscious. A smile appeared on his face. He stepped forward, took Zayer Ahmad's hand and kissed it. Zayer Ahmad was weeping, and in between his tears, he saw Mahjamal, who had fallen asleep like a baby. Such an evil heart has Busalmeh, who blocks the way to young handsome fishermen like Mahjamal and takes them to the bottom of the gray waters! Why is it that the curses of mourning mothers do not work? If sighs turned into flames and blazed up, they could dry up the seas. But where is the flame from the hearts of mothers? And what pain should Mama Mansur, the mother of seven sons, hide in her heart?

Above the waves, a bird was flying speedily. The weather was becoming calmer, and seawater sprayed on Mahjamal's face.

Mansur tore off a piece of the bottom of Mahjamal's shirt, washed Mahjamal's arm with the salty seawater gathered at the bottom of the boat, and wrapped it tightly.

Whether he was sleeping or unconscious, when Mahjamal came to his senses, the sea was no longer stormy. Its sound was a calm complaint, and he heard the fishermen faraway calling one another by name. Seagulls were flying in the sky, Mansur was standing in the middle of the boat, and Zayer Ahmad was using the can to bail the remaining water out of the boat.

When Mahjamal blinked his eyes and waved his hand, Zayer Ahmad and Mansur came beside him. Zayer laughed, caressed his head, and whispered in his ear:

"Your wound will heal soon; but you mustn't talk until we reach the village. Let him think that you are dead."

Mahjamal nodded quietly. Mansur kissed his forehead and whispered:

"We made it through."

Mahjamal smiled. Human words were ointment for his pain. He would never come back to the sea again, not even to fish. There, at the bottom of the sea, he had not seen anything resembling the affection on the land.

The memory of those drowned men, the memory of Mama Mansur's six sons and the man who wanted to hear him play a Fayez song and weep, chained him to the land, to the village. What a difference between Mansur's face and the faces of the six sons! Such strange sorrow that had nested in the eyes of the drowned men! No, he would never tell anyone about what he had seen in the depths of the green and blue waters. Let Mama Mansur remain ignorant of her sons still being conscious in their death, and how enthusiastically they are repairing their boat to come back to the village one day...

Rage toward Busalmeh was ablaze in his heart. If only he could strangle Busalmeh with his own hands! If only he could...! He sighed. Clumps of gray clouds scattered in the sky. A bird was flying in the distance. He traced the route of its flight. It was flying toward the village. The village! What was awaiting him?

The boats were coming together. The fishermen came toward Zayer Ahmad's boat, tired, but happy. Captain Ali had become old. He was not accustomed to the sea, and now the continuous fighting with the sea for nine days and nights had aged him even more. When Mansur saw him, he said:

"Doing alright, Captain?"

Captain sat on the hold:

"Not too bad, thanks."

He was silent for a moment. Looking at Mahjamal whose arm was wrapped reminded him of the pearl they had lost.

"We're going back emptyhanded."

Zayer Ahmad laughed:

"Don't take it so hard, Captain. Reckon that we got ourselves out of the water. What could be more precious than human life?"

The fishermen intentionally ignored Mahjamal. Up to the time that they stepped on the village soil, no one was supposed to even imagine that Mahjamal was alive. How could they be sure that Busalmeh could not read the minds of the fishermen?

In the morning of the tenth day, they saw Jofreh in the distance. Their hands raised up to the sky. The tiredness suddenly left their bodies. They warmed up. The men spoke loudly. Smiles would not leave their faces. The feeling of being alive and staying alive, returning to the village, to their land memories, made them restless. They rowed with vigor, and how slowly time passed, and how long the distance. Jofreh was standing on the seashore like a woman; and how the fishermen were powerless—they did not have arms long and strong enough to stretch across those blue waters—to inhale the scent of this woman, this waiting woman, and squeeze her in their arms.

Heedless of what was occurring in the hearts of the tired hopeful men, time dragged on, sluggish and like a termite; and they, if their feet would ever finally touch dry land, would kiss God's land and spatter the soil, the grounding soil of Jofreh, over their eyes. Alas! The sun, there in the sky, was not moving, or perhaps the arms of the tired men were exhausted, or the oars had decided to be disobedient.

Hurry up, hurry...

The bows of the boats beat restlessly for the village, and the oars hitting the water made a pleasant sound. The cove seemed so close, and Mansur stood up, shading his eyes with his hands, staring.

What had Mansur seen that made him stand and stare at the

village? Zayer Ahmad looked at him:

"Sit down, man! We'll get there."

Ignoring Zayer Ahmad, Mansur continued staring. His lips moved:

"Oh my God! They've put up black banners in the village."

They needed to travel some distance farther before the banners came to life in the eyes of Zayer Ahmad and Mahjamal. No doubt, Busalmeh had learned of their ruse and had begun what he wanted to do in the village. Whom had he killed? Whose life had he taken? He might have inflicted the lives of the villagers with consumption, or plague.

The men whispered with frightened, stifled voices in the boats. The joy of arriving on land turned into a confusing and silent sorrow. Everyone felt helpless, drained. Perplexed, Zayer Ahmad said:

"Put up the banners, the black banners."

Mahjamal was sitting, crouched in some corner. No one looked at him. The fishermen rowed. Strength had left their arms. Oh, if only the sun would stop motionless in the sky, time would not pass, and they would never reach the shore. If only Busalmeh would make them wander in the sea forever. If only Zayer Ahmad had thrown Mahjamal, when he was unconscious, into the sea. Busalmeh would not let go, and the thought passed through the minds of all the tired men: "One person to be sacrificed for all, or all to be sacrificed for one?"

The banners were getting bigger and bigger with every moment, and flocks of seagulls flew toward the village.

When the boats with black banners dropped anchor in the cove, the sound of wailing rose from the shore. The women in the village had seen the black banners, and they were not sure which of the men had failed to return.

Zayer Ahmad Hakim stepped into the water, followed by the

others. Mahjamal, who was at the end of the line, walked with his wounded arm. He had a fever. No one expected him, and the sound of the women's wailing grew louder every moment. The men were beating themselves on their heads and chests. On the shore, Kheyju chanted:

"The steed of our martyred saint has returned without its rider."

The men responded:

"Woe to us from this sorrow."

Zayer Ahmad could not recognize Kheyju's voice. Alas, black-hearted Busalmeh! Have you robbed Zayer of his only daughter? And has that voice that sang in the circle of mourning women on the nights of religious mourning been lost? Tears welled up in Zayer Ahmad's eyes, and in the eyes of the other men. How easily they had cast their lives to the wind, yearning for a pearl. How easily...

And what fire had this vagabond, who came at the end of the line of men, whose hearth and home had been cast to the wind, set to their being? When the fishermen reached the shore, the mourning intensified. Both groups, whether those whose hearts were on fire and were standing on the shore or the men who came out of the sea, hit themselves on their heads and chests and wailed.

Bubuni could not see Captain Ali. She was looking among the men, and she could not find him. Bubuni wailed, shook her hands at the sea, and in memory of the Captain who had been taken to the depths of the green waters on his only sea voyage, she screamed.

Captain Ali could not find Bubuni, his childless wife who stared at the village children with envy; and Kheyju could not see Mahjamal, the tall Mahjamal who had no kith and kin... Kheyju chanted and moaned, and Mama Mansur kept turning around and around and yelling:

"I am grieving, my tall handsome one, grieving..."

No one seemed to be among the men, and no man could find the woman he knew among the women. Everyone wailed.

Zayer Ahmad looked in front of him, suddenly hearing a familiar voice, a voice that moaned:

"Zayer... Zayer... Zayer."

Woman, and the overflowing river of her heart! Grief had erased Madineh's consciousness and senses. With the ends of her scarf loose, she screamed. Surprised, Zayer Ahmad stopped mourning. He grabbed both of Madineh's arms to stop her from pulling on her hair. He shook her and said:

"Madineh...Madineh, I'm here."

Madineh saw Zayer Ahmad. She looked at him, stunned. She took him in her arms, kissed his tired head and face, and sobbing, asked:

"Who did not come back from the threshold, the sea?"

Puzzled, Zayer Ahmad said:

"No one, Madineh. Everyone is safe and sound."

Madineh could not believe him. She scanned the crowd and saw all the village men. Others were still hitting themselves on their heads and faces. Madineh asked:

"Then, what was the black banner for?"

Zayer Ahmad answered:

"We put up the banners because of the banners in the village... Has anyone died in Jofreh?"

No one had died in the village. But when the men looked at one another and the women, laughing boisterously, embraced their men, Zayer Ahmad said:

"There may be some Divine wisdom at work. Now that you've warmed up for mourning, don't let it cool down. Beat your chests."

And he began to beat his chest. The mourning rituals went on in the village for another day and night.

6

The repentance wind—a wind that makes the sea repent and not pound the fishermen's heads with its high black waves—was blowing. It is the sigh from the hearts of drowned men, men who are sorrowful in their loneliness and sigh. Every year in the season of spring, the repentance wind glides the sighs in the hearts of drowned men across the surface of the sea and makes the sea take an oath to calm down, in order for fishermen to entrust their hearts to the sea without anguish and anxiety.

Mahjamal was sitting in the village square, in the gathering of men under the silk tassel acacia tree. He was straightening the bent tips of the fishing hooks, the sound of the wind reverberating in his ears.

But the sound was not merely the sound of the wind. For Mahjamal, who had heard the whispering of the drowned men and the six sons in the depths of the green waters, the sound was accompanied by a strange faint whisper, a whisper emanating from afar... Every once in a while, Mahjamal would turn to look at the sea, to hear more distinctly that vague sound that had concealed itself in the mantle of the wind.

The repentance wind had been blowing for two days, the wind

that took with it the worries of the fishermen every year and called on the blue waters of the sea to be calm. But in the silence that had fallen on the souls of the men of the village since that morning, a strange dispiritedness was evident in the sluggish movement of their hands, an unspoken expectation.

The men seemed to be busy with their work: one was removing the memories of the sea from the fish traps with a knife, another was tying together a new net, and a third was smoking a hookah. Mansur was making holes in the new fishing net float lines. But the echo of a distant, familiar sound settled on the faces of all the men, men who had their ears to the sea, a shadow that was taking shape with every moment.

Mahjamal glanced at the sea, and then at Mansur. A strange odor wafted in the village, and now Mahjamal could hear the sound clearly in the midst of the wind, a sound that came from the other side of the offing, the farthest point of the sea, and was getting closer.

Clearly, Mansur could not put his heart into his work. His hands picked up the fishing net float lines lethargically and slowly. His awareness and his senses were focused on the sea. Awkwardness in the presence of Zayer Ahmad seemed to force the men of the village to pretend to be busy. But Zayer Ahmad was not on the land; his glance traveled toward the horizon at the end of the sea.

A moment later, distraught Mahjamal surrendered to the sounds. He let go of the fishing hooks and sat facing the sea, in anticipation. Captain Ali felt heartened, tossed the pipe of his hookah aside, and settled calmly next to Mahjamal. No one talked, as though they had become delusional, as though each was thinking of something else. Several times, Mahjamal was about to say something, but he kept silent.

When they saw Mama Mansur, wailing and screaming, coming down from Zayer Ahmad's water cistern and ripping her collar and running toward the sea, Mahjamal realized that he was not mistaken. Mama Mansur had sniffed the scent of her sons from the sea. Now Setareh was also running toward the sea.

How quickly the six sons had repaired the boat! As though the scent of humans made their hands work more efficiently, and other drowned men whom Mahjamal had seen in his sea voyage to the depths of the green waters were coming to the surface of the water, as though walking on land. They were coming swiftly, without any fear or apprehension regarding Busalmeh, without turning around at every moment to look behind them.

With the color drained from his face, Zayer Ahmad said under his breath:

"Oh, holy saint... The drowned!"

Never in the life of the village, not in all these years, had the drowned come to the surface of the water this distraught, and all at once. It had at times occurred that one of the drowned would suddenly come to the surface of the sea, reach the shore, and call on his kinfolks to rush him to the village, and the people of the village, most sorrowfully, would place his dinner on the shore, throw his food for the day toward him, and he would leave a moment later, weeping. Often a drowned man would appear many years after his death, come toward the village, and call to someone, someone who no longer existed, someone who had been stolen by land death, or who from the sorrow for her drowned man had wailed and moaned so much that in her crazed state, she no longer recognized anyone, even if he was a drowned man.

The drowned always came alone. Apparently, in the depths of the green waters, suddenly their memories would drive them mad. In search of life, in order to find it, they would come toward the village, call out to someone, shout; but they could never hear the voices of humans, and they could never reach them.

This time, they had come as a group, all together. If it was not Busalmeh's trick, it was that the presence of Mahjamal in the depths of the green waters, his return, and the footprints of life that he had left behind had drawn the drowned to the village. The light of the sun shone on the drowned. They shaded their eyes with their hands and ran toward the village with a smile on their faces. And now, who would be able to restrain the women, women who had not seen their men for years and years, women who were distraught and hysterical, from heading toward the sea and walking into the water?

Someone had to hold Mama Mansur back, someone whose arms were stronger than a mother's love. Someone needed to grab Setareh. Someone had to hold Kheyju, to prevent her from rushing out of control into the water after male acquaintances from the village. But the drowned were coming, rushing toward the shore. They called their acquaintances by name, and they never reached a soul.

It was always possible that a drowned man would rebel against his own death, to suddenly appear on the surface of the water and come once again to live in the village. But everyone in the village knows that this is nothing more than a futile effort. A drowned man will never reach the village, even if he were to come to the edge of the shore, to the line between the water and dry land. A drowned man is chained by the blue and green waters of the sea. You see them rush toward the shore, traverse long distances, but never arrive. They are only on their way, on their way with astonishing speed, yet hopelessly.

Zayer Ahmad shouted:

"Save the women!"

Mahjamal saw Setareh running toward her man. They were two steps away from each other, arms stretched forward, but no matter how they walked toward each other, no matter how they struggled, they could not grab each other's hands. Setareh wailed and screamed... Borzu... Borzu... But Borzu could not hear her; the distance between him and Setareh was nothing other than the distance between death and life.

The way in which Setareh wailed and screamed was splitting the sky. Mahjamal rushed to the water. He grabbed Setareh in his arms from behind and tried with all his might to drag her to the shore:

"Setareh, don't make the drowned lose hope!"

But Setareh, anguished by the empty, cold days of her life,

wanted to take Borzu, who was her man at one time and was now one of the drowned, along with her back to the village. She was tired of her nightly sobbing. Mahjamal, grappling with her, was holding Setareh—who was strengthened by her strange womanly power—in his arms, but was unable to drag her with him to the shore. Setareh's feet were being dragged on the ground toward the village, and her arms were being pulled toward the drowned.

Further away, the boat of Mama Mansur's sons had reached the cove, and Mama Mansur was running toward them, with Mansur following her, confused and at a loss.

Mama Mansur's sons! Drowned men! How handsomely you have dressed. You have washed your clothes with the blue waters of the sea. You have rubbed your petrified faces with the green color of seaweed. You are coming toward life with coral branches and heaps of aquatic flowers. How well adorned you are, drowned men! You have not forgotten the custom of the denizens of the land...

Mama Mansur had reached the cove. She had grabbed the edge of the boat, and was trying to climb aboard. Her six sons reached their arms out toward her. They showed her the aquatic flowers and coral branches. In their strange movement, they were drawn toward her, but could never reach her. No one can reach anyone.

From behind, Mansur was holding his mother in his arms, trying to take her back to the shore and convince her that the six sons at one time had been her sons, but now they were of the drowned, and the drowned, no matter how dear and endearing, are strangers to life.

It was an astonishing turmoil. None of the men could subdue the women of the village, and the women ran toward their men until sunset, and finally returned weeping, weary, and crushed from their futile effort. They sat on the shore facing the sea and gazed at the drowned, who were running toward the shore without becoming exhausted, and calling out by name:

Setareh, Setareh, Golpar... Esfandiyar...

Borzu, Setareh's man, called his wife and children by name. Golpar pulled at her mother's scarf, pointing to her father, who was coming toward them, distraught. Esfandiyar had dropped on the sand, wailing and screaming.

Becoming accustomed to the presence of the drowned and regarding them as aliens was not a simple task. Even Bubuni, who did not have a man in the sea, sat on the shore crying, rocking back and forth like an ownerless boat on the sea.

The ones who had returned from their journey were stuck in their journey, and no one could be distant or close to them. The emotions that flared up in the hearts of the women of the village forced them to remain on the shore until morning.

Zayer... Zayer... Zayer...

The voices were sorrowful voices that would strip Zayer Ahmad of his strength. His knees trembled, and, ashamed of his inability, he wished his ears would be shut to the world. He had lost control. Frustrated and helpless, he walked around in the midst of the women of the village. How could he tell Mama Mansur to go back to her house and not listen to her six sons who had returned from their journey and who pleaded to return to their home and life? How could he say anything to Setareh, the woman who had lost her husband, the woman no one was strong enough to calm down, even on the shore? But tiredness and sleep enslave humans in their coils. The women were dozing off on the shore, at times suddenly awakening in fright, lest they had lost their men, lest the drowned had left.

In the morning, despondent and tired, the women awoke. No one felt like doing anything. But they needed to prepare some food for those who were running toward the village, tired, hungry, and thirsty. And it was Zayer Ahmad who explained to Madineh that, like all men in the world, drowned men understand hunger and thirst. Regarding women, sometimes one must speak in their own language.

The women of the village set out to work. They dug the ground in the courtyard of Zayer Ahmad's house. They built triangular fire pits with sea rocks, and they placed the cooking pots on them.

At noon on the shore, dishes of food were arranged in a row, and the tired drowned men came close and eagerly tasted human cooking.

After three days and nights, the repentance wind subsided. The people of the village forgot about their work and their lives, and stayed by the sea day and night in their despair. Tired and hopeless in their futile efforts, the drowned men were in the sea, looking, dazed. They had given up the idea of arriving, and there was a strange sorrow in their eyes that left humans no patience for any work.

At night, the women were heard on the shore, sobbing. Madineh moaned, distraught and miserable. Mama Mansur was not even moving anymore. She sat in the sand on the shore, dazed and stunned, staring at the eyes of her six sons, into which hopelessness had now found its way. Bubuni had forgotten about Captain Ali.

"No one should look into their eyes."

It was Zayer Ahmad who said that to the men in the village, and he crawled into some corner and wept, miserable and distraught. The despairing movements of the drowned men, their faces, and their eyes clearly revealed that they had come to believe in their own deaths. The drowned had crouched up, stunned, and, like the most confused deer in the world, looked at the village.

Zayer Ahmad was confused and distressed. He was of the land and life, and his heart was similar to that of other people in the village; but sitting by and watching the village melt from sorrow was not what any captain did, especially a captain who is in command of the ship and who must bring the sailors and passengers safely to their destination.

If the female crying and male pouting were to continue, that would mean the end of Jofreh. Even the children would die of grief. Perhaps the obstinacy of the drowned men to stay and look on so despondently and dolefully was what Busalmeh had instilled in them in order to destroy the village. No more than ten days had yet passed since the sea voyage, and it was quite likely that Busalmeh was vengeful and knew the untold secrets.

In a gathering of the men, Zayer Ahmad said:

"No matter what, they must leave."

But how could they make the drowned men—who had now crouched up within themselves and all of whose movements reeked of death and loneliness—understand that they had to raise anchor and leave to go to the depths of the green waters, men who could not hear the voices of the living and were entangled in their own alienation?

When the first woman in the village perished from grief, Zayer Ahmad, frightened, realized that everyone's turn would eventually come in the flour mill of life, and that in their sorrow, the women had lost their minds.

Zayer Ahmad never thought he would become fearful of his men, or that he would be helpless in their presence. It was late one afternoon when he sat on the top of the water cistern in consultation with the other men. Desperate and doleful, the drowned men looked at the village, a look that took Zayer Ahmad back to years and years earlier, to the day his boat caught fire before it reached the offing of the sea, the skeleton of his boat disintegrated under the flames of fire, and the boat slowly sank.

Zayer Gholam said:

"It is Busalmeh's doing. He is keeping them there intentionally."

That was the way to do it, even if it were not Busalmeh's doing. Life needed to be pitted against death; the women of the village needed to believe this in order to give up their incurable love. The drowned men still were hopeful about the shore; they still saw the women of the village. If the women would go back to their lives and work, who could tolerate being ignored, even if he is one of the drowned?

With the strange frightening whisper instigated by Nabati, Zayer Gholam's daughter, among the women of the village, they pulled their hearts away from the shore. To the women, it was now as clear as day that with the presence of the drowned men in the village and their heavy doleful glances, Busalmeh wanted to make everyone die of grief. Was it not true that every dead man at sea had a minder who would not allow him to get close to the village? There was no longer any room for doubt and hesitation, Busalmeh had restrained the minders of the drowned men.

From seeing eyes empty of love and kindness, empty of familiarity, the bones of the drowned men writhed in pain, they felt chilled, and they crouched into themselves. Distraught and sad, they waved the branches of coral and aquatic flowers in the direction of the village, and the movement of their hands was becoming slower and slower. The living were going about their own work and business, as though the drowned were like a weight on the lives of the people of the village.

None of the drowned men ever thought that his presence would one day make the village helpless or weigh down the living with fear and horror. Now they knew that they had a place in the memories of the living, and that they needed to leave and go their own way... But where?

One day, finally, they heard the voice of Mahjamal among all the voices:

"Go back... Go back!"

Many times, they had seen Zayer Ahmad yelling something and waving his hand toward the sea and the end of the horizon. And now, the voice of Mahjamal, who was a mermaid-human offspring, was showing them the solution; but where were they supposed to go, and how?

The six sons hopelessly waved their hands, pointed to the sea, and in a tongue-less tongue said that they had lost their way to death.

Until late at night, Mahjamal sat thinking beside Zayer Ahmad's men on the top of the water cistern. It was only he who could act as a guide for the dead of the green and blue waters of the sea. The way Zayer Ahmad looked at him, his pleading eyes, made Mahjamal once again set his heart on the sea.

In the morning of the fifth day, they saw the drowned men packing up their gear and lifting anchor. Mahjamal was hitching a boat to their boat.

When Mahjamal set the sail of the six sons' boat and turned the bow of their vessel toward the offing of the sea, in the gathering of the village men, Zayer Ahmad said:

"If Busalmeh smells it...?"

7

Two days later, they found Mahjamal at the edge of the sea, unconscious. The soles of his feet were cracked, and the skin of his shoulders fissured. The village men picked up his wounded body and took him to Zayer Ahmad's house.

No one knew what had happened to Mahjamal. The women of Jofreh, who had regained their wits, thought that in retaliation for the coldness and lack of kindness of the denizens of the land, the drowned had beaten him and tossed him into the sea. But the story that they heard from Mahjamal left everyone bewildered and laughing.

At sunset, before reaching the offing of the sea, Busalmeh had blocked the way to the drowned, and thinking that all the passengers on the boat were dead and within the domain of his power, he mocked them and began loudly laughing at them. He taunted them with the unkindness of humans, sprinkling salt on their wounded hearts. Mahjamal took advantage of a moment of Busalmeh's neglectfulness and tied him to the mast of the boat of the drowned men, so that in the morning, he could put Busalmeh on trial before all the denizens of the sea and execute him near the village. In the morning, however, with the shining of the sun, Busalmeh became thin; the sun had melted the fat in his body, and he was able to easily free himself from the ropes and escape.

The men and women of the village listened to Mahjamal's strange story and were certain that this time, he had lost his wits at sea.

8

Mahjamal had become the butt of the joke for the people of the village, and Kheyju, agonized by the hidden and open sneering of the people, pleaded with Nabati:

"How can you stand it? They're making fun of him."

But Nabati laughed boisterously. Tears had welled up in her small black eyes from the force of laughter, and along with the others, she also made fun of him. Zayer Gholam was the ringleader. He would sit in a friendly manner beside Mahjamal, rub his shoulder, and as he opened and closed the flap of his loincloth and winked at the others, he would ask:

"So, Mahjamal, what did you see when Busalmeh got free from the rope?"

And Mahjamal would explain that the six men suddenly disappeared, the surface of the sea was cleansed of the drowned, the skeleton of the boat collapsed, and as a hand came out of the sea slapping him, he dragged himself toward the village.

In the entire history of the life of the village, there had been no story in which Busalmeh had been tied in ropes. Busalmeh was never even captured in the stories, and now a vagabond gypsy and stranger, without having the slightest doubt about his wits, in clear daylight, and loudly, claimed that he had tied Busalmeh of the seas in ropes.

Indeed, what if Busalmeh were to hear his voice and become wrathful? The boisterous laughter of the men of the village, however, showed that no one underestimated Busalmeh. He ruled all the seas, and he controlled the bread and sustenance of all fishermen.

The village people laughed from the bottoms of their bellies, hoping that Busalmeh would hear their laughter. Behind this laughter was an odd request; the people were asking Busalmeh to be kind to them, to disregard the help they provided Mahjamal in getting back to Jofreh safely from the sea, not to cut off the bread and sustenance of the fishermen, and not to incite the sea to rebel against them.

The laughter was the laughter of supplication at the threshold of Busalmeh. By laughing at Mahjamal, the village wanted to soften Busalmeh's heart. Under Kheyju's angry eyes, Zayer Ahmad would keep silent and allow the game to continue, so that if some day Busalmeh discerned the trick and ruse of the village and learned that Mahjamal was alive, he would not be wrathful toward them, and only one person would be sacrificed, not the entire village.

And had it not been for the nocturnal weeping of the mermaid, one could easily see Mahjamal's fate. The man the village teased, the children chased, and others mocked.

* * *

One night, the village was awakened by a lonesome wailing sound. The sound came from the sea. Bubuni turned up the low wick of the lantern, came to the window, and saw her. A little blue mermaid was shaking her hands toward the moon, and weeping.

Terrified, Bubuni ran to the corner of the room. She saw Captain Ali sitting on his bedding, dazed and confused. She breathed a sigh of relief. Sleepily, Captain Ali asked:

"Who is it moaning at this time of night?"

Lantern in hand, Bubuni scanned the room with her eyes, looking for the can of salt. She said:

"It's one of the blue ones. Recite the salutation to the Prophet."

She herself recited the salutation loudly. When she found the can of salt, she brushed the ashes off the burning charcoal in the brazier, and poured salt on the fire; but the mermaid did not disappear. Facing the sea, she kept moaning and weeping all night long, into the morning.

In the morning, sleepy and confused, the people of the village were on the shore. They had made small campfires at the edge of the sea, and the women, with puffy eyes from sleeplessness and weeping, were sprinkling salt on the flames, and, brokenhearted, the mermaid moaned in misery. Zayer Ahmad walked among the people, confused and distraught. To him, it was as clear as day why and for whose sake the mermaid had come ashore. Zayer Ahmad had often told Mahjamal not to touch the blue mermaids, not to even get close to them, and now, given the mermaid's condition, no one knew what might happen to the village.

Based on all the signs that Zayer Ahmad Hakim had come up with in his solitude since the sea voyage, he knew that Busalmeh was toying with them, and that perhaps he intended to wipe Jofreh off the face of the earth, little by little. The sudden rush of the drowned to the village, the story that Mahjamal had made up—and it was as clear as the light of day to everyone that someone had gotten under his skin and fabricated the story—the mermaid rising out of the water and her wailing—which would seem strange even if it was not on the order of Busalmeh—every last thing indicated the blind rage from which Zayer Ahmad had imagined he had escaped.

The entire village knew that if a mermaid fell in love with a fisherman, she would rise out of the sea very soon, before the sun ripens the dates. Many days had passed since the sea voyage, and the presence of the blue mermaid in the Jofreh Sea and her moaning did not indicate love and kindness. It was quite likely that her presence was a calamity that had risen from the depths of the gray waters to obliterate the village from the face of the earth.

Busalmeh of the seas sometimes—when he is unable to force the denizens of the green and blue waters to perform a task—wakes the dead of the gray waters from their sleep of death.

Until they have gone to the depths of the gray waters, the dead of the blue and green waters are real men. The fire of expectation and hope that blazes up in the root of their soul forces them to indicate their existence with an action, a word, or even a small sigh. The dead of the blue and green waters have never been submissive and obedient, like slaves. Whenever Busalmeh wants to destroy something, to eradicate some country from the face of the earth, he awakens the dead of the gray waters from their sleep of death, the submissive and obedient dead who assume any form to appease to Busalmeh, in order to once again return them to the depths of the gray waters.

Zayer Ahmad bit his lips, and when alone, he writhed within himself. In the face of someone like Busalmeh, ruses are another form of struggle and denial. It was most likely that the times would have passed better than they had if he had severed Mahjamal's head and tossed it into the sea. It was most likely that this would not have disturbed the sleep of death of the dead of the gray waters, and the village would not have been enslaved to Busalmeh's wrath.

The helmsman of the ship must not yield to the desires of the heart. He must track the favorable winds, steer the rudder, and arrive at the anchorage safely.

Such was Zayer Ahmad and his strange doubts. Nonetheless, unwanted anxiety would not release its grip on him. He was afraid, he was afraid for Mahjamal. That morning, he had seen him terrified and pale-faced on the top of the water cistern, his lips trembling and his eyes looking toward the sea.

Mahjamal was sitting in the pomegranate orchard behind Zayer Ahmad's house, and the pain of having no one and being a stranger in exile was nearly cutting him in two. He had seen the mermaid in the morning and had recognized her. Her blue hair was disheveled and stuck to her forehead and cheeks, and large teardrops, like pearls, slid over her cheeks to her lips, which trembled strangely. She shook her hands rapidly in distress. She moaned. She said something, something the meaning of which humans could not understand, and Mahjamal seemed to be human. He was human, and he did not want to be taken to the depths of the green waters. He liked the land, the sun and the moon and the darkness and the light of its nights and days. Mahjamal had been afraid, and in order for the mermaid not to see him, he had taken refuge in the pomegranate orchard.

In solitude, Mahjamal prayed, appealing to the sky and the sea to take the mermaid to the depths of the blue waters. But her strange voice that sounded like wailing and screaming would not let go of him. She moaned continuously, and at times, unable to tolerate hearing the pain in the mermaid's voice, Mahjamal peeked from behind the wall of the pomegranate orchard and saw her facing the women of the village, moaning and pleading.

Aquatic Mahjamal, a captive of the land and the village, no longer understood the language of the mermaid. Distraught and confused, he looked at his own palms, hoping that, as in the past, he could read what was going to happen in the future; but his hands were as smooth and dusty as the village road.

The villagers stood on the shore. Nabati had turned dark from fear and was hiding behind Zayer Gholam who, heedless of the wind blowing the flap of his loincloth open, was standing there and looking at the mermaid. Setareh cried along with the mermaid. Outside the vision of Kheyju, who was standing there angry, Madineh was sitting beside Mama Mansur, taking long puffs on her hookah and moaning:

"Your days are turning dark, woman. Your days are turning dark!"

Mama Mansur, hesitant and worried, rubbed her legs:

"I am grieving, my tall handsome one, grieving."

Mama Mansur was afraid, afraid that the mermaid had come ashore for her only remaining son, Mansur. Unconcerned and carefree, Bubuni was chewing gum. She looked at the mermaid and wished she could cry like her, moving her head from side to side, distressed and in misery, so that if she quarreled with Captain Ali or found out that he, unbeknownst to her, was looking at the children of the village and sighing, she could begin to shed tears. No one could hear the wailing of the mermaid and remain calm. If only she could dishevel her hair like the mermaid and move her head from side to side, Captain Ali—whom Bubuni had now imprisoned in the house and who was looking at the mermaid from behind the bars of the window—would stay by her side forever.

The mermaid moaned for one entire day and night. Helpless and hopeless, the women of the village brought out their talismans. No salt was left in their houses. The women had sprinkled the last grains of salt on the fires, yet the mermaid would not disappear. The talismans did not work, as though something more powerful than all talismans in the world kept her in the waters of the village.

The following day, they saw the mermaid, gaunt and scrawny from the strange sorrow of love, dragging herself along the soft sand on the shore. The mermaid slithered on the sand; placing both hands on the ground, she slid her fish half on the sand and moved herself forward. Water dripped from her blue hair, and pain strangely rippled in her eyes. Sometimes, she stopped motionless, bewildered and pleading. She looked at the people of the village, who were walking backward upon seeing her, and again dragged herself along the sand.

Exhausted, she reached the dry land of the village at noon. Small pieces of stone had made wounds on her fish half. She would press her lips together, close her eyes from pain, and pant.

Love alone can make a human abandon his hearth and home, and love for a handsome fisherman alone can separate a small mermaid from the sea to the point of scooting along on dry rocky terrain and ignoring the pain and suffering of the land.

The sun scorched the soil of the village. The sky had turned white from the heat, and sweat poured from the heads and faces of the men of the village. The mermaid scooted on the hot soil, her fish half blistered, the water in her body evaporated; and in a halo of blue steam, panting from the heat, she was moving toward the silk tassel acacia tree. She was running out of breath.

When she reached the silk tassel acacia tree, she leaned her head against its trunk, and with her bewildered eyes, gazed at the legs of the women who knew the language of her heart and who were looking at her, weeping. Madineh rocked back and forth like an anchorless boat, moaning:

"Your days are turning dark. Your days are turning dark, woman. Don't go away from the sea."

Distraught and in misery, Setareh knew for whom the mermaid was looking, and she knew where he, Mahjamal, was hiding in the village; but her heart would not allow her to make a gesture toward the pomegranate garden, for Mahjamal to be enslaved at the hands of the mermaid. Without the presence of Mahjamal, the world was a desert for her, but the tears and moaning of the mermaid were destroying the light in her heart. When Zayer Ahmad saw the mermaid looking at the legs of the women so enviously and pleadingly, he realized that she was not of the dead of the gray waters, but the same small mermaid who was at one time supposed to become the bride of Busalmeh. Zayer Ahmad's back twinged. In that intense heat of the day, he felt a chill, and he saw the men of the village standing there irate and angry. Then he saw Zayer Gholam turning around with a meaningful look, and gazing at the pomegranate orchard, perhaps intending to let the mermaid know where Mahjamal was.

Zayer Ahmad cast a look at Zayer Gholam, and with his hand, pushed him behind himself, lest the mermaid see him and get a signal from him about Mahjamal's hiding place, even though, as did all the people of the village, Zayer Ahmad knew that when they come to the land, the mermaids ignore the gestures of the land men, and only ask about the man they are looking for from the women; and they want the women to exchange their legs with their fish half to be able to traverse evenly on the uneven land in search of the one they are longing for.

The mermaid rubbed her hand on her wounded fish half and pointed to the legs of the village women. The women held the corners of their scarves between their lips to prevent the sound of their sobbing from making the mermaid even sadder. Had it not been for the presence of Mahjamal's blue eyes and the fear of Busalmeh of the seas, who could withstand it? What woman could look at her pleading eyes and not give her soul to this strange lover from the seas?

Kheyju saw Madineh fall to her knees, crying and wailing. She grabbed her in her arms from behind and took her away, so that temptation would leave her soul and the mermaid would not make her surrender with the gestures of her hands and the pleading in her eyes.

In despair, pouting and saddened, the mermaid hopelessly placed her hands on the ground and began to move. The women averted their eyes.

It was sunset when she reached the middle of the village. She was thirsty. Her tongue had dried, and she was looking around, confused and lost. The women of the village took turns going to the sea, filling their large tin cans full of water, and pouring it on the mermaid, so that she could travel her path to her destiny less sorrowfully.

The mermaid paused motionless for a moment, looked around, and as though someone had called her, began to move toward the graveyard, a path that reached the dirt field and was rough and full of rocks. But the mermaid continued on her path without regard for the scrapes and scratches that the rocks left on her body. Her fish half was bleeding, and to prevent her mermaid body from coming in contact with small and large stones and thorns, Setareh spread her petticoats along her path.

Late at night, she reached the graveyard, in which there were only two old graves, a memento of the migration of the people of the village from Fekseno to Jofreh. Everywhere was moonlit. The mermaid went to the graves. Her body was bleeding and smeared with mud. Distressed and distraught, she pushed the grass and weeds from the tops of the graves with her small blue hands. She bent over the graves and put her ear to the gravestones.

She seemed not to have heard any sound from the heart of the ground, since she raised her head, confused and bewildered, and sniffed. She then turned toward the village, sniffed again, and looked at the women of the village who were standing under the light of the moon. A faint smile appeared on her lips. She sank into deep thought for a long while, and then suddenly slid toward the village.

When the mermaid with her small wounded hands pushed open one of the double doors of the first house and peeked into the courtyard, sleepy and sorrowful, the women of the village wept.

Zayer Ahmad, who was sleepily standing on the top of the water cistern listening to the cock-a-doodle-do of roosters that were crowing collectively, realized that before the mermaid had checked all the houses one by one and had found Mahjamal, she would not leave the village. All night long, Zayer Ahmad had quarreled with himself and the frightened, tired men, who wanted Zayer Ahmad to pull Mahjamal out of the pomegranate orchard and deliver him to the mermaid to take to the depths of the green waters.

At night, Zayer Ahmad had seen the men of the village hanging around the pomegranate orchard and peeking inside from above the wall. Zayer Ahmad had taken them by surprise in the pomegranate orchard. The men were sitting facing Mahjamal, staring into his eyes, and, without saying a word, were asking him to submit to the request of the village. Mahjamal had crouched up against the wall and breathed a sigh of relief upon seeing Zayer Ahmad.

The mermaid searched the village for seven days and nights. She opened the doors of the houses one by one and sniffed. Setareh poured seawater on her body day and night, and the village was adapting to her presence, to the wounded sorrowful presence of a female who would not tire in her endless search.

Adapting, this eternal savior, could return calm to the village. In their continuous chitchat, the women tamed the angry men, and Zayer Ahmad took the side of the women of the village, the side of his one and only daughter, Kheyju, who every now and then visited Mahjamal and gave him some food.

Even if the mermaid continues to search the village forever, one can still go on living. It is not implausible that, similar to women of the land, she would also give up her search and return to the sea.

The presence of red mermaids in clear daylight in the morning of the eighth day horrified the village. On that day, mermaids who in the depths of the green waters had heard the sound of the wounds of the blue one turned red from anger, rose up, and began to move toward the village sea. It was at that very moment that Zayer Gholam, along with the other men of the village, terrified by the presence of the red mermaids, ran toward the pomegranate orchard and came chest to chest with Mahjamal, who had seen the red ones and was trying to find a way to flee.

Zayer Gholam grabbed him by the collar and dragged him along like a sacrificial lamb. The commotion of the men resonated in Mahjamal's ears, and the fists of the frightened men pounded his head and face. Mahjamal was shouting:

"Reed flute! Reed flute!"

Setareh heard him and, frightened, ran toward Zayer Ahmad's house; and even though fear had dried her tongue, she conveyed to Kheyju, who was standing dumbfounded on the water cistern looking at the red mermaids:

"Reed flute!"

A moment later, the reed flute was in Setareh's hand and Mahjamal was in the village square. Zayer Ahmad had gotten himself there and drove the angry men away by shouting at them.

Mahjamal took the reed flute from Setareh. If the sound of sad Fayez songs turns the blue mermaids into red, would that not mean that the sound of happy Khayyam-style songs would quell the fire of the wrath of the mermaids?

Fearful and in anticipation, the village was keeping one eye on the sea and one on Mahjamal. Zayer Ahmad was at a loss. He could not come up with a solution... What was going on in Mahjamal's mind? If he played Fayez songs, the sea would roar over the village, and before long, Zayer and all that he had hoped for would be drowned. You who miss the land... Mahjamal... Mahjamal of the land, what are you doing?

Mahjamal had the reed flute to his lips and began to play a song:

"Swallow of the north wind..."[8]

Held breaths...were released! The breaths of women and men who had lost the way to their own happiness. The sound of the reed flute whirled around above the village like the silk skirt of a woman in love. It went toward the sea and enveloped the mermaids who had turned red from anger, and the men of the village gradually remembered the ancient words—words that took the past and the future of the world for naught and spoke of a moment in which humans, the jinn, and fairies breathe. Now...right now, neither has a tomorrow come nor a past that has passed...

With every word that flew from the tongues of the women and men of the village, the sea was becoming calm, the red mermaids were becoming a rainbow of light, and the blue lovesick mermaid was gazing at the harmonious rhythm of the feet of the women and men who, intoxicated by the sound of the reed flute and the Khayyam-style song, in a strange dance were shaking off their fears with their bodies.

The blue mermaid had reached an open area... Mahjamal's blue eyes were gleaming. Mermaids of different colors were turning blue and floating and dancing; they were going toward the offing, and the sound of the reed flute had taken away the consciousness and attention of the people such that they did not see that the wounds of the blue lovesick mermaid were healing, and her fish half, joyfully and so fresh, was reviving her inescapable desire to jump into the sea.

8- This is the first line of one of the most popular Khayyam-style songs. In contrast to sad Fayez songs, Khayyam-style songs are usually happy and often accompanied by dancing, particularly in Bushehr.

❧ 9 ❧

The fact was that this mermaid was unique among the mermaids of the world. She had broken the law of the hearts of the little girls of the sea, and she respected Mahjamal, the handsome fisherman, simply because of his lonely, loving presence on the land, or anywhere else he was in the world.

This distress of the soul and wandering of the mind was given to her by one of the six sons of Mama Mansur, with the words that, when Mahjamal had become the guide of the drowned, Busalmeh had taken him to the depths of the gray waters.

The mermaid was wandering in the seas day and night. In search of a piece of his soul, she traversed all the seas. She went among the eternal dead to the depths of the gray waters, disturbed their death of a thousand years, then, distraught and hopeless, she hastened toward the village, so that perhaps she could find some sign of him. And when she heard the happy voice of his heart, a broad smile of contentment appeared on her face, and she released the fisherman to walk on the land, to live, and to love.

This is precisely what lovers do in the world. They go beyond themselves and leave, so that the other, the one whom they hold as dear as life, can interpret his world in his own custom and ways. Yet, the tradesmen of the world, in their eternal give and take, in order not to be indebted and beholden, coil themselves around a human body like a snake around the neck of life, and extract the breath of a human being, such that he will sit in some corner, hollow and empty of all love and kindness, counting the numerous days of life, hoping for its end... But love is devoid of the trade of the tradesmen of the world; it translates into leaving, not staying, and into reaching beyond oneself.

As the mermaid jumped into the blue waters and left to grow old with her story of love, Setareh breathed a sigh of relief. The village forgot the past twenty-three days, as well as the future. It surrendered to the sound of the reed flute and the rhythm of the heart of humans. Then, exhausted and jubilant, it went into three days of slumber...

In wakefulness, however, the past slowly became momentous once again. Kheyju, who had understood the meaning of the presence of the blue one, like all women in the world who cannot tolerate hearing someone else's name without demeaning herself and breaking the cup of her patience, calmly and deliberately sang another song, in which there was no sign of the heart and love. From her perspective, the mermaid had been driven from the court of Busalmeh and thrown on dry land to spend a while in the village, in order to appreciate the value of the waters of the sea and to no longer set her heart on crazy things in the depths of the green waters.

Mahjamal had found a place in the eyes of the women of the village. And in order not to lose her fortitude and to prevent the intense jealousy that she had never before known any sign of in herself from grabbing her by the throat, Kheyju demeaned Mahjamal.

The sole daughter of Zayer Ahmad, during the days and nights of the mermaid, had seen Mahjamal, gaunt and thin, sitting in the pomegranate orchard; and, frightened by the slightest sound, he would be startled. Then, one day, as he was taking an earthen jug of water from Kheyju's hands, his hand had shaken and Kheyju had helped him to hold the jug of water to his thirsty lips, and Mahjamal had looked at her in such disbelief that Kheyju had let go of the jug and fled from that lonesome puzzling glance.

If a woman is a woman, she can easily read the thoughts and what is going on in the mind of the man through his eyes. During those days, Mahjamal had no refuge and was searching for kindness. The feeling of guilt and embarrassment at having caused the suffering endured by the village had left him gaunt. Kheyju had seen how the men of the village regarded the presence of Mahjamal as a sign of ill fortune. Those days, Mahjamal weighed like a heavy burden on the back of the village, and in order for the village not to drown, it wanted to remove that weight and throw it into the depths of the waters of the sea.

The longing to stay alive and be with the people on the land had forced Mahjamal to seek the warmth of some affection, and Kheyju had been bringing him food during his lonesome days and had sat next to him, and, without saying a word, had looked at him and seen his blue eyes restlessly wandering between the earth and the sky.

Kheyju already knew that Mahjamal, even with his manly presence, had an uncommon heart. Human inattention had plundered his soul. Nevertheless, she did not want the women of the village to think that Mahjamal was like the sun, the center of the universe, to her. Something strange formed a lump in her throat when she heard the stories of the women, the stories about Mahjamal and the mermaid, and the mesmerizing sound of the reed flute that had made the red mermaids dance.

The women of the village, however, did not bother with Kheyju's story. Wherever they were, they talked, cried, and laughed about the way the mermaid looked at Mahjamal, her smile, and about when she sniffed the graves.

Setareh was happy. She saw that Mahjamal held the village in respect. She had seen that he, that fisherman, that young offspring of strangers, had nested in the hearts of mermaids, and that this was the way of the true lovers in the world: they want others to honor the one cherished in their hearts.

Among the men, the situation was curious. Mansur would avert his eyes from Mahjamal's, and Zayer Gholam, embarrassed by his own fear and apprehension, hung around him, jokingly punched him in the arm, and clumsily tried to erase the bitter memory of the pomegranate orchard from Mahjamal's mind.

The fear of guilt and sin, the guilt that was born of the thought of surrendering and killing Mahjamal, forced the men of the village to be kind to him.

Mahjamal, who during the days and nights of the presence of the mermaid had seen himself demeaned in the eyes of the men of the village, with a faint smile, entrusted his heart and soul to the wings and feathers of their kindness; but in his heart, without showing it on his face, he told himself that on some other occasion, in its anger, the village would obliterate him.

Mahjamal had seen the fear of death and loss of life in the eyes of the men, and now he knew that for the denizens of the land, for humans, no jewel is more precious than life. Mahjamal had even seen the regret and hesitations of Zayer Ahmad; and, worried about the coming days, Zayer Ahmad sat on the top of the water cistern and looked at his men, who would not leave Mahjamal alone, without saying a word, asking Mahjamal to forget the days and nights of the presence of the mermaid.

Zayer Ahmad was aware of the doubts and the love and hatred of the men regarding Mahjamal. Love and hatred, like two plates of a balance scale, and with the heaviness and horror that thinking about Busalmeh created, shifted one way, then another. Every fear, every calamity that descended, hung Mahjamal by the neck in their minds, and then, they would bring him down from the gallows and console him.

Zayer Ahmad had seen Mahjamal's fear and fleeing during the days of the presence of the mermaid, and he could still easily read on his face the remnants of that fear, the fear of loneliness, of having no one, and of being driven from the land.

Mahjamal was sustained by the people of the village. For a long time, he was at someone's house every night and in another house every day. The men of the village gave him their shark tails,[9] fishing nets, fish traps, or new *dishdasha*s, and the women attended to cooking and preparing food for him.

Was Mahjamal—who was capable of making the mermaids such homeless refugees that they would break the law of the seas, and capable of forcing the red mermaids to come and go in the waters of Jofreh without their customary wrath and rebellion—not buttressed from somewhere, by some faraway force?

Mahjamal breathed in the velvety soft kindness of the village. Yet, suspicious of all that kindness, he would smile and remain silent. He now comprehended the character and the temperament of humans. He knew that in tranquility and calm, hope for life and staying alive as well as love and kindness grow; and in hopelessness and fear of loss of life, wrath and anger come alive.

Thus it was that he no longer went to Zayer Ahmad's house. He fled from Kheyju, keeping himself away from the sole daughter of Zayer Ahmad, in order to get close to Zayer Ahmad.

During the days after they returned from the sea voyage and after the invasion by the drowned and the wailing of the mermaid, Mahjamal had seen that Kheyju's thoughts and attention were focused on him. He had seen her worried and angry eyes, but... What did Mahjamal, an offspring of gypsy strangers, have that was superior to others that would make that sole daughter single him out from other men of the village? Did he have a house and possessions of the kind that makes humans happy? Was this not another plot by

---

9- According to the author, the people of Jofreh would dry shark tails, which became very hard, and which they used in fighting.

Busalmeh, so that Mahjamal in his loneliness and exile would extend a hand toward Kheyju and steal the sole daughter of Zayer Ahmad, and Zayer Ahmad in his loneliness, which is the blight of the lives of humans, would hold a grudge against him in his heart and, on a particular day and at a specific time, would submit to the request of the people of the village in whose hearts and minds a large white pearl continued to shine? No! It was quite likely that with the love and kindness of Kheyju, destiny intended to blacken the heart of Zayer Ahmad toward him; otherwise, who, what sane person, would relinquish his one and only daughter into the hands of a man who had the curse of Busalmeh on him, a man who had not risen from among the humans and had no place on the land, a man who was rooted in the seas and had a wandering, restless heart on the land?

Kheyju did not understand the way he behaved. Other than having been his companion during the bitter days of loneliness, she had not done anything. Confused and at a loss, Kheyju was grieving. She had lost her appetite, and Madineh and Zayer Ahmad could hear her voice when she was dreaming, as though quarreling with someone. She clenched her fists in her sleep, she gritted her teeth, and Madineh and Zayer Ahmad would sit by her bed and look at each other, perplexed.

Those were difficult days. Kheyju felt like she was burning, longing for some action on the part of Busalmeh. She wanted the people to once again drive Mahjamal away, for Mahjamal to become homeless, to flee out of fear, to become gaunt, scrawny, and distressed, and to have no one to warm his heart with a smile. Jealousy had made her distraught, jealousy of the generous kindness of the village, which she knew was rooted in all sorts of calculations.

When she stood on the top of the water cistern and saw Mahjamal going from one house to another, she would close her eyes. Jealousy grew in step with lack of attention and lack of kindness, and Kheyju could not believe that anyone would ignore her, the daughter of Zayer Ahmad, but Mahjamal would pass by her without paying the least bit of attention to her. She could not even imagine that Mahjamal would fall in love with someone else. She was unique in the village. Even that vagabond offspring of strangers knew of her lineage. She was the sole daughter of Zayer Ahmad!

In her despondent afternoons, Kheyju would accompany the women of the village to the Well of Loneliness, so that without saying anything herself, she could hear what others had to say about Mahjamal.

Nabati would be drowned in her own strange delusions and was afraid of Mahjamal. Whenever she mentioned his name, her face would turn dark from fear. She would bite her lip, recite a prayer, and blow around herself for protection. The incubus of Busalmeh dominated her mind and subconscious.

In disbelief and fear, others spoke of Mahjamal as out of reach. Given that Mahjamal returned from the sea voyage safe and sound, given that red and blue mermaids alike fell in love with him, he was not like other people of the village. He must get his power from somewhere, from someone. How was it that when they found him by the sea, no one saw his mother? How was it that he went into the sea along with the drowned? If Busalmeh did not attack once again, if he did not display his wrath, it was surely because Mahjamal was a favored one, or because Mahjamal himself was that something that the people on the land for years and years had gazed at the sky in anticipation of.

But in Setareh's silence, the yearnings of a lonely woman were unmistakable, a woman who did not want to blemish her rural honor with words. At the same time, Kheyju held Nabati in respect, even though Setareh called Nabati the angel of ill omen, since Nabati said that Busalmeh was sure to attack again, and that this time, since he was toying with the village, no trace of anyone would survive.

When those who are strangers to the sea are enslaved by storm and fall into the water, they are most likely to set their hearts on a broken piece of wood. The drowning Kheyju, who was unfamiliar with the sea and storm, prayed to see Mahjamal weak and in need once again.

Mansur and Captain Ali were busy building a hut for Mahjamal.

They cut the dried branches of the palm trees and brought them to an open space in the village. The hut was being built under the shade of the silk tassel acacia tree, where favorable winds invited the ship of the human soul toward tranquility.

Mahjamal, however, would not set his heart on such pretexts. The pretexts of life and happiness were crossed out with lines of doubt. A certain anxiety would not let him free of its grip. He could read nothing in his palm. The old signs did not even cross his mind. He walked in the darkness of his mind, and he was lonely, lonelier than humans on the land. He was an offspring of strangers who had come from the sea and abandoned him on the land... Mahjamal, aquatic Mahjamal, had himself consented to the contentment of the land.

The work on building the hut was completed. For the first time after twenty years of homelessness, Mahjamal had a shelter of his own. Confused and in disbelief, he looked at the dry palm branches of the hut. Sometimes he would sit, and sometimes he would stand, and he did not know what to believe: the generous kindness at the hands of the people of the village, or the anger and begrudging he had seen in their eyes.

A person, even if he is Mahjamal who has a mother in the depths of the green waters and a father who is one of the drowned, becomes happy when he has shelter. It was as though they had removed a heavy burden from his shoulders. The homelessness of his aquatic mind had not allowed him to know the meaning of hearth and home. He would lean against the dried palm branches of the hut and close his eyes. Solitude, the solitude that he never before had, an unfamiliar, agreeable feeling, and perhaps it was this strange sense of ownership that made humans fight for their lives and existence with all their might.

The village, with its generous donations, shared its possessions with him. His hut now had a straw mat and an earthen water jug, which was filled with water at the hands of Setareh. A brazier of charcoal was lit in one corner, and he had a bed cloth on which he could sleep comfortably at night.

On the first night, the men of the village stayed with him until morning. Madineh prepared for him a tiger-tooth croaker fish, and Zayer Ahmad sat in the gathering of the men and prayed in his heart that this unity and solidarity would remain in place to the end of the world.

Mahjamal no longer went to other people's houses. During the day, Setareh brought food from Zayer Ahmad's house, handed it to him, smiled strangely, and left. When night fell, the men of the village would not leave him alone. They stayed with him until late at night, talking about everything. They would make jokes, laugh out loud, and then leave.

No one made any reference to the sea, lest it would remind Mahjamal of the days of the mermaid; but Mahjamal was not happy about this silence of the men. Sometimes he looked at them with suspicion and skepticism. Why did none of the men of the village in their nighty chitchats ever mention the name of Busalmeh? Why was there no talk about the denizens of the sea? Why did they only laugh and show kindness toward him?

In contrast to The Drowned, in contrast to the aquatic-humans, humans have complicated minds. Anyone who has a pure and truthful heart, like a pond of water that reflects the cloud and the moon equally, has a strange and labyrinthine mind; and Mahjamal, aquatic Mahjamal, who had inherited the human mind, thought that the land and its offspring knew who he was, and they would not easily accept him. Mahjamal's aquatic mind was conflicted. He neither wanted to go to the depths of the green waters, nor was he comfortable on the land.

One night, the sound of the shuffling of feet awakened Mahjamal. Frightened, he looked outside through the dried palm branches of the hut and recognized Kheyju. He sat down, distraught and confused. Kheyju quietly knocked. Mahjamal was hesitant. He did not answer; but Kheyju would not give up.

Mahjamal was fearful. Of one's own human volition, at this time of night, no girl would come to any man's house. Mahjamal was certain that through Kheyju, Busalmeh was wreaking some sort of havoc and sedition. He covered his ears so as not to hear anything, to overcome what his body wanted and his heart desired, and the hesitations of his mind. Kheyju left in the dark of night, humiliated, and never forgave herself.

Kheyju was not the kind of woman to deceive herself. The despondence and the need that had gripped her by the collar at this time of night made her ashamed. To be enthralled by a man, and for that matter a man like Mahjamal, who was neither a rebel nor unruly, nor had he pierced the chest of a good-for-nothing with the bullet of a Brno rifle, was not worthy of her, worthy of Kheyju, the daughter of Zayer Ahmad, who despite the fact that she was born in Jofreh, knew her tribe and lineage well, and she knew that she came from a tribe that had not even surrendered to the stars in the sky.

Kheyju had grown up with her father's stories; and in her mind, love was accompanied by the sound of Brno rifles and the fight and flight of rebellious outlaws.

That night, the sole daughter of Zayer Ahmad sat on top of the water cistern looking at the distant stars in the sky and recalled her father's stories.

Who was this Mahjamal? A coward of a man whose lips trembled at the slightest breeze that blew from the sea, the color of whose face drained, and who looked at the village as though its inhabitants wanted to plunder his being. A man so attached to the land that no one ever imagined that he would someday become a rebel or have a rebellious tribe and lineage... No, rebels have strange black eyes; they are alien to fear and fright; they do not attach their hearts to the land; they do not settle in one place for so long. In the chaos of their lives, rebels are on the move. They move from this land to the next, from this frontier to that.

He could not be one of those. Jinn do not have shadows, but Mahjamal had one. Kheyju had often seen his shadow, which got smaller and larger, just like human shadows. No, Mahjamal was not a jinn. No jinn would stay alive before the eyes of humans for twenty years. Carrying the burden of human life on one's shoulders, even if by mimicking, is not a simple task. For sure, the jinn sometimes assume human form; but they disappear quickly, they go back into their own shells quickly. Humans alone can settle down on the land in their own skin for a lifetime. Not even Satan can endure human suffering, even though sometimes for fun and making fun, he gets under human skin.

Mahjamal was not that young stranger who one day appeared by the well in Fekseno, thirsty and tongue-tied, and with whom Fanus fell in love. He had nothing. Mahjamal was not death, either. Death takes human form on earth for a short time. During his twenty-year presence, Mahjamal did not cause any death. He helped the village. He often solved problems.

Then, what was this Mahjamal, with those blue eyes and roasted brown skin and his strange fleeing from her and his even stranger silences?

If only someone, some people, would also demand Mahjamal from Zayer Ahmad, so that like Fanus, Kheyju, also with a Brno rifle in hand, could shelter him and fight against the messengers of faraway lands.

That brave young teenage relative, Fanus, had been able to endure only under the joyous shadow of love... And she cried out, screaming such that it echoed in the Fekseno Valley, among mountains that reached the heavens, the only and the last utterances that she could relay to that young stranger.

And what should she relay? With what words should Kheyju call Mahjamal to herself? With which custom and ceremony could she wipe the doubt and suspicion from his blue eyes?

A rooster was crowing far away, and the sole daughter of Zayer Ahmad was weeping, brokenhearted, without seeing the tall shadow standing next to the pillar on the top of the water cistern, worried about her, from early evening to dawn.

Zayer Ahmad, who had respect for love and honor, these eternal twins, worried about his sole daughter, had followed her from the moment she knocked on Mahjamal's hut. Now the grief-stricken voice of unrequited love was filling his heart with sorrow.

The weeping of women reminded him of the tear-filled eyes of Fanus, his fourteen-year-old twin sister, who years and years earlier, on the charge of sheltering the love of a rebel man in her heart, was taken to the Valley of Sorrow, to be cut to pieces with sickles and axes.

How the pages of time had turned to overwhelm Zayer Ahmad with emotions in this strange dawn. She was weeping. Kheyju, the one who put the flaps of her scarf in her mouth so that no one could hear her nocturnal sobs, was Fanus, the one who was afraid her brothers would surrender the young stranger to the faraway rulers, the man about whose presence Fekseno was perplexed, the man who did not speak a word, and who had settled in their house and then suddenly disappeared when Fanus died, the man whom no one knew from where he came and, finally, where he went.

Zayer Ahmad broke his nocturnal silence; he coughed and stepped forward to quiet Kheyju's sobbing. Embarrassed, Kheyju turned around from her solitude, suddenly began to stand, and pulled her veil over her face:

"You're awake, Papa?"

"Thinking about Fanus is tormenting me."

Kheyju stood up. How fortunate when one's heart is one with her Papa, and how shameful when a daughter deprives her Papa of sleep for the sake of a gypsy offspring who has no kith and kin!

Upon seeing Zayer Ahmad and his eyes that had suffered from sleeplessness, Kheyju regained her anger. She kissed her father's shoulder, and irate because of the night that had brought her nothing but fatigue and sad thoughts, said to herself that no matter what Mahjamal was, jinn or human, life or death, it made no difference. No matter where she saw him, she would pound him on the head with a club. What was the meaning of going to his hut at night?

What did she hope to gain? What secret did she have to reveal? In their surrender, women lose everything; and what was the use of this heart, this useless heart, when it dishonored a woman?

If only she could take one of the Brno rifles that Zayer Ahmad had concealed between the walls of the house and, before sunup, pierce a hole in Mahjamal's chest... If only...

❖ 11 ❖

Matters did not get that far. Fate acted differently. One afternoon, as the people were sitting in their houses and, flustered by the hot weather, fanning themselves, the earth shook. A strange sound reverberated in the village, and all the people jumped out of their houses, terrified.

The ground was shaking. The palm trees were trembling, and the silk tassel acacia tree, as though suffering from dizziness, its branches and leaves shaking, seemed to be collapsing sideways on the top of Mahjamal's hut. The huts were falling apart. Confused and at a loss, the people were standing in the courtyard of Zayer Ahmad listening to the strange sound from the ground and looking at the yellow dust that had covered the sky of the village. Busalmeh seemed to have put the village to sleep for a while. He had put the people to sleep, so that they would be preoccupied with the happy things in life, would get used to peace and quiet, to the nights of storytelling in Mahjamal's house, to the days of companionship and kindness by the sea, to the weaving of fishing nets, and to the seagulls and the blue sky.

Everything was chaotic and confusing. The water cistern had cracked. The earthenware water jugs were drained. Plaster on the walls of the houses was falling off. Walls were cracking, and dizziness had so overtaken the essence of the people that even when they closed their eyes, the world was spinning around their heads. One day, two days, three days... No, the world did not intend to calm down. With their mouths open and eyes before which everything trembled, the people looked to Zayer Ahmad; and Zayer Ahmad understood the meaning of the people's glances and their silence. What could he do? How could he calm the ground? Zayer Ahmad did not want to think about what was passing through the minds of the people of the village. For men such as Zayer Ahmad, in whose heart kindness and love have a home, often admitting inability and weakness might be more acceptable than reluctantly grabbing onto the only remaining solution engraved in the minds of others. Zayer Ahmad would keep silent. He would not open his mouth to utter a word, as long as the men had not said anything. But who could overcome the restlessness of the land? Busalmeh had blocked the path to the dead of the land, who, horror-stricken and frightened, were running under the hot soil of the land, bumping against one another and grabbing one another by the collar to find their ways to their graves.

This time, Busalmeh had pitted the village against the dead of the land, the dead who went to the depths of the blue waters of the sea during the week and only returned to the land on Friday eves, so that their children, who lived on the land, would say a prayer over their graves and tell them about their troubles.

The sound was the sound of their jumbled yelling, asking Zayer Ahmad to appease Busalmeh, not to keep them forever in the labyrinthine tunnels under the ground.

Zayer Ahmad would block his ears in order not to hear the voices of the dead of the land; but the horror-stricken eyes of the people, which were gazing at some spot of the ground every moment in anticipation of the dead rising from the ground and grabbing them by the collar, deprived Zayer Ahmad of peace and quiet.

Zayer Ahmad was fearful, fearful that his maternal uncle and his mother—who had been buried in the graveyard of the village in the early years after the migration—might so badly lose their minds in their death that they would rise from the heart of the ground and force him to surrender Mahjamal to Busalmeh.

An entire week had passed when Friday arrived, and the world continued shaking; Zayer Ahmad realized that this time, Busalmeh would not stop, and as long as Mahjamal's blood had not colored the soil of the land and the water of the sea, the dead of the land would have no peace.

The village could not sleep. Fearing that they might suddenly find themselves alongside all the dead in the world, at night, the people would sit in Zayer Ahmad Hakim's courtyard, horrified, and stare at one another. The moon and the stars in the sky were lost behind a yellow dust, and the people heard the howling of wolves from the outskirts of the village.

Nabati, who thought that the end of time had come and the world would shake so much that it would shatter to pieces like a glass jar, Nabati, who was worried about pieces of her body being torn apart, developed diarrhea and became so thin and gaunt that Zayer Gholam, foaming at the mouth and fuming, put her on his shoulders, took her to Zayer Ahmad's house, placed her on the ground before Zayer Ahmad's feet, and shouted:

"What are you waiting for, Zayer?"

In Kheyju's ears, Zayer Gholam's voice was most beautiful. With a smile on her lips and her head dizzy, she stood there looking at Zayer Gholam and Nabati, who appeared to be taking her final breaths.

Mahjamal was nowhere to be seen. In the minds of the people of Jofreh, once again, Mahjamal was gaining significance. Those who had been kinder to him were even more fearful; and in order to compensate for their sin and avert Busalmeh's wrath away from themselves and the village, they thought more about killing Mahjamal. Mahjamal had to pay with his life for his presence in the village. The dead of the land had to find their lost path to the sea and to their graves, and the land had to become calm.

In her loneliness, Setareh wept. She wept night and day, remembering the sky, which had been blue at one time, remembering the dead of the land who could not find their way anywhere, and for the sake of the loneliness and lonesomeness of a man who was cast away around the shrine of his holiness Sire Ashk without even one loaf of bread, and who had no one to talk to and erase the sorrow from his heart. In the days when the world was calm, Setareh had been able to see him under every pretext, to observe his blue eyes closely, and all this was enough for a woman of good reputation who had lost her man.

At night, they could hear the chirping of the roots of the palm trees. It was as though in their extreme anger, the dead of the land were clawing and chewing at the tree roots with their hands and teeth. The silk tassel acacia tree moaned night and day. It was most likely that thousands and thousands of young dead people had grabbed its disheveled roots, pulling them in different directions.

Zayer Ahmad was on the verge of madness and had lost control of everything. Bewildered, he looked at the village, seeing the astonishing consensus about killing Mahjamal, that sign of ill omen, seeing that they were sharpening their sickles, picking up the shark tails hanging on the walls, and looking angrily at him, the man who was still hesitant.

Zayer Ahmad already knew that the village was finished. Fourteen days had passed, and the dead were wandering, some in the sea and some in the depths of the cold dark soil.

No dead person would easily surrender to bewilderment and mental confusion. Often, in their yearning for calm and quiet, their yearning to rest for a moment without concerns and without life on the land disturbing the calmness of their own death, and in order to view the world without worries and anxiety, humans long for their own death.

How long can one side with love and kindness when death has opened its mouth and Busalmeh is squeezing the throats of the living and the dead in his claws?

The minds of the villagers were exhausted, and Zayer Ahmad knew that sooner or later, the dead of the land would carry Jofreh on their shoulders and, with the unity and solidarity that terror and fear creates among humans, toss the village into the sea.

When the people of the village saw the first dust-covered dead person who had stuck the upper half of his body out of the ground, weeping and shaking his hands toward Zayer Ahmad, without concealing their anger and wrath, they attacked what was left of Mahjamal's hut and set all he possessed on fire. The flames had not yet subsided when the dead person who had risen from the ground sank into the ground, and Zayer Ahmad consented to the killing of Mahjamal.

But who would listen to Zayer Ahmad, who knew that the dead person who had risen from the ground was one of the dead people of the gray waters of the sea, not one of the dead people of the land, since even though the dead people of the land and death become bedfellows, they never forget its bitterness. The coercion that is rooted in death and dying makes the human soul eager for love and life. Even humans who have died and whose eyes have been strangers to sunlight for years and years are not happy with the death of another. Zayer Ahmad knew that all this was due to the ruckus of Busalmeh's wrath. In fear and horror, the village had lost its mind.

Mahjamal, with his aquatic blue eyes, was a sign from the sky for Zayer Ahmad. The more Busalmeh, who is the sign of darkness in the world, insisted on his demands, the more he used all his power and might to grab Mahjamal, in Zayer Ahmad's mind and heart, the more dear Mahjamal became.

Kheyju was happy, and Zayer Ahmad looked strangely at his daughter, as though he wanted to communicate to her that she should save Mahjamal in any way she could.

When the men of the village gathered around Zayer Ahmad on the ground that was shaking, Kheyju was sitting in a gathering of women further away from the men. But Zayer Ahmad spoke so loudly in the gathering of villagers about the plan to kill Mahjamal that even Setareh figured out that he wanted to urge Kheyju to let Mahjamal know about it.

The following night, which was a full moon and twenty-one days had passed since the shaking of the ground in the world began, the men of the village were going to bring Mahjamal with his hands tied from the Shrine of Sire Ashk to kill him by the sea.

Kheyju went to the Shrine of Sire Ashk at night. For twenty-one days, she had controlled her heart not to take any food to Mahjamal. Twenty-one days earlier, she had seen him running toward the shrine with a bagful of bread...

Now Kheyju was going once again, to see him frightened and in need.

This time, Mahjamal was happy to see her. His dust-covered face blossomed into a smile. The shaking of the earth and the heavens for twenty-one days had made him despondent. He had not heard a human voice for twenty-one days; he had not seen the face of a woman.

Frowning and firmly, Kheyju said:

"Don't stay here; tomorrow night, they intend to take your life."

Without waiting for an answer, she left.

What pleasant music is the human voice! What an intimate friendship the human scent creates in the world! The world is beautiful because of human existence; and how forlornly the land, which is the mother of humans, drives him, aquatic Mahjamal, away from herself...

The lump in Mahjamal's throat lifted. The aquatic man was weeping. The entire world without the presence of land and humans was no more than a lonely house of exile. No, he did not want to go to the sea. He did not want to become intimate friends with the denizens of the sea, and he knew that even if he is to be killed, the soil would not take his aquatic body in trust. His fate—he who had a mother from the denizens of the sea and a father who was one of the drowned—had been sealed differently... Mahjamal had raised his hands toward the sea, calling out to his aquatic mother...

"Let the soil of the land be kind to me... I call on you in the depths of the green waters... Use your aquatic magic... Make the land and the denizens of the land kind to me..."

❧ 12 ❧

Hearing the voice of Mahjamal, the aquatic mother, who was sitting in a gathering of the blue mermaids of the sea, felt proud and elevated, and in expectation of his arrival, she laughed at the drowned men. It was the blue lovesick mermaid who heard his lonely voice in exile, and she brought the news to the blue mermaids who were still intoxicated by the sound of the reed flute and were dancing in their own imaginations. Thus it was that they blocked the way to the first large ship and enslaved it to the storm, dropping its cargo into the sea, and made the small and large waves swear on the hearts of lovers to bring the cargo of that ship to the shore of Jofreh.

All night until morning, the village tossed and turned in bed and sighed. How slowly time was passing, and how late the night of the full moon was arriving.

Waiting for the moment of being rid of the presence of a man whose ill fortune had been toying with the village for a long time and who had deprived everyone of rest and sleep, the people were listening to the chorus of roosters, and moments passed slowly.

Perhaps to shorten the day, they came out of their houses at dawn and went to the shore. The world was still shaking, and some colorful things were bobbing up and down on the ripples of the sea. They advanced cautiously, shaded their eyes with their hands, and tried to forget about the dizziness of the world and see what was on the water. The waves were pushing three boxes toward the shore. The surface of the water was covered with fruits, red apples, large oranges, and lemons, which they had never seen in their lives.

A sea filled with colorful balls and wooden boxes made them imagine that dizziness had impaired their vision. In their minds, they could not figure anything out. They were all watching each other out of the corners of their eyes. Finally, without saying anything to one another, staring at the surface of the water, they waded into the sea. Everything seemed real.

Shading his eyes with his hands, Zayer Ahmad Hakim watched and was puzzled. He had never seen people's minds so distraught that they all saw the same thing. From the silence of others, Zayer Ahmad had realized that, like himself, they were thinking that what they saw was merely a delusion, that they were imagining it. He did not know what to say. He could not believe his own eyes. The shaking of the world had deprived him of his power of judgment.

But the children of the village, who were not that concerned about the shaking of the world, cast caution to the wind, gathered up the colorful balls, and came back to the shore, shouting. Everything was so real that the whole village rushed toward the fruit, picked up the three wooden boxes, and brought them to Zayer Ahmad's house.

Busalmeh and his unrelenting wrath were forgotten for a moment. Zayer Ahmad cautiously grappled with the locks, and when he could not figure out what to do, Captain Ali and Mansur went at it, and as the ground was shaking the earth, they attacked the locks of the boxes with hammers.

The village suddenly pulled back. The boxes were all filled with pretty bottles full of sherbet. The people stared, bewildered. Slender-waist bottles, round and wide bottles, in all sorts of colors, and to prevent the bottles from colliding and breaking because of the shaking of the world, Zayer Ahmad immediately divided all of them up among the people of the village.

Zayer Gholam was the first villager to open the lid of his bottle with his teeth, and he gave a mouthful of it to Nabati, who, gaunt and frightened, was sitting next to him. Nabati's face became rosy a moment later. She stood up laughing, and took a lemon from the hand of Golpar, Setareh's daughter, and bit into it.

With the exception of Zayer Ahmad, who was still puzzled, the men and women, upon seeing how Nabati felt, downed what was in the bottles.

The world was shaking. The village was happy and cheerful, and Zayer Gholam had taken off his loincloth and was singing and dancing stark naked. His testicles would enlarge, swell up, and the children who had gotten over their fear and had drunk from the magical sherbet, touched Zayer Gholam's testicles, which were getting firmer with every moment, and they got their old wish.

Nabati laughed boisterously. Captain Ali was hugging Mansur and kissing him. Bubuni was punching Mansur on the head and face. Mama Mansur had picked up a stick, shaking it at the sea. Madineh was singing lamentations for Fanus and the mermaids, shaking her head and moaning. Setareh was wailing loudly, searching among the crowd, looking for someone with familiar blue eyes.

Drunkenness and sobriety, even should the distraught drunkard be Setareh, a rural woman of good reputation... Suddenly, Setareh began to yell, "Mahjamal, Mahjamal," and the village in its drunkenness began to weep. Where was Mahjamal, Mahjamal who was kind and handsome, who had suffered step by step along with the village? Who were those who set his hut on fire? Why did they do that? Which hand emptied the kerosene can on Mahjamal's hut? Who lit the fire? Which wicked person?

Setareh moaned and screamed, and Mansur, who was hugging Captain Ali, was punching the Captain on the face:

"He did it! He set it on fire...set it on fire..."

The words came out of Mansur's mouth heavily and sluggishly.

Bubuni had grabbed Mansur's collar, and Setareh had Captain Ali's hair in her fist. They were all beating and kissing one another.

Zayer Ahmad was at a loss. He was watching the people of the village, who seemed to have gotten the devil under their skin. The jinn that had been waiting in ambush in the bottles had robbed the villagers of their minds. Zayer Ahmad had tried several times to take the bottles away from the hands of the men of the village, but they seemed not to recognize him. Zayer Gholam had punched him on the chest, and Mansur had raised his bottle to hit him on the head.

Kheyju put an end to the commotion. As though driving a herd of unruly horses, she shook her hands toward the Shrine of Sire Ashk, and while trying to hold herself firmly on her feet, she yelled, "Mahjamal," and she headed in that direction.

The villagers had a difficult time finding the direction to the Shrine of Sire Ashk, as though some force had blocked the way to the shrine. Several times, they ended up at the Well of Loneliness, and eventually, with a gesture from the hand of Zayer Ahmad, who was shouting and showing them the way, with arms around one another's necks, shedding tears and singing, they set out toward the shrine.

The sound of the crowd had brought Mahjamal outside in fear. He was puzzled when he saw them. The crowd bumped into one another, wept, and laughed. Frowning and struggling to hold herself firmly on her feet, Kheyju was approaching him, and Mahjamal, who was standing there perplexed and dazed, as though having lost his mind, remained there so long that the sole daughter of Zayer Ahmad began to jump toward him. She grabbed him by the back of his neck, punched him on the shoulder, and staggering, took him along. On the way back, the women and men of the village drunkenly kissed him and pounded on him. In front of the crowd, stark naked, Zayer Gholam was snapping his fingers and dancing. The children were clapping.

When Kheyju arrived at home, she threw Mahjamal at Zayer Ahmad's feet and stared into her father's eyes. Smiling and silent, the crowd looked at Zayer Ahmad.

Mahjamal and Zayer Ahmad were the only two sober men in the village. Mahjamal was confused and puzzled. Zayer Ahmad was shaking his hands toward Mahjamal, pointing to the empty bottles, and did not know what was what.

The crowd's silence did not last long. Zayer Gholam dropped down weeping and kissed Zayer Ahmad's hands and feet, then pointed to Kheyju and Mahjamal. Holding a stick, Mama Mansur pushed the women of the village aside and came toward Zayer Ahmad. She held the stick firmly over her own head and stared into Zayer Ahmad's eyes. In her drunkenness, Setareh was weeping, kissing the hands and feet of Zayer Ahmad, Kheyju, and Mahjamal; and Madineh, away from everyone's eyes, headed toward the sea. She sat in the midst of the blue waters of the sea; and perplexed, she watched her legs, which were turning into the fish-like half of a mermaid. In its drunkenness, the village had forgotten Madineh.

Confused and puzzled by what had occurred, Zayer Ahmad faintly smiled. Now that the village had lost its mind, why should he not act wisely and recite the marriage vows? For Zayer Ahmad, it was as clear as day that an amazing force supported Mahjamal, a force that regarded Busalmeh as naught.

When Zayer Ahmad took the hands of Mahjamal and Kheyju and recited salutations to the Prophet and his family three hundred and thirteen times, the women of the village burst into tears; and, comfortable with what had been done, he thought that from then on, Mahjamal would no longer be regarded as a sign of misfortune in the village, and that even if only out of respect for him, as he was his son-in-law, no one should regard Mahjamal's presence as an excuse for the calamities from the sea.

Dancing and celebrations continued for one night and day. The women sang, and Zayer Ahmad had no idea where they had come up with those songs, nostalgic songs about the past, about a stranger who came to Fekseno one day thirsty, and Fanus, the bravest and most passionate girl in Fekseno, fell in love with him. He was a man regarding whom ultimately the rulers of faraway lands demanded that the people of Fekseno, who held love dear, hang from the gallows on the charge of being a rebel and an outlaw. Zayer Ahmad knew that many of the women who were singing the songs so fervently and passionately at the time of the migration were not yet even a gleam in the eyes of their parents on this dusty land... Do women make up such love songs in their own minds? And do these stories, these love stories, find their way into the hearts of their little daughters with the milk of their mothers?

* * *

In order to collect his thoughts for a moment, Zayer Ahmad came out of his house and went to the shore, where he saw Madineh floating and swimming in the water like a mermaid. Madineh was so preoccupied with the sea that she seemed not to recognize him. Alarmed, he hurried into the water, shaking his hands toward Madineh:

"Have you lost your mind, woman?"

As though not having heard him, Madineh stuck her head under a wanton wave, and Zayer Ahmad heard girlish laughter, the laughter of a fifteen-year-old girl who had at one time captured a small mermaid. Leaping forward, Zayer Ahmad came to her, and Madineh, in an incomprehensible language and with words which only came out of the mouths of mermaids, said certain things, and Zayer Ahmad shook his hands helplessly.

Could the jinn in the bottles that had raided the lives of the people of the village drive a person so out of her mind that this old woman would see herself as a young mermaid? Zayer Ahmad had doubts about his own mind. Surely, the harsh smell of the magic sherbet had disturbed his mind.

Zayer Ahmad stepped forward, and Madineh, frightened, fled with her fish-like half.

It was late afternoon when Zayer Ahmad took Madineh, whose fish-like half glittered, out of the blue waters of the sea and brought her to the shore, panting. As he was putting her on the soft sand, he saw with his own eyes that her fish-like half disappeared, the lines and signs of time appeared on her face, and she began wailing, helplessly, painfully, and forlornly.

"What am I doing here?"

13

After the commotion and chaos of the bottles and taking Madineh from the sea, the village slept for two days. Mahjamal and Zayer Ahmad were worried about the day of wakefulness to come. The two sober men of the village did not know, once the people did wake up, whether or not they would have regained their wits.

In the morning of the third day, they heard the sound of the moaning of those who had awakened from their two-day sleep. Women took out ceruse from their coffers, soaked it, and rubbed it on their own foreheads and the foreheads of their men, their fathers, and their children.

Mama Mansur moaned from her aching head. Nabati was holding her head between her hands, screaming. The men wrapped their heads with fishing net threads, and without recalling what had happened to the village, set out for the house of Zayer Ahmad Hakim.

When they saw Zayer Ahmad and Mahjamal busy repairing the cracks of the water cistern and Madineh and Kheyju gathering the broken glass, they regained their memories. It was only then that they became aware that the ground had calmed down and the world had stopped shaking. They remembered the magic sherbet, and Mansur and Captain Ali longingly stared at the sea and sighed.

Like the days of good fortune, the sea was blue. No boxes could be seen, and no waves brought the colorful balls of the world as gifts on its crown to the Jofreh shore.

Mahjamal must have broken the sorcery of Busalmeh. A fisherman had been able to make Busalmeh's constant wrath ineffectual and escape with his life. The villagers caressed Mahjamal with their eyes, asking him and his immortal being to bless the world. The sea was not going to bother the fishermen any longer. Because of a celestial force, Busalmeh had lost his power and might.

Now the village could deal with the destruction with peace of mind, with all that had happened because of the rebellion of the dead of the land. Mahjamal could see praise and appreciation in the people's eyes. He was happy, and he was sure that his aquatic mother had helped him.

Mahjamal was building his hut when Zayer Ahmad told him that it was a divine marriage vow, and that he could live with his sole daughter Kheyju in one of the rooms of Zayer Ahmad's house. Finally, Kheyju, who had wrapped her head tightly in her scarf and would not look at Mahjamal out of embarrassment, swept the small plastered room that had a window toward the sea. Madineh, who was moaning because of her aching legs, set up the bridal chamber in that room; and the women, in the dusk of sunset, joined together the hands of Mahjamal and Kheyju; and without waiting behind the door of the bridal chamber for the proverbial handkerchief to prove the bride's virginity and the groom's virility, early in the evening, they returned to their own houses and went to bed.

Once the bride and groom were alone, Mahjamal sat in a corner in distress. Overwhelmed by some strange unknown fear, he looked at the door and walls. He did not know how he was supposed to begin. Never in his life of twenty years had he been alone with a woman for this purpose, and now, the air felt heavy to him. Something was blocking his throat, and he was flustered by the heat... The daughter of Zayer Ahmad had an odd look in her eyes. She was drawing him to herself with the strongest hook in the world. Restless, Mahjamal knew that the scorching heat that burned his body was because of the presence of Kheyju and the flame in her eyes. He wanted to flee from that plastered room with its heavy yet desirable air, and to be freed, freed from the presence of a woman whose lips were trembling and whose eyes squinted and who said:

"It's late. Let's go to sleep."

She lay down on the far corner of the bedding that was already spread out, on her side, with her back toward Mahjamal, who was sitting and whose warm breathing she could hear.

But he was not sleepy at all. A strange, unknown scent wafted in the room. He could not distance his blue mind from the woman, whose stifled sobbing he could now hear. Mahjamal turned to his side and saw Zayer Ahmad's daughter. She was leaning her head against the wall, crying. A moment later, he was sitting beside her, looking at her like a bewildered child. He wanted to say something, but a lump blocked his throat.

"Go to sleep."

"Where?"

"Wherever you want."

There was no anger or hostility in Mahjamal's voice. Like all women in the world who often learn things on their own, Kheyju realized that her blue-eyed man did not know the customs and ways of the world. In the midst of sobbing, she opened her lips into a smile, grabbed Mahjamal's hand, and pulled him into bed.

It was as though he was riding on the blue waters of the sea when a pleasant breeze blows from the north and gentle wanton waves appear on the surface of the sea, and the fisherman, wishing to reach the shore, rows joyfully and with delight. Sometimes his hands are doubly strong and he pushes his chest forward fully, bends and bends, and drives fast, and a moment later, pulls back and calmly, calmly rows. The woman was an amazing sea. Mahjamal was riding his boat forward, rowing, reaching the shore, and knew that from then on, the land would accept him.

All night long came the sound of giggles from the direction of the sea. At times, a blue light shone within the frame of the window, a light that intoxicated and mesmerized Kheyju, as though an aquatic woman was laughing in the depths of the blue waters.

14

The people spent a great deal of time attending to the village. The restoring of life and calmness had increased the strength in their arms. They raised the walls that had crumbled, rebuilt the destroyed huts, repaired the doors and windows, and at times, gazed at the sea and sighed.

Zayer Gholam got up every day at dawn, went to the shore earlier than everyone to answer the call of nature, gazed at the sea, and could see nothing.

Children played, never leaving the seaside. They chased one another along the shore until sundown, jumped into the water, and concluded their days waiting for things to come from the sea, but nothing came.

Assuming that Mahjamal had something celestial and was capable of protecting Jofreh against all calamities from the sea and the land, the village had surrendered to calm and tranquility. Mahjamal had gone through the sea voyage, the invasion of the blue and red mermaids, and the days of the presence of the drowned and the shaking of the earth, and it was most likely that due to his presence on the soil of the village, none of the people of Jofreh would suffer any harm.

But when one night, suddenly the cries of Nabati reverberated throughout the village and awakened Zayer Gholam, Mahjamal came to believe that before having his covetous eyes on what the land bestows, man becomes enslaved by his fancy and imagination.

In her dream, Nabati had seen Busalmeh chewing on the village; she was caught between Busalmeh's teeth, and woke up as she was crying out. She told Zayer Gholam that the village was in Busalmeh's mouth and that soon everyone would be smashed to smithereens between his teeth. Horrified, Zayer Gholam looked around, then went to Zayer Ahmad's house in the middle of the night. To render the chaos of Nabati's imagination ineffective, Zayer Ahmad Hakim pointed to the sky and the sea and said that no one could swallow the place where he lives, even if it is Busalmeh, and that even if his head could reach the Pleiades, his hands could not reach the sky. He said that the sky and sea show that Jofreh is sitting magnificently where it is, and it is the same place that has existed for years. If Nabati's dream were true, he would also have to appear in the dreams of other women.

Waiting for Busalmeh to appear in the dreams of the other women of Jofreh, Nabati every morning went to the other women in the village, hung around them, and listened to their songs and stories; but eventually, she would go back home, despairing and angry.

Weary of Nabati's dreams, Zayer Gholam eventually came to the conclusion that the magic sherbet had caused the numbness and confusion at the roots of Nabati's brain.

The village had regained its life. Every morning, the pleasant sound of women singing came from the sea, women who were washing their dishes and clothes, and in their songs they pleaded with the sky and sea to keep Jofreh in place to the end of time, not to deprive the hearts of calm and kindness, and to return the fishermen from the sea with full baskets. In the late afternoons, the women of the village in their most beautiful petticoats went to the Well of Loneliness. Kheyju, the sole daughter of Zayer Ahmad and Mahjamal's mate, went to the well along with the other women, sometimes even earlier, to speak with the trapped Maiden in the Well about her happiness and good fortune. She spoke about Mahjamal and his odd caring and kind behavior, because she, the Maiden in the Well, upon hearing stories about happiness and good fortune, would forget about her own misfortune of remaining in the well. It was not fair for any new bride to forget her, the one who was to remain in the well until the end of time.

One day at dawn, alone and bewildered, Kheyju went to the Well of Loneliness. Jofreh was still asleep. Occasionally, a rooster crowed at the other end of the village. The color of the sea was the color of Warsaw silver, and the seagulls were asleep. She did not want to believe it; she did not want to again remember what she was feeling. But perhaps the Maiden in the Well would know how she felt. Kheyju was repulsed by the smell of Mahjamal. In the middle of the night, she had suddenly felt he was a stranger. She had refused his craving, and under the pretext of having a headache, she had pulled away from him. For a woman who had been in union with a man no more than a short while, this was a strange feeling. When Kheyju reached the well, fearful of her own temperament, she stuck her head into the well so that others would not know that she was distancing herself from Mahjamal and his voice, that she would turn her face away when she saw his blue eyes. Rather than hearing a voice of astonishment and distress, Kheyju heard laughter coming from the bottom of the well.

"Daughter of Zayer, may your offspring live forever. May your progeny survive."

Zayer Ahmad's sole daughter put her hand on her belly. She would fill the world full of Mahjamals, men with roasted skin and blue eyes, sons as tall as he. Then she stood up, happy and joyful. She threw a fistful of wheat into the well, and went back home.

The world was beautiful. God's sky was blue, and the baskets of the fishermen were filled with fish. The women sat around the clay bread oven and tossed the branches of the Bibi Maranjan plants into the oven. The fire flamed up. Madineh would stare at the flames to tell the women's fortunes. The women laughed and chased one another like children, and Kheyju carried the heavy burden of life with her.

In his life of twenty years, Mahjamal had frequently seen the women of the village carry within themselves the beautiful burden of life, but he had always passed by this sealed secret obliviously. Now, with every dignified and stately step that Kheyju took, with every breath that she breathed, his soul was filled with unfamiliar joy and happiness, a curtain was drawn aside from before his eyes, and he understood the secret of existence. The world belonged to Mahjamal. His roots were being spread in the land. The desire to build, stay, and work flared up in his arms and made him strive to work hard. Some restfulness needed to be brought to this heartfelt, delightful restlessness. He would have to erect a veranda with high pillars for the wind from the sea to ricochet in it and invite one's heart and soul to calmness. Mahjamal brought rocks from the sea, and Mansur and Captain Ali went with him to help. Other men also helped, in order for Mahjamal to honor the existence of his child by building a veranda across from the plastered room.

Zayer Gholam, who knew that Busalmeh had lost his magical power regarding Mahjamal, helped to build the veranda even more than the other men of the village; and Nabati, who still had her eyes focused on the sea and was waiting for a sign of the wrath of Busalmeh, would tell her father not to do it. She would warn him that the veranda would collapse on the heads of the men, and that Kheyju was going to give birth to a strange beast, and the village would become a spectacle for the whole world.

15

Finally, one autumn day, after the veranda had been erected and the women were washing dishes in Zayer Ahmad Hakim's Pothole near the shore, Nabati stood up suddenly, yelling happily, and pointed to a small white boat that was coming rapidly toward the village.

Frightened, the women abandoned their dishes, and before they reached the sand on the beach, the white boat passed them by speedily and stopped in front of Zayer Ahmad Hakim's house, under the silk tassel acacia tree where Zayer Ahmad's boat was on the ground on its side.

The women went to Zayer Ahmad's house. The men of the village assembled on the top of the water cistern and stared at a boat with no people in it that could move both on land and sea all by itself. Nabati was laughing; Zayer Gholam was looking at it suspiciously; and the men of the village were at a loss. Zayer Ahmad recited salutations to the Prophet and his family under his breath. Watching his mouth, the men of the village also recited the salutations, but the white boat did not disappear. The people of the village were standing on the top of the water cistern trying to peek. The children, wiggling restlessly and being drawn toward the boat, finally, without listening to their mothers, came out of Zayer Ahmad's house, gathered around the boat, and touched it, mesmerized.

When three tall, blond men with blue eyes emerged from the white boat, the children began to walk backward. It was unclear where in the world these aquatic men had come from. It was not certain that they were humans. From the top of the water cistern, Zayer Ahmad could see everything. Was Busalmeh toying with the drowned? Had he given them the power to reach land to drown the village? Or were they perhaps the denizens of the sea coming to the village in human form?

Mahjamal knotted his brow. He had seen the three men before, somewhere faraway. Mahjamal! Aquatic Mahjamal! Where have you seen them? Mahjamal put his hand on his forehead, his mind had been plundered, and on his palms, there was no sign or letter. With weary eyes, he looked at the blond men, who were smiling at the children of the village. The blond men spoke in the strangest language in the world, and they waved at the children, smiling. The children, who had not yet gotten over their fear, were standing at a distance, staring at them. When the first man said something to the other two and went back into the boat, the men of the village looked at Zayer Ahmad.

Zayer Ahmad could not understand what they were saying. The mouths of the people of the village were left open. Zayer Gholam, who had now come closer, saw that a man came out of the boat carrying a briefcase. He opened it and offered the children large red apples. The children suddenly got over their fear. They stepped forward and took the apples.

Zayer Ahmad breathed a sigh of relief. Now he knew that the tall blond men were not of the drowned, and that they could not be denizens of the sea. The blond men were kind; they touched the heads and shoulders of the children. They smiled.

Zayer Gholam, who had now gotten over his fear, snapped his fingers, straightened his loincloth, and, winking at Captain Ali and Mansur, said:

"Senigel, denigel, menigel, boo..."

A moment later, with the exception of Zayer Ahmad and Mahjamal, everyone gathered around them, and it was unclear where Zayer Gholam had found one of the empty bottles, which he showed to the blond men, all three of whom happily patted Zayer Gholam hard on his shoulder and gave him three of those magic sherbet bottles. After saying things which no one understood, they got back into their boat, drove into the water, and went all the way to the offing of the sea.

When the white boat reached the offing and disappeared from the view of the people of the village, nostalgically, the men sat on top of the water cistern and thought about the tall blond men who had come from the sea, and who spoke in the strangest language in the world, kind men on whose faces a smile never disappeared, and on whose white boat they could travel on land and sea and go anywhere in the world they wished to.

Suddenly, the hearts of the men of the village were filled with a heavy sadness. Hookahs were passed from hand to hand, and they regretted having so easily lost the offspring of the other side of the world; and had it not been for the bottles of magic sherbet, they could perhaps eventually have concluded that what they had seen was no more than a delusion, and that never had men of such kindness and good looks existed in the world.

Mahjamal's mind was distraught. Words and images fled his mind, and he did not know how to tell Zayer Ahmad what was in his heart, tell him that he had seen those men somewhere far, far away from the village.

At nighttime, when Zayer Ahmad was sitting in the room with five sashed windows and Madineh was dishing out the food, Kheyju heard a sound, a trembling, incomprehensible, childlike voice. Astounded, Kheyju touched her belly, and imagining that the summer heat had impaired her mind and senses, she picked up the straw fan and looked at Zayer Ahmad, who was leaning against the wall, not paying any attention to her.

Zayer Ahmad, who after the arrival of that strange boat had seen

Mahjamal confused and distraught, was playing with his long, thin fingers, and he knew that thinking about those men who suddenly disappeared in the sea had caused Mahjamal to be distressed.

When Kheyju heard that childlike voice the second time, surprised, she grabbed Mahjamal's hand and shook it. Mahjamal eagerly placed his ear on Kheyju's belly and said, "Thieves?" Madineh left the frying pan full of fish and listened to the childlike voice and said, "Leaves?" In disbelief, Zayer Ahmad leaned closer, baffled, and recited a prayer under his breath.

The world was becoming complicated. Mahjamal laughed, and Zayer Ahmad nodded his head, remembering the days when Mahjamal was a child. Zayer Ahmad's grandchild, who had not yet come into the world, was giving warnings, a singular son who had inherited soothsaying from his father. And what tricks the thieves in this day and age use to fool you! They come to you on a boat that was made by the greatest sorcerer in the world in such a way that it would easily come like the wind from sea to land, and they smile at you to once again finish you off at night and plunder all you have.

Kheyju brought out the religious mourning ritual drums. Mahjamal and Zayer Ahmad pounded on the drums on the top of the water cistern. Time passes quickly. The entire world must be warned about the presence of the blond thieves.

Bewildered, the people of the village came to Zayer Ahmad's house. Zayer Ahmad brought Kheyju to the top of the water cistern. The women, listening to the unborn grandchild of Zayer Ahmad, puzzled as to whether they heard "thieves" or "leaves," bewildered and frightened, looked at Zayer Ahmad, who, tired and soaking in sweat, was standing next to Mahjamal. The people of the village had focused their eyes on Zayer Ahmad's mouth. But the men of Jofreh had not assembled. Bubuni, who was standing in front of Zayer Ahmad, pointed to her house, and set off ahead of everyone else. When Zayer Ahmad reached Bubuni's house, he saw Captain Ali and Mansur who, along with Zayer Gholam, were busy with the bottles. Angrily, Zayer Ahmad grabbed Captain Ali by the collar and lifted him up, and the women smashed the bottles and dumped cold water on the heads of their drunken men. They assigned watchmen for the village on the same night.

Two days later, that strange boat reappeared; and this time, as well, no one could stop the children. Clubs in hand, the men were sitting in front of their houses, waiting for a gesture from Zayer Ahmad's finger to attack the blond thieves and drive them out of the village. Zayer Ahmad's intention was to send them on their way back to their own land wishing them well, and to explain to them in a reasonable language that he had figured out what their intentions were, and that the village had nothing, not even sighs to trade for moans. The blond men, however, brought out from that strange boat a man stretched out on a board, and worriedly placed him on the ground. Clubs in hand, the men of the village did not move, but the women of the village came out of their houses and approached the boat. When Zayer Ahmad reached the boat, he was taken aback. The man stretched out on the board was dead. Zayer bent over the corpse, looked at his face, and with a gesture of his hand, the men of the village put their clubs down on the ground.

The blond men said some things, and with their hands, pointed at the dead man, then at the ground. Guessing, Zayer Ahmad figured out that the blond men wanted to know where the graveyard was. Now having gathered around the white boat, Zayer Ahmad said to Mahjamal, "I guess they want to bury their dead man." The women of the village began to cry and wail.

Noon was approaching, and a dead person, no matter who he was and from what part of the world he had come, should not be kept wandering on the ground any longer. Zayer Ahmad Hakim set out for the graveyard, and the men of the village, following their ancestral tradition, took turns step by step carrying the rectangular board on their shoulders. The sound of "there is no god but God" resonated throughout the village.

A grave farther away from the graves of the people of the village was dug. Those three men put their fingers on three spots on their chests, and recited something under their breaths. Tired Zayer Gholam, who had dug the grave, said:

"Zayer, they're also human; they're praying."

Captain Ali, who still thought Zayer Ahmad was upset with him, wiped his tears and looked at Zayer Ahmad, hoping to appease his heart. Zayer Ahmad recited the prayer for the dead under his breath, and the three men stuck two sticks together and placed it in the soil above the dead man's head. Wailing and crying, the women pushed the men aside and stood around the grave in a circle. Hitting her face, Mama Mansur sang:

"When away from his homeland a king dies

He is taken to his grave in agony and sighs."

The sound of the wailing of the women of the village reached the sky. To make sure that the dead man would not burst out crying, the women hit themselves on their faces. Every one of them called him by a different name. "I grieve, my tall, handsome one, grieve. I never saw you in your bridal chamber, brother, I grieve; I grieve."

Stunned by the mournful crying and the dancing of the women, the blond men were shaking their heads. They squinted, looked dazed and amazed, and stared at the women, sometimes saying something to themselves under their breaths. Exhausted, Zayer Ahmad pointed to the village and started to walk.

How could one treat people who have one of their dead buried in your soil harshly? All the clubs were put back in the coffers, and the people of the village, ashamed of their previous thoughts and intentions, avoided looking into their eyes, hung around them, offered them everything they had, and slapped their own foreheads as a sign of mourning for the young man who had died.

The three men had their dinner on the top of Zayer Ahmad's water cistern, surrounded by the people of the village. The village had arranged such a banquet, which was unprecedented. Everyone had brought something from their own houses. People had killed and cooked their chickens and roosters, so that the dead man would not think that he had been buried in a strange land where he had no one.

Late at night, the blond men brought some things out of their boat and gave them to the children, things that the people had no clue as to what they were, and with gestures, they conveyed that they would come back again. Then, weeping, Zayer Gholam kissed the men's faces, and the men of the village took turns kissing the faces of the blond men one by one.

When the blond men went to their boat, the sound of people reciting salutations to the Prophet and his family echoed throughout the village.

16

Everyone seemed to feel a responsibility concerning the dead man. Burying a person without ceremonies, a human being who had been brought into this world by his parents, was beyond the comprehension of the people of the village. Soon after, they brought out the black banners. They had a wake in Zayer Ahmad's house and sang lamentations. The people of the village wept and beat their chests so much that Zayer Ahmad was embarrassed regarding the warning of his yet unborn grandchild. Nabati fainted three times. Setareh was beating her chest and crying. Out of respect for the dead man, Bubuni did not chew gum. And Zayer Gholam sang lamentations and spoke about the character and virtues of a man who had never hurt the heart of any creature, a man who had fought Busalmeh many times, who had taken food to the drowned at the bottom of the sea, who had fought the red mermaids for the sake of the living fishermen of the world, and one day when he had been caught in the belly of a shark, most courageously and bravely, he had been able to open the mouth of the shark with his powerful hands and save himself. Alas, the land had lost just such a man.

For a long time, the people of the village talked about a man who was kinder than the kindest human being on the earth, and whose death had caused the mermaids to go into mourning.

In the face of the upheaval of the spirit of the villagers, Zayer
Ahmad kept silent. Perhaps Madineh, who could hear the sound of
the sighing of the mermaids from the other side of the offing, was
right. Maybe there were no thieves. In grappling with himself, in his
heart, he swore that, whether "thieves" or "leaves," he would never
listen to things said by an unborn child. It was as clear as day that
by using the voice of a child, Busalmeh wanted to humiliate him
before the people of the village, and this belief was enhanced when
one night, before the blond men showed up again, Zayer Ahmad
once again heard the voice of his unborn grandchild. Upon a gesture
by him no one gathered around Kheyju. Kheyju, however, heard the
baby's voice, speaking in the strangest language in the world, as he
was hopelessly wiggling around in her belly. Tired of all that she
was hearing, Kheyju pounded her belly with her fist and heard the
unborn child's final words:

"Don't say I didn't tell you."

Zayer Ahmad's grandchild, who was fated to spend the years of
his life in the lands on the other side of the world away from Jofreh,
no longer spoke, until after he was born and later began speaking;
and the members of the household were free of his tongue for quite
some time. Zayer Ahmad, however, did not cast caution to the wind.
He summoned Mansur, Captain Ali, and Zayer Gholam, and warned
them that no one was allowed to take the magic sherbet from the
blond men.

Dismayed, Zayer Gholam left Zayer Ahmad. Close to noon, when
that magic boat that could travel both on the sea and land appeared,
he made an agreement with Captain Ali and Mansur that, concealed
from Zayer Ahmad, they would be nice to the blond men and obtain
from them the sherbet that took away one's senses and mind and
emptied the heart of worldly sorrows.

17

This time, the three blond men were accompanied by a man who had reddish brown hair and carried a large briefcase, the handle of which he was holding tightly. Atop the water cistern of Zayer Ahmad's house, he opened the briefcase like a sorcerer, smiled at the people of the village who had surrounded him, and took out small and large boxes. He gestured to the children to gather around him, turned the eyelids of the children up with his finger, and as he was saying something and nodding his head, he poured medicine into their eyes.

Zayer Ahmad had begun to serve as the medicine man many years earlier with the arrival of a man who had been shot in the village of Melgado, and what the man with reddish brown hair did erased his doubts and suspicions, and he came to believe that children before they were born, similar to the dead of the gray waters, were obedient to Busalmeh.

The village remembered its old aches and pains. Wishing to test the ability of the physician with reddish brown hair, Zayer Ahmad would point to the men and women of the village, and in the oldest language in the world, explain their pains and suffering. The man who could not stop smiling calmly examined them, took some things out of his briefcase, and handed them to Zayer Ahmad to give them to the people of his village. Zayer Ahmad was bending over the medicine, and would not take his eyes off the long thin fingers of the man. When the man, without asking for anything, gave him his large briefcase, Zayer Ahmad smiled like a baby, and slapped the man on his shoulder.

Late at night, the men of the strange boat left. The villagers stood on the shore with lanterns until they could no longer hear the strange boat, and the small red light that was stuck on the entrance to the cabin of the boat disappeared in the darkness.

What things the offspring of the other side of the earth knew! The villagers laughed. The memory of the four kind men was being engraved on their minds. Bubuni restlessly hung around Zayer Ahmad. Among the things of the men who had come from the other side of the world and who were even more knowledgeable than Zayer Ahmad, could there be anything for a woman who could not have children?

How could she make the men of the strange boat understand that her baby oven was cold? They needed to be kind to the men from the other side of the world. Captain Ali needed to become friends with them, to invite them to their house.

In Zayer Gholam's eyes, the world was beautiful, more beautiful than ever. He would open and close the flap of his loincloth. He laughed in front of the women boisterously, and spoke in the language of the strange men. Concealed from Zayer Ahmad, he had been able to obtain a bottle of the magic sherbet from the blond men.

For Mahjamal, the world was chaotic and incomprehensible. He had seen the men of the white boat somewhere, somewhere far away, somewhere close. He remembered their eyes, eyes that were not kind previously, eyes that were vindictive and made you sad. But if he had seen them in the depths of the gray waters, if they were twins of the dead of the gray waters, then where did all this love and kindness, such boundless generosity and humane smiles, come from?

Woe if the human is afflicted by suspicion. He rocks to one side or another at every moment like an anchorless boat, and eventually surrenders to the high shadowy waves and sinks to the bottom of the muddy waters.

Mahjamal did not know what to do. What should he do in the face of the men of the strange boat? Should he join them, or flee from them? Should he tell Zayer Ahmad what was in his heart, tell him that he had seen them in the depths of the gray waters?

They came once again. There were six of them, with strange and outlandish equipment. Away from the village, they measured the land. They stuck some things into the ground, dug out the soil from the depths of the ground and sniffed and examined it. Each one of them was busy doing something. One was writing, another was bent over a map, a third one was measuring the ground, and three others were sinking a large metal pole into the ground so deeply that Zayer Ahmad, worried, rose to his knees and held the hand of one of them, so they would not torment the land any more. He was afraid that the large metal pole would pierce the skull of the dead of the land.

Tired, at noon they stopped working and jumped into the sea, and then Zayer Ahmad rinsed them off with the fresh water from the water cistern. The women of Jofreh saw their white naked bodies and came to believe that they were the sons of the sun.

The sons of the sun ate their food in the house of Zayer Ahmad, and once again began to walk in the village. They went to the other side of the Shrine of Sire Ashk until they reached the slopes of the mountains. Captain Ali finally showed them Bubuni, and with gestures told them that she could not have children and asked the men from the other side of the world to treat her with some medicine. The six men laughed and said things that Captain Ali did not understand. The blond men pointed at the village children and shook their heads. The villagers accompanied them from this corner to that corner of Jofreh.

Kheyju's mind and senses, however, were focused on Mahjamal, who was watching the blond men silently. In her mental arguments with herself, Kheyju was unable to get anywhere. Numerous questions remained unanswered: Why are they measuring the land in Jofreh? What do they want the soil for? Are they going to gradually settle down in Jofreh? Why do they show the village children to one another and laugh? In fact, where have they come from, and where are they going?

Distraught because of Mahjamal's silence, Kheyju tried to listen to her baby, but she heard nothing. If only she had not pounded on her belly with her fist. Kheyju was afraid, afraid of the strangers; and she was not happy with the villagers and what they said, thinking that the blond men were the sons of the sun, that they thought that the blond men would soon build a large water cistern behind the Shrine of Sire Ashk and bring trees from the other side of the world to Jofreh to make the village as green and pleasant as their own village.

Zayer Ahmad accompanied the six men all around the village and saw that they shook their heads and pointed to the black feet and disheveled hair of the children. He told the mothers to wash their children in the sea and have them wear nice clothes. Zayer Ahmad did not want the children to be the cause of degradation and humiliation for the village.

The blond men filled the village with souvenirs. The women put the tinsel wrappers of the candies that they gave the children on the walls of their houses. Even though the doctor with reddish brown hair had not come, the blond men gave Zayer Ahmad a package of various medicines with which he could treat the people of the village; and late at night, when they left, the scent of kindness and good fortune wafted in the village.

The world was beautiful, and no one thought about anything. The sons of the sun had said that they would come back to the village again. It seemed that the men of the strange boat had robbed the mind of the village, as though the world had begun with their arrival. At night, the men of the village sat in the room with five sashed windows and told stories about those blond men. On Friday eves, the women of the village sat beside the grave of that stranger who had died and recited the prayer for the dead, and they lit a lantern over his grave so he would not feel forlorn.

Nabati, Zayer Gholam's daughter, was happy. She was sure that those men had come from Busalmeh. She knew that the bad denizens of the sea had disguised themselves in human form to sniff every handspan of the soil of Jofreh. Day and night, with every breath, Nabati was thinking about Busalmeh, and she kept her eyes on the gray sea.

But Bubuni still had not given up hope. It was quite likely that this time, the men of the strange boat might bring something that would make Captain Ali stay home. Captain Ali and Zayer Gholam would sip from the bottle of magic sherbet; and concealed from the eyes of Zayer Ahmad, they sat chatting on the mounds of dirt by the road until late at night.

When the men of the strange boat came to Jofreh for the last time, the village saw the strangest box in the world. It was late afternoon when suddenly the white boat rose from the sea, stopped under the silk tassel acacia tree, and three men dismounted carrying a large box. Tired and smiling, the men went to the room with five sashed windows, and before the eyes of the villagers, they clicked the button on the box. One of the men turned a knob, and the magic box spoke in the strangest language in the world. The villagers stepped back, bewildered, the blond men laughed, and the sound of the magic box became louder. To make the fear of the villagers go away, the blond men touched the box, smiled, and said things the meaning of which no one knew.

The world was complicated. Zayer Ahmad, who saw that his men were afraid and indecisive, came forward, looked at the magic box up close, and was at a loss about the ways of the world and what went on inside it. It was unclear how many people were living inside it. One of the men turned a knob. A man and a woman were laughing, and a child was crying. Had a sorcerer imprisoned them in the magic box? Did the blond men want the village to help them free the people who were under the spell? Suddenly, there was the sound of the footsteps of a man and a woman, who were laughing loudly, and another woman who was saying something quietly. Then the sounds became distorted and confused.

Zayer Ahmad frowned, and the blond men's smiles suddenly disappeared from their faces. Through gestures, Zayer Ahmad asked them who had imprisoned those helpless people. One of the blond men laughed loudly, slapped Zayer Ahmad on his shoulder, took his hand, and placed it on the magic box. It was wood, just wood. Zayer Ahmad closed his eyes and pulled his hand back. The man turned the knob of the magic box, and suddenly a man's voice said:

"The time is seven forty-five. This is London."

The men of the village stepped forward. They held their breaths, and Zayer Gholam looked at the blond men, bewildered. The whole world knew that this was Jofreh. In a broken voice, Zayer Gholam put his hand on the shoulder of one of the men, and said quietly:

"This is Jofreh, Jofreh."

The whole village together said that this was Jofreh, and the blond men laughed loudly, hit the magic box hard with their hands, and said some things that no one understood.

Finally, one of the blond men clicked the button of the magic box, and the box became silent, and the village breathed a sigh of relief.

That night, the blond men stayed in the village. They gave several boxes of medicine to Zayer Ahmad, took a walk around the village, and in the morning at cockcrow, they went away in their strange boat and left the magic box for the people of the village.

The village was left with something strange and heavy. Who could ignore the magic box in which men, women, and children sang? Wherever the people were in the village, and whatever they were doing, their minds were preoccupied with the magic box. At night, when they gathered around Zayer Ahmad, as though they had no stories or memories left, they looked at one another, broke the silence with single coughs, and stared at Zayer Ahmad. The magic box had cast a spell on the village.

Zayer Ahmad's mind was totally preoccupied with concerns about Madineh, who having lost her appetite could not eat anything, and in front of everyone, wept for the men and women who were under the spell. Hungry and with sleep-deprived eyes, without speaking a word, Zayer Ahmad's wife sat beside the magic box, and tears rolled down her cheeks.

Madineh was afraid that the people in the magic box would die without food. How long could a human being breathe, hungry and thirsty, in a place that confined?

Like all wise men in the world, Zayer Ahmad was a captive. A woman, even if she is Madineh, can make her man lose control of everything.

Finally, on one of those sleepless nights, Zayer Ahmad cast caution to the wind, brought the magic box among the people, cautiously pressed the button that the blond men had pressed, and the magic box made crackly noises. Zayer Gholam, who had been more restless than all the other people in the village and who had been coming to Zayer Ahmad's house day and night under a thousand pretexts, turned the knob, and the entire village heard the voice of a woman who was singing the saddest song in the world, loudly.

That night, the people stayed in Zayer Ahmad's house until morning, and in the morning, in order to send the people back to their own houses, Zayer Ahmad pressed another button, and the magic box went silent.

❧ 19 ❧

The voice that sang in the magic box was the strangest voice in the world:

"To the city of my beloved..."[10]

The women of the village liked her forlorn voice, and sang her songs under their breaths.

The whole village sat beside the magic box day and night, and Mahjamal, who could not figure out the world, at midnight on a cold winter night when everyone was sleeping, in order to figure out what the magic box was, opened the back of the magic box, and was perplexed, with his finger in his mouth. There was no one in there, only thin wires that lit two lamps. Mahjamal, who felt that the world was becoming more complicated day by day, closed the back of the magic box tightly, and concluded that the one whose magic power is the greatest in the world had chained the voices of the humans.

The next sad morning, the magic box with the voice of a woman who sang, "O nightingale, begin to wail,"[11] went silent. Madineh

---

10- Translation of the Arabic "Ala Balad El-Mahbub," a popular song by the renowned 20th-century female Egyptian singer, Umm Kulthum.

11- Popular early 20th-century Persian song, the lyrics of which were composed by the poet laureate Bahar, sung by female Iranian singer Qamarolmoluk Vaziri.

developed a fever right away, and Zayer Ahmad placed the magic box beside her head, so that she could get up half asleep and half awake and turn its various knobs and not find her way anywhere.

The village waited until high noon for some sound to come from the magic box. When their expectation went unfulfilled, bored and sad, they went back to their own houses; and it was only then that the village realized that during that time, three of the prettiest children of the village had gone missing.

The village fell apart. They searched every handspan of the village; the young men went down to the bottom of the Well of Loneliness several times, but they did not find any children.

The Maiden in the Well told Kheyju, who had stuck her head into the well: "The children are not on the land." Distraught and miserable, Kheyju got up from the well.

It was as clear as day for the village that the Child Snatcher had come to the village while they were preoccupied with the magic box and had taken the children. Setareh, who had lost her five-year old son, screamed and wailed and fell on her knees before Zayer Ahmad, begging him to do something. She pleaded with the men and women of the village; but the more they searched, the less they found.

Mahjamal was not happy with what the villagers were saying. Strange things were going on in his mind. The blond men pointing at the children of the village, their comings and goings for no reason, everything was indicative of a different story. Mahjamal had often seen that the blond men looked at the little five-year-old son of Setareh, a little boy with curly black hair and big green eyes.

Mahjamal was taken by surprise by Kheyju in the middle of the night. He had placed his ear on her belly to perhaps hear something. Kheyju pretended to be sleeping. She herself had also frequently tried to listen, to perhaps hear something. The voice of the Maiden in the Well would not leave her alone: "The children are not on the land." Then, where were they? Had they been taken away by the Child Snatcher? Zayer Ahmad's grandchild kept silent, and Kheyju was infuriated.

Zayer Ahmad, however, who regretted his own negligence, gave orders that with the setting of the sun, no child was allowed to stay outside his or her house.

Nabati had seen with her own eyes that the Child Snatcher had risen from the sea with long strides and walked around the village, a tall scrawny man whose face was the color of silver, whose head reached the sky, and whose hands were so long and thin that they could enter the cracks and kidnap any child that he wanted. The silvery eyes of the Child Snatcher, who had obviously been sent by Busalmeh, had mesmerized Nabati.

"I could not scream."

The Child Snatcher was holding the children in his long narrow arms and fled toward the offing of the sea. The sound of the magic box had not allowed anyone to hear the screaming of the children.

The Child Snatcher would never have come from the sea, and it was as clear as day that one of the evil denizens of the sea had assumed the form of the Child Snatcher and attacked the village.

With what Nabati said, it was as clear as day for everyone that the Child Snatcher had taken the children of the village.

Bubuni, who was afraid that one of the blue mermaids disguised as the Child Snatcher would take Captain Ali away to the depths of the green waters, without mentioning Captain Ali's name, went to Madineh, who was upset with the world and was still playing with the knobs of the magic box. Fed up, Madineh convinced Bubuni that the mermaids never disguise themselves as someone else, and they remain in their female form to the end of time. Madineh, who was smoking a hookah and singing lamentations, despondent because of the women and men who had died from starvation in the magic box, without showing it on her face, was convinced that Bubuni was eventually going to lose her wits someday.

During the times of misfortune and pain, who else other than Nabati could listen to Bubuni's complaints? Joyous about what had occurred, Nabati became certain in her belief that the blond men were sons of Busalmeh, and finally one of them had attacked the village disguised as the Child Snatcher.

Sitting beside Nabati, who was giggling, worried about the mermaids and the sea, Bubuni would tell her that from then on, she would accompany Captain Ali everywhere in the world, and would never let him out of her sight.

The Child Snatcher erased from the people's minds the memory of the magic box, which no longer talked and sang. From the fear and horror with which the Child Snatcher had afflicted their lives, the women of the village would stay awake until morning, hold their children in their arms, and at the slightest sound, sit up.

The children of the village, who used to play in the alleyways and on the shore until late at night, now deprived of their nightly games, developed fevers, and Zayer Ahmad Hakim became very busy. With the box of medicine, he went from one house to the next until the children got used to the new law, and at sunset, quietly and obediently, upon seeing the sun sinking into the sea, they went to their houses.

With the four children who were born in the village, the world calmed down; but the Child Snatcher had stolen those three missing children without even returning their corpses.

Zayer Ahmad Hakim's grandchild was born on a clear morning, right at cockcrow. Mama Mansur and Madineh had stayed awake all night beside Kheyju, in pain with sweat pouring from all four corners of her body. Zayer Ahmad's grandchild did not intend to come out that easily, as though he wished to inform the entire universe of his arrival. Mahjamal, who had lost his soothsaying power after the sea voyage, was awake and restless all night long, hearing Kheyju's pained moans. Fear and fright nested in his heart, and he pleaded with the sea and the sky, while Kheyju walked around slowly and sluggishly and pleaded with Mama Mansur and Madineh to save her.

Mahjamal was at a loss. If humans are born amidst such suffering and bitterness, if pain pierces its hook into the soul of pregnant women and drags them toward the shores of death, then how is it that no one abandons the world, the number of children of the land increases every moment, and women take sperm from their mates every year?

Kheyju was biting her lips. A strange howl emitted from her closed mouth, and Mahjamal sunk into himself, confronted with the mystery of the land, and made a pledge to himself never to be intimate with Kheyju and never again to pour all the pain and suffering of the world into her body.

Mahjamal, aquatic Mahjamal! Negligent of human temptations, in the middle of the night, he took refuge to the Shrine of Sire Ashk, where he moaned, looking at the sky and the sea. He was suddenly frightened: what if Busalmeh wanted to retaliate, to expose the secret of his life, and with a child that had a fish-like half, make him a spectacle among the people? Mahjamal would hear the moaning of the daughter of Zayer Ahmad, would block his ears, and could not forgive himself for that brief moment of being liberated in the rapture of pleasure on the land.

Kheyju had lost all her strength. Her hair soaking wet and disheveled was stuck to her cheeks, and she could not take even one step forward. Madineh and Mama Mansur were rolling her on the ground, a stifled sound emerging from their throats:

"Push! Push!"

Up to the sandbag was a long way, a bag on which she would have to sit, legs open, straight up. She would push to have a piece of her life travel its journey to the land. Could she take one step, just one step?

Finally, in the throes of pain shooting throughout her entire body, she reached the sandbag. She sat on her knees trying to support her body. No, she could not. Let me give birth lying down... She lay down, slowly and painfully. The sandbag, her pillow. Her languid eyes on Mama Mansur, with a gesture of her hand, she asked her to press on her belly with her foot. Mama Mansur pulled back. She had never helped anyone in the village to give birth with a kick. Kheyju moaned:

"Do you think this is a human child?"

Lethargically, Kheyju took Mama Mansur's hand and placed it on her belly. Kheyju's listless, trembling voice had frightened everyone. A moment later, when she became unconscious, Madineh and Mama Mansur were still frightened and pressed her protruded belly with their hands.

It was at cockcrow that Zayer Ahmad's first grandchild, the sound of whose crying reached the end of the world, opened its eyes to the world. The newborn, a boy that Zayer Ahmad named Bahador, cried until noon. Without calming down even for a moment or closing his eyes, he screamed, and his voice became silent only when, shouting and yelling, Bubuni ran to Zayer Ahmad's house, pointing to the sea.

A mermaid was waiting in the cove, looking at Zayer Ahmad's house, distraught and confused.

Tormented by Bahador's screaming, upon seeing Bubuni and Zayer Ahmad, who were standing on the top of the water cistern, Mahjamal looked at the sea and recognized his aquatic mother; and without saying a word, he picked up Bahador, who was still crying, walked into the sea up to the cove, hesitating for a moment, and before reaching the mermaid, washed Bahador in the sea water. Holding a coral branch, the mermaid came toward them. Mahjamal was frightened. With his hand, he gestured to his aquatic mother to stay where she was, and he held Bahador up in the air and showed him to the mermaid from a distance. In her sorrow, the mermaid smiled, then disappeared.

The lump in the throat of the mermaid burst on the way, which made her cry, and Mahjamal saw the water of the sea rising. He smiled bitterly, and knew that he had saddened his aquatic mother.

Mahjamal went back to the house with Bahador, who had now calmed down and was looking with his strange blue eyes. Bahador's crying showed that he was born of the sea. His being born of the sea, however, was not that clear; he did not have a fish-like half that would have frustrated the sole daughter of Zayer Ahmad.

Kheyju was at a loss regarding the strange love of Bahador for water. In the course of the day, she had to wash his hands and face with the salty seawater so he would not drive the entire village crazy with his bellowing.

After cockcrow, Mama Mansur went to the houses of two other pregnant women, and was busy with them until sundown. Then, dead tired and beat, she went home with a bowl full of dates and some flour. All she thought about was the boys of the village, boys who were born as though they wanted to fill the place of the missing children.

When she turned into her alleyway, from behind the stucco house, she heard whispering. Quietly, she went and peeked from behind the wall, where she saw Nabati and Mansur rolling around on each other.

Late at night, when Mansur came home, without looking into his eyes, Mama Mansur punched him on the chest and shouted:

"You have to get married."

Mansur stared at her. Mama Mansur spat in his face:

"Thug!"

Mansur got the clear impression that his mother had seen everything, and silently consented to get married.

❄ 21 ❄

Zayer Ahmad recited the marriage vows. He himself had no idea what he was reciting. When you are fourteen years old and migrate from one place to another, when you have no more than a few weddings in your memory, what you later recite as marriage vows cannot be very much trusted. Zayer Ahmad recited the salutations to the Prophet and his family, and he knew that God understood his intention.

At the time of the migration from Fekseno, other than a few young people of his same age along with his maternal uncle and mother, who were now resting in one corner of the graveyard, no one else was with them. All that remained in his memory of God and worshiping God consisted of the ceremonies and beliefs of the people of Fekseno, who several times every year were faced with invading tribes, and more than being adherent to ceremonies and beliefs, were concerned about their lives, their very existence, about how not to humiliate themselves before anyone in the world in order to live and survive on God's earth, in order not to be harmed by and not to harm anyone.

The women, however, seemed to be more bound by their beliefs. The sound of scrubbing pots and dishes and pulverizing plant seeds could be heard throughout the village. The face of the sea along the shore was full of people. The women and children of the village would walk around on the sand and pebbles along the shore, collect small seashells, string them up, and make necklaces and bracelets for themselves.

The wedding of Mahjamal and Kheyju had been ruined due to the fright and fear of Busalmeh in addition to the headaches that were the result of that magic sherbet. Now the village wanted an elaborate wedding celebration in which everyone would be joyful for seven nights and days and transmit their happiness in a loud voice to the ears of the sea and the sky.

Mama Mansur visited the women to pluck their facial hair and help with their makeup. In Zayer Ahmad Hakim's house, along with the other women, Kheyju prepared collyrium and applied it to Nabati's eyelashes. She tried her clothes on Zayer Gholam's daughter to see which ones were more becoming. Nabati was at a loss. Annoyed by all the kindness, she would close her eyes. Human commotion and joyfulness withered her soul. Silent and pale, she walked around among the women. She was tired of the goings on of the world. When the women spoke to her about the wedding night and the consummation of marriage, she shuddered. Kheyju would tell her about having children, and she was horrified. Fear seemed to have roots of a thousand years in her being. She was scared of the wedding night, of the handkerchief that was supposed to be handed to the women who would stay all night until morning behind the door of the bridal chamber, to prove her virginity and the virility of the groom. The daughter of Zayer Gholam would try to control herself, so as not to faint and collapse in front of the others; pain would shoot through her head, her teeth, and her entire body. Mansur was for the most part concerned about his own reputation. Distressed and regretful about what he had done, he went around in circles and could not get anywhere. Lust hollows human bones like guinea worms, and leaves no memento other than regret. Lust ruins the human soul.

The day before the wedding, tired of his mental arguments and anguish, Mansur went to Zayer Ahmad's house. The color was drained from his face, and his lips trembled. If only Zayer Ahmad would blame everything on Mansur's youth and be kind to him and give him a bit of that red medicine[12] that the blond men had given him to treat wounds! If only he would forgive him.

Mansur sat in front of Zayer Ahmad, and slowly told the story of his shame. Zayer Ahmad listened to him in silence. A moment later, he stood up. He was not looking into Mansur's eyes, as if there was no one else in the room with five sashed windows. Zayer Ahmad took his shark tail off the wall and gestured to Mansur.

They passed by the women of the village who were sitting around the clay bread oven. Upon seeing the two men, the women's faces blossomed into smiles, and without being able to hide their happiness, with their ululation, they saw off Mansur, who was accompanying Zayer Ahmad to the Shrine of Sire Ashk.

It was quite possible that Zayer Ahmad wanted to tell Mansur the secrets of being a man. It was quite likely that he might force him to take an oath at the Shrine of Sire Ashk before the eternal witnesses of the world, the sky and the sea, to be a man with his wife and life and to love Nabati to the end of time. The women were teasing Nabati, who was sitting beside Kheyju, and no one saw the shark tail that Zayer Ahmad had tied to his waist under his long gown.

Zayer Ahmad held Mansur under the shark tail, and, in fear for his reputation, Mansur did not emit the slightest whimper. He only said briefly that one day, the magic sherbet that he had received from the blond men, concealed from Zayer Ahmad's eyes, had made him so lusty that he tore apart his own and the village's honor and chastity, and he had dishonored Nabati, the daughter of Zayer Gholam.

Zayer Ahmad Hakim, who knew that if Zayer Gholam learned about the shameful story of his daughter, without any fear and apprehension, he would cut her throat from ear to ear, gave a small bottle of the red medicine to Mansur. Agile and feeling good, without remembering the stabbings by the shark tail, Mansur went

---

12- Mercurochrome.

to Nabati, whose heart Busalmeh had blackened and who was about to lose her mind and senses from fear.

The following night, Setareh, Bubuni, and Mama Mansur stayed behind the door of the bridal chamber in order to ululate and inform the village about the handkerchief that indicated Mansur's virility.

Mama Mansur—her face covered with the sweat of shame and tormented by strange and outlandish guesses and conjectures, before her son went into the bridal chamber—had sharpened a knife and handed it to him to stab his finger when the time came, to stain the white handkerchief with blood. However, now self-assured, Mansur threw the knife on the ground, stood face-to-face with his mother, and looked at her angrily.

Ashamed of her suspicions, Mama Mansur kissed his eyes and believed that he had done nothing to be a cause of shame.

When Mansur handed the handkerchief soaking in the red medicine to his mother, all three women ululated. It was dark, and no one could see the handkerchief clearly; but the next morning when Mama Mansur looked at the handkerchief in the light of day and recognized the color of the red medicine, she bit her tongue and said nothing, so that she would not be humiliated before the village. Never removing the grudge from her heart against Nabati to the end of her life, she began her resentful silence by punching the chest of her daughter-in-law at noon.

Mama Mansur did not deserve to be regarded as a stranger by Mansur in the early days of his marital life and for her son to take the side of the newcomer, she who had raised her sons without a man, a guardian, all on her own, she whose six sons had been swallowed by the sea.

Mama Mansur took the handkerchief stained red with the medicine and hid it at the bottom of her trunk, thereby starting her life of ill thoughts and suspicions regarding Nabati.

But the mind of Nabati, who had been relieved of the torment of the wedding night, was distressed by another sorrow. Something moved in her belly, and she could not exhale. Whatever it was or was not, if Mama Mansur drove her to the cracks and corners of the house with her evil-eye glares, if the sudden headaches would make her desperate, if she had given herself to Mansur before their wedding, if something was moving in her belly and wanted to make her a spectacle in the village, it was all because of the presence of a man who was still alive and breathing in the village, heedless of Busalmeh's wrath. Nabati was certain that Busalmeh was entering the souls of each and every one of the people of the village and subjugating them; and if Busalmeh had marked her above all others, it was because of her fondness and love for Mahjamal at one time, a man whom no one knew from the start from where he came. Had Mahjamal been pure and innocent, he would have parents, like all other humans on the land.

Some strange dark grudge grew in Nabati's heart, and she was furious that the village had forgotten about Mahjamal, and that Kheyju, the close confidante of her teenage years, was spending a calm and tranquil life beside that cursed man. She knew that eventually Kheyju would pay for that union. She knew that Mahjamal was like fire under ashes. She was fearful. She would remember the strange days after that sea voyage, and she was dazed within the rationale at which she arrived in her loneliness. Busalmeh would this time act slowly and quietly, like termites, to destroy the village. In her loneliness, she pleaded with Busalmeh of the seas, she begged him, and she reminded him that she was not like the others, that she remembered everything and would take the side of Busalmeh to the end of her life. She did not regard herself as deserving of the wrath of Busalmeh. When away from others, she would punch her belly to destroy the cause of her shame, and she would ask Busalmeh to save her, to relieve her from disgrace and death, and to support her to the end of the world.

One day, following her excruciating nightly pains, she woke up at dawn and went to the sugarcane field with its undergrowth around the village, went at herself, and then buried the baby that looked human under the dirt in the undergrowth and stuffed some sheep manure in her body. Close to noon, bent over from pain, under the burden of a load of firewood, pale and lethargic, she came home, and for ten days under the pretext of menstruation, she slept away from the heat of Mansur's body.

She was freed from the disgrace and humiliation that was about to plunder her life. Busalmeh had accepted her pleas, had given breath to her breath, and she would compensate Busalmeh's kindness at an opportune time.

After ten days, once she was free of pain, she gave her body to the salty gray water of the sea. An ugly wind was blowing from the direction of the offing of the sea, and Nabati was yelling her words in the wind, asking Busalmeh to never forget her. In the dusky air as she was preparing to leave, she heard a sound. She turned around and saw a tall woman who had covered her face with the sand of the sea. She had strange red eyes. Nabati recognized Yal. Her heart skipped a beat; she knew that she had come from Busalmeh. With a smile that opened her muddy lips, Yal came forward. She stretched both her hands toward Nabati pointing at her chest, with her index finger drew a circle on her chest, and took out Nabati's heart. She looked at it for a moment. Her eyes sparkled, and in a voice that seemed to come from the depths of the earth, she said:

"You shall no longer love anyone in the world."

When Yal took Nabati's heart and disappeared, Nabati sat down on her knees. She was tired, as though she had been walking on her feet all her life to get there, in the midst of the gray waters and the ugly tumult of the wind that blew from the offing of the sea.

When Nabati set out for the house of Zayer Ahmad Hakim, the sun had drowned in the sea. There on the top of the water cistern, Mansur and Mahjamal were straightening the wire of the fish traps. Two lanterns by their side pushed the darkness of the night away. When she saw Nabati, Kheyju came out of the room with five sashed windows.

"Nabati, are you out of your mind coming back from the sea at this time of night?"

Nabati gave her a faint smile. She sat down on the stairs of the water cistern soaking wet. Kheyju poured a bucket of rainwater over her head to freshen her. Mahjamal picked up a lantern, placed it at the side of the stairs, and, looking at Mansur, said:

"My good man! In the darkness of night, Yal searches around in the seas. You were just married the other day."

Mansur laughed, and Nabati was momentarily at a loss. Had

Mahjamal figured out that she was not the previous Nabati, that she was another Yal who, on the order of Busalmeh, had to live on land among the people of the village?

Since the sea voyage, Mahjamal had been afraid, had been fleeing from the people, and had not predicted any of the calamities. Exhausted, Nabati put her head on a stair of the water cistern. Smiling, Kheyju patted her belly.

"Hey, Nabati! Any news?"

Sluggish and heavy, Nabati lifted her head, and without looking at her, laughed. Kheyju sighed deeply. She had been neglecting the close confidante of her teenage years. She had never seen Nabati this tired. How soon people's lives distance them from one another! Bahador, her seven-month-old baby, a baby that frustrated her with his non-human love of the sea, would not allow her to return to her past memories.

Bahador always sat facing the window that opened toward the sea. At night, when the sea was occasionally calm, he stayed awake until morning, bellowing. Sometimes he talked to someone and laughed; and Mahjamal was not at all surprised by the little boy's behavior. A kind smile would appear on his lips, and as though recollecting some precious distant memory, he would nod, and keep silent in response to Kheyju, who called to him out loud to get him out of his faraway thoughts and daydreams.

Zayer Ahmad Hakim held his blue-eyed grandson dear. He told him stories. He already knew that Bahador was not fond of guns and gunfire and the stories of Fekseno. When he wanted to take him back to his own past with Fekseno stories, Bahador would frown and put his small hands on Zayer Ahmad's lips to make him stop talking. But with stories about mermaids, his eyes sparkled, and Zayer Ahmad would be taken aback. No seven-month-old child in the world could be so attached to the sea and mermaids for no apparent reason. At times, Zayer Ahmad thought that the breath of the mermaid who was sitting in the cove during the birth had had an effect on the newborn.

Zayer Ahmad could not figure out the complexity of the world, and did not take it seriously, until one night he was awakened by Kheyju's screaming. The moon had lit up everything like broad daylight, and Bahador was gone. Zayer Ahmad Hakim's ten-month-old grandson was missing. When, horrified, everyone was searching the house from top to bottom and Kheyju was hitting herself on the head and chest and thought that the Child Snatcher had taken Bahador in the middle of the night through the bars of the window, Zayer Ahmad happened to look at the sea by the shore and saw his ten-month-old grandson, who was sitting beside a mermaid, as the mermaid was caressing his head.

From then on, Zayer Ahmad instructed them to put Bahador to sleep in a fish trap placed next to the window, or tie his hand to his mother's when sleeping.

Zayer Ahmad Hakim was happy with the world. He had come from Fekseno to protect his progeny away from the fights and flights of the time, away from the sound of the guns and the moaning of Fanus, and now the village was passing its days without headaches. Every morning, Zayer Ahmad visited the people who regularly got sick since the appearance of the strange white boat in Jofreh. The box of medicine seemed to have brought sickness to the village. In the life of the village, Zayer Ahmad had never seen so many women and children being afflicted with invisible ailments. Every morning, patients with imaginary ailments came to Zayer Ahmad to receive syrups and pills for their new sicknesses, and Zayer Ahmad, worried about the medicine running out, eventually rationed the pills.

At night, the men of the village would gather around Zayer Ahmad on the top of the water cistern, and embellish their imaginations with feathers and wings. Recollections about the blond men were often included in their stories, kind blond men who had a dead man buried in the soil of the village; and surely they were now on the other side of the world sitting on the top of the water cistern of their own village and talking about Jofreh. The men of the village had examined the magic box many times, and, disappointed because of its eternal silence, they would sit back. Sometimes, the men went to the sea, close to the offing, spread out their fish traps and nets, and came back. Everything was calm, and Busalmeh, regretting his ruses, had retreated. But Nabati knew that Busalmeh was preoccupied with other villages, and that whenever he found an opportunity, he would once again grab Jofreh by the throat. No one, though, was concerned about her delusions and stories.

Life was good, and at night from the rooftops came the sound of the panting of men and women who were busy building the world, and the sound of the giggling of children who pretended to be sleeping. Babies were born, and the houses and huts became larger.

Setareh worked day and night in Zayer Ahmad Hakim's house. She took care of Bahador, and held him in her arms and kissed him, as he gazed at the world with his strange blue eyes. She was comfortable and content. She could see Mahjamal. Kheyju had become more dear to her. Previously, when she had gone there with her daughter, Golpar, it was out of need to sit at Zayer Ahmad Hakim's supper cloth; but now she considered it her own home. She swept that large courtyard. She took their clothes to the sea, to the place that was known as Zayer Ahmad Hakim's Pothole, washed all of them, and came back to the house without feeling tired. She carried firewood from the sugarcane fields around Jofreh, and sometimes when necessary, she brought sea rocks on her back. She delivered medicine for Zayer Ahmad to the people's houses. Her daughter, Golpar, was growing up in Zayer Ahmad's house. Following the incidents that had occurred in Jofreh, Zayer Ahmad had ordered the men to rebuild Setareh's hut. In the eyes of Zayer Ahmad, Setareh was a woman who did not want to take a bite of food from someone else's supper cloth without working hard for it.

Zayer Ahmad had come to believe that no other incident would ever again disturb the calm and tranquility of the village. Every morning, the women gathered at Zayer Ahmad's Pothole, washed their dishes, and chitchatted. In the late afternoon, the voices of women who were returning from the Well of Loneliness singing reverberated in the village.

Zayer Ahmad occasionally walked around the village. With a

smile on his lips, he visited the houses and huts and recalled the days in the distant past when, exhausted, they had come from Fekseno, and looking at the sea, they had decided to build the village on God's earth. Upon seeing Zayer Ahmad, the children would stop playing. Zayer Ahmad would pat them on their heads and shoulders, and sometimes he would call a mother to take her child to the sea and wash him from head to foot. Who knew? It was quite possible that suddenly a white boat from the other side of the world would come, and its men would see the unkempt child and shake their heads.

When Zayer Ahmad walked around the village, he would see Bubuni with a broom in her hand, sweeping outside her house and sprinkling salt. A smile would appear on his lips, and in his heart he would pray for Bubuni and all the women of Jofreh to make God's land prosper with their children. The village was not in need of anything. It had a large clay bread oven. It had the holy Shrine of Sire Ashk, in which the people gathered on the days of religious mourning. The village was clean, and every morning at dawn, the people went to the shore close to the sea to answer the call of nature. There was no begrudging and hostility in the village. The people took care of one another. Mama Mansur would lend her millstones to other people. Everyone who came back from the sea brought the fish they had caught to Zayer Ahmad's house to be distributed among the people of the village. When Madineh milked the goats, she gave the women of the village yogurt, cheese, and whey. No one was left to themselves in the village, and the water cistern was full of fresh water all year long. Even though the hands of the sky were sometimes dry and without rain, the people were patient and thrifty.

Zayer Ahmad walked happily around the village. He would think and ponder over his plans. Would he be able to build a large water cistern away from the village, near the Shrine of Sire Ashk, so they would have water in reserve for when there was a drought? Would he be able to build a wall in front of the sea, so that when the mermaids wept, it would not flood the village? But building any wall would require stones, Zayer would tell himself. And how could he convince the people of the village to go far away from Jofreh to fetch stones?

For a long time, the people had raised their houses using rocks from the sea. No one would go close to the mountains.

Thirty-five years earlier, they cut the stones from the mountains to build a house. In those days, the world was quiet, and the sound of the singing of the men resonated in the mountains, "Hel lu heleh mali...," along with the sound of the shovels and pickaxes that struck the mountain. There was the sound of happiness and life. Until one day, a strange iron bird appeared in the sky, a bird whose sound was louder than thunder and lightning. The bird seemed to want to hunt them. The sorcerer who was sitting in its belly brought it precisely over their heads, and without flapping its wings, it circled above their heads. The men of the village were fleeing, and the bird was chasing them. When the bird got frustrated by the men and could not circle anymore, it dropped its bird droppings on the ground, which made the stones break apart from the mountain, threw a lot of dirt and debris in the air, and the sound of thunder filled the world. It was because of the droppings of that same bird that Zayer Ahmad's maternal uncle fell to the ground, his whole body bleeding, and died in Zayer Ahmad's arms. From then on, no one went toward the mountains, and all the houses were built with rocks and stones from the sea.

Zayer Ahmad walked around the village. Where was Jofreh located in the world? Where were other villages? Years and years earlier, during their migration, they had moved at night in order not to leave any footprints behind. They crossed mountain passes and mountains that had never before heard the sound of human footsteps; and then, suddenly, without having planned it, they arrived here, on this hot land.

Neither Zayer Ahmad nor any of those who had accompanied him from Fekseno was ever able to find the way they had come, and the only contact Jofreh had with the outside world was a man who came from behind the mountains once every few months. He would unload his stuff right there on the mountain pass, and Zayer Ahmad would go to see him.

That man, who many years earlier disturbed the calm of the

women of Jofreh and was the cause of the death of Zayer Ahmad's mother, on his very first visit, upon arriving in Jofreh and unloading his stuff from the camel, happily took out from the middle of his bric-a-brac small, round mirrors and distributed them among the women before the men even knew it. Zayer Ahmad's maternal uncle, who was still alive, began yelling and took away the mirrors from the women's hands, then accompanied the man with his stuff to the mountain pass and made him swear that he would never again set foot in Jofreh.

Zayer Ahmad's maternal uncle, however, was unable to save the life of Zayer Ahmad's mother. She had been able to look at the mirror and see Fanus, still distraught and bewildered. She died three days later; and for a long time, the people paid no attention to the man who came once every few months and away from the village yelled, "Kerosene! Kerosene!"

When Zayer Ahmad's maternal uncle died because of the droppings of that bird, Zayer Ahmad decided that the nights of the village should not pass in darkness. He went to the mountain pass, and without any discussion, he began the bartering of fish for kerosene.

Such was Zayer Ahmad, with his hopes and dreams. He hoped that someone would become literate in the village, someone who could understand God's words. The Koran that his maternal uncle had brought with him from Fekseno smelled of time. Its binding was broken and its pages were tattered. For a long time, Zayer Ahmad would look at its script, dazed and at a loss, and he would sigh. God Himself knew that he was a servant without guilt. To make up for all the things he did not know, Zayer Ahmad would say, "In the name of God," and recite the salutations to the Prophet and his family.

The alertness and the lively minds of the women of the village, however, would not allow the days of religious mourning to pass by coldly. The things that these astonishing creators of the world did! The women would sit around a cradle in which they took turns placing their babies one by one, rocking it, and singing lamentations. They made a headless effigy of a commander with cotton. A hand severed from the arm and a masked woman clad in black, who would search door to door in Jofreh on the days of mourning for the one killed, and lanterns that brightened the dark nights of Jofreh... This was the way they mourned the Night of Lonely Strangers.

On the days of the Ashura[13] religious mourning holiday, Jofreh was filled with seagulls. The birds sometimes sat next to the men and looked at them, as they were beating their heads and chests, while the women wailed. No one knew how or when these lamentations came about in the life of the village.

Zayer Ahmad would contemplate, smile, and tell himself that a world without women is nothing but a desert, and it was only the hands of these creators of the world that could make the desert prosper. Zayer Ahmad prayed that the sky would protect the women of the world and keep them pure, even Nabati, who was getting scrawnier day by day and distancing herself from the village.

Zayer Ahmad would sometimes get off course and go to Mama Mansur's house and chat with Mansur, hearing him complain:

"She talks to herself. She thinks the village is cursed. She's afraid Busalmeh is going to take me one night to the depths of the gray waters..."

Women and their strange and odd imaginations. Was it not Madineh who during the first five years of their married life wore black because of that little mermaid? What was Zayer Ahmad thinking when he chose her as his mate, Madineh, the distraught girl of Fekseno, who after the death of the mermaid was going mad and wanted to drown herself in the waters of the sea? Oh, the energy that Zayer Ahmad had spent, and how he was drained until he was able to take her away from the sea! And then, after their wedding! It seemed that, regarding all of them, when they become one with a man, their delusions and imaginations would flare up. How she was

---

13- The 10th day of the Islamic lunar month of Moharram, the anniversary of the martyrdom of the Third Imam of Shi'ites, Hoseyn. For Shi'ites, Ashura is the most important religious mourning day of the year. The Night of Lonely Strangers, "Sham-e Ghariban" in Persian, is the evening of Ashura.

trying to force Zayer Ahmad to sleep with one of the mermaids; how she was waiting for the mermaids! But time extinguishes the fire in the largest clay bread oven in the world. Madineh was no longer worried. She did not have delusions. There is no woman in the world who would not spend half of her life with delusions and imagining things.

Zayer Ahmad walked around the village happily. There had been no death in the village for a long time. As a child, he had heard that the plague, cholera, and consumption had wiped out an entire village. But Jofreh was healthy, healthy and clean. It had a clear blue sky on which at times the clouds drew designs and images, and stitched it to the land with long threads of rain. No jinn went through Jofreh. The denizens of the sea were calm, and even though the medicine of the blond men was gradually running out, with guesses and conjectures and by smelling the medicines, Zayer Ahmad had been able to figure out their plant sources, pulverize the wild plants with a mortar and pestle, mix them with the medicines, and give them to the people of the village with imaginary ailments.

Zayer Ahmad was certain that in fighting Busalmeh, the God of life had gained victory, and that He was protecting the village from up there in the sky.

One night, however, the screaming of Madineh and bellowing of Bubuni disturbed Zayer Ahmad's peace of mind and the calm of the village.

❖ 23 ❖

Madineh was the first person to see a corner of the moon turning red. An ugly black hand was holding the throat of the moon and squeezing it. The moon was struggling, thrashing about. It was panting. Madineh was screaming toward the sky. The world was becoming dark. In the absence of the moon, the stars were coming closer. The black claws pressed harder. The moon was coughing; its tongue was tied. The women of the village were clawing at their own throats. Their breathing passages were blocked. The mermaids were coming to the surface of the water, screaming and moving toward the village, and Bubuni was yelling.

Horror-stricken, the people came to Zayer Ahmad's house. Soon the moon would die in the sky and fall into the sea, and Busalmeh would not give back its corpse. Zayer Ahmad did not know what to do. The mermaids were approaching the shore of the village.

"They have lost their minds. Oh holy saint! Look how they're coming!"

Confused and bewildered, as though a thousand shady waves had pounded on their backs, the mermaids were coming toward the village. When they reached the shore, they kept pushing one another on the sea pebbles, gliding over one another's bodies, and coming.

When she heard Zayer Ahmad's voice, Madineh stopped screaming, thinking, the mermaids are coming to the village in search of the moon, and if they find out that the moon has died in the sky, they will suddenly die of grief on the land. When Madineh brought out the drums from the small room next to the room with five sashed windows to pound on them and tell the mermaids that the people of the village had not hidden the moon, the women, even though they did not understand what she was doing, accompanied her near to the shore. With such strength of hand, the likes of which no one could remember up to that day, Madineh began pounding on the drum, and suddenly the world filled with the sound of the drums. Someone was using Madineh's mouth and singing:

"Mama Zangeru, let go of the moon

Let go of that full moon."

The women pounded on the drums. Mama Mansur and Bubuni brought copper pots to the shore, and a pleasant voice from Madineh's mouth said that Mama Zangeru had to let go of the moon, that the moon is the symbol of light and love, the moon that the God of the skies lights every night in some corner of the sky to show the way to the night travelers.

The women played the drums, Madineh sang, Mama Mansur pounded on a copper pot, and Bubuni shook her hands toward the sky and danced. Nabati sneered at the efforts of the women of the village; and the men of the village on the top of the water cistern looked at the women, while no matter how hard he tried to recollect something from his memories, Zayer Ahmad could not come up with anything. None of the men of the village knew about Mama Zangeru. The women repeated the refrain of Madineh's song, and in the midst of the fear and fright of the village, Zayer Ahmad was reaching the conclusion that the women of the world were in contact with the invisible world, a world to which the men of the village had no access. Zayer Ahmad contemplated that women, from the time that the Creator of the World creates them in order to continue the human race, from the time that He places a womb in their belly, have something superior and better than men. They are the main guardians and protectors of the world.

The women pounded their drums and copper pots and wash basins. They danced and sang so much that eventually that ugly, black hand released the moon. Exhausted and bright, the moon sat in the sky. The sea suddenly turned blue, and the mermaids smiled.

The blue mermaids were retreating. Mahjamal saw his aquatic mother, who was summoning Madineh with a gesture. Madineh, whose clear, bright voice reached the end of the offing of the sea, let go of the drum and approached the aquatic mother. Mahjamal saw that his aquatic mother put a necklace made of green and blue stones of the sea around Madineh's neck, smiled, and along with the other blue mermaids, went to the depths of the green waters.

Who was this Mama Zangeru? That night, no matter what ploy he used, Zayer Ahmad was unable to separate Madineh from the women of the village. Moreover, it was quite possible that if he asked who she was and the village learned that the medicine man of Jofreh did not know about Mama Zangeru, that would be the end of his long-standing respectability. From Nabati, who did not feel well, Zayer Ahmad was able to find out what the women of Jofreh had in their hearts.

Distressed by the victory of the women of the village, for a long time, Nabati had to listen to the female chitchatting around the clay bread oven, at Zayer Ahmad's Pothole, and at the Well of Loneliness: Mama Zangeru is the mother of Busalmeh, and like her son, she is ugly and evil. She hates the sound of drums, and upon hearing the singing of women who live on the land and who are healthy, brave, and beautiful, she gets dizzy. If she decides to take the sun one day, the women need to beat on the drums and dance so much that Mama Zangeru will get dizzy and fall into the sea.

Indeed, what if she were to take the sun and choke it in her claws? What if the dancing and singing of the women of Jofreh does not work, or if Mama Zangeru, that decrepit old hag who hates light, falls on the village while suffering from dizziness? Zayer Ahmad felt something blocking his throat. He would sit beside his men on top of the water cistern and gaze at the sky. He could see Mama Zangeru chasing the stars to catch and strangle them. Seeing the meteors flying through the sky, he would shake his head and sigh. It was now as clear as day to him from whom those wandering stars were fleeing, and he hoped that the Creator of the Sky would never bring the day when Mama Zangeru would be victorious and the stars would become wandering and homeless.

To make certain not to afflict his men with his own extreme anxiety, Zayer Ahmad would keep silent. He was afraid to lose control of everything. He carried the burden of his astonishing horror with him all alone; all night long until morning, he stayed awake facing the sky, and no one in the household dared to ask him how he felt. Zayer Ahmad's vigils, his strange silence, and his lack of appetite that was depleting him day by day had so preoccupied the minds and consciousness of everyone in his household that they became negligent of Bahador, and no one could figure out how he had been taken to the shore at nighttime in his fish trap.

* * *

One clear morning, everyone was awakened, terrified by Kheyju screaming. Bahador was not there, and nothing could be seen on the sea. There were no mermaids, and the sea was calm and silvery.

It was either because of Kheyju's screams or Mahjamal's yelling that suddenly the people saw Bahador smiling and coming slowly from the end of the village with coral branches in his hand. His smile was so clear and transparent that Mahjamal could figure out where Bahador had been; but Kheyju, who was worried about her strange son, slapped him on his face, and Bahador threw at her the pearl he was hiding in his fist.

It was unclear what stories the people would have fabricated about the pearl if suddenly a putt-putt sound had not been heard from a distance and a man riding something that made the putt-putt sound had not been approaching from the road.

◈ **24** ◈

Terrified by that sound, everyone went silent. The children took
refuge in their mothers' arms, and the women of the village waited,
their faces drained of color. Zayer Ahmad and Mahjamal were at a
loss. Perhaps the world was going to turn upside down once again;
perhaps the world was going to shake once again.

They perked their ears toward the sound. It was coming from the
other end of the village. The people there abandoned their houses
and gathered in Zayer Ahmad's. He saw with his own eyes that a
man riding something with two horns that made a putt-putt sound
was coming toward the village. The man was holding tightly to the
two horns of the putt-putter, not to fall off. There was a little cabin
behind the man, which swayed this way and that along with the
putt-putter.

When the man reached the village square under the silk tassel
acacia tree, his putt-putter stopped making a sound. It ground its
teeth two or three times and suddenly became silent. The man
released its horns and pressed something with his foot. The putt-
putter just stood there, and the man dismounted. Zayer Ahmad
could see him standing in the middle of the square, looking around.
There was no one in the alleyways and back alleys of the village.
The doors of the houses were half open, and Zayer Ahmad could see

the man in the square looking at the half-open doors and windows, surprised. The man stood there in the square hesitantly for a moment, and then slowly began to walk. When he reached Mama Mansur's house, he knocked on the door. Hearing no sound, he went toward Captain Ali's house. One of its double doors was open. He peeked inside the house, knocked, and, disappointed, returned to the square and yelled:

"Hey, chief!"

Zayer Ahmad took a deep breath. When they heard the man's voice, the children got over their fear, jumped out of their mothers' arms, and in the blink of an eye, they came out of Zayer Ahmad's house, went to the square, and stood some distance away from the man and his putt-putter.

Upon seeing the children, the man laughed, hit his thigh, and said:

"I swear to God, I thought I had come to the land of the jinn."

He walked toward the children, and they stepped back. The man had a thick black mustache, his shirt collar was open, and he had a leopard tattooed on his chest. He asked:

"Where are your parents?"

The children stared at him, and at the leopard on his chest. Baffled, the man turned his head and looked around. The women and men of the village were watching him from a distance, on the top of the water cistern. When the man saw them, he cheerfully yelled:

"How's it going, chief?"

And he waved his hand toward them.

A moment later, Zayer Ahmad and the others came down the stairs of the water cistern and went to the square. The crowd behind Zayer Ahmad stood some distance away from the man.

Unsure of what to do, hesitantly he asked Zayer Ahmad:

"What's the name of your village, chief?"

Calmly, Zayer Ahmad said:

"Jofreh."

Moving his hands, the man said:

"To tell you the truth, I was passing by; I thought I'd as...ask how you all are."

The villagers watched Zayer Ahmad's mouth in silence, and Mahjamal was staring at the putt-putter. With a cough, the man cleared his throat:

"I wa...was thirsty... Do you ha... have a sip of water?"

Silently, Zayer Ahmad looked at Captain Ali. In order to fetch a bowl of water, Captain Ali separated from the crowd. The man, without thinking about his thirst, went to the little cabin behind the putt-putter. When he came back, his hands were filled with colorful candy. Hesitantly, the children came forward, and when the man tossed a few pieces toward them, they happily bent down and picked up the candy from the ground and opened the tinfoil.

What the man gave them was even better than the candy of the blond men. It was sweet and stuck to your teeth like chewing gum. Despite all this, the children were still terrified by the leopard on the man's chest; and the man, who was following the eyes of the children of the village, hit his chest, laughing, and made funny faces for the children. The children giggled, and before long, they gathered around the putt-putter.

The little cabin behind the putt-putter was full of merchandise of all sorts. Now having gotten over their fear, and seeing that the man was busy conversing with Zayer Ahmad, the children touched the putt-putter, went around it, laughed out loud, and finally peeked into its little cabin.

The man had come from the port, a city behind the mountains. He was a businessman who went to villages near and far and sold merchandise. The port was not very far away on the putt-putter. The city was several times the size of the village, many people lived in it, and there were many putt-putters there.

The villagers listened in silence; and to prove his claims, the man opened the door to the little cabin and took out colorful, curved hair combs. The combs were handed around. Bubuni stuck four colorful combs in her hair and, with a smile, stood in front of Captain Ali, who was returning with a bowl of water. Nabati suspiciously took one comb. Without taking a comb, Madineh stared at the man, then shifted her wandering eyes and stared at the putt-putter.

Frightened by Madineh's look, Zayer Ahmad grabbed the man's hand and led him to the side of the putt-putter:

"Mir... Do you have mirrors?"

Surprised at the sweat that had beaded up on Zayer Ahmad's face, regretfully, the man said, "No."

Zayer Ahmad breathed a sigh of relief, wiped his forehead, and whispered to the man:

"Here, no one must look into a mirror."

Puzzled and confused, the man placed his hand on Zayer Ahmad's shoulder:

"Rest assured, I have never seen a mirror in my life."

To set Zayer Ahmad's mind at ease, the man showed him all the merchandise in the little cabin. Assured, Zayer Ahmad led the man toward the men of the village.

What was that thing that the man had brought to the village? The putt-putter had no resemblance to a horse or a camel. Donkeys and mules also looked different. What did they feed the putt-putter? How could it stand on the ground in place without even a bit of movement?

The men touched the putt-putter one by one, examined it, and, amazed, realized that the skeleton of the putt-putter was made of iron. The man—on whose lips a faint smile had appeared from the things the people of the village were saying—looked at Mahjamal, who was standing beside a little boy with blue eyes, away from everyone else, looking at the sea out of boredom. It was as though he did not take his presence and the putt-putter seriously, as though he was waiting for him to go on his way and leave the village. To strike up a conversation with Mahjamal, the man walked toward him. Having gone no more than a few steps, he heard a sound. He turned around. The putt-putter had fallen on its side, and the children had scattered the merchandise all over the ground and were now playing with a stack of papers.

Frightened momentarily, the man hurried toward the children; but then he remembered that these people, who were separated from the rest of the world, were of no danger to him. Embarrassed by his own alarm, he stacked up the papers, placed them on his belly and buttoned up his shirt, all the way to the top.

The man quickly collected himself, took the bowl of water that Captain Ali was holding toward him, and drank it to the last drop. He then rode on his putt-putter, circled the square several times, and even gave a ride to the braver and more daring children of the village and allowed them to hold onto the horn of the putt-putter and honk it.

Amazed and gleeful, the entire village looked at the man and his putt-putter. To ward off the evil eye from the putt-putter, Bubuni took out one of her talismans and hung it from the putt-putter's horn, and Mama Mansur rubbed her spit on it.

The man with the leopard on his chest, whose name was Ebrahim, stayed in the village until noon. He went around the village on his putt-putter, and he saw no gendarme station or any sign of law and law enforcement.

The people of this village did not know the meaning of money and buying and selling, and when Ebrahim the Leopard showed Zayer Ahmad a one-*tuman*[14] bill and tried to explain to him what

---

14- Unofficial currency of Iran, equivalent to ten *rials*. Prior to the Islamic Revolution in Iran in 1978-1979, seven *tumans* were approximately equivalent to one U.S. dollar.

money meant, he could not get his point across. Zayer Ahmad took the bill, and it reminded him of a piece of paper which years and years earlier his father had stuck on the wall of the room in Fekseno. On that piece of paper, there was the picture of a man with a bald head, and on this one, the picture of a young man.

When Ebrahim the Leopard got on his putt-putter to leave, he told Zayer Ahmad that he would come back to the village once every seven days and bring them everything they needed.

Ebrahim the Leopard pressed his foot on something, and the putt-putter made a putt-putt sound and started moving. The village loudly recited a salutation to the Prophet and his family so see him off. Ebrahim the Leopard was following the straight road along the sea to leave, where he saw three thirsty men of the village with bottles in hand, and smiles on their lips.

Zayer Ahmad was happy. The world had suddenly become big to him, a world with strange and odd things that no human being could figure out. The city would be interesting to see, a place full of putt-putters, where the people sold their things in a place called Bazaar, and it had places to which people went when they got sick and schoolhouses in which children became literate. Also, it was most likely that in a place like that, they would know Mama Zangeru, could figure out her tricks, and would be able to do something that would cause her to pack up and go on her way, like Busalmeh.

In the mind and imagination of Zayer Ahmad, Mama Zangeru would be captured and shackled in thousands of chains, and the fishermen of the world would take the black-hearted old hag to the offing of the sea and send her to the depths of the gray waters.

Dreams and liberation. A human who is unable to fly the bird of his imagination to the other side of the world will wither from sorrow. When Zayer Ahmad would take Mama Zangeru to the depths of the dark waters, he would return to the village. He wanted Jofreh to also have a schoolhouse, and in order to test Ebrahim the Leopard and find out whether he was actually a human or a small monster who had disguised himself as a human, he had asked him to also bring a Koran for the village.

The people tossed and turned in their beds until late at night. Bubuni would not leave Captain Ali alone. This time, if Ebrahim the Leopard came back, they needed to go to the city with him and visit the house of the doctor to treat her incurable ailment. In the minds of Captain Ali, Zayer Gholam, and Mansur, bottles of the magic sherbet were being filled and emptied. But Nabati knew that neither was that stranger with the leopard on his chest a human nor had he come from a place called City. He was certainly sent by Busalmeh to misguide the village, and then turn into a leopard and rip Mahjamal apart.

The village was stunned and dazed for a week, dreaming of the city. A new world was taking shape in the minds of the villagers, a world full of putt-putters, colorful candy, and foot covers that saved the soles of their feet from the scorching hot sand, foot covers like the ones they had also seen on the feet of the blond men.

With the temptations of the unseen world, Mahjamal once again slept away from Kheyju, away from her who once again was disgusted with Mahjamal's odor, which made her dizzy. The villagers looked at the road with every sound, and sighed waiting for the sound of the putt-putter.

The aquatic man stared at the stars in the sky and talked to himself. He was bewildered. The strange rough journey that he had accepted on the land with his heart and soul among the humans, and the things that Ebrahim the Leopard had said, and the commotion that had been created in the village all seemed to have suspended him between the earth and sky. Greedy humans, curious humans! Still, Mahjamal could not understand the character and temperament of humans.

❀ 26 ❀

On the seventh day, they heard a sound from afar, and this time, two putt-putters entered the village. The second putt-putter was new and did not have a little cabin behind it. A man with a salt-and-pepper mustache and a permanent smile was riding it. Ebrahim the Leopard had buttoned up his shirt all the way to his collar, and the leopard on his chest was not visible. No matter how much the children stared, they could not see anything.

Ebrahim the Leopard had changed. He did not make funny faces, did not pat anyone's head or shoulder, and more than anything else, he looked at the other man. When the man got off the putt-putter, Ebrahim the Leopard brought out the souvenirs from the little cabin, which the children snatched from his hand in the blink of an eye. The man shook his head and laughed.

The men gathered in the room with five sashed windows. The Koran that Ebrahim the Leopard had brought passed from hand to hand. Zayer Ahmad was happy; he patted Ebrahim the Leopard on the shoulder, and the other man looked on silently. Zayer Ahmad's grandson, Bahador, was sitting next to Mahjamal, near Zayer Ahmad. Kheyju and Setareh were serving tea to the men and replenishing the tobacco of the hookahs. Ebrahim the Leopard told Zayer Ahmad that the other man was an old friend of his who would like to do something for the village if he could. Zayer Ahmad nodded smiling, and the man coughed and began to talk. With his appealing voice, very calmly and slowly, he said that human beings must help one another to make life easier and for no one to remain hungry and for everything to be provided for everyone equally.

With sparkling eyes, the man was looking at the men of the village and speaking about resources that he had in the city and friends who could solve many of the problems of the people of the village. When the man finished what he had to say, Zayer Ahmad told him: In the village, the air, the land, and the sky belong to everyone. Women bake bread and plant vegetables, and the men go to the sea. Only Busalmeh torments the fishermen, and sometimes Mama Zangeru takes away the moon and makes the sky dark. Even though Mahjamal had broken the spell of the power of Busalmeh, his mother, Mama Zangeru, who could fly in the skies and grab the throat of the stars and throw them into the depths of the gray waters, was now the source of all the fear in the village, the fear that someday, Mama Zangeru would grab the sun and strangulate it or would herself fall upside down on the village. And woe to everyone if Mama Zangeru were to fall on the village, because no one would be left alive. But—may the wind and Satan become deaf and not warn her about it—it is even possible to pull Mama Zangeru down to the ground with chains. Of course, in the village of Jofreh, the women have a solution. Once they even forced her to leave us alone. But Mama Zangeru had a vindictive heart. At night, she bewildered the stars and deprived Zayer Ahmad of sleep.

Beads of sweat had appeared on the man's temples. His eyes were strangely dazed, and his mouth was open, like that of a fish. Ebrahim the Leopard was biting the corner of his lip, and his eyes were sparkling with concealed laughter.

Zayer Ahmad cleared his throat, then took a glass of tea from the tray and continued: Once the business of Mama Zangeru is taken care of, Busalmeh will become wrathful. We will certainly need to build a wall in front of the sea so that when Busalmeh is angry, the waves will not roll over the houses, and the red mermaids will not be able to dump the water of the sea over the village...

The man, who was quietly biting his lip, pleased that he had found a topic that he could discuss, interrupted Zayer Ahmad and said that it was necessary to build a dam. Zayer Ahmad repeated the word "dam" a couple of times and looked at Mahjamal, who was listening without a sound, and he looked at the other men of the village, who seemed to be repeating the word "dam" under their breaths in unison.

When he saw everyone confused and puzzled, the man, who had found an opportunity to explain the meaning of the word "dam" to them, took out a piece of paper and drew the shape of what he had talked about on the paper. He said that the village should rest assured that the dam would not create a distance between the people and the sea and that it would merely stop the wrath of Busalmeh and weaken the strength of the waves.

Zayer Ahmad took a deep breath and spoke about his other wish, which was to build a big water cistern in order for the village not to suffer from thirst.

Late in the afternoon, Zayer Ahmad showed the men the magic box that no longer talked, and said that the entire village could bear witness that many men, women, and children were in the magic box who no longer talk and sing for some reason that is not clear to anyone. The man, whose eyes sparkled again and was quietly biting his lip once more, promised Zayer Ahmad that he would make the magic box talk, come the following week. Then Zayer Ahmad showed them the box of medicine, which by now no longer had any medicine left in it. The second man, who knew a lot of things, read the writing on the containers out loud in the language of the blond men and promised that he would get boxes full of medicine from a doctor he knew in the city and bring them to the village.

At sunset, Ebrahim the Leopard and the other man got on their putt-putters; and at the end of the village, they saw Zayer Gholam, Captain Ali, and Mansur standing in the middle of the road. Zayer Gholam showed them the empty bottles of the magic sherbet. Ebrahim the Leopard burst out laughing and slapped Zayer Gholam's shoulder.

"Next time, chief."

The next morning, Zayer Ahmad Hakim, carrying a broom, set out for the Shrine of Sire Ashk. He placed the new Koran on the wall shelf, and, happy with the world and with life, he swept the place and went back home, hoping that no calamity would befall the village and that the presence of God's book would be able to instill reason and sanity in Mama Zangeru's head.

At nighttime, the women and men of the village assembled in Zayer Ahmad's house and resumed telling their stories. The second man, whom Ebrahim the Leopard called Morteza, had given promises to Zayer Ahmad. The dam would definitely be built. If the people made an effort and all worked together, the water cistern would be easy to construct. Morteza had said that if the people unite, not even Mama Zangeru and Busalmeh could do anything. The second man had spoken so fast and waved his hands so much that Zayer Ahmad had not had the opportunity to tell him that the villagers always went to the sea together, they always were sorrowful together, they always were frightened together, and they always danced and prayed together; but they had been unable to get over the wrath and uproar of Busalmeh and the anger and begrudging of Mama Zangeru.

Nevertheless, it was obvious that Morteza knew a lot of things about the world. The people had listened to him all day long, and even though they did not understand much of what he said, they had all seen the way Zayer Ahmad kept nodding and agreeing with what he said.

Late at night, the villagers left Zayer Ahmad's house. All night until morning, Kheyju tossed and turned. The baby was wiggling in her belly, and she knew that by the time her children grew up, the world would not be so confined. That very night, Kheyju asked Mahjamal to go to the city on the putt-putter as soon as he could, and tell her what he saw with his own eyes.

Putt-putter... Putt-putter... Putt...

The seven nights and days seemed to have no intention of coming to an end. Everyone's attention was focused on the village road. Even Zayer Ahmad no longer was preoccupied with the sea. The people had lost their dreams and imaginations. The putt-putters had robbed the village of reason. In her imagination, Mama Mansur made flour from wheat, baked bread, and gave the bread to Ebrahim the Leopard to take to the port and sell. And the fishermen in their sleeping and wakefulness dreamed that they took their fish to the port on putt-putters and came back with baskets full of souvenirs. Bubuni, with colorful curved combs in her hair, saw herself as even more beautiful than the mermaids; she felt reassured, and was now less concerned about the sea and the mermaids. Captain Ali, Mansur, and Zayer Golam gazed at the road restlessly, waiting in anticipation day and night, waiting for those crystal bottles filled with the magic sherbet.

❖ **28** ❖

The two men arrived on the weekend on two putt-putters, and to Zayer Ahmad, who wanted to know what had happened to their shin and forehead, told a story that no one believed.

Had the magic box not come to life again and sang, the broken forehead of Morteza and the limping leg of Ebrahim the Leopard could once again have revived the fear and horror of Busalmeh in their hearts and robbed the village of its wits. But when Morteza took out some things from a small box and put them into the magic box, the village forgot about the wounds of the two men. Everyone gathered around Morteza; and Zayer Ahmad and the other men of the village saw with their own eyes that no one was living and dancing inside the magic box. When the magic box came to life, Zayer Ahmad understood that it did not have the power to sing. Morteza was impatient and was not in a good mood; and Ebrahim the Leopard was not looking into the eyes of the three men of the village.

"A man should keep his word," he said. "I broke my promise."

Concealed from the eyes of Morteza, who was showing the box of medicine to Zayer Ahmad, Ebrahim the Leopard promised the thirsty men that he would take them to the port with him and show them a place that was filled with magic sherbets, a place that has sherbets that can make the men drop and can send Busalmeh and all his kith and kin to the next world with one gulp.

29

The magic box was singing. Zayer Ahmad had turned the knob all the way up, so that even a person who lived in a house at the other end of the village could hear it. The voices of some people echoed in the sky of the village. No one knew where in the world they were sitting, or in which country they lived. No one could hear the fluttering of the wings of the seagulls any longer. The world was full of sounds and voices, unfamiliar, strange sounds.

A woman was singing, "To the city of my beloved..." Mahjamal noticed that the women of the village were no longer singing. He could not even hear the sound of their anklets, and a strange feeling of nostalgia arose in his heart. Something was being lost, even though Mahjamal did not know what it was, and the people of the village seemed not to care about it.

The evenings of the village were spent on top of the water cistern of Zayer Ahmad, and the people still turned the knob on the radio with wonderment and listened to various sounds. The nightly chitchats of the men and women of the village were being replaced with silence. Something strange and invisible connected the minds of the people to the radio. Sometimes a faint distant voice would say, "This is Tehran," and everyone would bring his or her ear closer to hear that voice more clearly, a voice that reported about different parts of Iran, even though they did not know where those places were, and about the fortunate young Shah, even though they did not know who he was.

Kheyju was in a different mood. With the radio becoming alive once again, she was no longer worried about Bahador. The mermaids rarely came to him, and Kheyju considered the absence of the mermaids as a good sign. At night, she allowed Bahador to sleep any way he wanted and to look at the sea as much as he wished. The sound of the magic box had distanced the mermaids from the village. Zayer Ahmad Hakim's first grandchild could not figure out the world, and did not know why the mermaids had suddenly disappeared, and why his aquatic grandmother no longer came to see him, his aquatic grandmother who had one day hugged and kissed him at the end of the village beside the sea, and had told him that whenever he would stare at the water of the sea, no matter where she was in the sea, she would come to see him. Even Zayer Ahmad, who told stories to Bahador until late at night, was no longer preoccupied with him. And Kheyju, who now had a swollen belly, would point to the sea and would sit him down facing the sea in order to be free of him. Bahador was bored. Something in the village was changing, something that Bahador could not understand.

Nabati was pregnant, and Mansur stayed with her most of the time, to prevent the two women in his house from quarreling and tearing each other to pieces like fighting cocks. Theirs was a hostility that Mansur could not understand, a hostility that made Mama Mansur get on Nabati's nerves and made her yell and scream. Zayer Ahmad had mediated several times, spoken to Mama Mansur, and now he was so drowned in his dreams that he had even forgotten about Mama Zangeru. No one dared to break the stream of Zayer Ahmad's thoughts.

The village was getting bigger, the number of children was increasing, and one clay bread oven alone was not enough to meet the needs of the people of the village. Zayer Ahmad had the women and the men of the village build another clay bread oven at the other end of the village, in which the women in the northern part of the village could bake bread without having to wait their turn or borrowing bread from other houses at night.

If it was possible to build a clay bread oven in the village that easily, why should every house not have its own bread oven?

The minds of the villagers were becoming enslaved in the coils of building and possessing.

* * *

Ten days had passed, and the putt-putters had not come. Where were they? Something strange gave the villagers assurance that the two men would return. Everything was real and clear: places on the other side of the mountains, boxes of medicine, magic boxes that sang, and women who were giving birth.

Kheyju's labor pains began early. She was sitting with the other women beside the clay bread oven preparing chunks of dough to be flattened when the pains made her scream; and as Mama Mansur and Madineh held her under her arms to help her get to the house, she delivered her little baby right there under the silk tassel acacia tree. Just standing there, Kheyju opened her legs for the impetuous, hasty baby girl to fall to the ground. Madineh wiped the little baby girl with the flap of her petticoat, cut her umbilical cord with the knife that Bubuni brought, and was amazed by the little baby girl's strange silence.

The little girl did not cry. She was staring at the world so intently with her large black eyes that, even though still in pain, Kheyju anxiously looked around. The world was still as it always was. The sky was blue, the ground was dusty, and the sound of the magic box was shouting in the sky of the village that certain people wanted to sell out everything to the aliens.

To bring the women of the village out of their dumfounded state, Mama Mansur slapped the baby girl on the face, and she, whose name they chose to be Maryam, sighed with tearful eyes and turned her face away. Mama Mansur, who was shocked by what the newborn had done and thought that she was born without a tongue, put her finger into Maryam's mouth and realized that, like all babies in the world, she did indeed have a tongue.

The females' pinching and slapping her made no difference. In silence, Maryam looked at the world most eagerly, and did not bother with her father's surprised eyes, as he was worried about the water of the sea rising and he saw that she did not pay much attention to the sea, and even her aquatic grandmother had not come by the shore in the early days of her life.

Years later, when Maryam was sitting in a cave next to Mahjamal in the Fekseno Mountains and listening to his stories, she heard from her father that in the early days after she was born, without the villagers paying any attention or being preoccupied with the sea, the water of the sea rose, and every night Mahjamal heard the voice of his aquatic mother, who was crying for her second grandchild of the land.

But very soon, one thing became obvious and clear to everyone. Maryam was incredibly fond of the magic box, and Mahjamal had even seen her turn the knob of the box with her small weak fingers and listen to that faint distant voice, her big black eyes opening and closing from being so amazed. In his mental squabbles, Mahjamal was frustrated and would sigh for having lost his soothsaying power. The world was dark for him, since he did not know what fate had in store for his children.

One month passed, and the two men from the city had not come back. The village resumed its fancies and fantasies. The Koran that Ebrahim the Leopard had brought showed that they were not the denizens of the air or sea disguised as humans. The wounds on the forehead of Morteza and the limping leg of Ebrahim the Leopard indicated that they were not the dead of the gray waters. Then, where were they, the two men? Who had shut the road to them? Zayer Ahmad became certain that the bad denizens of the sea had this time been toying with his guests and had made them forget the way to the village. Regretting what he had said to the two men, Zayer Ahmad went around in circles and swore not to ever again open his heart to any stranger who happened to drop by.

The villagers did not know what to do. The new world would not let them live as they had before. The flat, round loaves of bread that Mama Mansur had baked became moldy. The teeth of Bubuni's combs broke, and she was unable to fix them, not even with fire. Captain Ali, Mansur, and Zayer Gholam kept their eyes on the road and yawned. Nabati was certain by whom and for what those men had been sent.

The sound of the magic box had become faint and the villagers were afraid that it would run out of power again. No one seemed to remember the village without the sound of the magic box. But Madineh looked at the sea happily. When no one comes to the village and the magic box shuts up, the mermaids would come to the surface of the sea and she could see them again, combing their long hair and singing in Zayer Ahmad's Pothole. Madineh would sit beside Bahador, and when any sound came from the sea or when a wave turned and twisted, she would grab Bahador's hand and with her finger, point at the sea.

The village was paying no attention. It had lost its aquatic memory. No one was setting his heart on the sea, and the men pretended to be preoccupied under some pretext or another. But such preoccupations did not distract Mahjamal. He could see the ripples becoming lively.

One morning at dawn, just as the village was losing all hope, Ebrahim the Leopard, riding in a very large cabin that had an even larger room without a ceiling behind it and had four wheels and two eyes, entered the village, which immediately amazed and astounded the people. This thing was called a pickup truck and could go to the city faster than the putt-putter. There were many of these trucks in the port city, which were used to deliver merchandise to villages near and far. If the people of Jofreh wanted, Ebrahim the Leopard could even bring stones and cement to the village, build a water cistern, and build a dam in front of the sea. In exchange, his friends, who were chiefs in the port city, wanted nothing other than for the people to consider them their friends. And now, without taking anything from them, Ebrahim the Leopard had come to take them to the port city and show every part of it to the people of the village of Jofreh.

The children gathered around the pickup truck, touching its eyes and climbing on its head and body. The village was so fascinated by the pickup that they all had completely forgotten to ask where the men from the city had been all that time, and why Ebrahim the Leopard had come alone. Ebrahim the Leopard, who saw that the men and women were getting ready to leave, was at a loss. On the order of Morteza, only the men of Jofreh were supposed to be taken to the city, and now even if he made several trips, he could not take so many people to the city by sundown.

"Zayer, let the men come this time. Tomorrow will be the turn of the women and children."

With a gesture of his hand, Zayer Ahmad sent the women of the village away from the pickup truck, and went back to Mahjamal again, who was not keen on going.

Zayer Ahmad had to stay with the women and children, and they could not entrust the men of the village to Ebrahim the Leopard alone and hope to God all would be well. Thus, even though hesitant and disinclined, Mahjamal took the long white shirt that Kheyju was holding in front of him, and went behind the wall of the house to change his clothes.

When he came back, all the men of the village were on the truck, and Ebrahim the Leopard was sitting in the little cabin chewing on his mustache and waving to the children.

The pickup truck drove off with its strange noises and the smoke that was coming out of a pipe. To make sure that the children were not upset, Ebrahim the Leopard circled the village square two or three times, and turned the lights on and off several times, and while continuously honking the horn, he followed the road and disappeared at the end of the village.

30

The men of the village were stuffed in the back of the pickup truck, and every once in a while, with fear and amazement, they stretched their necks to see a world that they had never before seen. Mahjamal was sitting next to Ebrahim the Leopard, looking amazed and baffled. The roads of the city were black and smooth, and the pickup truck moved like a boat on a calm sea without struggling or shaking. Men riding putt-putters and people sitting in all sorts of pickup trucks were passing by speedily. Everything was moving. Some people were walking on the sides of the roads. No one stopped to ask someone else how he was doing. The sound of the honking of putt-putters and pickups was deafening the ears of the world. Ebrahim the Leopard was happy; he was drumming on the steering wheel with his fingers and could not stop smiling. Mahjamal was at a loss.

"Has anything happened?" he asked Ebrahim the Leopard.

Ebrahim the Leopard lifted his hand from the steering wheel and laughed boisterously:

"No! Like what, chief?"

It was as though Mahjamal had come to the land of stories, stories devoid of mermaids. The city was full of noise and movement. The sound of the city was not the sound of seagulls and the storm of the sea, and the movement was not the movement of the north wind or the repentance wind.

Ebrahim the Leopard let them off in a large square, filled with people:

"Well, here we are. Mingle with the crowd."

Mahjamal looked at him, stupefied. Ebrahim the Leopard patted his shoulder:

"Don't be scared, chief. They are our friends, celebrating."

Upon seeing the men from the village, the crowd made room for them. Tricolored cloths were hanging on the doors and walls, and there were white banners in the hands of the people in the square, with something written on them and which they waved. There was a pool full of water with a pipe sticking up that sprinkled water all around. The people in the square were all clean and tidy. Women without headscarves, old and young, were standing there smiling at them. Sometimes they whispered something in each other's ears, nodded, and made room for them.

Mahjamal kept blinking. He had never seen so many people in the world. He had never seen a pipe that sprinkled water around without any hand doing something. And those tall green trees! It was as though he was dreaming, or he was on a long journey.

The men of the village were so confused that they did not know when and how Morteza went to the top of a platform with a long rod in front of him, a rod the top of which was round, and its sound, stronger than thunder in the sky, was deafening.

"Comrades..."

Morteza held that thing in front of his mouth and coughed. His cough was louder than Busalmeh's. The crowd went silent. Then Morteza said things, and Mahjamal looked and listened, confused.

There was no talk of a wedding celebration. The voice exploded over the heads of the crowd. The men of the village did not know with whom Morteza had a quarrel and why he was yelling; and bewildered Mahjamal did not know how Morteza could raise his voice so easily to reach the other side of the world. Morteza's voice was so loud that Mahjamal thought it would surely reach the village, and that Zayer Ahmad and the women of Jofreh who had been left on their own could easily hear it.

Mahjamal could hear the word "Busalmeh." The crowd had turned around and was looking at them. Sorrow and sympathy waved in their eyes. There was no similarity between that calm and unconcerned voice and this angry and begrudging one, and all this did not smell good. Regretting having come, Mahjamal saw the men of the village, who were holding onto one another, feeling so unprotected.

With the final shouting of Morteza, fists flew into the air, the crowd yelled, and the white banners waved in the wind.

When Morteza was finished speaking, he came down from the platform and walked toward Mahjamal, whose head was spinning from the strange sound of the crowd, his eyes jumping back and forth. Morteza grabbed his hand, patted him hard on his shoulder, kissed him, and asked about Zayer Ahmad. It was at that moment that a man with some gadget in his hands came to them and adjusted the equipment toward Mahjamal. Smiling, Morteza was holding Mahjamal's hand in his hands. A bright white light spread over Mahjamal's face. The equipment made a clicking sound, and Mahjamal closed his eyes. The light spread over his face several times. The last time that Mahjamal opened his eyes, he saw the people in the square running away.

Some men dressed in identical clothes were chasing the people and grabbing them and dragging them away.

A moment later, there remained Mahjamal and the empty square. The men who wore hats and had clubs in their hands, for some unknown reason, were beating the men of the village.

To where could they flee? Where was the village? Why should

they be under the strikes of those clubs, clubs that hollowed your bones? No one had ever even seen quarrelling in the village. No one had raised a hand toward another. In the life of the village and in the course of Mahjamal's strange life, Zayer Ahmad had resolved everything. Where was their Zayer Ahmad?

The men of Jofreh had no quarrels or arguments with anyone. They have not done anything wrong. They have only come to see the city.

No one would listen. Mahjamal was shouting and uttering that which could initiate reconciliation, but the club-wielders did what they did, and with every word that Mahjamal said, they attacked and beat him even more.

There was no way to escape. It was as clear as day that the club-wielders would not be convinced with words. With the first fist of Mahjamal that struck one of them, the men of the village figured out what to do.

31

When he opened his eyes, he was in a dark, tight cell, his whole body was swollen with shooting pain, and he could hear the strange sound of the rising of the water of the sea. One of the mermaids was crying. It was not his aquatic mother. He knew. Every moment, when he was unconscious, Mahjamal had seen his mother, who was awaiting his entry into the depths of the blue waters of the sea, sighing. The one who moaned all night, the one who was shaking her hands all night long toward the moon and was asking the moon and the sky to show her where Mahjamal was to ease his suffering for having chosen the land was the blue lovesick mermaid. In the midst of his pain, Mahjamal smiled. At the moment when he suffered from pain and injury, he liked to hear the voice of the blue mermaid. He liked someone calling him by his name. He was lonely. Lonely and forlorn.

What Mahjamal had heard from the humans as they were punching and kicking him was incomprehensible to him. It did not connect him to the land. It distanced him from the scent and the voice of humans. Traitor to the country...to the homeland...foreign spy. How could one be a traitor to the water and land? Where is the homeland that one can sell? And who was the foreigner? Over what have the humans risen to fight each other? The promise of which pearl has pitted them against one another? He missed the kind human voice of the village and Zayer Ahmad. Where was Mahjamal? Where have you come, aquatic Mahjamal?

He felt a lump in his throat, and he wept. The human voice is blue, and the human glance is green, but the pained, lonesome howling...

Aquatic mother! Put your spells to work. Dump the water of the sea on this little room...

❧ 32 ❧

Three days later, Mahjamal was standing before a short stocky man with a Genghis Khan-style mustache and a red face, who was looking at him, smiling. Mahjamal suddenly felt a chill that shot down his spine. Where had he seen him?

The man was one of the dead of the gray waters, one of the dead of the muddy waters. One could not tell how many long years he had been living on the land to complete his mission and return to his sleep of death. Mahjamal had seen his double among the dead of the gray waters. Silently, Mahjamal stared at him. He had the same eyes and the same grin!

The man stepped forward and placed his boot on Mahjamal's swollen foot, shifted all his heavy weight to the right foot. Mahjamal bit his lip, the salty taste of blood filled his mouth; and staring into Mahjamal's blue eyes, the man stepped back:

"Well, so you are from the Tudeh."[15]

Dizzy from pain, Mahjamal said that he was from Jofreh and

15- Reference to the Tudeh Party, which was initially a leftist party that later became the pro-Soviet communist political party that played an important role during the movement for the nationalization of the Iranian oil industry. It was banned in Iran following the 1949 assassination attempt on the Shah.

not from Tudeh. Having heard the same statement for twenty-four hours, the man felt a shooting pain in his temples. He pounded on the desk with his fist and shouted that he did not know why all the Tudeh Party members say they are from Jofreh. Shouting, the man swore on the epaulet of His Majesty that he would make all the people from Jofreh talk, and cleanse the soil of the homeland of every traitor. Mahjamal had been hearing this word for three days: Epaulet... Insulting the epaulet, swearing on the epaulet... The soldier's epaulet. The epaulet of His Majesty... What was epaulet? Where was Zayer Ahmad, to tell him its meaning? Was epaulet one of the names of God, a name that some people resort to in order to beat up the people of Jofreh?

The man turned around and sat behind his desk. In his silence, Mahjamal looked at him, dazed and confused. Where had he seen those tiny black eyes and that face, reddened by meaningless shouting?

"So, you say you are not from the Tudeh?"

Obviously, Mahjamal was from Jofreh. But what had the people of the Tudeh village done that he was looking for them from door to door?

The man took a cigarette from his pocket and lit it. His movements were sluggish and slow, as though he was sitting in the depths of the gray waters. Mahjamal suddenly felt a chill. The same grin, the same eyes, eyes that were staring at him... Where had he seen him? In the depths of the muddy waters?

The man picked up a piece of paper and began asking his endless questions: date of birth, place of birth, names of father and mother. Mahjamal could not understand. He had never in his life imagined that someone would ever want to know the names of his parents and accuse him of something. What could he say? And silence made Major Senobari shout at the top of his lungs.

The minds of the dead of the gray waters are empty of the memories of the blue waters of the sea, and the double of the man in the depths of the dead waters could never inform him of what had passed in the depths of the green waters. Hesitant and worried, Mahjamal delivered the story that the women from Jofreh had told about him.

"Aha! So you came from an orphanage."

The man was laughing, chewing on his mustache, and jotting down something very fast. He asked again: date of birth... date of joining... date of... date of...

Desperate and helpless, Mahjamal could not convince him that he was from Jofreh, that he had two children, and that he was Zayer Ahmad Hakim's son-in-law.

"Last name, the last name of your parents!"

Mahjamal put his hand on his throat and swallowed his saliva. Pain shot through his entire body. He was feverish.

"I told you, I'm the son of gypsy strangers."

The man nodded.

"So, you are Mahjamal, last name, Gypsy-son, from Jofreh."

The man turned around and looked at the map on the wall behind him. He had been searching for a dot named Jofreh on the map for twenty-four hours. For him, Jofreh was a skeleton in the closet. Coming from somewhere called Jofreh, a place no one knew about; assembling in the square and participating in the rally of a political party that would soon be banned; clashes with the honorable government agents; resistance in the interrogations; and acting as if they had no idea what was going on. No, one could not believe their simplicity and their innocent looks. If he could make this traitor group confess, he would travel a hundred-year-long road overnight.

The man was sitting upright in his chair, and in his daydreaming, he was reaching from the rank of major to that of colonel, and from that of colonel to brigadier-general.

And Mahjamal was seeing his aquatic mother, who was slowly

approaching the village at night, grabbing Bahador's and Maryam's hands, and taking them to the depths of the green waters. I hope Zayer Ahmad ties Bahador's hand to his own at bedtime. I hope Kheyju doesn't leave Maryam by herself. He was cold, like the time he was standing among the drowned men, like the moment when he had disturbed the sleep of the dead of the gray waters.

"Sign this!"

With his hands linked behind him, the man was standing next to his desk.

"Mahjamal Gypsy-son, from Jofreh. Sign it."

Mahjamal looked at him, dazed and stunned. His lips moved slowly:

"What?"

The man yelled:

"What? You won't sign it?"

He held the piece of paper in front of Mahjamal's eyes.

Mahjamal's blue eyes were wet. He moved his hands as though he did not know what to do, and he looked at the sheet of paper.

"I can't read and write."

The man suddenly went into thought. How well the enemy can disguise their faces, and pretend to be oppressed and innocent. Mahjamal's eyes were blue, and the white skin of his face had surely turned dark under the sun of the south, and then there was this simple rural speech of his! When foreigners speak Persian, this is all they can do. The famous German spy, Wilhelm Wassmuss, also knew Persian. He was familiar with local southern dialects. Whatever country they are from, they get training in special courses. Each person is trained for one country. And as for his being unconcerned and carefree...! When you have your back covered and you know you have support from somewhere, then why worry? But I, Major Senobari, will soon make you sing like a Russian nightingale in the city square.

The investigation of the men of the village of Jofreh resumed. How long had he been living in that village? What did he talk about? What ideology was he advocating to the people?

But Mahjamal had grown up on the lap of the villagers, and according to what they said, his lineage was gypsy. The drowned could hear his voice, and he had played Fayez songs at the wedding of Busalmeh and had calmed the red mermaids with Khayyam-style songs... He had even been able to capture Busalmeh at one time...

Major Senobari was at a loss. The stories of the men of Jofreh were of no use to him.

❧ 33 ❧

In the village, confused and lost, Zayer Ahmad would stare at the road. The women brought out their talismans once again, and hung them on the windows facing the sea. They did not converse. Something was blocking their throats. They walked in the village quietly, so that no one could hear the sound of their footsteps, so that no one would know that they were alive. They were afraid they would give an excuse to Busalmeh; Busalmeh would calm down if he did not hear the sound of their breathing. The women would sit in the courtyard of Zayer Ahmad's house, smoking hookahs and weeping. Busalmeh had plundered the village. With that strange pickup truck, he had swallowed the men of the village as a group. This time, Busalmeh had dispatched the Little Giant, who could turn into any shape, even a putt-putter or a pickup truck.

Nabati hissed like a shark, and she muddied the water of the village. Despite all her promises and agreements with Yal and Busalmeh, they had taken her Mansur, and she blamed all this pain and suffering on Kheyju, who lived with a cursed man. Nabati grappled with Kheyju, and Zayer Ahmad's daughter grabbed her by the hair, rolled her on the ground, and dragged her to the side of the clay bread oven. Mama Mansur became involved in the fighting and took Kheyju's side. The daughter of Zayer Gholam had stabbed her soul; she was a bad omen, and she had brought nothing but loneliness and misfortune to her house. Zayer Ahmad separated the angry women from one another.

"Have you lost your minds? Mama Zangeru has pitted you against each other."

If the women of the village had not driven Mama Zangeru crazy, if with their dancing and the sound of their drums they had not deceived her, the village would not have faced such a day and such conditions.

The days passed agreeably for Madineh and Bahador. The lovesick mermaid had been moaning for three days, while the village was so preoccupied with its own sorrow that no one heard her crying. Late afternoons, when the mermaid would sit in Zayer Ahmad Hakim's Pothole, Bahador would go to her, play with her blue hair, and would see Madineh looking at him from the edge of the water, her eyes bright and happy. Zayer Ahmad's grandson was happy that the village did not pay attention to him, and that he could stay in the sea for as long as he wanted.

Bubuni could not figure out what Busalmeh was doing. She knew no matter where Captain Ali was, he was not in the depths of the blue waters. The mood and the condition of the mermaid made it obvious that Busalmeh had chained the men of the village somewhere far away, far away from the blue and green waters. When the lovesick mermaid disappeared and the sea by the shore was filled with starfish and small dead fish, Zayer Ahmad also became certain that the men of the village were not in the depths of the blue and green waters. What had risen from the sea showed that one of the blue mermaids had lit her talismans under the aquatic fire to find the fishermen. If the fishermen are not in the depths of the blue and green waters, then where could they be?

Zayer Ahmad went around in the village, and he did not know how to explain to the women that it was all Mama Zangeru's doing, that she had taken the men to the sky and put each one in some corner on a star, so that, like their women, they would also die of the grief of loneliness.

Finally, on the fifth day of bewilderment and wondering, a khaki-colored pickup entered Jofreh. It went from one end of the village to the other and then stopped under the silk tassel acacia tree. Two men wearing khaki-colored clothes got out. The women were peeking at them from behind the windows and the walls, and the children in the blink of an eye ran over there and surrounded the pickup. One of the men asked:

"Where are the men?"

One of the children answered: "They're lost."

Without saying anything to Zayer Ahmad, who was coming out of the courtyard of his house, the men got into the pickup and left.

Where had the men come from, and where were they going? How could anyone not talk to Zayer Ahmad Hakim, and just pick up and go? The world was chaotic and confusing, and the land and the sky were complicated. Zayer Ahmad set his heart on the sea. The waves of the sea can go everywhere in the world, find the lost men, and bring the news about them to the village, concealed from the eyes of Busalmeh and Mama Zangeru.

The women of the village slaughtered their chickens and put their cooking pots on the fire for the good denizens of the sea and the drowned; and at noon, up to their necks in water, they dumped the food from their cooking pots into the cove and sat facing the sea in Zayer Ahmad's house. Perhaps a sign would come from the sea and tell the village what has happened to their men.

The children saw the sign before everyone else. Ten days had passed since the absence of the men, when the children of the village came to Zayer Ahmad's house shouting that they had seen something black on the sea that kept coming up and going under.

Before Zayer Ahmad could reach the shore, Kheyju and Mama Mansur pulled the corpse out of the sea. It was a young man whose hands were tied behind his back and who had been shot in the heart. He was not from the village, and no one recognized him. He was young, and his face was so calm that the women thought he had been killed in his sleep.

When the women of the village brought the dead man to the edge of the sea, Zayer Ahmad arrived, and he recognized him, a young stranger who had appeared years and years earlier at the well in Fekseno, hungry and thirsty. This was the end of the world! They were killing the lovers of the world. Standing beside the corpse, Zayer Ahmad was at a loss. The same dark face, the same large eyes and long eyelashes, and the same straight hair that sometimes fell on his forehead.

The lovers of the world do not grow old...

Collapsing within himself, Zayer Ahmad said nothing; and the women of the village buried the man in the silence of the night; and awaiting the corpses of their own men, they sat facing the sea.

34

Two weeks later, with the arrival of Ebrahim the Leopard, the village breathed a sigh of relief. Ebrahim the Leopard was limping, he had become thin, and he spoke hurriedly. The men of the village had been arrested. Along with others, they had engaged in riots in the city square against the government. Mahjamal had beaten up the government people... No one, if he is wise enough, would quarrel with the government.

For the village, it was as clear as day that the government was Busalmeh, or his double who ruled on the land and who had promised the large pearl to some of his men if they arrested the men of Zayer Ahmad's village.

No one would let Zayer Ahmad get into Ebrahim the Leopard's pickup and go. Suspicion and mistrust were flaming up in the eyes of the women of the village. Seeing the serious hesitation of the women, Ebrahim the Leopard placed his hand on the Koran and said that the government is the crown on the head of everyone. He swore on the epaulet of His Majesty that he was not in charge of anything and that he had no problems, and that the government had released him, and from then on, he would have nothing to do with any group, and that if he has risked his life and come to Jofreh, he had come only because of the bread he had broken with Zayer Ahmad.

Ebrahim the Leopard, who had begun to weep, said other things as well, which the women of the village could not comprehend, and in order to stop a man that big from crying, they consented to Zayer Ahmad's departure.

35

Zayer Ahmad got out on a smooth, black road. Ebrahim the Leopard pointed to a building:

"Go. I'll be waiting for you right here."

Not even in stories had Zayer Ahmad witnessed a house like this, as though they had placed four ships on top of one another. He was terrified that he would get lost. What if he got lost in this big house, or they would not let him leave and return to the village, like they did to Mahjamal?

Should he go back and make Ebrahim the Leopard take him to the village? But what will happen to the men of the village, and how could he explain it to the sorrowful women? In front of the door, he saw many women and men who went forward when a voice called them, and each took a number. A man in a hat in blue clothes was pushing them, bullying them, and shouting at them. Everyone's attention was focused on the numbers, and no one looked at Zayer Ahmad.

When Zayer Ahmad went into Major Senobari's office, it was quite a while after noon. Zayer Ahmad told Major Senobari that he had come from Jofreh, that his men had been captured, and that now he had come to take them back with him.

Major Senobari, who now knew that Jofreh was a real name and place on earth, smiled:

"The charges against the men of the village of Jofreh are serious, and the government will not allow their release that easily."

Thirsty and tired, Zayer Ahmad said that he wanted to speak to the person who was the government himself, and to tell the government what he knows about the men of the village, and say that the men of the village had never done anything bad in the world, and that in his life of so many years, he had never seen anyone quarrel with anyone else. The women of the village were sad. They could not put their hearts into any work, and the children kept looking at the village road...

"I am the representative of the government. Speak to me."

In Zayer Ahmad's mind, the world was coming to an end. Major Senobari was the representative of the government, and the men of the village would be released on bail and with official deeds. Driving toward the village, Ebrahim the Leopard was shifting gears and talking:

"A deed is a piece of paper that shows which house belongs to which person. A wise person is a person who has everything he owns registered, so that someday, someone cannot take them away from him."

The world was becoming confusing. Staring at the windshield of the pickup, Zayer Ahmad could not figure out what was what. It was as clear as day that the people had built their houses with their own hands, and everyone in Jofreh knew which house belonged to whom. Thus far, no one had gone to someone else's house by mistake. Bewildered, Zayer Ahmad's lips moved; he was talking to himself.

Ebrahim the Leopard promised to bring the officials of the Bureau of Registry to Jofreh in order for everything to be settled soon.

The officials of the Bureau of Registry arrived just as Nabati was screaming from labor pains, and Mama Mansur would not consent to stay beside her. Madineh was forced to help her give birth to a scrawny, feeble baby, who was born breached.

The officials soon realized that the people of this village had no birth certificates and that prior to having their houses registered, they needed to have their own presence in the world registered. Zayer Ahmad walked with the officials from house to house and hut to hut.

It was not possible to calculate the dates of birth of the people of Jofreh. Even the largest calculators in the world would be confused by Zayer Ahmad's explanations: Mama Mansur was born twelve springs before Fanus was cut to pieces in the Fekseno Mountains; Bubuni, during the year that birds were falling from the sky and fluttering on the ground; Setareh, when the edge of the sea by the shore was filled with tiger-tooth croaker fish; Madineh was born when the sun shone more than ever in the world one scorching hot afternoon in Fekseno; and Bahador, when the mermaid cried until noon in the sea.

The Bureau of Registry officials, whose eyes opened wide and who were biting their lips, no longer listened to what Zayer Ahmad was saying. Upon seeing every person in the village and hearing his or her name, they wrote down some date for his or her birth. Thus, Mama Mansur became the same age as Nabati; Kheyju was born the same year that the scorching hot sun was shining in Fekseno; and Bahador and Maryam were born on 25 July 1951. Soon after, with two types of documents, the people were able to prove to the strange chaotic world that had invaded the village that they existed and breathed in their own houses.

In order to have the men of the village released, Zayer Ahmad went to the city many times. Finally, on one of those hot summer days when sweat was pouring from every nook and cranny of his body, he grabbed Major Senobari by the collar, threw all the documents on his desk, cursed and insulted the government and everything else, and, fed up with all the futile coming and going back and forth, yelled that the business of the people of Jofreh had nothing to do with the Tudeh and the government, that they were fishermen and they only wanted to catch fish and go on with their lives. As though taking everything as a joke, Major Senobari was laughing and trying to free his collar from the hand of that tall old man. It was 23 September 1953,[16] and the city was calm. Under the domain of the power of Major Senobari, not even a bird dared to chirp, and Major Senobari with peace of mind would be able to return all the men of the village to their hearth and home, with the exception of Mahjamal.

It was now clear to Major Senobari that Mahjamal had nothing to do with the banned party; but the double of the dead of the gray waters could not let go of Mahjamal. Something flared up inside him that called Major Senobari to a challenge, which impulsively made him think of Mahjamal. He was searching for a way to interrogate him, to torture his aquatic body on the rack. Mahjamal's glances, his strange silences, his tolerance for pain, and the sorrowfulness that suddenly would nest in his blue eyes, in fact, Mahjamal's very being, tormented him. No matter where they are, the dead of the gray waters act the same; they yield to Busalmeh, and the presence of Mahjamal disturbs their sleep of death.

The village was happy, and Kheyju was sad. She was unable to do anything, and she could not comprehend what Zayer Ahmad and the men of the village said. In some place, they beat the people, they question them, and the government calls everyone to account... The government... Kheyju would sit listening to what the men of the village said, and could not make any sense of the world. Setareh stayed close to her to erase the sorrow in her heart. Bahador was preoccupied with the sea. And Maryam in her infinite solitude would turn the knob on the magic box and hear that everything has been put in order, and the young fortunate Shah had returned from his journey, celebrations and festivities were going on throughout the world, the country's advancement and progress continued, and soon, general amnesty would be issued and those who had repented would be pardoned.

16- On 19 August 1953, a joint plan by the British government and the American administration to overthrow the government of Prime Minister Mohammad Mosaddeq, who nationalized the Iranian oil industry, and to return the Shah to power was carried out, martial law was established, and a large number of the opponents of the regime were arrested and jailed or executed.

"Imperial pardon..."

All the way to the village, the wind carried the voice of Major Senobari, who was standing before the prisoners, none of whom were political and all of whom had been arrested on the streets. Major Senobari was reading the decree of general amnesty, and anger swelled in Mahjamal's soul. Busalmeh of the land devoured the tall handsome young people. Who would get the pearl? Who was the bride of Busalmeh of the land?

When Mahjamal put his fingerprint at the bottom of a long piece of paper on Major Senobari's desk in order to be released, a smile appeared on Zayer Ahmad's face, and he remembered the day when they were enslaved by Busalmeh's wrath and Mahjamal had not wanted to have his index finger cut off.

Zayer Ahmad and Mahjamal went from this room to that room until sundown, putting their fingerprints at the bottom of countless pieces of paper, and finally when, tired and beat, they were getting into the pickup, they had both come to the conclusion that the government people were more fond of paper and dates than of human life.

❖ 36 ❖

Pearl! A large pearl! Humans on the land and on the sea were after that large pearl, and need darkens the human heart. Mahjamal's vivid mind would not leave him alone. It was as though in the heat of the events, he had not had the opportunity to believe what he had seen. The chaos of the storm subsides, the sea recovers, and the particles of pain and suffering settle into Mahjamal's soul!

He had also sat and listened to Zayer Ahmad's stories. He knew what the walls of Zayer Ahmad's house concealed inside them. The repeated nightmare of Zayer Ahmad's Brno rifles... The nightmare of magazine bullet loaders, which he had never seen in his life... A hand would tear apart the walls of Zayer Ahmad's house, grab the Brno rifles from the time of migration, and eyes would weep... Even the double of the dead of the gray waters is a human being. His hands would tremble, the Brno would fall on his feet, and then the strange sound of crying would rise. He would wake up frightened, and sit up soaking in sweat. Kheyju would hand him a bowl of water:

"Go to sleep, Mahjamal. Everything has passed. It's over."

But fear and terror would not leave him alone. He loved humans; his heart would not consent to seeing anyone's blood being spilled on the ground.

Mahjamal had seen that a human being can go mad from pain, can become a lunatic, and can laugh even though his body is furrowed with wounds. They had taken a young man from his cell, and when he had returned, he did not recognize Mahjamal. He could not recognize anyone. He laughed, and Mahjamal could see that his eyes were empty of the gleam of memories.

Ashamed of what humans do to themselves, Mahjamal would sink into his own silence...

For the people of the village, the world had become complicated and incomprehensible, and in their vague imaginations, Busalmeh had been replaced by Major Senobari and the government. In their gatherings in the evening, for a long time, the men talked about what they had witnessed. They would gather around Zayer Ahmad, and their stories were coupled with astonishment, pain, and laughter. At times, Zayer Gholam mimicked Major Senobari and his agents. He would open and close the flap of his loincloth to remove sorrow from the eyes of the villagers. Everything had become confusing in the minds of the people. Busalmeh of the land was no less than Busalmeh of the seas. The dreams of the women and the thoughts and plans of those who intended to become involved in trade prior to the story of the putt-putt riders had been disturbed. Thinking and dreaming about the bottles had been completely erased from Zayer Gholam's mind.

Nabati was not on speaking terms with Kheyju; and she would quarrel with Mansur, telling him that he should not go to Zayer Ahmad's house. Bubuni had sworn to herself that she would never let Captain Ali step out of the village. And Ebrahim the Leopard, who did not find the conditions in the port city favorable to him and wanted to get himself lost and concealed somewhere, came to the village more often, spent many nights in Zayer Ahmad's house, and could not take his eyes off Setareh's daughter, Golpar, who was watching Maryam or playing with Bahador on the edge of the sea.

In Zayer Ahmad's heart, however, there was a different tumult. The paved and uniform roads, the reflecting pools at the centers of the squares, and the pretty houses would not leave his mind. If he could make the road to the village smooth, he could build a large water cistern and solid pretty houses that would not collapse, not even from storms and rain. Ebrahim the Leopard, who had sold his pickup and came on his putt-putter, would tempt him that perhaps with the same little cabin he could bring stones and plaster to build the water cistern. Ebrahim the Leopard could take some things from the village to sell and use the money to buy plaster and cement. Perhaps he could urge the men of the village to approach the stony mountains and, as was the custom in the old times, carve the stones out of the mountains. Perhaps the village could stay outside the quarrels of the government and go on living.

"A big reflecting pool, like that pool..."

Mahjamal was at a loss. Time and forgetfulness! How easily a human being forgets his suffering and sorrow, and how easily the bird of imagination flies over the bitter memories and nests in a place that was not seen in the heat of battle and suffering. Mahjamal did not think that in his exhausting going back and forth to the port city that Zayer Ahmad had been able to see anything. But apparently, a human being in the heat of pain and suffering lessens his sorrow by absorbing beautiful images, and once calm returns, the beautiful images are aggrandized and appeal to his mind and senses, like the capricious fish in the sea.

Zayer Ahmad's daydreams were interrupted by the arrival of an old man accompanied by three women clad in black. The old man walked bending over, and his small black eyes wandered around, bewildered. He turned off his car under the silk tassel acacia tree, came to Zayer Ahmad's house with the women, and showed him the photograph of the young man who had one day risen from the sea with his hands tied behind him and a bullet in his heart. Zayer Ahmad said:

"It looks exactly like him."

He took the picture from the old man.

Death cannot leave its footprints on images and photographs. If Madineh or Mama Mansur were to see the photograph, the village would fall apart under the crying and weeping of the women. It was him, the same stranger who years and years earlier, when Zayer Ahmad was fourteen years old, had come to Fekseno.

The lovers of the world do not grow old, the lovers and rebels of the world...

Mahjamal saw the trembling of Zayer Ahmad's hands and the knotting of his brow. When Mahjamal along with Zayer Ahmad and the women in black reached the graveyard, he smelled something, a kind, painful, and familiar scent, the scent that he had heard about for twenty years in Zayer Ahmad's stories. The tall handsome young man of Zayer Ahmad's stories had died. It was a story that had ended, in order for another story to begin.

The people of the village, who had just remembered that they had not mourned the dead man, brought out the black banners, and before the horrified eyes of Ebrahim the Leopard, who suddenly got on his putt-putter and fled, they went into mourning. Three days after the departure of the women in black and the old man, a truck full of soldiers arrived in Jofreh, and Zayer Ahmad saw Major Senobari, who went straight to the graveyard. Before the worried eyes of Zayer Ahmad and the women, who had not let their men appear in front of him, Major Senobari ordered the excavation of the grave and the removal of the corpse, but none of Major Senobari's agents saw the faint smile that appeared on the lips of Zayer Ahmad and the women of the village. When they dug out the dirt of the grave, they found nothing but small coral branches and large ear-shells that could only be picked in the depths of the blue waters by the hand of the dead of the land.

"Where is the body?"

Zayer Ahmad pointed to the coral branches and made every effort to make Major Senobari understand that the dead only are in their graves on Friday eves, and in the course of the week they go to the sea and become companions of the corals and the fish of the sea. Stunned and confused, the soldiers were listening to what Zayer Ahmad was saying, but Major Senobari would not give up.

"Three days ago, a number of people came here..."

"The dead have kinfolk."

Major Senobari knew that the old man and the women in black had left Jofreh emptyhanded, the village had been in mourning for three days, and no one had touched the dead man's grave. But, who had given Zayer Ahmad permission to bury the dead without a permit?

Surprised, Zayer Ahmad's mouth remained open. To the same degree that what Zayer Ahmad said was incomprehensible to the soldiers, the questions of Major Senobari indicated his confusion and lack of understanding of the ways and customs of the world. In his entire life, Zayer Ahmad had never heard that he needed to get a permit to bury a dead man.

"The dead do not belong to anyone. They belong to the land."

Major Senobari exploded:

"Enough of that foolishness! Tell me where the corpse is!"

When Zayer Ahmad silently pointed his index finger toward the sea, Major Senobari screamed loudly:

"Arrest him..."

But Kheyju did not give the dead of the gray waters a chance to shout again. She stood face-to-face with Major Senobari and ululated combatively.

The women, whose hearts were bleeding about what had happened to their husbands, their faces enflamed with anger, ululated, shook their hands, and with a strange dance that symbolized war and belligerence, surrounded Major Senobari.

It was that strange dance of the women of Fekseno when they inevitably rose in defense! A smile appeared on Zayer Ahmad's lips. Humans inherit so many things! This was Fanus, Fanus singing in the midst of the women of the village, ululating and dancing. The world was repeating itself, in a different form, a different shape and face.

Stunned, Major Senobari stepped back, and ordered the grave to
be refilled with dirt.

Zayer Ahmad calmed the women with a gesture of his hand.
With a face enflamed with anger, Kheyju left the graveyard with
the other women. Without looking at Zayer Ahmad, Major Senobari
began to walk through the village from one end to the other; and
finally, when he reached a hill by the sea at the end of the village, he
pointed at it and said:

"We will build a guard station right here."

The soil that makes the dead so restless that they go to the sea
during the week and those living on it who raise such a ruckus in the
city must be kept directly under the government's watchful eyes.

❦ 37 ❦

It took an entire year before the guard station was established in Jofreh. The entry of soldiers with shovels and pickaxes did not smell right. The women of the village would tear down the walls at night; they would grab the collars of the soldiers, who spoke in a variety of accents, and no one could stop them, not even the gunshots fired into the air, which terrified the seagulls. Zayer Ahmad went to the port city many times to ask the government to leave Jofreh alone and not to hoist strangers over the heads of the village of Jofreh.

"The country's order and security must be maintained."

"But what does the village of Jofreh have to do with the country?"

In the midst of anger and joy, Zayer Ahmad soon learned that the villages of Jofreh and Fekseno and thousands of other villages and provinces were part of a country, in which order and security had to be established. The world was big, like the sky, and the village of Jofreh was but a small star in this strange sky. Searching in his recollections for disorder and lack of security, Zayer Ahmad finally concluded that order and security did not have any specific meaning, and that anyone could define them as he saw fit.

One day when Major Senobari saw Zayer Ahmad in his white skullcap waiting for him, he threatened him and said that he was disrupting government business, and that if the women tore down the walls of the guard station one more time, he would arrest all the men of the village and imprison them on the charge of smuggling.

Ebrahim the Leopard came to the rescue of the people and Zayer Ahmad, and explained to them the meaning of the word "smuggling." Mansur was overjoyed. On the sea, they go to faraway countries and bring foreign goods and sell them at high prices. Smuggling became etched on Mansur's brain, and it was he who first thought about building a large boat with which he could travel to Zanzibar and Gujarat.

Finally, the guard station was built near the Well of Loneliness. In the late afternoons when the women went to the well, as they reached the front of the guard station, they pulled their scarves over their faces. The breath of male strangers wafted in the village. With their presence, everything was changing in the village of Jofreh. The women would return from the well silently, as though they had lost their voices and had forgotten their songs. The mermaids had vanished. Seagulls flew over the sky of Jofreh at higher elevations. The gunshots fired into the air had scared them away.

Madineh was worried about the mermaids, and Bahador, after keeping his eyes on the sea for days waiting to see his aquatic grandmother, developed a fever and collapsed. Having exhausted his knowledge of how to treat him, on the insistence of Ebrahim the Leopard, Zayer Ahmad took Bahador to the port city and became acquainted with Dr. Adeli, an exiled colonel who had a Number 4 haircut, an oval face, and a moonlit complexion, and who always shouted at his patients, who came like a flood from the surrounding villages upon hearing that he had been exiled there. Zayer Ahmad told the doctor the story of his village; and the exiled colonel, fascinated by Zayer Ahmad's simple mind, examined Bahador but could not figure out what was wrong with him. Medical tests did not indicate anything, but as Zayer Ahmad spoke, Bahador's eyes became bigger, his pulse went up and he became restless, sweat beading up on his forehead. Dr. Adeli soon concluded that the blue-eyed grandson of Zayer Ahmad Hakim had an unusual attitude toward the sea and mermaids. Without letting Zayer Ahmad know what he had determined, the doctor promised Zayer Ahmad the he would go to the village of Jofreh, talk with the soldiers, and treat the incurable ailments of the people of the village, ailments that they had developed only after the guard station was built.

Dr. Adeli, for the first time in his forty years of life, was faced with patients who were sorrowful about the blue color of the sea. Madineh, who along with her aquatic grandson missed the mermaids, told Dr. Adeli that since the time of the absence of the mermaids, she had lost half of her heart, as though the walls of the guard station had collapsed on half of her heart and smashed it with dirt and debris. Madineh said that she could not remember the shape of the mermaids anymore, even in her dreams, and that as soon as she closed her eyes, she saw that the dead of the gray waters were building a guard station in the depths of the green waters. Kheyju, who had lost her memory and forgotten the songs, pleading with the exiled colonel, wept for the first time in front of everyone.

Mahjamal bit his lip and did not tell Dr. Adeli that day and night he heard the sound of weeping from the depths of the green and blue waters of the sea and from the land. Setareh said that the world was too confined for her, and that in her sleep and when she was awake, she saw a seagull on fire, a seagull that went all the way to the offing of the sea and fell head down into the strange waves.

Dr. Adeli, who was spending Friday, his day off, until sunset in the village of Jofreh, saw the people of the village, gave them some medicine, and in the late afternoon on his way back, he was so worried about the mermaids and the blue color of the sea that, like always, he forgot to think about his own exile and wandering, and about the things that he missed in that faraway city, the capital.

* * *

The guard station issued its first decree on the day that the men of the village were getting ready for winter fishing. A soldier on the shore fired a shot into the air. The head of the guard station rode on a boat to the cove and told the men, who were lifting anchors, that from that day on, fishing was allowed only with the permission of the guard station.

Zayer Gholam dropped the anchor into the water, and, yelling, stepped into the water:

"What about sleeping with our own wives? Does that also need permission?"

Tears had welled up in the eyes of the men of the village. In Mahjamal's mind, the mermaids were screaming. The women of the village, who had gathered on the shore with the sound of the shot, saw their men coming despondently out of the sea, and they went to Zayer Ahmad's house.

"The government wants to kill the people with hunger."

Accompanied by the men of the village, Zayer Ahmad went to the guard station; but Kheyju along with the other women had arrived there earlier. Kheyju, the first person from the people of Jofreh to enter that little room, grabbed a young scrawny soldier by the collar and, screaming, lifted him off the ground. Stunned and confused, the man was disarmed without realizing it. Yelling and screaming, the women attacked the guard station, and the soldiers, trying to avoid confrontation with the women, ran away with their weapons, when suddenly the sound of gunshots filled the air. Moments later, the doors and windows of the guard station were broken, and the head of the guard station begged and pleaded with Zayer Ahmad to calm the women.

It took quite a while before Zayer Ahmad spotted his sole daughter and knew that from among all the moments of the Fekseno stories, the sound of the neighing of Brno rifles and the story of Fanus was the only thing that had remained alive as a memento in his mind. He grabbed the rifle from her hand and sent her home. Zayer Ahmad, who had come to Jofreh long ago searching for tranquility alongside the blue sea, and had buried the Brno rifles of the men who accompanied him in the walls of his house hoping not to hear the sound of gunshots to the end of time and to have his offspring grow up away from the tumult in the world, saw that the world had not turned as he had wished. His sole daughter and the singing women of his clan, desiring to be like Fanus, had practiced with rifles and shooting in their minds.

Mahjamal was taking Kheyju away. His forehead was knotted, his lips were pursed, and he did not know that Zayer Ahmad was watching the strange quivering of his lips. Kheyju and the singing women of the village were right. It was as though it is human fate to rebel and revolt in order to protect what one owns. Today, they take the sea from you, and tomorrow, it would be hard to walk on the ground without permission.

Is human fate to live and fight? Wrestling with his new beliefs, Mahjamal took Kheyju home, and he tossed and turned in bed until late at night from the sound of the lashes that were administered to the body of the soldier who had been disarmed. Finally, with sleepy eyes, he and Zayer Ahmad went to the guard station. They were whipping the soldier behind the guard station.

"The gun means the honor of the soldier."

And the soldier who had lost his honor was crouched into himself, his body turning and twisting, and the head of the guard station was standing there counting the lashes. He was not listening to Zayer Ahmad or to Mahjamal, who felt pain shooting through his temples and who had submitted to pleading, asking the head of the guard station to stop being angry and to let the soldier go.

Had it not been for the heavy shadow of the women of the village, who had quietly formed a circle around the guard station and the soldier in the dark of night, and had it not been for the fiery eyes of Kheyju, that young Lor tribal soldier would have most likely joined the world of the dead, and the village graveyard would have received a new guest.

"We are the agents of the law, Zayer."

The law... The law... Zayer Ahmad thought that everyone has a law for the law, and the law of the village cannot be the law of the guard station, and everyone interprets the law on the basis of the bread that he eats.

That night, Zayer Ahmad applied ointment to the injured body of that young man. Madineh fed him with her own hands. And Kheyju and the other women of the village, facing the sea until morning, prayed for the soldier, who had a mother in some faraway land and the government had brought him here for his compulsory military service.

❧ 38 ❧

Mercenary general, kill me, for spilling my blood you'll pay
May your bad name and ill repute last to Resurrection Day.

One month later, the voice of the young soldier who sang in a strange accent made the women of the village sad. In search of her six lost sons, Mama Mansur gave food to young soldiers, who sang every sunset in Gilaki, Kurdish, and Azeri dialects. She patted their heads with kindness to fill the void of her seventh son, Mansur, who was distancing himself from her day by day. No longer did anyone pull her scarf over her face when she was passing by the guard station.

Every day in the late afternoon as the sun sank halfway into the sea, the women of the village sat under the silk tassel acacia tree listening to the sad songs of the men of the guard station, songs with the scent of the sorrow of being strangers in a strange land.

Their voices ignited a fire in Setareh's heart. She was near to Mahjamal and far away from him; her rural female honor would not allow her to say a word. Setareh wept, and Kheyju, laughing, wanted to wipe the sorrow of Setareh's lost man from her heart. With her strange secret of love, Setareh would listen to Kheyju, who talked about Golpar, who was now ten years old already and Ebrahim the

Leopard brought her all sorts of gifts from the city.

One night when Ebrahim the Leopard was staying in Zayer Ahmad's house, tired of recollecting his memories of the city, Mahjamal asked him:

"What happened to Morteza, that friend of yours?"

The color drained from Ebrahim the Leopard's face, and he swore that he had not seen Morteza for a long time, and that in fact from the very beginning, he and Morteza did not drink from the same trough, and that Morteza was the kind of person from whom one had to run away like from the plague, because such people destroy your hearth and home.

Silently, Mahjamal nodded, and he realized that even though Ebrahim the Leopard looked like a bear, he was no more than a straw man.

Ebrahim the Leopard, who no longer thought about anything that had to do with politics, had bought a bigger pickup truck, and he continued to travel to villages near and far. He came to Jofreh every week, and brought the things that the head of the guard station had ordered.

The village was worried about the things that Ebrahim the Leopard unloaded in front of the guard station. The people would gather around Zayer Ahmad in a panic.

Perhaps the government intended to build a high wall in front of the sea, so that no one could see the sea any longer. Now that the fishermen did not listen to what the law said and went fishing winter and summer without the permission of the guard station, it was quite possible that by building a solid concrete wall, similar to the prison walls that Mahjamal and the other men of the village had seen in the city, they wanted to put the sea in prison.

But when the soldiers of the guard station, with their bare upper bodies, mixed plaster and cement and dug the foundation for another room behind the small room of the guard station, the village breathed a sigh of relief. The guard station was going to become bigger, and this had nothing to do with the people of the village and the sea. The head of the guard station was happy about the peace and quiet of the people of Jofreh. Unconcerned, the women passed by the guard station to go to the well, and every day at sunset, Mama Mansur gathered everything she had to take a wooden container of bread and copper pots full of food to the guard station. Major Senobari would soon be coming for inspection, and if the new room was ready, another star would be placed on the shoulder of the head of the guard station.

One morning at dawn, the village woke up fearful and horrified by what had happened to the guard station. The head of the guard station was standing helplessly on the heap of aquatic pebbles and did not know which pickup truck had dumped that many pebbles behind the guard station in the middle of the night.

Zayer Ahmad brought him out of his futile fantasies.

"It's the work of Falaknaz..."

"Find him!"

The women of the village bore witness that they had seen seagulls in the middle of the night showering pebbles on the guard station, and to prevent the head of the guard station from bursting his larynx from shouting, they spoke about a man who years and years earlier was shot in Melgado, and late one afternoon he had gotten himself to the village in order for Zayer Ahmad to put some ointment made of plants on his wound, and with the rising of the sun, he flew away in the form of a seagull.

The shovels and pickaxes fell out of the hands of the soldiers, and the confused head of the guard station went to his small room to report the attack of the seagulls to Major Senobari, who was always waiting for the slightest news from Jofreh.

❈ 39 ❈

Major Senobari was certain that it was the doing of the women of Jofreh, and that the pebbles had been dumped on the walls not by the seagulls but by the rebellious women, basket by basket, women who easily rip all affairs apart and bow to no one other than the sea. Major Senobari tossed the letter of the guard station on the desk and told the soldier who was standing at attention in the doorframe:

"Let's go!"

Soon, the port city would be connected to the villages near and far and would preoccupy the women of the village so much that they would forget Busalmeh, the sea, and the mermaids.

The soldier, who came in still holding his hand in a salute, asked:

"Jofreh?"

Major Senobari said:

"Road building."

Three months later, the people of the village of Jofreh heard strange sounds that would deafen the ear of the world.

Ebrahim the Leopard, who would take the people of the village in turn to watch the end of the world, said:

"They're building a road to the coastal villages."

Zayer Ahmad had opened his lips in a smile. With every sound, a door would open to his village. Soon, traveling to faraway cities would be like jumping into the water of the sea. The cities of the world were getting close to Jofreh. Zayer Ahmad would go with Ebrahim the Leopard, get off halfway, and spend many hours watching the workers who were slashing the mountains with the strangest equipment in the world. Late in the afternoon when he would return home, he would get bored. He would wash the dust off his body in the water of the sea and then sit on the top of the water cistern, waiting for the next day; and without listening to his men, in his heart, he prayed for the asphalted road to be built as soon as possible. Zayer Ahmad was so preoccupied with the road and road construction that when the head of the guard station showed him the government memorandum and told him "you must have permission from the guard station to go to the sea," he was not taken aback at all.

Apparently, certain people from the coastal villages had been able to travel to distant lands under the pretext of fishing and take certain men across the maritime borders. A great deal of merchandise was being bought and sold in the bazaars of the city by smugglers who went to the sea under the pretext of fishing.

While explaining all this to Zayer Ahmad, who was not paying much attention to what he was saying, the head of the guard station did not miss the gleam in Mansur's eyes.

The friendship between Mansur and the head of the guard station was solidified by a bottle of booze, which was finished in their gathering of two concealed from the eyes of Zayer Ahmad Hakim. Mansur took advantage of Zayer Ahmad's inattentiveness and convinced the men of the village that they had to obey the law of the guard station and not quarrel with the government people.

Thus it was that the village submitted for the first time to the government law.

The sea, however, had no intention of being obedient. It suddenly turned black, foamed up, and screamed like a woman who had lost her husband. Its waves went up into the air, and one night rolled over the guard station and the village. Zayer Ahmad received the punishment for his neglectfulness. He had neglected the sea and set his heart and hopes on the land. The sea is a vengeful lover; like a fourteen-year-old girl, it demands your complete attention. The people lived in water for forty days and nights. The beds, the straw mats, the pots and pans, and everything was on the water. With the tumult of the waves of the sea, the soldiers came out of the guard station in a panic, and those who remained inside were taken by the waves to the offing, to the other side of the sea. No one heard their cries as they were pleading and asking the people of the village to rescue them from the sea with its one thousand hands.

The head of the guard station had been able to escape and had gotten himself to the silk tassel acacia tree in the village square. He had climbed the tree and stayed there for forty days and nights, eating the leaves of the silk tassel acacia tree and the small fish that Madineh would catch from the water and give to him. From up there, he would see the women of the village, who prayed with talismans in their hands, and Bahador, whose eyes shone with tears and who was playing with the hair of a little mermaid who had died.

During the first days of Zayer Ahmad's indifference to the sea, Madineh had been able to turn his attention to it. On the first day of the rebellion of the sea and the mermaids, weeping, Madineh got herself to the foot of the silk tassel acacia tree and said that the mermaids had been saddened by being away from the fishermen, one of them had died from sorrow, and the world would never calm down unless the government law would pack up its possessions and leave the village of Jofreh, so that the village could breathe without the mediation of the guard station.

Holding onto the trunk of the silk tassel acacia tree with her hand, for forty days and nights, Madineh told the story of the red and blue mermaids to the head of the guard station and drew the shape and face of Busalmeh for him in the air. The head of the guard station—who had lost his wits because of the sound of the waves and the storm and the screaming of the women, and who was shaking down to his heart and bones from the fear of the shape and face of Busalmeh—to rid himself of Madineh's stories, swore on the epaulet of His Majesty that he would do anything he could to appease the mermaids throughout the world. In the midst of the sounds of the storm and waves, Madineh yelled the news to the women of the village, who were standing up to their chests in water and who were ululating, facing the high waves.

When the weather calmed down, the people gathered what was left of their houses and counted the number of the missing. The guard station was missing along with seven soldiers, but the village had lost no one, except for the scrawny, feeble son of Nabati.

The sea had taken Nabati's son. She blamed no one but herself. Nabati had forgotten the promise she had given to Busalmeh. Cooperation with the guard station meant cooperation with Busalmeh. It was Major Senobari who jailed Mahjamal, and Busalmeh had implanted in the hearts of the soldiers the idea of coming to the village. And then, she, who had been chosen by Busalmeh, cooperated with the women of the village and tore down the walls of the guard station and cursed and insulted the government soldiers. Regretting all she had and had not done, in her nightly crying, Nabati talked to Mansur, talked about her lost son, reminded him of the old stories, and tried to make Mansur surrender to her pain and suffering, and to her beliefs.

The corpse of the little mermaid was a matter of concern for everyone. The women of the village washed her hair and face. Madineh and Setareh rinsed her with fresh water from the cistern, and Madineh placed her in a grave next to the grave of the stranger. But when for the seventh time Mahjamal saw the mermaid getting out of her grave and falling down under the silk tassel acacia tree, stretched out on the ground, he stepped forward, picked up the little mermaid, went to the cove, and took her in a boat to the offing and tossed her into the blue waters of the sea.

Confused and dazed, the head of the guard station performed his duty as a soldier at the first opportunity. He went to the Gendarmerie to report on the strangest happening in his life. In a frightened voice, he said that he had seen with his own eyes that the sea reached out with its hands like a human and took the guard station with seven sleepy soldiers who did not know where they were going. He swore that he had seen with his own eyes the mermaids who were weeping in the sea and pounding on the walls of the guard station with their fists. He had even heard the voice of Busalmeh, and as he was standing there at attention, sweat dripping from him, he told Major Senobari that he had seen the most beautiful creature in the world in the village of Jofreh, a little mermaid who had come out of her land grave several times and had finally become calm when back in the sea.

Major Senobari sentenced the head of the guard station to twenty-four lashes on the charge of yielding to fantasies and superstition in an age when the country was on the path of advancement and progress. He then sent him on a new assignment, in addition to sending ten more soldiers to Jofreh to build another guard station.

One day, the soldiers arrived in the village in the morning. They greeted the young and the old; and quietly, without anyone hearing the sound of their footsteps, they got busy building the guard station, and they shared whatever they had brought with them with the people of the village:

"The sentence for disobeying the law is execution..."

No one in the village wished for the pale and frightened soldiers to be executed. The people, who were busy rebuilding the village without paying attention to them, gathered around Dr. Adeli, who had come with a semi-truck full of blankets and food.

Dr. Adeli listened to Madineh, who was prepared to give him the necklace she was given by the aquatic mother to stop the law of the guard station; and he also saw the head of the guard station, who asked him to speak to Major Senobari to have the place of his assignment changed or to allow him to forego the enforcing of the law of the guard station regarding the village. The exiled military colonel, Dr. Adeli, under whose feet the dead ear-shells made a crunching sound, went from house to house, observed the village, which looked as though it had been submersed in water, and revived the idea and the dream of the dam in Zayer Ahmad's mind.

"The government must help…"

Astonished, Mahjamal looked at the doctor:

"The business of the government is not to build. So far, it has accomplished nothing but destruction."

Nabati, who was standing next to Mahjamal, reported what he had said to the head of the guard station that night; and the terrified head of the guard station fled from Mansur's house, leaving Nabati behind, stunned and dazed.

Ignoring Mahjamal, who said that building a dam would give the government a pretext to destroy the village, Zayer Ahmad began going back and forth to the port city.

The Department of Roads had dug some distance into the heart of the formidable mountains, but it had not yet reached the village. For an entire year, Zayer Ahmad went from one government department to the next, talking about the sea and its wrath, until one day when his index finger became heavy and as stiff as a stick and he could not put his fingerprint at the bottom of any piece of paper, tired and drained, he came to the village and told the women of the tribe to all go and hold a sit-in in front of the Governor's Office.

Ebrahim the Leopard came to Jofreh several times, loaded up the women, and took them to the port city. The women sat on the hot black road, not moving from there for a week, until finally the governor, who realized that the women were about to cause a riot in the city, told Kheyju, who was the leader of the group:

"The government can only grant permission for this dam to be built, but it will not provide any other assistance."

The entire village was mobilized to build the dam. Stupefied by the human temperament, Mahjamal would sit on the top of the water cistern, squashing his anger with fishing nets; and he could see that the village, inundated with stones and cement, was separating itself from the sea. The smell that came from the mountains was not pleasant. Human hands disrupt, construct, and destroy everything. The fear that had engulfed Mahjamal's soul was not the fear of constructing. Human hands were helpful, provided a vague, unknowable smell would not make Mahjamal's mind distraught. There was no doubt about Zayer Ahmad's intentions. He loved the land and the people. He wanted the village to prosper; but the greater world would put a greater burden on one's back. Mahjamal would flee from suffering, from what was unknown to him, and Zayer Ahmad would get his old wish.

Zayer Ahmad's knowledge of practicing medicine had advanced with the efforts of Dr. Adeli, as he sometimes sat in a small room downstairs from Dr. Adeli's office and treated the patients that the doctor would send to him. And with the money he received from the patients, he was able to convince Ebrahim the Leopard to bring stones and cement to the village with the new vehicle that he had bought.

The head of the guard station, who was not pleased with the storm, sent his soldiers to help, soldiers who, like the people of the village and like the head of the guard station for a long time, had come to believe in Little Giant, Busalmeh, and the mermaids, and had filled the doors and the windows of the guard station with all sorts of talismans.

Six months later, the dam was built. During that entire time, Madineh and Bahador were worried about the dam going up and were afraid that suddenly it would go so high that the sea to the other end of the world would be lost. During the days of its construction, Madineh had pleaded with the head of the guard station, so that perhaps this time, through the government that had created so much commotion in the village, he would do something to prevent Jofreh from becoming distanced from the blue waters of the sea, and to prevent Bahador, her aquatic grandson, from becoming more depressed day by day. The head of the guard station, who was no longer considered a stranger, confused by the stories of the mermaids and Busalmeh, sat next to Madineh and became her chitchat companion, and told her that a short wall would never stop the mermaids, and that if someday a small mermaid was unable to climb up the wall, he himself would pick her up and bring her to the village.

When the dam was built and with a smile of satisfaction Zayer Ahmad declared the completion of the work, the head of the guard station, who was sighing, yearning to hold a mermaid in his arms, with eyes that sparkled from happiness, went to Madineh:

"I will pick her up in my arms, I promise on my honor!"

The head of the guard station had lost his military temperament and character to such an extent that one day when Major Senobari came to the village without prior notice, neither recognized the other.

Wearing a *dishdasha*, the head of the guard station was sitting on the dam next to Madineh, his rifle aimed at Jinn-Haunted Cove, waiting for Yal to come up. He was looking at the sea, soaking in sweat.

Two days had passed since a pregnant woman was in labor pains and Mama Mansur sitting beside her could do nothing. Hoping to save the woman's life, Madineh had gone to the guard station:

"Yal is not letting the baby be born."

To find a place in the hearts of the people of the village, the head of the guard station was determined to shoot Yal on the sea and show the whole world that the men of the guard station adhere more to the law of the village than to the law of the government.

Upon seeing the jeep of Major Senobari, the soldiers who were scattered around the guard station, each busy with their fishing nets and gear, fled into the guard station terrified, and turned the place upside down to find their uniforms, which they could not find. Shocked, Major Senobari saw Zayer Gholam wearing a sergeant's shirt, and sitting with a group of village men was Mansur wearing a pair of soldier's pants that were too short for him. When Major Senobari reached the guard station, he was taken aback. All sorts of talismans were hanging from the door and the walls, and none of the soldiers, who had loincloths wrapped around their lower halves, would agree to remove the talismans from the walls.

On that same day, Major Senobari took all of them to the city, assigned Sergeant Sinayi along with several soldiers to the guard station, and ordered them to report to the city regarding every incident, on a daily basis.

The rumors about a sergeant and soldiers who had lost their minds as a result of seeing mermaids and jinn in the village of Jofreh spread throughout the city, passing from mouth to mouth. The women of the city would cautiously approach the women who came from villages near and far to sell their vegetables and eggs in the bazaar. Once they made sure that they were not from the village of Jofreh, they would breathe a sigh of relief.

The young men of the port city who stood next to Tavakkoli's booze shop and downed their tea glasses full of booze while standing up, once Tavakkoli closed his small booze shop, would stagger to the rooftops. Yearning to see a mermaid even if for once and go mad forever, they would sigh and stare at the road on which at sunset on some days Zayer Ahmad would disappear with Ebrahim the Leopard.

The men looked at Zayer Ahmad Hakim—the medicine man of the poor people who came to the city twice a week, to that small room downstairs from the office of the exiled colonel to treat the patients who were dozing off on the sidewalks, waiting for him, with respect and fear. The silver hair, the tall stature, and the clean and neat clothing of Zayer Ahmad, and the calmness on his face, sometimes diminished the fear; and thus it was that the men of the city came to Zayer Ahmad for the treatment of the wounds, trachoma, and stomachaches they did not have.

Old men who slept the final nights of their lives in their cold beds of loneliness and ailment, with a thousand pretexts, would approach Zayer Ahmad Hakim and spend tremendous amounts of money to hear something about the mermaids. Zayer Ahmad, who could not figure out their countless questions, with a tired smile, would speak about the mermaids and what he had or had not seen himself, up to the last moments before sunset.

One day, the young men who did not get anywhere with their nocturnal sighs, and every day woke up with hangovers from the bottles of booze, cast caution to the wind, and in a rented car, shadowed Ebrahim the Leopard, finally reaching the village and the road that passed by the Shrine of Sire Ashk.

The hungry young men with an infatuation that made their bones tremble stared at the sea and saw nothing but a little boy who was on the edge of the water, bending down over the sand obliviously gathering live ear-shells, and sometimes reprimanding the creatures that hid themselves in their shells with the invasion of his tiny hands.

When the sun sank into the sea and Bahador disappeared before their eyes, they suddenly heard the sound of their rented car, and saw that the car was moving on its own toward the city, without anyone at the steering wheel. The terrified young men from the city began to run away in the opposite direction. They passed the Admiral Building and the Midnight-Jinn-Haunted Building, and they clearly heard the jinn, who were playing cards, following suit.

Three hours after midnight when, tired and soaking in sweat, they reached the city, they came face-to-face with the government patrols, and in order to be rid of them, told them the story of their failure.

The next morning, when the officials went to Jofreh to find the rented car, their hands and hearts were trembling. They avoided looking into the eyes of the men of the village, who were following them, confused and lost, and they turned their backs to the sea, fearing the rise of the jinn and the mermaids.

After one week of fear and trembling and searching the fire pits of the houses, under the beds, and inside the dried up wells, the officials returned to the city, their shoulders drooping in disappointment.

A few months later, Ebrahim the Leopard was selling the dismantled parts of the car that was rumored in the city to have been taken to the depths of the green waters by the mermaids, and without anyone becoming suspicious of him, he demanded cash for them. From then on until years and years afterward, other than government officials who were forced to come to the village of Jofreh, no one set foot in Jofreh, with the exception of sick villagers who were drawn there by the reputation of Zayer Ahmad Hakim's medical practice to find some cure for their incurable wounds, worms that had penetrated to the depths of their bones, and tumors as hard as stone that had embedded themselves in their bodies.

They came with chickens and roosters, bags of yogurt and fresh cheese, handwoven straw mats, and baskets of dates from Dashti and Tangestan, sat on the top of the water cistern or in the courtyard, and left their horses and camels under the silk tassel acacia tree to look at the sea with bewildered eyes.

It was on one of those days when a camel became intoxicated from the blue color of the sea; frenzied and with a torn-off bridle, it rushed toward the sea; and in order to reach that blue color, it went all the way to the offing of the sea and never returned.

Among all the things that the people from Tangestan brought to Zayer Ahmad's house was a small fawn with thin, feeble legs and eyes that made Setareh weep for an entire twenty-four hours, since she was reminded of that stranger who had one day disappeared in Fekseno. Setareh would hold the little fawn, whose name was Tara, in her arms, feed it goat milk, and on the nights that she spent in Zayer Ahmad's house, she would put Tara to bed next to her and look at its sad eyes until late at night.

Zayer Ahmad's knowledge of medicine was improving every day, using the medicine that he brought from the city, and with the help of Setareh and Kheyju, he used several meters of cloth that had been soaked in alcohol to stick into the wounds of the patients in order to extract puss. He poured medicine in their eyes that had turned red from pain. With his long, thin fingers, he would turn up their eyelids and insert blue-colored patches, which Dr. Adeli had given him and which melted after a while.

In the evening, Mahjamal would sit and listen to the stories of the men from Dashti and Tangestan; and to safeguard himself from the wrath of Kheyju, who for the third time would once again get nauseated and was carrying Zayer Ahmad Hakim's third and fourth grandchildren, he would sleep right there on the top of the water cistern or in the courtyard on the mats or rags of the people who had traveled on twisting and turning roads and across strange salt deserts to come to Zayer Ahmad Hakim. The world was in disarray. The stories of the men from Tangestan ripped his aquatic curtain of delusions, and he would come out of his blue aquatic mind. The world was gray, gray and black. There were women who had arrived at Zayer Ahmad's house either on foot or on the back of their men, women from the bottoms of whose petticoats blood was still oozing out. There were eyes that had suddenly gone blind, swollen bellies that sounded like the drums of mourning, large eyes of children which were popping out of their sockets, famine and the burning or scorching of the harvests, the fight and flight of the rulers of faraway territories... No, there was no pearl. The hand of Busalmeh of the land had reached the farthest point in the world, and the dead of the gray waters were scattered everywhere.

Mahjamal would sit and listen to the nightly stories of the men from Tangestan. He would get heated; something cried out in his heart. The dead of the gray waters were scattered throughout the world in order for their doubles in the depths of the muddy black waters not to wake up from their sleep of death. It was not only Major Senobari who had given his breath to the breath of Busalmeh. When on occasions he came to the village at night and sat smoking cigarettes with the men from Tangestan, Dr. Adeli would tell Mahjamal about what he had seen in the capital city on the days of arrests. In one of the nocturnal tales of the men from Tangestan, Mahjamal heard the name of Niru. A spark shone in the eyes of that old man from Tangestan, and a smile appeared on the lips of others when they heard the name of Niru. That night, when Maryam was sitting next to her aquatic father, and amazed, she was listening to the narrators of her future stories, she saw tears in her father's eyes for the first and last time, and she saw that he turned his face toward the dusty moon that was sitting in the sky, faraway and clueless, and sighed.

Mahjamal heard stories about Niru, who had wounded sixty-six gendarmes, who had nailed the chests of four colonels to the seat of their Dodge with his bullets, and who had put Major Senobari's arm in a sling that hung from his neck for a long time. Niru was the man who was a homeless fugitive wanderer of mountains and deserts, the man whose name was elevated higher with each moment and each hour in the songs of the women and stories of the men from Tangestan. The eyes of the men from Tangestan would light up upon hearing the name of Niru, and as though sheltered by a mountain, they would forget their pains and ailments.

In his own mind, Mahjamal was searching for the tribe and lineage of Niru. He would ask the villagers. He would ask about Niru's ancestors, to perhaps be able to link him to a fisherman who had been captured by the blue mermaids one stormy night.

The world was full of the dead of the gray waters, full of those who would take the most handsome humans as a reed flute player to Busalmeh's wedding. They were all searching for that large pearl of the world.

Had Mahjamal not lost his soothsaying powers, with a look at his hot palms, he could perhaps see the fingertips that burned waiting for the trigger of a Brno rifle, see how he himself would be elevated in the songs and stories of the people of Dashti and Tangestan and how in his nocturnal journeys, he would escape safe and sound and continue his life because of the signs that unknown supporters would place on the tops of mountains and hills to warn him of the dangers near and far, so that he would escape safely and continue with his life.

The flood of patients and the stories of the land had made everyone neglectful of the sea, and the people of the village spent so much time thinking about the stories of the people of Dashti and Tangestan that they did not notice when the land opened its mouth from dryness, the water of the sea receded, and the sea retreated to the other side of the cove.

41

Soon the village was filled with the carcasses of thirsty seagulls that fluttered and died from lack of water. At night, from the sea came the sound of the crying of the drowned men, who had smelled the drought, and the women of the village sometimes saw the mermaids appear on the surface of the sea and toss white seashells toward the village. The women would rush toward the seashells, open them up, and drop a drop of fresh water found inside into the mouths of their children.

The drought reduced the visits to the village. Tired camels with blistered lips would die before they reached the village, abandoning their sick riders in the middle of untrodden trails under dried palm trees.

The land cracked. With blistered lips, Madineh was worried about the small blue and yellow flowers that sprouted, and Kheyju, in the midst of grappling with dizziness and thirst, delivered her twins, two girls who were so different from the very start when they were born that Mama Mansur, the village midwife, was stunned, with her finger in her mouth. One had fair skin and black eyes, and the other, a dark face and blue eyes.

In the midst of her nocturnal nightmares, Kheyju would be

awakened and would cry out, "Water!" With his head numb from sleeplessness, Mahjamal would repeat what he had said before:

"The water cisterns are full of water."

The dark water in the water cistern, however, had no resemblance to the crystal clear rainwater. Worms wiggled in it and climbed its moldy walls.

Worried, Zayer Ahmad fixed his eyes on the sky. Jofreh had grown larger. Some of his patients had built huts and decided to stay there, and there were too many children to count. This drought could chase everyone away from the village and turn Jofreh into a floodplain. Why had drought afflicted the life of the village? Had the sea become angry with the village and no longer wanted to give the vapors of its belly to the skies? Zayer Ahmad would look at the retreated sea and could not figure out the world. Finally, it was his wife, Madineh, who reminded him of a distant, lost memory, and showed him the solution. How long had it been since the villagers, all together, had given their bodies to the hands of the waters of the sea?

Wednesday was the day on which Zayer Ahmad did not go to the port city to practice medicine. Before the stunned eyes of Dr. Adeli and the guard station, he made the people of the village sit stark naked in the sea and cleanse themselves under seven high waves and make the sea swear to be kind to the land and the people of the village of Jofreh, to open its threshold to the people, to send the vapors of its body toward the sky, and send the rain toward the land.

The soldiers who were witnessing the ablution of the naked women of the village in the water hid in the guard station from some unknown fear. Sergeant Sinayi wrote a detailed report. Dr. Adeli, who was standing by the shore, could not avoid looking at Kheyju, who, bare naked, was giving her firm white body to the water. A strange hubbub reverberated in the sea, and Dr. Adeli's mind could not figure out anything, and could not understand the meaning of the chant of the naked people of the village as they floated on the water. And Zayer was unable to help him understand. Words were older than the earth, and no one, not even Zayer Ahmad, knew the meaning of the chant that he was singing.

After one week had passed and there was no sign of rain, to bring a few drops of water to the village, Zayer Ahmad became a wanderer in the port city. He went from one government department to another, but who would give water to "disreputable" people? Zayer Ahmad, who saw no connection between being disreputable and lacking water, with his unmatched stubbornness, many times went after those who knew about water. Many times, he spoke to the tired drivers in the Mihan Tour Bus Company terminal, who gathered together yawning, and whose lips had turned black from their intimacy with opium pipes: "The whole world has run out of water, Zayer. You need to get help from the mermaids." Without turning around to see the laughter of the wakeful drivers, Zayer Ahmad would return to the village.

The city pipes had plenty of water, even though in the afternoons of those days when Zayer Ahmad practiced medicine, when he opened the faucet, it grumbled like Busalmeh, and it would take a while for a narrow stream of water to come out.

Finally, on one of those days of drought, the exiled military colonel, Dr. Adeli, reported to Zayer Ahmad that one of Her Highnesses, a princess, was coming to visit the city. Dr. Adeli told Zayer Ahmad, who still did not understand how rain could have anything to do with Her Highness:

"A letter, you need to send a letter."

42

Colorful flags were hanging on the doors and walls of government buildings, and Zayer Ahmad was going around the city with Captain Ali, who constantly came to the city under the pretext of finding a tanker of water. Those flags of all sorts indicated that Her Highness was an important person. Upon seeing the flags that were waving in the wind, like a child who could not stop laughing, Captain Ali figured out the power of Her Highness, and he told Mansur that anyone who was able to open or shut off water to a group of people must be more powerful than Busalmeh.

Other than Mahjamal, who would not agree to such petition games, all the people of the village put their fingerprints at the bottom of the letter that Dr. Adeli had written. Mahjamal told the exiled colonel that a person who was able to make the water pour from the sky with a petition and rescue the village from thirst needed to tell everyone where she had hidden this power up to now, and where she had been during this year of thirst.

Using Ebrahim the Leopard's pickup and the camels of the village, the people went to the port city and stood alongside the road on which Her Highness was supposed to pass. The men beat the drums of the Shrine of Sire Ashk, and the women beat on their tin cans and chanted: "Ma o meskamo."

Zayer Ahmad did not know how these ancient words, which were from the dialect of their ancestors, were coming out of his mouth and the mouths of the people of the village. All day long, the people of the village of Jofreh, without realizing it themselves, shouted in the strangest and oldest dialect of the world: "We want water." Perhaps it was an expression of the ghosts of the people of Dashti and Tangestan, whose lips for years and years had blistered from thirst, along with the language of the people of Jofreh, who shouted their thirst in the ears of a princess who no one was sure would hear the voices of the thirsty ghosts of the land.

A bird, which Ebrahim the Leopard called an airplane, was flying in the sky over the asphalted road, scattering flowers along the route. A man was sitting inside the airplane, just like the man who at one time had dropped the droppings of his bird on the mountains near the village and killed the maternal uncle of Zayer Ahmad.

The officials, who were pleased with the large crowd along the route of Her Highness, mingled among the people of the village of Jofreh in civilian clothes, and no matter how they tried to tell them to applaud and say "long live the Pahlavi Dynasty" when Her Highness was passing by, they did not get anywhere.

Kheyju, who had secured her twin daughters Hamayel and Shamayel on her back and like the other women was beating hard on the tin cans, saw a scrawny feeble-looking woman with a frozen smile on her lips in a shiny black car, waving her hand slowly.

When Her Highness the Princess passed by with a smile on her lips, the security officials and Major Senobari breathed a sigh of relief, and they had an audience with Her Highness in the office of the governor of the city, the steps of which were covered with carpets.

Her Highness, who was sweating from the heat and who was constantly touching her long, curved eyelashes, asked:

"What were those people saying?"

The head of the security agents was frightened for a moment, when Major Senobari came to his rescue. Major Senobari had heard the yelling of the people loudly and clearly:

"We want the Shah."

In order not to be outdone by Major Senobari and to please the Princess, the head of the security agents then explained the beliefs of the people who played the drums, and about the mermaids, and the sergeant, and the soldiers who had lost their minds upon seeing the mermaids. Sweat beaded on Major Senobari's face; he felt a chill. Soldiers are supposed to obey their superiors, not the mermaids. His eyes were fixed on Her Highness's mouth. Her Highness, however, curious about the mermaids and people who went into the water all together stark naked, totally ignored the lack of military discipline. Major Senobari, who was no longer worried about a reprimand, to avoid displeasing Her Highness, said that naturally the mermaids fell in love with princes, that which the people of the village of Jofreh said was not worth a pittance, and that no mermaid who has any brain would set her heart on a fisherman with only the shirt on his back.

And thus it was that Her Highness's two hour visit was extended to a week, in order for her to search in a helicopter and with small and large binoculars above Jofreh and the Jofreh Sea to find one of the mermaids, which would be handcuffed and taken to Tehran to be dropped in her large swimming pool, so that she could show her off at her countess dinner parties to the domestic and foreign guests as being a gift from the people of the south.

The Navy was mobilized for an entire week. Large and small battleships and boats like that of the blond men searched the entire Jofreh Sea handspan by handspan and did not find anything. Having lost all hope of finding a mermaid, Major Senobari assigned his agents to search every house in Jofreh, since quite possibly, they had hidden a mermaid in a backroom of one of their houses.

For Mahjamal, the world was coming to an end. Rage scorched his entire being, and with his blue eyes that were flaming, he looked at Zayer Ahmad, who had not listened to him and had pleaded at the unholy shrine of Her Highness who performed no miracles. Zayer Ahmad, who was surrounded by men clad in white and gendarmes, and who regretted what he had done, pleaded with Busalmeh of the seas.

"Roll the waves of the sea over the village."

But Madineh knew that Busalmeh of the seas would laugh at the village. Zayer Ahmad's wife could hear the sound of his strange laughter day and night, laughter that shook the walls of the village, and forced her to plead with the women:

"The talismans! Place the talismans under the fire."

In their strange fright, the women of the village sat by the flames of the fire and moved the red hot talismans with tongs.

What if they were to take the mermaids?

Mama Mansur, whose heart bled because of the sea, for the first time since the loss of her six sons, looked at the sea and realized that she liked its blue color. Regretting her jealousies, Bubuni became thin, and whispered in Madineh's ear that if the mermaids did not surrender to the strangers, she would bring one of them to her house and every morning comb her hair with perfume and oil.

Depressed, the villagers looked at the sea, which was full of battleships, large and small.

On the seventh day, Major Senobari—who had not anticipated that much courage on the part of the mermaids who, despite the presence of Her Highness, dared to go to the depths of the green waters just as Her Highness, frowning and upset, was boarding the airplane—promised Her Highness that he would find one of the mermaids and bring her to Tehran in handcuffs. It was at that moment that Her Highness promoted Major Senobari to the rank of colonel, and dismissed the head of the security agents from his position for no reason. While she was absolutely fuming because of the illiterate mermaids who rather than falling in love with princes set their hearts on fishermen, she boarded the plane and never again returned to that city.

$\diamondsuit$ **43** $\diamondsuit$

The people of the village, who were about to go mad from the noise and the tumult of large ships and battleships, which they had seen for the first time in their lives, forgot all about thirst. When the sky and the sea were cleansed of the large and small battleships and helicopters, they breathed a sigh of relief.

But other than beseeching the sea, beseeching does not end well. For a week, the people of the village would hear the sound of boisterous laughter from the sea. The red mermaids were ridiculing Zayer Ahmad and his village. At night, they would appear on the water with drums and tin cans under their arms, and similar to the people of the village who had shouted for Her Highness, they shouted, "We want water," and laughed and laughed. The sound of the laughter and the drums of the red mermaids deprived Zayer Ahmad and his people of sleep. With his own eyes, Zayer Ahmad had clearly seen that scrawny, feeble-looking woman walking in front of the red mermaids, waving her hand, and making funny faces. The village already knew that the Princess was the double of the dead of the gray waters.

Those days, the world was dry and the sky, clear. Fish were tossed to the shore from thirst, the trunks of the trees were cracked, and everyone's lips were blistered. In the city, the water tankers hushed the afternoon grumbling of the dry, empty pipes.

Eventually, Dr. Adeli was able to come to the aid of the village and bring a tanker of water to Jofreh and ask Zayer Ahmad to give the people their daily ration of water cup by cup. One tanker of water, however, could not quench the thirst of the people of the village, and it was Kheyju who finally pleaded with Geli.

On one of the cold nights of the drought, when the freezing wind was wreaking havoc, the stones were cracking, and the seawater was frozen, the women of the village assembled along the shore, placed big pots on a fire, and made wheat porridge.

The next morning, at dawn, Kheyju had all the people of the village each eat one bite of the wheat porridge, so that in whoever's throat a bead was caught, that person would become Geli and carry the millstone of Mama Mansur on her shoulder from house to house.

The bead was caught in the throat of Nabati. They made her wear a tattered old dress, placed the millstone on her shoulder, and all began walking through the village. Kheyju was the leader, and she sang:

Our houses, they are caving in
Quick, quick, rain, rain

We've got so many mouths to feed
Oh God, send us rain again

The people went around in the village from house to house and hut to hut until sunset. They even visited the guard station, where Ebrahim the Leopard brought them water in big barrels. Finally Nabati, who had been crushed under the weight of the millstone, put the millstone on the ground and shouted as loud as she could that the village of Jofreh was cursed and the drought would never end.

Mama Mansur, who saw that Nabati was making the daily prayers of the people ineffective with her curses, grabbed Nabati's long black hair, wrapped it around her hand, and pulled her, bloody and beaten, up to the side of the clay bread oven.

It was in that very fight that Mansur and Nabati figured out that Mama Mansur knew the story of that false handkerchief, and to prevent her from casting their reputations to the black wind, they packed up their stuff and went to the house of Zayer Gholam.

Ten days later, the rain began to pour, the ground became saturated, and the water cistern filled. The women remembered the songs they had forgotten. The children held their hands under the large raindrops and laughed boisterously, and Setareh searched around in the house to see if there was a leak. A story in her ever-in-love mind would force her to hold a piece of cloth in front of the leak. Zayer Ahmad, who had never figured out what the women of Jofreh did, would silently look at Setareh, sigh, and say to himself that the drought had forced him to understand the worth and value of water. Setareh, however, in response to Maryam, who followed her step by step and helped her to stop the leaks, said:

"When water is dripping somewhere, it means that a lovebird is thirsty for sure."

It was this very sentence that years and years later made Maryam, who was about to complete the preliminary first two years at the university and among numerous fields had placed a checkmark beside medicine, set aside medicine, despite what her grandfather, Zayer Ahmad Hakim, had said, and wander from college to college.

The regulated drops of IV solution that dripped above the head of a patient had forced her that day in the hospital of a far-away city to shut off the IV solution, and in response to the strange yelling of her professor, tell him Setareh's story, which left the professor confused and stunned.

Zayer Ahmad heard Setareh's story from Maryam, who was telling it to him quietly on one of the nights when the rain was pouring down more calmly. Maryam had looked at Zayer Ahmad with her big black eyes, her arms around her grandfather's wrinkled neck, and wanted to know whether or not he believed Setareh's story. Zayer Ahmad kissed Maryam's black eyes and said that Setareh was right for sure, since Setareh was a woman, and women knew about the world of the unknown.

When the rain stopped, Setareh's story was passed from mouth to mouth. The little girls and women of the village, even Mama Mansur, who had been suffering from back pain for some time, carrying tubs full of plaster, searched for leaks and blocked all the cracks and holes in the village, and they made the men climb the trunks of palm trees and shake the palm branches that had dried up from lack of water, so that water would not drip from them. Exhausted and soaking wet, Setareh would grab the branches of the silk tassel acacia tree and shake them until her head began to spin and the leaves became dry, as though the hot summer sun had shone on them.

* * *

At dawn on a day in late winter, the arrival of a wounded man, who had concealed two Brno rifles in his saddlebag and who was sleeping on the back of a horse and had covered the hooves of the horse with cloth in order not to leave any footprints of himself behind, distracted the minds of the villagers from the dripping of water.

The man had been shot in the Melgado Mountains. On foot, he had made it to Fekseno, and there the people had told him about their cousins and about Zayer Ahmad Hakim, whose reputation as a medicine man had even reached Fekseno, and they had given him a white horse to get to Jofreh.

Zayer Ahmad recognized the white horse with a long mane and eyes heedless of the hardships of the world. Delavar had gone missing ten days after they had settled in Jofreh, and now it had come back with a wounded, cherished rider, without time having left any marks on it.

The village was happy, and Zayer Ahmad, more than anyone else. Fekseno was still there, and the cousins, alive. A guest is a blessing, and even more of a blessing if his name is Niru.

Zayer Ahmad removed the bullet from his side. The people in his house stayed awake beside him until morning. That night, the neighing of the white horse, which suffered pain in sympathy with Niru's, deprived the guard station of sleep. The village prayed all night until morning for the sea and the sky to keep him away from the death that had spilt his side. It took a week before Niru was able to sit on his feverish knees facing the window on the plastered veranda and, along with Mahjamal, stare at the sea.

Mahjamal sat and listened to the nightly chatting of Niru for a month. He became familiar with Chieftain Ali and the braves of Tangestan, and with Lion Mohammad, who had in the end escaped to the sea on a boat. With his black eyes, Niru would stare at Mahjamal's blue eyes, and rub his forehead with his hand:

"This is our story..."

It was Mahjamal and his astonishing fear of death: If it comes, what if it comes before he has told me all that he needs to? In sleep and wakefulness, every moment, he stayed beside him restlessly with a bowl of water and a piece of bread. When Niru was sleeping, Mahjamal would place his head on his broad chest to make sure that he was still alive on the land. With his eyes, he admired him; and when he suffered from pain, he would push back the man's black hair from his feverish forehead. Where had Mahjamal come to? No path to return to the depths of the blue and green waters remained. But why return? Was the excitement and hope that he had seen in the eyes of the patients when they talked about Niru any less than the sparkle in the eyes of the sons of Mama Mansur at the time when they wanted to return to the land, return and reach that which the human heart loves?

In their loneliness, the denizens of the land and the drowned do the same. They keep the fire of hope burning in their hearts, and the presence of or the chatting with someone redoubles their zest for life. The people of the land are the people of time. The drowned, however, in their efforts never reach life.

The flyers that had been distributed about the capturing of Niru reached Jofreh as well. One day, the people saw some individuals posting announcements on the door and the walls of the guard station and the stucco houses. Mahjamal, who had been sleepless all that night and was now dozing off beside Niru, was awakened by Maryam's voice:

"Papa! The walls are filled with pieces of paper."

Until noon, no one figured out what the pieces of paper were announcing. Zayer Ahmad was at a loss, cursing himself and his village for no one in it being literate.

At noon, a young soldier who had come into the village looked at a piece of paper stuck on the wall and read it:

"They are looking for Niru."

Then, looking around and making sure that no one else was listening, he told Zayer Gholam, who was looking at the paper over his shoulder:

"They have set a price on his head."

The entire village knew that Niru was staying in Zayer Ahmad's house. The sound of his dry, choking coughs, despite all his caution, had made it known to the people of the village; but everyone pretended not to know, lest the wind should carry their voice to the guard station. Even on the evenings of storytelling on the top of the water cistern, wittingly or unwittingly, they would not look in the direction of the room with five sashed windows, and often they went back to their own houses earlier than usual.

Setareh knew that Zayer Ahmad had taken a risk, and that Mahjamal would be on his way. She saw a long journey in his eyes. She knew every sign in the eyes and face of Mahjamal quite well.

With her head raised high, Kheyju envisioned a bloody battle. She sighed for all those guns that were covered with dust in the guard station. In her fantasies, Kheyju saw Mahjamal's name being repeated in the nightly stories of the men of Tangestan, just like Niru's name.

Nabati had heard the story from Zayer Gholam and Sergeant Sinayi, who on many nights drank booze with Mansur and Captain Ali. She pretended to have a stomachache and, for the first time after a long time, she went to Zayer Ahmad's house to ask about that horse that, she had heard, had left the village of Jofreh at one time and had now come back after so many years on its own.

No one suspected her. But with Mahjamal turning his glance and attention toward the small room next to the room with five sashed windows, Nabati became suspicious; and after having visited there for ten days for the treatment of an ailment she did not have, early one morning, at dawn, under the pretext of fetching water from the Well of Loneliness, she went to the guard station and told Sergeant Sinayi that in Zayer Ahmad's house, with her own eyes, she had seen Niru, who was holding his side.

The fact was that she had heard the sound of coughing from the room with five sashed windows. She had held herself back with difficulty from leaping toward the room shouting. Mahjamal had smiled a familiar smile, and without fear and without feeling the oddity of Nabati's presence, he had gone to the room.

The next morning, Zayer Ahmad's house was under siege by men wearing high boots on their feet and holding guns in their hands. Colonel Senobari was on the top of a vehicle shouting into a megaphone.

Stunned and confused, the people of the village were looking from the windows and the rooftops of their houses at that large old house with its colorful glass windows, which would now shatter with the uproar of the machineguns in the hands of the soldiers, like thousands of dogs barking, and fall onto the ground. Both Mahjamal and Niru had barricaded themselves with the two rifles that Niru had brought with him in the room with five sashed windows. Colonel Senobari, who wanted to make sure to capture Niru alive, continued the barrage of bullets at the doors and windows.

The dead of the gray waters had come to the surface of the sea, and the people from behind the windows and on the rooftops saw the double of Colonel Senobari on the sea, slowly opening his eyes, which were puffed up from sleep and laughing. The red mermaids were looking at the village from a different corner, whispering in one another's ears, and the people of the village of Zayer Ahmad, for the first time in their lives and the life of the village, saw Busalmeh. Busalmeh, who once and for all had been defeated by Mahjamal in the seas, was now laughing with his big, black snout, making the hairs on the bodies of the people of the village stand on end.

The blue mermaids were not there, and the water of the sea was slowly rising.

When two days and nights had passed and the bullets of the Brno rifles ran out, the villagers became certain that the lovesick mermaid had made the industrial workers of the drowned in the depths of the blue and green waters build furnaces, and with the drowned anchors left there over the course of years and years, make bullets that were compatible with the old rifles of Mahjamal and Niru. In the dark of the night, Setareh saw with her own eyes that the mermaids brought the Brno bullets to the edge of the shore, and from behind the pomegranate orchard, Kheyju would take them to Mahjamal and Niru.

In the morning of the third day, Nabati mingled with the women and learned the secret of the resistance of Niru and Mahjamal. She informed Colonel Senobari, on whose order a row of soldiers stood facing the sea at night, shooting their bullets toward the sea. Bubuni, who had developed a severe headache from the sound of the bullets, saw many mermaids who were wounded. One of the mermaids turned red and took a soldier to the depths of the muddy waters.

After three nights and days, when the people of the village had lost all their sense of time and place, Niru, who had saved his last bullet, handed the Brno rifle to Mahjamal and pointed to his own forehead. Mahjamal trembled. He could not. Without Niru, the world was so empty and meaningless that Mahjamal saw himself wandering in an empty and futile void. Niru's month-long sojourn, the sound of his nocturnal coughs, the warmth of his stories, his homelessness and wanderings in the mountains and deserts, and the strange chime of his voice that sounded as though he constantly had a fever would not allow Mahjamal to consent to killing him. Mahjamal had turned white, the color of the long mane of the horse that had carried Niru to Jofreh.

In the midst of the clamor of bullets and the bewildered eyes of Zayer Ahmad, who saw that everything was being destroyed, Kheyju took the Brno rifle from Mahjamal's hand and, before Madineh could get there, aimed it at Niru's heart. It was not right for Niru to fall into the hands of the law, into which the men of the village had fallen at one time.

Years later, Kheyju told Maryam, who had crouched up in some corner during those days of horror, that she had never shot a bullet in her life and that Niru fell to the ground because of a stray bullet that came from the sea.

As they were taking Zayer Ahmad and Mahjamal away, the stunned people of the village heard Busalmeh of the seas laughing boisterously, and on the surface of the sea, the dead of the gray waters were yawning with satisfaction.

In the village, Madineh lay in some corner, drained of all energy, and Kheyju was on fire from anger and helplessness. It was as though the laughter of Busalmeh had put a spell on the people of the village. No one made the slightest move until the military trucks disappeared at the end of Jofreh. It was only Maryam, the second grandchild of Zayer Ahmad Hakim, who ran after the trucks with her scrawny small legs, shouted the name of her father, and eventually stood there, helpless and hopeless, in the middle of the road.

Depressed and despondent, the people of the village were looking at the white horse, Delavar, whose long mane was disheveled in the wind, neighing toward the end of the village, toward the place where the trucks had left with Zayer Ahmad Hakim, Mahjamal, and Niru, who was at one time a denizen of the land, who loved humans, and who refused to play the reed flute at the celebration of any Busalmeh.

45

For a long time, gray warm smoke was emitted from the place where the bullets had hit. The smell of gunpowder drifted everywhere, and there was nothing the women of Jofreh could do. Ebrahim the Leopard would not consent to make his vehicle available to the men of the village in search of Zayer Ahmad and Mahjamal. To avoid being harassed by anyone, he did not come to the village for a month, and during that time, Zayer Gholam gave a beating to Nabati, his daughter, who was in her last month of pregnancy and who had confronted him, trying to prevent her father from accompanying the men of the village. Mansur listened to Nabati and Sergeant Sinayi and did not leave the village. Captain Ali, however, used the Tavakkoli booze shop as an excuse and went to the port city with Sergeant Sinayi, and concealed from him, went to Dr. Adeli to deliver the news of the village.

The situation was far worse than whatever Dr. Adeli might be able to do anything about. The news that the exiled colonel brought to the village would intensify the anxiety of the people. Mahjamal had a previous criminal record; Zayer Ahmad had sheltered the enemy of the government; and both had fired shots at government agents.

Kheyju, however, could not just sit and twiddle her thumbs waiting for some news that Captain Ali or Dr. Adeli might bring

from the city. On one of those days of anxiety and waiting, Kheyju
told the women of the village that they should go to the city to sit
in front of the court and not move until they get some news about
Mahjamal and Zayer Ahmad. With bundles of loaves of bread, the
women set out for the city at night on foot, reached the port city
at high noon, and held a sit-in in front of the court. Heedless of
the blisters on her feet, Kheyju went to the offices all on her own,
stood in front of this or that desk, told her story of sorrow, and
finally shouted: "What law is there that would not allow treating a
wounded man?" But no one seemed to have ears with which they
could hear. The government officials would push her out of their
offices, and Kheyju would scream in the narrow, dark hallways.
There was nothing that the daughter of Zayer Ahmad could do on
her own. She would have to go to the women of the village and make
all of them shout. On the third day, in order to prevent the people of
the port city from setting out for the court for no good reason other
than to sit there and watch the women of the village, who were all
singing together, "Mama Zangeru let go of the moon," Kheyju was
allowed to visit Zayer Ahmad behind the prison bars. Zayer Ahmad,
who had lost a lot of weight and could hardly breathe, asked his
sole daughter to take care of the village and the patients who came
from the mountains and valleys, not to be impatient, to stop being
obstinate, and to let the law go through its normal process.

46

In the one-year absence of Zayer Ahmad, the affairs of the village were managed by Kheyju and Mama Mansur. With the help of Setareh, Kheyju took care of the patients from villages near and far, washed their wounds, and, whenever she did not know what to do, would go to Dr. Adeli's office and ask him for help. The smooth-shaven face of the exiled colonel and its pleasant scent awakened a strange yearning in the heart of Kheyju, a yearning that lightened the heavy burden of the absence of Zayer Ahmad and Mahjamal. Dr. Adeli, who came more often to the village, smelled like the city, the scent of something inaccessible and new, and it was on one of the same days of questions and answers that the doctor's white hand with its long, slender fingers touched Kheyju's hand; and in order for the daughter of Zayer Ahmad not to collapse into the arms of a man who was looking at her amorously, she sat on the ground, hid her face with her hands, and wept loudly. The doctor, whose fingers were clearly trembling, lifted Kheyju up, and it was precisely at that moment that Setareh arrived and reported that two sham patients were sitting under the silk tassel acacia tree.

Kheyju was fed up with the phony patients who had no ailment and who came dressed as villagers just to collect information. She would avenge her heart by giving them medicine that gave them diarrhea.

Mama Mansur, who did not want the lamps in Zayer Ahmad's house to be extinguished, had settled in one of its rooms. She had brought her millstones with her, to make sure that the house was filled with people, as usual. The men of the village provided food for the village, and with the exception of Mansur, who was busy building his big dream boat with the help of Sergeant Sinayi, in the afternoons, everyone came to Zayer Ahmad's house, sat on the top of the water cistern, as in the old days, had bread, milk, and tea, and informed one another of the news. The charges against Zayer Ahmad were not serious. But, as for Mahjamal, he would soon be sent to the capital city to be put on trial, and for his fate to be determined.

On the magic box, on which the news of the world was reported out loud, nothing was said about Mahjamal. The men of the village gathered around the magic box many times, perked up their ears, and finally reached the conclusion that the magic box was nothing but a lie, and that nothing it said was worth a copper coin.

Some strange excitement and enthusiasm was drawing Dr. Adeli more often to the village. To cover up his enthusiasm from the eyes of the simple people of the village, the exiled colonel took the side of caution and visited other villages, as well, pretending that he had the same relationship with all the people. His behavior, however, was at times so amateurish that no one could overlook his extreme friendship and kindness regarding Zayer Ahmad and the village of Jofreh. He was actually the one who one day looked at Maryam and Bahador and saw that they had grown big enough that they needed to go to school.

School and literacy, despite the fact that she could no longer look into the eyes of the exiled colonel, gave Kheyju a wakeup call. In the midst of the commotion of treating the patients, going back and forth to the city, and wandering between the court and the prison, once she heard the sound of a bell, she stopped in the middle of the street. She was with Captain Ali and Setareh. Like a sleepwalker, she followed the sound and reached the door of a building, out of which came children with braided hair and in uniforms, leaving the school like a herd of deer. Kheyju waited until a woman came through that large gate. The woman, who was kind, like a mermaid, put her hand on Kheyju's shoulder and told her everything she knew.

A week later, Maryam and Bahador were attending school. No one in the village agreed to do the same. The Child Snatcher might snatch the children on the way. Kheyju sought the help of Ebrahim the Leopard, who now came more often to Jofreh; and knowing that he did not have to be worried about becoming entangled in the problems of Zayer Ahmad and Mahjamal, he consented to spend the nights in the village and take the children to the city during the day and bring them back in the late afternoon. Ebrahim the Leopard would have been happy to pay the expenses for Golpar's schooling; but Setareh, whose heart was still in mourning because of the Child Snatcher, did not consent to Golpar going.

47

Finally, one day, Zayer Ahmad came through the big gate of the prison. The salty scent of the sea and the village! He detected the scent of Kheyju and Setareh, who were waiting in the corner of the square.

With the arrival of Zayer Ahmad, a smile appeared on the lips of the people of the village. Zayer Ahmad was the soul of the village. They would sit around him until late; they obeyed him with their hearts and thanked the sea and the sky. Dazed by the love and kindness of the village, once alone, Zayer Ahmad took an oath to never allow Jofreh to go to its knees and never to allow the people to become needful of strangers.

In the evening, all eyes in the village were on Zayer Ahmad's mouth; but the tall old man with his silver hair looked at them with his kind amber eyes and could not make his heart consent to disturb the heart and soul of the village, to tell them that before his own eyes they had placed Mahjamal between blocks of ice, that they had kept him thirsty to watch his feebleness and misery, that they had deprived him of sleep, and that they had tied him in the middle of a tire and rolled it... No, let the heart of the village be calm. Zayer Ahmad rubbed his high forehead with the biting coldness of his hand to wipe the beads of sweat before they became visible. Then, as in the past, he coughed and broke the silence.

Mahjamal was going to be transferred to Tehran. The news was brought to Zayer Ahmad by Dr. Adeli. It was at dawn when the people of the village, women, men, and children, and even the city people who had heard stories about Mahjamal and the village of Jofreh, gathered along the route to see Mahjamal. When he came out of the door, his hands were cuffed to the hands of two gendarmes. His sunburned face had become gaunt, and he looked at the crowd with two callous blue eyes.

Where is the kindness in Mahjamal's eyes? Setareh bit the edge of her scarf to stifle her sobbing. They had changed his shirt. He wore a prison uniform, and his ribs were protruded. His beard and mustache had grown long. He looked at the crowd, a crowd he did not recognize.

An old woman beat her chest:

"Your poor mother..."

The voice of love and kindness! Mahjamal's eyes lit up. He was in need of the blue voice of humans. He looked at the old woman, and his glance drifted over the crowd. The salty scent of the sea and the village! Where were the people of the village? The flood of sunlight into Mahjamal's eyes! He blinked, and looked once again. The world was alive. The sea still sent its waves to the shore, and the seagulls still flew over the village. A strange joyfulness drifted into his heart. He loved the world, the village, the city, and the land.

Without a sound, silently the people of the village stood there. He pushed back his memories. He would collapse to his knees if he looked at the people of the village one more time. Just like on that sea voyage, a strange sorrow gripped his throat. He wanted to be among the people in the village. But Busalmeh was determining his fate, and he did not know how to play the reed flute; he would not attend the celebration of any Busalmeh. If only he could free himself! He was afraid he would lose his manly strength and begin to sob. Only look at other people; they do not awake any memory in your heart. But why have they come? In their eyes was the same sparkle that was in the eyes of the men from Tangestan when they spoke about Niru. He felt warm. He can, he can be free. Human strength gathered in his mind and thoughts. Human beings! Eagerness and excitement ran through his soul. Humans and the land have accepted him. The true offspring of the land have never lived in comfort. They have carried the burden of heavy suffering on their shoulders, suffering that they accept with their hearts, in order to disobey Busalmeh. For a moment, he remembered what one of the prisoners had said. The man who steals fire to give it to humans. That's it! That is what the whole world is. He turned around, briefly glancing toward Zayer Ahmad. What a man! What ability! He wanted to extend his arms, embrace him, and kiss his shoulders twice. A glance at his hands in chains with two gendarmes beside him. Another glance out the corner of his eye at Zayer Ahmad, and a smile that gave Kheyju reassurance. Zayer Ahmad saw Mahjamal's smile and was at a loss. What is he smiling about?

He got into the jeep, turned around, and it was at that moment that he saw Maryam. During the prison days, Maryam had frequently listened to the radio hoping to hear some news about her father, but had not heard any. In school, she had pretended to be thirsty, and with a glass in her hand, she had fled.

Two days later, when the gendarmes raided the village and searched for Mahjamal in every nook and cranny, and they had their boats patrolling the sea, Zayer Ahmad understood the meaning of that smile, and the meaning of what Mahjamal said on the sea voyage. When Zayer Ahmad wanted to cut his finger off, Mahjamal had said: "Not my finger."

The village came to life. The women snickered at the helplessness of the government agents, and the children in the village square under the silk tassel acacia tree, in the stories they made up, divided into two groups, Mahjamal and his supporters, and Colonel Senobari and his gendarmes.

Just before reaching Rudak Hill, a small teahouse where tired travelers stay, Mahjamal got off the jeep with the two gendarmes. Glancing at the sun, which was setting behind the mountains, he said that he wanted to perform his afternoon prayers. They took off his handcuffs. He performed ablutions for prayers, stood facing Mecca, and in the final prostration of the prayer, he filled both his fists with dirt from the ground, threw it into the eyes of the two gendarmes who were sitting on each side of him, and fled.

The wind carried the salty scent of Mahjamal to villages near and far, and those who had sighted eyes saw the bowls of water and containers full of bread and dates along the rarely-trodden paths and depressing mountain passes that had been left on the roads for Mahjamal's hands to reach for them whenever he was thirsty or hungry.

Mahjamal stayed in the slopes of mountains and in caves for twenty-five nights and days. He ate mountain plants and drank water from the springs, and on the twenty-sixth day, he knocked on the door of a hut, which was half open, and said hello to an old woman, who was soaking bread in liquid whey. The old woman smiled, placed a separate bowl in front of him, and told him about the strangest news of the world, and about a rebellious outlaw who had hundreds of riflemen, who was brave, and whose heart was one with kind farmers, who would distribute bread and water and land equally among the people, return kidnapped little girls to their homes, invade prisons and free those in shackles, place loaves of bread by the houses of widows and orphans, and...

Mahjamal was at a loss. He did not know that rebellious outlaw, and he did not know how to track him and reach that Mahjamal that the people of the villages near and far had fabricated.

At dawn on the following day, the old woman, who had stayed awake all night, gave him some food for his journey. As Mahjamal was climbing the slope of the mountain, he saw the old woman running like a teenager toward another village.

The story of Mahjamal passed from mouth to mouth...

Mahjamal was of the world of the unknown. He was and was not everywhere. If clusters of wheat grew taller, if palm trees bent down because of their burden of dates, if springs bubbled with water, it was clear to everyone that Mahjamal had passed through there. With his presence, sick people left their sickbeds, and women gave birth to healthy children; and wherever he passed through, the drought would retreat, a palm tree that had dried up years before would become green, springs would bubble with water, and, with his voice, a narrow brook would track him from the heart of the mountain and follow him.

The villagers saw the narrow brook with their own eyes, which babbled pleasantly, and its amazing blue color had enchanted everyone.

The soldiers and the gendarmes who searched the entire regions of Dashti and Tangestan handspan by handspan, looking for him dead or alive, were left bewildered in the midst of the stories. Mahjamal was no different from Niru, who had escaped from prison one cold winter night with a bullet in his heart. Mahjamal was Chieftain Ali, the rumor of whose death they had spread falsely in Dashti and Tangestan, so that no one would any longer beseech any human being for help. Mahjamal was the son of Lion Mohammad from Tangestan, who one day jumped into the sea and disappeared.

Mahjamal also heard these stories, and he respected Lion Mohammad of Tangestan. He would ask about what he looked like. Could the blue and green waters of the sea change a human being that much? What was the difference between the land faces of the six sons of Mama Mansur and the faces that the green and blue waters had made of them? Was the man he had seen one day at the bottom of the sea, who was heartsick for the land, Lion Mohammad? At times, Mahjamal was certain that he himself was the son of Lion Mohammad of Tangestan, who was taken one stormy night by his aquatic mother to the depths of the blue waters to start the progeny of one of the mermaid-humans who had to live on the land.

❖ 49 ❖

Two years later, one midnight in Jofreh, Delavar, that white horse, neighed and stomped its hooves on the ground, and Kheyju knew that somewhere near or far Mahjamal had been shot. It was summertime. She secured Maryam to the back of the saddle, took the medicine from Zayer Ahmad, asked whatever she did not know from Dr. Adeli, and gave the horse a free rein. After four nights and days, Delavar took her to a cave in which Mahjamal was wheezing, with a bullet in his chest.

Maryam did not have the heart to watch Kheyju remove the bullet with a knife that she had heated over the flames of a fire. She turned her head and looked into the dark, cold cave at the rifles and the canteens that were hanging from the wall of the cave, which had all been taken as booty from various guard stations. They stayed there for two months, until Mahjamal was able to lean against the wall of the cave. It was on one of those nights that he told the story of his aquatic mother to Maryam, who had skipped one grade in school. Mahjamal, whose voice had become husky like the voice of Niru and whose forehead was hot, took Maryam's small hands and placed them on his forehead.

"When you go back to Jofreh, go to the sea."

Kheyju told Mahjamal the news from the village: In his mind and heart, Bahador is still preoccupied with the sea, not with lessons and homework. Madineh's legs ache; she yells from pain at night. Mansur has launched his big boat on the water, he has several crew members, and he owns a stucco house near the guard station and a shop in which Nabati sells merchandise to the people. Ebrahim the Leopard wants to marry Golpar, Setareh's daughter.

When Kheyju returned to the village, Madineh was still moaning from the pain in her legs, and Zayer Ahmad had been unable to convince the Department of Education to build a school. "No matter on which door I knocked, it did not work." Kheyju, who was taking off her scarf and putting the horse saddle on the ground, took a deep breath. Building two little rooms did not require any moaning and groaning. From that very day, they could start; even if with sea rocks, the walls could be raised...

A month later, past the Shrine of Sire Ashk, a two-room schoolhouse was built. The people of the village walked around its half-finished walls.

"A bell! All it needs is a bell."

Zayer Ahmad gave the necessary instructions to Captain Ali, who was ready to go to the city at any hour of the day or night:

"It has to be big, the biggest bell in the world."

The bell that Captain Ali brought back was the strangest bell in the world. All the men of the village gathered together to move it, and it took one month to build a high cement wall that could hold the weight of the bell.

Zayer Ahmad, who considered the sound of the bell to be more beautiful than the sound of the call for prayers, rang it. All the villages near and far were awakened at the sound of it, and the children listened in amazement to a sound that called out to them.

On that strange day, the people of the village of Jofreh saw small mermaids who naughtily stuck their heads out of the water and sprayed water on one another, and it was on the same day that

Busalmeh's head became dizzy; he brought his head up from the depths of the muddy waters, and a fisherman, who had been caught between his teeth years and years earlier, was able to free himself, come to the village of Jofreh, and decide to stay there.

When the children of Jofreh assembled in the school, it was then that Zayer Ahmad took a look around him and sighed deeply. No one in the village knew how to read and write. Before Zayer Ahmad set out for the port city, however, the jeep of the Department of Education arrived carrying a few men. The director of the Department of Education, who had heard the sound of the bell at dawn that morning, and it still resonated in his ears, clapped his hands happily:

"It needs to be inaugurated."

Bubuni, who did not know the difference between inaugurated and discombobulated, these days was looking at the road that led to the city. The going back and forth to the city of Captain Ali had increased the worry in her heart, and she got the news to Zayer Ahmad, who was preparing to go there. Zayer Ahmad came to the school, and without understanding what inauguration meant, he conferred that authority on the director of education.

"We have no teacher."

The director of education placed his hand on Zayer Ahmad's shoulder:

"We will inaugurate it when the time comes."

Thus it was that a school with two rooms was inaugurated one month later, on 26 October, the birthday of the Shah, in the village of Jofreh. That morning, the people were awakened by the crackling sound of a loudspeaker. One man was laying electrical wiring over the wall, other men were pounding small flags on the walls, and colorful lamps were lit. An iron machine was grumbling in the corner of the schoolhouse. Captain Ali said, "I'm sure Her Highness is going to come," pointing to the lamps and flags.

The people of Zayer Ahmad's village, who had gathered around the school, stepped back, terrified.

Zayer Ahmad anxiously remained beside the Shrine of Sire Ashk, watching men who were placing four-legged stools in the courtyard and a table with a large picture of His Majesty next to it, a picture which he had frequently seen in government buildings and in prison, which had made him think that the affairs of the city could not go on without that picture. Another truck was unloading boxes of fruit and sweets.

All the hard work of the village was going to waste. Her Highness and Colonel Senobari were going to come now, and everything would be ruined. They might once again remember the blue mermaids and start searching the houses and the sea. Zayer Gholam went to his house and took out his large hatchet, and the other men hid their shark tails under their *dishdashas* and sat waiting, away from the school, next to the Shrine of Sire Ashk.

The sound of the loudspeaker traveled far and reminded the men of their first trip to the city:

"In every village now, a school has already been built..."

The director of education was speaking, without anyone having come from the capital city. He talked about the people who up to yesterday believed in the jinn and mermaids, and now, because of the advancements of the country, they were pursuing the acquisition of science and knowledge.

The director of education was shaking his hands and yelling. Those who were sitting on the chairs applauded and yelled "hooray"; and Zayer Gholam, who saw that the building of a school had been able to bring such advancements to the country, smiled with delight. He leaned his hatchet against the wall of the shrine, and he was slowly opening and closing the flap of his loincloth toward the director of education. Zayer Ahmad, who had become very skeptical because of the bitter experiences of recent years, was praying for the inauguration to be finished soon, without a calamity befalling the village and the school.

At noon, the director of education installed the sign for the 26 October School over the door of the school, then all of them got into their cars and left. The people of the village had to spend an entire day cleaning up the trash and the fruit peelings that they had left behind.

❧ 50 ❧

The sound of the bell even reached the ears of Mahjamal. He had returned exhausted from some battle. In the valley were the corpses of those killed in the battle. His riflemen were sitting behind a rock, and Mahjamal was leaning against the mountain, heavy-eyed. He had learned that they had suddenly surrounded his hiding place, and by morning, he had barricaded himself behind one rock, and then another. Now he was leaning against a rough rock, about to doze off. Ding-dong. He opened his eyes and heard the sound. With a smile, Zayer Ahmad, the strange silver-haired old man, was in front of him! He was shaking his index fingers toward him.

A smile appeared on Mahjamal's lips... Sleep flew from his eyes, a breeze was flapping the bandana on his face, and he could smell the scent of mountain flowers.

Zayer Ahmad! How he wished to see Zayer Ahmad again! That old man with his kind amber eyes follows his own path and goes on. His heart is fresh, the world still amazes him. In contrast, he...he cannot figure out anything.

He rose up on his knees, remembering his twin daughters, Shamayel and Hamayel. They are not alike. What are they doing now? They are probably sitting on the shore, playing with sea

pebbles, without having heard any story from the mouth of
Zayer Ahmad. And Zayer Ahmad cannot tell them a story; he is
preoccupied with building, constantly struggling and striving, tying
a cloth of supplication to everything that is new. Success is the great
human need, and Zayer Ahmad is constantly in search of something
to provide tranquility for the village. But Zayer Ahmad's love of life
stands against Busalmeh's lust for life and death. What a battle!
What a strange battle has begun in the world. The battle of love and
lust, life and death. Zayer Ahmad and Busalmeh.

The morning light was illuminating the valley. Down there, human
bodies empty of life had fallen; and yesterday at this time, wishing
to trap him and receive their prize, they were turning their futures
upside down. Mahjamal looked. His riflemen were exhausted, their
heads on their rifles, sleeping.

When he slid down, he waved to a young rifleman who was
running after him: "Stay right there." He went into the woods. It
was as though something was drawing him, a distant, faint voice,
a voice he had heard years earlier in Jofreh, the voice of the tribal
Lor soldier. His heart trembled; he stopped hesitantly. He wanted
to step back, but, no, he had to go. He had to reach the final point.
He stepped forward and reached the soldier, fallen in the woods, his
black hair disheveled and his eyes open toward the sky. Upon seeing
him, a small bird fled. You are free from the shackles of profit and
loss, you have become free. Mahjamal sat down. The soldier's lips
seemed to move.

"Mercenary general, kill me, for spilling my blood you'll pay."

The power of love might often fall on the improper path to
reach its end, to reach death. Woe if the head hits the sea rock of
reality! The intellect rises in opposition to love. What have you done,
Mahjamal? You have had no lust for life. From which people have
you taken away the love of life? "Do not close my eyes, the sun is so
pretty."

He pulled up the back of his shirt. Perhaps he could see the scars
of the lashes that landed on his back in Jofreh that night. Suddenly

ashamed of his unavoidable deeds, he tossed his rifle and bent down... He was lost. Time had replaced him with someone else. Where is aquatic Mahjamal? A lump exploded in his throat. He wept without embarrassment. He wept for the character and disposition he had lost.

An hour later, his riflemen pulled him out of a blue lake.

If an aquatic-human cries away from the sea, his tears form a blue lake from which the constant sound of the crying of a human with his hand and feet in chains can be heard from the depths of the blue waters. Mahjamal was near Melgado, his hands and feet in the chains of an obligation that had forced him to do other deeds.

◈ **51** ◈

The children wandered idly around the school until December. The director of education had totally forgotten which schools he had inaugurated, and where. Zayer Ahmad was at a loss, with his finger in his mouth. "Jofreh! The village of Jofreh!" The director of education nodded, "Aha, the jinn and the mermaids," and he seated Zayer Ahmad on the chair to have him talk about the mermaids. But Zayer Ahmad had nothing to say. The color of the sea was gray, and the gray sea loses its sight and becomes blind. Then it might do just anything you can think of; it might even roll over the Department of Education. The director of education was sinking into his chair.

Finally, on 22 December, a woman with long straight hair and big black eyes entered the school with a suitcase. Her name was Azar, Azar Mottaqiyan, but no one called her by her last name for as long as she was in Jofreh. Azar stayed in Zayer Ahmad's house, and the school became a place for the children to sit on the benches every now and then. Azar was the principal, the teacher, and the assistant principal in charge of discipline. All day long, she handled the children, and at night, she delved into her far and wide hopes and dreams and the pictures she had from foreign countries, which she showed to the women and kept them entertained.

It was on one of those nights when Kheyju learned that many

people sent their children abroad for education, to become professors. Zayer Ahmad could not properly explain the meaning of professor for Kheyju. Azar also was not very much preoccupied with professors. She knew more about the freedom and equality of women and men than the lives of professors.

Azar, who was insistent that the women of the village must also be educated, was unable to persuade Golpar to go to school:

"I'm already grown up. It's time for me to have my own home and life."

As though it was the wedding of a mermaid, they had set up the bridal chamber in a hut, one like the home of the mermaids. Green and blue pieces of cloth covered all the palm branches, and Golpar was sitting in the bridal chamber next to Ebrahim the Leopard, who was twisting his mustache. The children hung around the hut.

The village was happy. It had been a long time since the sound of clapping and ululating reverberated in the village. The men played stick games, and, concealed from the eyes of Zayer Ahmad, Mansur had emptied several bottles of booze with Ebrahim the Leopard and other young men.

But from that evening until the next morning, the wind, which was about to unhinge the doors and windows, carried the sound of the pleading cries of Golpar, depriving the people of the village of sleep. When the screaming of Golpar became so heartrending that not even the Child Snatcher could recognize her, Maryam, who had prayed all night for the Child Snatcher to come and rescue Golpar from the claws of Ebrahim the Leopard, fell asleep in pain and anger, and in the midst of sleep and wakefulness, she promised her aquatic grandmother that if she grew up someday, she would never get married.

In the morning, Maryam was awakened by the screaming of Setareh, and she saw Golpar wrapped in a bedding-wrap cloth with her golden hair hanging down. Ebrahim the Leopard fled from her grandfather, Zayer Ahmad Hakim, who was ready to kill him, and never again returned to the village.

Golpar flew away like a seagull and was gone, and the village was clad in black. On one of the nights of mourning, Azar gathered all the girls of the village, even Hamayel and Shamayel, in her room, and, still crying, she told all of them that the laws of the country were ridiculous, and that no one should get married before the age of thirty. She said that a sane person would only get married when she fell in love, and not in love with a person like Ebrahim the Leopard. The children, who could not understand what she was saying, ate her candy, and it was only Shamayel who stared into her big black eyes, and then asked at what age the deer get married.

Azar had seen that Shamayel would never stay away from the deer. She had seen her many times talking to Tara in the corner of the courtyard. The incidents that occurred in Jofreh so rapidly every day had caused absentmindedness and forgetfulness, and had made Zayer Ahmad and Kheyju neglectful of the children. Not much could be expected of Madineh either; she was suffering from her aching legs, and her eyes still teared up remembering the head of the guard station who wanted to kill Yal with his rifle.

That night, Shamayel could not fall asleep all night long because of what Azar had said. Among the deer, the foolish rules and arrangements that were common among humans did not exist at all; they could love each other and easily get married to each other. Shamayel wished to marry Tara, for herself and Tara to wear green clothes, to have plates full of sweets and henna, and for everyone in the village to clap and play stick games. But Shamayel was not like Golpar, to leave and not show up again. Shamayel would stay in the village. She would not go to anyone, not even to God. She would play with Tara right there in the courtyard, and they would eat sweets together.

* * *

Not even forty days had passed since Golpar's death when Captain Mansur's big boat with the sailors who had come from ports near and far was launched into the water, and Zayer Ahmad Hakim, who was standing beside the dam, remembered the days when still a child, Mahjamal ran to him and told him that his big boat would catch fire.

This time, however, Mansur and several young men from the village got on the boat. They fired up the engine and, without anything catching fire, went to the other side of the offing of the sea and disappeared before everyone's eyes. Before the journey, Mansur had visited each and every house in the village and, ignoring Nabati's yelling, he had taken the orders for what they needed and had set out for the Emirates on his big new boat, on the mast of which the women had hung hundreds of talismans.

Nabati had gained weight. She sat in her store from morning to sundown, and her son, Abdu, wore the most beautiful clothes, which Nabati ordered from the city. Abdu did not get along with the children of the village. Nabati did not want her one and only son to play with a bunch of "gypsies."

Sergeant Sinayi's jeep full of merchandise would be unloaded once a week behind Nabati's store; and Nabati, with the information that she would glean out of the customers, reported the news of the village to Sergeant Sinayi. She had been the one who, during the few days' absence of Kheyju, had said that she had gone to see Mahjamal.

During those days, from the presence of the soldiers who kept his house under surveillance and the phony patients, whose number had increased, Zayer Ahmad could figure out that someone was reporting to the guard station about the village and his house. But how could he suspect the people of the village? Who was it that was severing his or her own roots? Zayer Ahmad had become suspicious of Azar, who was still talking the women's heads off about the freedom and equality of men and women who lived in foreign countries; but a simple calculation made him realize that this was not the doing of the simple teacher of the village. Azar was not interested in the story of Mahjamal. She did not believe in the mermaids. Dreaming about traveling to faraway countries, she had come to this village to save up some money and someday leave this "backward country." Azar—who every night opened the suitcase that she had packed with things that she had bought for living in faraway countries to show them to the children and the women of the village—could not have been the one who reported about Kheyju's absence. At that time, Azar had not yet arrived in the village.

One night, before Mansur set out for the Emirates, Zayer Ahmad had become suspicious of Mansur's sailors, who were strangers, and he went to talk to Mansur. It was then that he saw Mansur drinking booze with Sergeant Sinayi and Captain Ali. Zayer Ahmad did not hesitate. He still had not lost the strength in his arms. He went after Mansur and Captain Ali with the shark tail that hung on the wall. Mama Mansur, hearing the yelling of Mansur, got there in a hurry and began grappling with Nabati:

"Shrew!"

For the very first time, Zayer Ahmad witnessed heinous words coming out of the mouths of two women of the village. Depressed and distressed, he went home and could not sleep all night. The women's character had changed.

On the following morning, when drunkenness had fled from the heads of Captain Ali and Mansur, after hearing about Zayer Ahmad's concerns, they promised no longer to be drinking companions of Sergeant Sinayi. It was as clear as day that in their drunkenness, they simplemindedly had mentioned what went on in the village to Sergeant Sinayi. It was for the same reason that Zayer Ahmad asked Mansur to go on his sea voyage earlier, so that on the sea, he could rid himself of his nightly booze drinking.

Those days, Bubuni, who was more worried about the city than the mermaids, would not consent to Captain Ali leaving. Bubuni did not want Captain Ali, who was the only captain in the world who knew nothing at all about being a captain, to go to a strange land. Her face was wrinkling more every day, and in her heart she was becoming more neurotic. She was afraid Captain Ali would not return to the village anymore.

* * *

Two weeks after Mansur's departure, an incident occurred that brought sorrow to the people of the village. Away from the eyes of Nabati, Abdu opened one of the packages of ten that Sergeant Sinayi had brought from the port city, saw himself in the mirror, and, bewildered, picked it up and ran to the house of Mama Mansur. Unwittingly, Abdu handed Mama Mansur's death to her. He gave the mirror to Mama Mansur, who was sitting beside the millstones grinding wheat into flour.

Twenty-four hours later, Zayer Ahmad shadowed the coming and going of the soldiers, who were looking for Abdu. He followed them and reached Mama Mansur's house, where he saw her in the final moments of her physical life. The mirror was shaking in Mama Mansur's melting hands, and Abdu was screaming in the arms of a soldier. No doubt remained for Zayer Ahmad and the other men of the village that this time, Sergeant Sinayi had come with a jeep full of mirrors to destroy the women of the village.

The women, who were beating themselves on their heads and chests because of the expiring of Mama Mansur and the turning of the last parts of her body into tears, remembered their past sad stories. And in order for the women not to go to that store that was selling death, this time, Zayer Ahmad went there hurriedly.

Nabati, who had forgotten about the story of the mirrors for a long time, heard about it when her store caught fire, the mirrors had been smashed, and, scared by the wrath of the men of the village, her "Sergeant Major" Sinayi and his big and small soldiers had stuffed themselves into the guard station.

Kheyju rescued Nabati from the hands of Zayer Gholam, who wanted to cut off her head and throw it into the clay bread oven, and took her to her own house. Nabati did not stay in Zayer Ahmad's house, and for the first time, someone stood up to Zayer Ahmad. "I will make a complaint. I will make a complaint against all of you."

Until six months later, when Mansur's big boat appeared at the offing of the sea and dropped anchor on the other side of the cove, the village was the place of the comings and goings of individuals who were searching for the person who had set the store on fire.

Not knowing how to explain the story of the mirrors to them, Zayer Ahmad was finally frustrated and agreed for the village to pay Nabati the damages, which had been calculated by Sergeant Sinayi.

The arrival of Mansur, who had already figured out at sea that the village was not calm, however, made the plans of Sergeant Sinayi like images drawn on water. Having heard his mother's sighs at sea, Mansur realized that his mother had been upset with him in her death, and in order for the drowned to recite prayers for her and for the mermaids to weep for her death, he had tossed two palm branch sacks full of dates into the sea.

Mansur held Nabati under the shark tail and tore to pieces all the papers of the bill of indictment that were in Sergeant Sinayi's handwriting and had Nabati's fingerprint on them, shut the door to Nabati, who had violated the village's sanctity and respect, and asked Azar to write a letter declaring the withdrawal of the demand of the owner of the store for damages.

Zayer Gholam picked up the letter in Azar's handwriting, went house to house, and showed it to all the people of the village, and in the evening, he sat on the top of Zayer Ahmad's water cistern, kissed Zayer Ahmad's hand, and in the midst of sobbing, he thanked the sky and the sea for once again having restored peace and reconciliation to the village. Zayer Gholam, who had been avoiding looking into Zayer Ahmad's eyes for a long time out of embarrassment, stayed in Zayer Ahmad's house that night, and up to the moment that he became insane and started walking stark naked in the village, he never again saw Nabati, nor went to her house.

Mourning for his mother, who had not been buried in the land, Mansur canceled his nightly appointments with Sergeant Sinayi; but the guard station was there, along with its permission for going to the sea. He could not make his heart give up on profits and losses. Sergeant Sinayi had opened a place in Mansur's life. The temptation of the foreign markets on the other side of the waters finally shut his eyes to the world, and it was Mansur who gave the control of his boat to a man sent by Sergeant Sinayi. Neju, a captain who knew every handspan of the sea, looked for passengers who paid enormous amounts of money to flee across the border.

The village was changing. Azar sighed in contentment, and she was happy about the sailors on their return home having filled the houses with radios, pineapples, and colorful slippers. The story of the mirror and the strange death of Mama Mansur, however, took a long time before it left Azar's mind. It was during those days that Azar patiently sat and listened to Madineh, who was moaning from leg pain and who covered her ears not to hear all sorts of voices on the radios. Madineh's voice appealed to the heart of Azar more than the voices of the men and women on the radios, and she hid her small mirror at the bottom of her suitcase and never brought it out, until the time when Setareh and Maryam buried Fanus's bones in Fekseno Valley. It was on that day that Azar, without knowing why, opened her suitcase, saw herself without worry and anxiety, with the same big black eyes, long smooth hair, and oval face, as she was sighing, waiting to travel abroad.

Mansur's boat went on foreign journeys twice more. At night, from Mama Mansur's house, in which the sailors now stayed, came the sound of the boisterous laughter of the men who had returned from their sea voyages and were bothering Bubuni with the strange things they did. Sometimes Neju put on a long blue dress and stood behind the window where Bubuni was standing, worried, awaiting Captain Ali's return from the city.

"The jinn, Zayer... The jinn are stoning me."

Bubuni's hands trembled, her cheeks having sunken, as she spoke about a strange sound that she would hear at night. Zayer Ahmad had frequently told the sailors not to torment the heart of a woman who was drowned in her delusions; but Zayer Ahmad had lost control. The world was being lost to the sounds of the small and large radios. For a long time in the city, he had seen the comings and goings of the people who had come to Jofreh one day in a strange boat, men and women who dressed alike and were the same height and shape, and one did not know what they were doing there during those hot and humid days.

Zayer Ahmad's patients, who no longer talked about the mermaids, came to his practice as a matter of habit, and they spoke about blonde women with blue eyes and about oil wells that had been found in the vicinity. Zayer Ahmad was lost in the midst of the presence of blond people in the city, the oil wells that had opened their mouths in villages near and far, and the road building company, which had once again started its operations and was rapidly building a road to Jofreh.

Finally, one morning when Zayer Ahmad's breath was trapped in his chest, he saw that the road had reached close to the village. Here and there on the vacant land, workers had built houses for themselves, and trucks full of stones and cement were loading and unloading alongside the road. Zayer Ahmad, who at one time wished for the village to be connected to the whole world, tired of the invasion of noise and news, in the middle of the night, heard the neighing of the white horse in his sleep next to Shamayel and the deer, whose black eyes were gazing at him in the dark, hoping to escape the strange news that the wind was carrying. There was no good news. One village had been swallowed by oil. They had bought the people's houses for a pittance. The comings and goings were monitored. Mahjamal had set fire to the pipelines that were supposed to take natural gas from Kangan to foreign countries on the other side of the waters, and the government issued identity cards in the oil-rich regions for the inhabitants and planned to build barracks in the vicinity for the Air Force and the Navy.

Zayer Ahmad was afraid that oil might also be found in his village. He had gone to the Well of Loneliness several times to sniff it, had sniffed the water from the well, and when he was alone, he had dug the corner of the courtyard with a shovel and had tasted the soil. Zayer Ahmad, who had built the village with his sweat and blood, was so enslaved to his sorrows that when Setareh said that she had been hearing the horse neighing for a week, he agreed with her and said nothing.

In a black dress, with her gaunt face the color of moonlight and eyes that had sunken because of Golpar's death, Setareh got ready to head off for the mountains.

Zayer Ahmad did not think it expedient for Kheyju to go on that journey. With the fire set to the natural gas pipelines and the wounding of foreigners who had settled around Kangan in prefabricated houses, the number of phony patients had increased, and this time, the villagers knew that Colonel Senobari had promised the capital city that he would deliver Mahjamal, dead or alive.

No one was able to stop Maryam, not even Azar, who at night would tell her stories about faraway countries. A strange incredible force made her sit behind the saddle of Setareh's horse and set out for the mountains, after four years.

❧ 52 ❧

Along their route, Setareh and Maryam passed by dry river beds, bridges that storms had brought from thousands of parasangs away, and large white rocks that Satan places on the path of humans. At night, they passed by outlaw rebels hiding in ambush behind branches, waiting for the gendarmes; and finally, they reached the Fekseno Mountains. They took the winding path and went to the Valley of Sorrow, the valley in which Fanus's bones still moaned after so many years.

Mahjamal was not wounded; he was distraught and tired. His voice was that of a ship-wrecked captain who had lost his guiding star, a tired desperate captain who in his profound despair was looking for a way to escape.

"We have lost our way..."

He had arrived in the Valley of Sorrow of Fekseno twenty days earlier. At night, he had escaped from the government forces, hoping that the voice of that Lor tribal soldier would leave him in peace. For a long time, he had been shooting at the mountains and hills; then he would retreat in his fight and flight, leaving his bewildered friends behind...

"Our business is not to take life."

"But there is a bounty on your head."

"What a head, such a frenzy!"

Mahjamal among his supporting companions, tired and sleepy, with a sarcastic smile on his lips, a sarcastic smile that had not let go of him for a long time... His companions' glances at one another... Mahjamal withdrawn into himself with knots in his wandering mind and waves and waves of thoughts that would not leave him alone... Everything had come to this point. My head, my neck, my self. I and Colonel Senobari. Colonel Senobari and I... And all of this, for what? The caravan that you started, the command of open fire that you gave, and now no one pays attention to the gesture of your hand. They only pull the trigger. From where to where have you come?

No, he did not want to be a caravan leader, the caravan leader of death...

A long time earlier, he longed to live among humans, to hear the human voice, to see the rising and setting of the sun. But now, he was caught in something like that strange feeling that at one time in the sea had caught him by the throat and was forcing him to go. But where?

Were all those he had seen during those strange years denizens of the land? Does this not mean that a human being on the land, who is drowned in stories and sorrows, can be of the drowned, fed up with life? What are you, yourself, Mahjamal? Of the land, or of the drowned?

Once, in a place of ambush, he had heard a soldier who was yearning to return to his place of birth sing a lamentation:

I packed up my bags and set out for the port
All in the dark of night
How foolish I was to give up my love
All in the dark of night.

The voice was not the voice of the people of the land. It seemed as though the world breathed completely in the depths of the green waters. And who was Busalmeh? It often can happen that a person unknowingly occupies the seat of Busalmeh; and if he is not mindful, his hands become totally contaminated.

"I am lost, Setareh."

Maryam had never seen her father so broken and sad:

"We have brought you seawater."

She wrapped her small arms around his neck.

Mahjamal kissed the forehead of the little girl.

Setareh slowly emptied the goatskin full of water over his body. The man who had lost his way, like a withered mountain flower that suddenly comes to life, was rid of the headache that had gripped him, and he fixed his aquatic eyes on Maryam.

"We must leave this place."

Twenty days earlier when they had reached the Valley of Sorrow at dawn, he had heard the voices of his companions:

"We are finished! No escape route."

For twenty days, he had heard the cries of a fourteen-year-old girl, without being able to do anything. Familiar loving hands, the hands of a woman who burned, yearning, that alone could break the spell of that valley and show the way to the rebels who had lost their way. And where are the hands of a woman yearning for love?

Setareh and Maryam found Fanus's bones from among the bones of hyenas and leopards that had been shot and deer that had fallen down the slopes of the mountains, and buried them on a silvery day; and it was at that very moment that in the village, Azar suddenly took out her mirror and looked into it, and Bubuni, who was searching for Captain Ali in the city, saw herself in the mirror, and other women of the village saw their own faces in earthenware jugs and bowls of water without the screaming of a fourteen-year-old girl causing them distress.

The spell was broken; and twenty-four hours later, with the

valley filled with sugarcane and yellow peacocks, Mahjamal and his riflemen, following Delavar who knew the way, left Fekseno's Valley of Sorrow, so that the wind blowing in the sugarcane field would not revive the old memories and stories in the minds of his riflemen, and the moaning that reverberated with the wind in the valley would not wrap them around on its lap like a whirlwind. The restlessness of the sugarcane field and the yellow peacocks that followed Mahjamal and his companions for some distance were indicative of a distressed heart. Mahjamal looked at his riflemen. Perhaps behind these tired frowning faces the heart of a lover was beating, perhaps many of these young people would not abandon the group, embarrassed by his presence. Or does Setareh perhaps have a heart that is in love? Mahjamal remembered that Setareh had lost her man very young. When a woman is able to gather the bones of a person in love, that means that her hands have remained lonely, yearning for the bosom of a man. Mahjamal was at a loss. It was as though he was seeing Setareh for the first time.

53

Forlorn in the darkness of night, waiting for the moon to rise, with eyes on the dark blue sky filled with stars, he was sitting when he heard a rustling sound. It was the long skirt of a woman, dragging on the ground. He turned his head and saw the silhouette of Setareh. What is she doing here at this time of night? Without fear of the eyes of a stranger, Setareh pulled off her headscarf. Her hair reached her waist, braided, and massive. And a few steps away from the goatskin full of water that was hanging from the branch of a tree, Setareh placed her mouth on the opening of the goatskin.

Something was pushing the darkness back. The reflection of moonlight on the whiteness of Setareh's neck... Mahjamal pressed his eyes shut. The strange desire to stand up and go toward the woman with whom he had grown up... Setareh held the cup of her hand under the mouth of the goatskin. She poured a fistful of water into her collar, and reached into the gap of her dress. The air turned warm. A scent wafted everywhere, a scent that swept over that of the night-scented stock flower. Setareh was undoing the braids of her hair, one by one, and the hair cascaded to her waist... Mahjamal did not move. He did not breathe. The rising moonlight placed before his eyes everything naked, revealing that a woman in the mountains, sheltered by the slope of the mountain, was removing her clothes from her body to entrust her body to the water, to the hands of the water.

Mahjamal's knees were trembling. Should he go? Or has she gone? Who is going toward whom? Was it Setareh who was coming, or he, who was on fire, trying to reach Setareh? The flames of the fire seemed to uproot Mahjamal's body. He had no control, not even of his feet; and something was caught in his throat that blocked the way to the words he wanted to utter. What did he want to say? The scent of a filly wafted everywhere, a scent that intoxicates the rider.

As Setareh began to fall, Mahjamal caught her in his arms. He felt the warm breath of the woman on his neck. A horse neighed far away. Was this a neighing of craving, or of fleeing? The rider greedily bent over the horse. The limbs were in the business of steering and riding. Mahjamal bent over to sniff with his entire body. The scent of a filly, alone and thirsty... He brought his head to her ear; the face was hidden in the long mane, and once again he would raise his chest to breathe and be energized, to gallop. To caress and gallop until morning, until dawn, when the crested lark sings...the crested lark, that capricious bird in love.

54

Maryam, with a backpack full of her father's stories, and Setareh, lonelier than ever, returned to the village.

One day later, the white horse that in the course of coming back would not obey Setareh went missing, and no one was surprised. The smell of oil and hot tar permeated everywhere, and Zayer Ahmad thought that, like all the animals who escaped to the desert from the smell of oil, it had run away.

Not to distress the minds of the people of the village, Setareh never said a thing about the man who had lost his way.

The asphalted road, for the completion of which Zayer Ahmad had counted the days, passed by the village. The names of several villages in which oil had been discovered were becoming household names. The workers, who had smelled the oil and had left their cities hoping to find work, without paying attention to the strange myths of the people, without fearing the mermaids and Busalmeh, had built little shacks alongside the road near the village to entrust their bodies to the water of the sea.

The road to the city was short; and, happy with the world and the smell of oil that wafted in the sky, Azar would gather the women of the village in her room:

"Jofreh will soon be filled with skyscrapers."

Amazed and enjoying what she said, the women of the village sat and listened to her. Kheyju could not take her eyes off Azar's mouth, and, with a thousand excuses, she would go to Dr. Adeli to get answers to questions from the exiled colonel that Azar did not know. Madineh was worried about the skyscrapers rolling over the sea, and Shamayel did not know whether or not the skyscraper could cure her Tara, which had become dizzy from the smell of oil.

Zayer Ahmad did not believe what the village teacher said, but humans are capable of anything.

Zayer Ahmad Hakim was regretful. The invasion of the movement and noises in the village disturbed the calm of the world ... strange noises that made Madineh constantly cover her ears and made her face crumble from the delirium of movements. Anguish was the heartache companion of Zayer Ahmad, anguish about Madineh, anguish about Bahador who, gaunt and scrawny, would stand facing the sea, so that even perhaps for once he could see the sea as blue and the mermaids on the water. But the blue mermaids had apparently gone to the depths of the green waters because of the smell of tar and oil and the strange noise and commotion of the radios and cars. The village was getting big, and was falling apart. In his mind, everything was crumbling. Claws bigger than Busalmeh's were squeezing the throat of the village, scratching Zayer Ahmad's head and face, and disturbing his memories. Zayer Ahmad's anxiety intensified when the belly of one of the village girls, Khatun, swelled up, and her mother, assuming that she had a tumor in her belly, brought her to Zayer Ahmad.

Zayer Ahmad Hakim, who stayed awake and wept for the lost times that night until morning, without uttering a word to anyone, soon realized that the swelling that moved under his hand was not a tumor but a baby, four months into the pregnancy.

"Khatun is pregnant with a baby from the sea."

The women of the village, who had not yet lost their power of storytelling, and Khatun's mother, who was looking for a piece of broken board so as not to be drowned in her own shame, grabbed onto what Madineh, who talked nonsense yearning for the bygone days, said and gathered around her. The village had to go into the water, and from right there, throw sea stones at the strangers.

Madineh would shake her long thin finger at the women of the village, hold her face that was crumbled up from pain toward the sea wind, and talk about the sea that had a grudge against the village and wanted to ruin the reputation of the women of Jofreh, so that the village would not treat just any stranger who came from behind the mountains as an acquaintance.

But the times were strange. Madineh stood all alone in the middle of the gray waters, dragging her ailing thin legs, which every moment were about to separate from her body and go toward the offing of the sea, along the sea stones, and calling out to the women of the village one by one; but no one responded to her, and no one went to her aid, so that they would stone the strangers from there. Zayer Ahmad's strange old wife, on whose face tears mingled with the sprays of water, in her insanity and simplemindedness, realized that the world no longer revolved around the pleasure of mermaids.

Khatun's pregnancy, no matter from whom or where, kept Hamayel, Kheyju's little girl, from sleeping and eating.

With her own ears, Hamayel would hear Khatun's mother cursing the sea in front of acquaintances and strangers for having ruined her own and the village's reputation. In the gathering of the women by the clay bread oven, Khatun's mother would suddenly rise up on both her knees, grab her own collar facing the sea, and curse, weeping. Kheyju and Bubuni would calm her down; but a moment later, as though misery afflicted her body, she would heave a sigh again and resume her moaning and cursing.

In the gathering of the tired men of the village as they were sitting beside Zayer Ahmad on top of the water cistern, the conversation was all about the sea that had become filled with the sperm of strangers because of their nocturnal presence.

The whispering of female strangers, the suspicion and hesitation in the things that Kheyju said, and the dismayed face of Zayer Ahmad, whom Hamayel had seen weeping when alone, made Kheyju's little girl run away from the water, terrified, and not swim in the sea for the rest of her life. The sea can ruin virgin girls, ruin the reputation of the village and Zayer Ahmad, and pretend that it does not even know it at all. Pouting and frightened, Hamayel would look at the sea, and in her nightmares, she would see that suddenly the mountains throughout the world would roll over, and small stones would begin to move toward the sea and bury the sea of the village.

Bubuni—who in those days did not feel well and was going mad because of the absence of Captain Ali and his frequent visits to the city—helped deliver Khatun's baby, and Khatun's mother, in the same way that Khatun had taken the baby from the sea, in the middle of the night, entrusted it to the sea and set the minds of the people of the village at ease.

Years later, when Maryam came back to Jofreh, she saw a woman who had become old from the madness of love, and who was playing with the heap of paper that she had collected from here and there in empty Jofreh, and was asking imaginary people to read for her the letters that had arrived from Tabriz, since she was not literate, to be able to read them.

If the sea is able to impregnate a little girl and make a village silent in its sorrow and place a smile on the lips of strangers, if the sea is able to place human sperm in the belly of a little girl...

Bubuni, who had lost her teeth, not from fear, but from being enslaved to the habit of her life, and still every now and then swept all around the outside of her house up to the edge of the sea hoping to have Captain Ali return to his hearth and home, had set her hopes on that little window, on the sea that had made Khatun pregnant.

In the early days, with embarrassment, she tracked the tired men, marked the location where they swam, and the next morning under the pretext of washing dishes or fetching water, she would walk into the sea and sit right there in the water and ask the denizens of the sea, even the red mermaids and Busalmeh, to plant a baby in her old womb. Waiting to take a baby from the water, Bubuni stayed in the sea so long that the people of the village would see her all day sitting in the gray sea, pounding her fists on the small waves.

Finally, in one of the late afternoons of Jofreh when the sun had sat on the water, despite all his lunacy, Zayer Gholam saw Bubuni riding one of the waves of the sea all the way to the offing of the sea. Zayer Gholam figured out that the strange wave that swam and went on the sea under the command of the blue mermaids had come up to the cove to take a woman, who for her entire life had been enslaved to the fear and envy of mermaids, to the depths of the green waters and make her a companion of the drowned.

Zayer Gholam yelled mutely and pointed to the sea, but no one paid any attention to Zayer Gholam, not even Captain Ali, who had just returned from the city and whose body had the scent of a perfumed woman.

The men and women of Jofreh searched throughout village, but they did not find her. Zayer Ahmad Hakim, who had kept his eyes on the sea for a long time and was flustered by the half-finished utterances of Madineh, who claimed that she had seen Bubuni riding a wave, did not believe Zayer Gholam, who had grown old in his madness of ill repute, a madness that began with Mansur's taking refuge to the house of the women of all the men in the world and the opium dens of the city, and reached its zenith with the elopement of Nabati and Sergeant Sinayi.

Before he went mad, in the middle of the night one night, Zayer Gholam gave shelter in his house to eleven young men who wanted to cross the border at night. On the final night of their stay, the young men told him about what went on in distant cities and about a cleric who had been exiled by the government.

On the appointed night, Neju, the captain of Mansur's boat, came in a small boat up to the dam and took the young men in five groups of two each time. When he came back the sixth time to take the one remaining man, when the man asked for the password that he had arranged with the tenth man and saw that Neju kept silent, he figured out that Neju did not know it. He then fled through the window and disappeared in the dark.

All night long, as the passengers were going to meet their deaths, Zayer Gholam had heard the sound of distant fighting from the sea and had reassured the young man on whose face suspicion had nested. After that night, he fell into a strange silence in order to prevent Zayer Ahmad from seeing the shame in his eyes, and under the pretext of having an aching leg, did not leave his house.

It was too late once Mansur found out that Neju was an agent of Colonel Senobari. Chewing on his mustache and with a smile on his lips, Colonel Senobari pointed his revolver at Mansur's sweaty temple:

"Shut your mouth!"

Tired and as though he had been swimming against a strange wave and not reaching anywhere for years and years, Mansur climbed down the stairs of a department that had no sign over its door; and it was right there that his regret at not having paid attention to Zayer Ahmad's suspicions gripped his throat so tightly that he went straight to Tavakkoli's booze shop, and from there to the small dark houses of the city in which the women of all the men in the world lived, as they danced to various tunes, placed tea glasses full of booze on their foreheads, and without spilling a drop, bent backward at their waists.

All the riches that Mansur had amassed and possessed were cast to the wind within less than a few months at the hands of Taji, a woman whose scent intoxicated the men in the world; and Mansur stayed there and was lost, to the extent that when Captain Ali lifted him up, drunk and wasted, from the top of Taji's legs and told him that Nabati had eloped with Sergeant Sinayi, he did not even blink. It was on the same day that in Jofreh, Zayer Gholam, embarrassed in the presence of Zayer Ahmad, who was weeping like an abandoned child, lost his wits, ran toward the guard station, and began what he would never forget, to the end of his life.

The soldiers in the guard station had already become accustomed to seeing an old man who would take off his loincloth, wiggle his hips, and wave his member toward the guard station. No one could restore Zayer Gholam's wits, not even Dr. Adeli, who would sit, stunned with his finger in his mouth, next to Madineh, whose screaming deafened the ears of the village.

Madineh's legs, as though separating from her body and running toward the sea, would not stay with her body. A strange, painful waiting nested in her eyes. At times bewildered and pleading, she would grab Dr. Adeli's hand, and show him a small wave that was coming toward the shore. Dr. Adeli would search in all the magazines that he received from abroad and could not find any sign of the ailment with which the wife of Zaher Ahmad Hakim was afflicted.

With injections that he said were the newest and strongest scientific treatment in the world, Dr. Adeli would make Madineh fall into the sleep of a hare. With half-open eyes, Zayer Ahmad Hakim's wife would sleep facing the window, tears pouring out of the corners of her eyes. She seemed to be afraid that if she fell asleep, she might miss something. Despite all this, she would not scream, and the village could focus its attention on Captain Ali, who had come to Jofreh with a woman named Zari, who washed her hands night and day with soap and made Captain Ali brush the teeth he did not have.

Four months after Bubuni left with the sea waves, Ms. Zari, who wore high heel sandals, came to Jofreh. Captain Ali hired several workers to repair Bubuni's house and build an additional room in the corner of its courtyard in which Zari could place her sewing machine and give sewing lessons to anyone who wanted to learn.

The women of the village, those who were from Jofreh in the old times, out of respect for a woman who had left with the waves of the sea, never went to see Zari. They killed the temptation in their hearts of seeing the sewing machine that could make clothes for the entire village in one day, and in the hot middays of the village, when they stuffed themselves into their houses away from the heat of the sun, they covered their ears, not to hear that strange sound. But the homeless girls, those who had become homeless because of the oil and had settled in this and that corner of Jofreh waiting for the oil wells to run out, came to Ms. Zari to, on her instructions, take off their petticoats and put on clothes that required less fabric and were befitting of proper people.

Zayer Ahmad Hakim, who could not stand to look at Captain Ali, clenched his teeth and did not say a word, lest he would drive away one of the men of the old times. The mind and conscience of Zayer Gholam, however, had been erased from this-worldly calculations and bookkeeping, and the presence of any stranger reminded him of his plundered life.

Ms. Zari—who had forced Captain Ali to always close both double doors and had asked others to knock—one hot afternoon in the summer, fainted when Zayer Gholam climbed the wall and in the courtyard, before the eyes of the homeless girls, shook his member.

The recurrent image of Zayer Gholam climbing the house walls and jumping down stark naked, the whispering of the women of the village who pointed at her from a distance, and the men of the village avoiding Captain Ali, even whose accent had changed, made Ms. Zari flee Jofreh along with Captain Ali at night, and never return to the village.

The world was filled with sorrow, and speed and noise had opened their mouths like a Busalmeh and were swallowing the village.

With sunken cheeks and sad amber eyes, Zayer Ahmad would sit on the top of the water cistern all alone, thinking about the lost world, about Zayer Gholam who wandered around the village disheveled and mad, about Mansur who was lost in small dark houses and whom Zayer Ahmad was never able to find, about Mahjamal who had become a wanderer of mountains and deserts, and about Madineh with her half-open eyes who slept facing the sea and from the corners of whose eyes tears drifted down.

Zayer Ahmad Hakim was so concerned about the village and its sorrows that he never noticed that Azar had bought Ms. Zari's sewing machine, that Maryam's and Hamayel's and Shamayel's clothes had changed, and why Kheyju did not wear petticoats and was beating Bahador, who was bending over a geographic map.

Bahador, who had ripped his heart away from the empty gray sea, dreaming about traveling to faraway lands that were full of mermaids, would bend over the map that Azar had bought for him and put check marks on the coastal places.

Shamayel was worried about her deer, which was wasting away from the smell of the oil and looked at the world with the eyes of someone who was seeing something for the last time. Shamayel would tell her heartfelt sorrows to Tara, tell Tara about the beating she received from Kheyju and her shouting at her. No one knew where Kheyju had found so much soap with which she constantly washed Shamayel's hands and asked her not to hang around an animal that might have all sorts of diseases. Hamayel had worn out Azar's ears, and now she already knew that only women could give birth to children, that a woman would marry someone, have her belly swell up, and then deliver a baby to the "society," and for that matter, a backward society. In any case, it would not make any difference whether a person would get pregnant with a baby from the sea or from someone she married. Having children was not the right thing to do; it would be a catastrophe. If one were abroad, at least something could be done. There, children have a future, but here...

If a person was a boy, he did not have to worry about anything. Hamayel played with boys. She wore the boys' clothes that Azar sewed for her, and despite all her contentment about becoming a man, she would not go to the sea.

Kheyju could not figure Hamayel out. She would frequently pull down her pants to make sure that she was just a little girl, and from her mother's neuroticism, Hamayel took refuge to Setareh, who, before she spontaneously burst into flames in the courtyard of Zayer Ahmad, would give the news about Mahjamal to Kheyju.

The last news that Setareh gave to Kheyju was ten days before the strange sad news that put Zayer Ahmad in bed. Colonel Senobari had gone with helicopters and all sorts of equipment to the regions where Mahjamal was fighting. Colonel Senobari was forcing Mahjamal toward an impasse, step by step.

It was precisely three days later that Madineh became such a cause of concern for Zayer Ahmad that he could not think, even for one moment, about what Kheyju said and her worries about aquatic Mahjamal.

No injection could calm Madineh down. The strange convulsions of Madineh's scrawny painful legs increased so much that Zayer Ahmad asked Bahador and Maryam to stay beside her night and day, and hold her legs to prevent her from fleeing toward the sea.

"I can't figure it out, Zayer."

Exhausted, Dr. Adeli rubbed his high forehead and told Zayer Ahmad that a stronger sedative would make Madineh's heart stop.

❖ 55 ❖

Madineh was not herself, and Zayer Ahmad did not want to cause further confusion in the mind of the doctor, a kind exiled colonel who occasionally thumbed through foreign magazines in front of him and told him about the advancements in the world, and who was teaching Kheyju how to read and write.

Madineh was not herself. Even that which went by the name of Madineh with her painful legs sitting before him was not real. It was the aquatic shadow of Madineh, and her long white hair had the salty scent of the sea.

Had Zayer Ahmad married the shadow of a mermaid? Was that sad salty scent of the sea that always wafted in his bed at the time when Madineh was young, slipped into his arms, and wrapped her arms around his neck, as though fleeing from something, was that scent that of the sea, or the scent that the shadow of a mermaid that she carried with her? How long could the shadow of a mermaid remain on the land away from its source? Zayer Ahmad's mental squabbles did not get anywhere, until midnight on one of those strange nights of Jofreh, when Bahador, who was sleeping next to Madineh, heard a voice, a familiar kind voice that awakened him. He sat up facing the sea, which was lit up by the full moon, and looked. It was the mermaid, the same one with whom he had sat in Zayer

Ahmad Hakim's Pothole many days combing her hair. The mermaid was moaning and moving toward the land. Bahador was looking silently, and he saw Madineh, his grandmother of the land, who had risen on her two elbows and was gliding toward the window.

When the mermaid came out of the sea, glided on the ground, and reached the window, Madineh placed her hand on Bahador's mouth and spoke in the language of mermaids to his aquatic grandmother, whose light had now made everything blue. The aquatic grandmother shook her hands toward the mountains, grabbed Madineh's legs, and pulled them toward herself. With a smile, Madineh nodded, took her legs out of her hands, pointed to the sea with her hand, and drew the shape of a small mermaid in the air. Tired, the blue mermaid said something, nodded her head, and went toward the sea.

When she came back, she was accompanied by the lovesick mermaid. The aquatic grandmother, pointing, showed the mountains to the lovesick mermaid and disappeared in the sea.

Upon seeing the lovesick mermaid, Madineh was revitalized. She passed through the bars of the window, took the mermaid's hand, and suddenly there was the sound of the storm and the waves. The sea waves rolled over Madineh and the mermaid, and Bahador heard his grandmother moaning.

The next morning at dawn, Zayer Ahmad found Madineh next to the window outside the house. She did not have legs, and her fish-like half sparkled. Maryam was standing beside her, crying. Before she completely lost her speech, in a language of that of mermaids and that of humans, Madineh asked Zayer Ahmad to release her in the depths of the green waters. Zayer Ahmad, who did not understand every other word that flew out of Madineh's mouth, spent all day trying to convince her to be buried in the village graveyard. But Madineh, about whom Zayer Ahmad did not know even to the end whether she was a denizen of the land or a shadow of the denizens of the sea, was not convinced. In the late afternoon, while Azar was befuddled and bewildered and Maryam was screaming, Zayer Ahmad placed Madineh, who no longer spoke, on a boat, took her to the end of the sea, and released her to the depths of the green waters, so that, as Maryam said, she would go there, become the grandmother of the fish, and tell them stories from the land.

Zayer Ahmad, who now knew why Madineh in the course of all those years braided her white hair toward the sea and why her leg pain was so bad that she could not endure it any longer, in mourning and regretting all his preoccupations, and repulsed by the sound of the horns of the oil tankers that impeded hearing the voices of the blue mermaids, remembered that old story about the blue mermaids: sometimes when they miss a fisherman who is far away from the sea, they grab the legs of the women denizens of the land or the legs of the shadows of the denizens of the sea, and wander in the deserts in order to warn him about the great deception that is imminent. Bent over under the burden of events, Zayer Ahmad would look at the gray sea and sigh, missing Mahjamal, who had one day risen from the sea.

Ten days later, at high noon, Setareh, who was calming down a restless Shamayel in the courtyard of Zayer Ahmad's house, heard the neighing of a horse and suddenly burst into flames, and in order not to contaminate others with that strange fire, she ran.

No one could stop a woman who had opened her arms like a seagull and was running. Pressing her lips together from pain, she ran, and sparks of fire fell from her body so much that finally, in the form of a seagull on fire, she flew toward the offing of the sea, and Zayer Ahmad and the tired people of the village saw with their own eyes that seagull on fire descend at the offing and disappear in the waves, precisely where Madineh had gone to the depths of the green waters. In her last glance at the land, the seagull on fire could see the soldiers of Colonel Senobari on the walls of the Old Castle firing a barrage of bullets at aquatic Mahjamal.

❖ 56 ❖

The fact was that the lovesick mermaid, who had made herself a wanderer of the deserts to warn Mahjamal about the great deception, was never able to see him again.

Repulsed by the actions he had been forced to commit, Mahjamal would flee. Those who walk on the land are mortal, but why had he fired those finishing shots? Why should aquatic Mahjamal become the fated destiny of those who, out of misfortune and need, would consent to be in pursuit of him? Humans on the land are the warp and weft of one another, and no one can ever be of the land and live in seclusion and not become involved in the sphere of the destiny of another. You become entangled without even knowing it. Your hands become stained with the blood of humans that you could have loved. What did those hungry and thirsty rural offspring with blistered lips want of him and his reputation? Power, or the achieving of that which is the right of humans? And what are humans searching for? What is Colonel Senobari after? Who knows the truth?

The truth perhaps was the forlorn song of the man from Tangestan that Mahjamal heard one day when he was on his way to Melgado to rest in the Old Castle for a moment.

He was worn out. His riflemen were already each a Mahjamal,

and they were busy with fight and flight. Mahjamal had eaten some mountain plants for food, and now he was hiking the rocky paths of the mountain in his bare feet to reach the Old Castle in Melgado. He had been living in the mountains and on the slopes for a long time. He had saved his last bullets for himself, so that no one could put his body and soul on display.

As the last rifleman was leaving, he had shouted at him, and he had wept like a child. Mahjamal was in need of human presence; he did not want to remain alone.

"We can live right here."

"Live, on mountains and slopes?"

"If one is going to live, any place is a place for living."

But, not every place was a place for living. Relieved and forlorn, Mahjamal was coming down the mountain, going to Melgado, the people of which had shut the gates of the Old Castle to the world, and only with the intention of going on pilgrimage, he would go to a blue lake from the depths of the waters of which the voice of a man whose hands and feet were in chains could be heard, a lake that had suddenly risen from the land.

He reached the slope of the mountain, exhausted. It was late afternoon, when wayfarers need to hurry. He turned right onto a rocky path. A strange scent wafted in the air, the salty scent of the sea when a fisherman in a small boat is alone on the other side of the offing. And he was alone, and had let loose his fishing line to the bottom of the waters of the sea, hoping a tiger-tooth croaker fish would bite his hook. But woe if a tiger-tooth croaker fish were to nibble twice within a short period of time and spiral-shaped lightning would flash in the sky. Then, if you are not absentminded and know that a storm is on the way and the drunken camel on the horizon will soon unload its heavy load of rain on the head of the fisherman...

He was alone in his small boat, and the tiger-tooth croaker fish had nibbled twice, and the lightning was flashing in the sky, and everything was moving away in a thick fog...

I am worried and anxious on a road faraway
That before me is a road even farther away.

On the ground, Mahjamal stood in the middle of the rocky road, when he heard the sorrowful voice of a man. The voice was familiar. He hastened in the direction of the voice and recognized Khadar, the driver from Tangestan. He had spread a blanket next to his truck, and with his back leaning against a rock, he was singing. He had seen the man earlier on in the Old Castle, a man who before reaching Melgado would distribute what he had on his truck along the road among the villagers. A good name is worthy of the human soul, and this man from Tangestan, with a smile on his lips and hands ready to do everything he could, had made a place for himself in the hearts of the men of Melgado. He liked his voice and his happy laughter, and the book of poetry he had in his heart. At night, whenever he arrived in Melgado, he sang beside the campfire.

But why is this voice, which is surrounded by the silence of the mountains, so sad? If a human being has no sorrow in his soul, how could he sing so sadly?

On the road, I am left behind by this caravan
I am most lost and confused by all I have done.

He had a lump in his throat, Mahjamal. The man from Tangestan was singing the song of his heart, the song of the sorrows of a man who had risen from the sea and remained distanced from that which he held dear at one time.

The man from Tangestan, who had gotten up and seen him, was laughing, probably to bring happiness to Mahjamal's heart.

"Hey, Mahjamal!"

Mahjamal wrapped his arms around his neck to smell the human scent.

"I was going to Melgado. I thought I'd take a short nap on the way."

Sunset had arrived, and Mahjamal was sitting beside the man from Tangestan who, driving on the unpaved road with difficulty, drove slowly on the turns of the mountain passes, and along the way would ask questions, so that he would have more memories of the outlaw rebel Mahjamal in his mind.

"They have blown up the gas pipelines."

A meaningful smile on the lips of the man from Tangestan, and Mahjamal's wounded heart:

"Sing that same poem, the one you were singing."

The man from Tangestan looked at him in disbelief. He turned the steering wheel, pressed his lips together, and looked at the horizon, whose tresses were bloody. He had long wished to see Mahjamal alone, and tell him what he knew. But now...

Did that mean that Mahjamal did not want to hear what was happening on the plains? Did that mean that he did not want to know where Colonel Senobari was, what he was doing, and in which direction he had pointed the barrel of his gun? And what about if he would tell him about Jofreh, about Zayer Ahmad, about what has happened to his village, and about Madineh?

"The village is not the village it used to be."

Mahjamal sighed. He did not wish to hear anything, from anyone or anywhere. The past was passed, and the village was a distant story of which he did not want to hear anything.

"Sing...the same one you were singing."

Once again, from the corner of his eye, Khadar looked at Mahjamal, who looked like anyone else in the world but that which people had heard about him: disheveled, with a distraught face, furrows in his brow, and sorrowful lips pressed together.

Khadar sang all the way to Melgado. At midnight, when the guards opened the gate of the Old Castle to both of them, he had concluded that in the course of his life, Mahjamal had never pulled a trigger.

One week later, the guards saw his truck, which had stopped by the walls of the castle in the dark of the night. Mahjamal, who kept an eye on the outside through a small window, looked at the truck, which had a tarp over its load, smiling. Where have you gone, man from Tangestan?

At midnight, at the time of the changing of the guards, a guard who had sold out to Colonel Senobari made a strange owl sound, informing the soldiers who were waiting in ambush under the tarp cover, and Colonel Senobari, who was dressed in the clothing of the people from Tangestan, quietly entered the castle, and the soldiers sat in ambush on the walls of the castle.

At cockcrow, Mahjamal, who had been dreaming about the sea all night, was awakened. He was on the sea. A whirlwind had picked him up from under the silk tassel acacia tree and was moving on the sea toward the offing. Floating mermaids were whirling around the whirlwind, and his aquatic mother was coming toward him with bouquets of sea flowers.

Mahjamal opened and closed his eyes in the semidarkness of the room. A cock crowed far away, and he was on the land, in the Old Castle, on the soil of Tangestan. He smiled. He got up to feel the breeze and came into the courtyard of the castle. A cool breeze was making ripples on the reflecting pool in the middle of the castle courtyard. He sat at the edge of the pool. Remembering the waves of the sea, he cupped his hand, put it under the water, and hearing a sound, he looked at the wall of the castle.

It was a cock crowing. Apparently, it had wounded him. He pressed his hand to his side. Would anyone become wounded with the singing of a bird? Blood was jetting out between his fingers. The cock crowed twice more. He fell on his side. Oh, life was denying him... But what a morning, what a silvery and blue day it was. His heart yearned to see the world as long as he could. He kept his eyes open with difficulty, and saw them on the walls of the castle. The last image of the land! Men with covered faces were aiming at him, as though they had no fear of dropping him to the ground... Alive, do they want him alive? Blood... Red shawl of blood on his shoulder...

An effort to get up... His ears were shut to the tumult of the world. He could no longer hear the sound of triggers. For an instant, Niru, with his black eyes hardened from pain... He looked at him. What did he want to say? The strange games of the world, and... Life that... is full of misunderstanding. He wanted to yell, to shout, I... But what was left to say? He wanted to say that he has never been tainted, ever... But what does tainted mean?

Mahjamal would yield to the song of humans. And who were those who fired the shots? Undoubtedly, many of them have the love of a woman in their hearts, and dreaming about going back to their hearth and home, they play the reed flute at Busalmeh's wedding... The reed flute players at Busalmeh's wedding? Anticipating a large pearl? What delusion! What false delusion! Bullets were making a circle around him, and he writhed in pain within himself. His arms did not function, as they continued firing from the top of the walls of the castle. He wanted to shout, to stand up and shout, but he could not. He struggled to rise. Using his uninjured shoulder, he moved, and before the terrified faces of Colonel Senobari's men, he stood on his knees, and, drenched in blood, yelled:

"There is no pearl!"

He collapsed. Pain was plundering his mind and his consciousness. He wanted to test his mind. He had heard that when death approaches, human memories are plundered.

He was in the village, in the depths of the green waters. How a human being struggles to stand on his knees and shout into the ears of others the truth that he knows. But what was the truth? In the midst of pain, a bitter smile appeared on his lips. Was the truth the song of the man from Tangestan, or the struggle of the drowned to reach...? Reach where? No, the truth was perhaps that the world was at the bottom of the green waters, and humans were the drowned. What an effort he had made to reach from the depths of the green waters to the village, what a struggle to live on the land! And where was he now?

He was soaking wet, with sea water or with blood? The scent of the strange sea flowers hit his nose... The sound of the storm and the waves... He opened his eyes. The sons of Mama Mansur were gesturing for him to come closer, to repair the ship and return to the village.

Death had arrived, and he wished to sing. To sing the song of Khadar, the man from Tangestan.

On the road, I am left behind by this caravan
I am most lost and confused by all I have done.

He could not; he was one of the drowned. A faint smile on his lips:

Human fate is to lose...

Finally, in order to free Mahjamal from the pain and suffering of the land, his aquatic mother diverted a bullet that was aimed at his leg and made it land on his forehead, and Mahjamal, who in his life was enamored by the song of humans, fell to the ground motionless.

57

Of the two guards who had sold out to the colonel, one went mad and the other fled into the mountains and mountain slopes. The people of the Old Castle, mesmerized by the perforated body of Mahjamal and the blue smoke that emitted from where the bullets had pierced, silently let the agents of Colonel Senobari toss his body in the back of the truck of the man from Tangestan, whom they had imprisoned in a guard station in the vicinity of Melgado.

Whether from Mahjamal's presence or the pain of which he suffered in his soul in the final moments of his life, the Old Castle became all green. The phantom of a wounded man remained in the castle. And the crystal green color of the stones of the castle made the people of Melgado so fretful that they packed up their belongings and took refuge in the mountains, in order to be free from the strange song that Mahjamal wanted to sing in the final moments of his life: an incomprehensible song about the love of life, in which pain and suffering ricocheted. And whatever heart it landed on, it made the person weep for the land and its joys and pleasures.

Years and years later, however, the camel drivers and their offspring who passed through Dashti and Tangestan, when they reached the Old Castle, could hear the white horse neighing toward the gate of the castle in expectation of a rider, and they saw a woman reddened from anger and pain who had lost her way on the land and, bewildered, circled around the castle. That mermaid who had been distanced from the sea is the same woman whom sometimes the newly arrived travelers to Dashtestan consider to be the land fairy of the poet Fayez, the same fairy who made Fayez a wanderer of the plains.

That fairy, whose heart was scarred by sorrow, was fated to moan in bewilderment in the deserts forever and to lament the loss of a fisherman who was of a mermaid-human race and who should have lived on God's land for three hundred years, and then turned into a wave of the sea.

Had the bullets of Colonel Senobari, who became a brigadier-general afterwards, changed the natural law of the mermaids? Had Mahjamal died?

58

The village was occupied by men who had come to find the corpse of Mahjamal, which had apparently disappeared just before the village of Shumbeh, a corpse that turned so blue when the bullets of Colonel Senobari emptied it of its human life that, terrified, Colonel Senobari had closed his eyes, and one of the guards of the Old Castle had fled.

Those left in the village, abstaining from speech, ignored their presence. The people of the village went about their daily lives, and even if they came face-to-face with the agents, they would not step aside. They would walk straight forward until that stranger with a rifle on his shoulder moved aside. Even with the constant shots fired into the air, they would not divert their eyes; and thus, silently, they came to Zayer Ahmad's house; and since there was no sign of Mahjamal on the land, they sat facing the sea for seven days. They saw the fish of the sea coming to the shore, throwing themselves on the sand, and then mourning and sorrowfully returning to the sea. Dumbfounded by this chaotic world, Zayer Ahmad, who had become bedridden, remembering distant and recent memories in his loneliness, would burst into tears, and to avoid being questioned by his grandchildren, who looked angrily at the uninvited guests in boots, he concealed his sorrow from them.

Zayer Ahmad would remember the days when in the port city he went from this to that government department, and those distant days, which were so far away from his memory that they seemed to have occurred on the other side of time, the days of Busalmeh and the shaking of the land in the world, the days of mermaids and the drowned. Zayer Ahmad held the memory of the days of the mermaids and the wrath of Busalmeh dear, and yearning for the return of the world to those days, he would sigh.

But time steers on a linear course and never revolves around itself like the earth, the pictures of which Bahador would show him. The earth was round and it revolved around both itself and the sun.

Zayer Ahmad was stupefied by this strange world, and he did not know what to believe. The world seemed to step forward in long strides; but what was being crushed under those steps? If, as Dr. Adeli said, the world was making advancements, then why would the mermaids be too afraid to come to the surface of the water? Why was the world chaotic?

"Time never returns to the past."

This was the last thing that Dr. Adeli said to Zayer Ahmad on one of those occasions when he was not cautious and came to occupied Jofreh. The exiled colonel, who would give his foreign magazines to Maryam and Bahador and would sit for hours beside Zayer Ahmad and speak about the advancements in the world, during the same days was summoned to the capital city with a letter, and Zayer Ahmad never saw him again, and the office of his practice was left empty for a long time.

After forty days and nights of the occupation of the village of Jofreh, Brigadier-General Senobari called his men back to the city and swore on the epaulet of His Majesty that he would take his heart's revenge on the disobedient people, who did not know anything, and would destroy and annihilate that village.

The village became quiet, and there remained Kheyju and Zayer Ahmad, whom the exhaustion of years and years had suddenly aged and whose heart was so tender that every time that Kheyju shouted at the children, his eyes filled with tears.

Death, even if it is the chaotic death of Mahjamal, does not kill the habit of life in the human heart. Azar would make arrangements to register the children in the city. Zayer Ahmad's medical practice office in the city, which had been left empty for a long time, was swept and cleaned by the women of the village in order for the children to gather in it at noon, have bread and halva made of sesame seed date juice for lunch, and return to school. Every day, one of the women of the village would accompany the children, stand by the road, and get into a pickup truck that brought the workers; and at sunset, when the same truck went to pick up the workers, the children would return to the village.

Winter passed with difficulty. In the midst of the rain and storms that had suddenly come and made the ground muddy, the children were sometimes forced to stay in the city for several days. Kheyju's comings and goings to the city did not get anywhere, and the director of education did not allow Bubuni's house, which was left vacant, to be made into a high school. Missing the exiled colonel, Kheyju pleaded with Dr. Najafi, who had just come to the port city and who knew Dr. Adeli well; but he was not like the exiled colonel. He had come to these areas only to treat patients, and he did not want to become involved in affairs that were no business of a military colonel.

Zayer Ahmad could not do anything; but before the day came when Zayer Ahmad would leave this chaotic world, he was forced to go to the city several times. Bahador had told him that two of the girls of the village were not going to school; they played in the alleyways by themselves, and when they heard the school bell, they would go to the office of his medical practice. On that day, Zayer Ahmad gathered up all his energy, went to the city, and on the route of the children who went to school, he stood in ambush, when he saw Chiru and Peykar, who turned and entered an alleyway. Zayer Ahmad, who had never even annoyed a female, caught both of them, took them to the office, and right there, suspended them inside a water cistern in the courtyard of the office and held them there until both became unconscious.

Years and years later, when Chiru, who had become a high school teacher in Shiraz, told stories to her daughters, she would mention a man by the name of Zayer Ahmad Hakim, who, despite the fact that he could not read and write, had such respect for education and books that he was prepared to hang everyone in a water cistern to make sure that they would never shirk their lessons and homework.

* * *

Electricity had reached the vicinity of the village, but the children of Jofreh had to do their homework under the light of lanterns in the evening. Azar—who in her daydreaming would bring electricity to Jofreh, tear down the houses, and in their place build multi-story apartments—went to the City Hall and Electricity Department many times, but to no avail. Some mysterious hand would not allow electricity to come to Jofreh. Zayer Ahmad, however, astonished by human ability, would listen to Maryam, who talked about a man who had been able to bring Busalmeh of darkness to his knees, and Zayer Ahmad would recall Mahjamal, who had at one time defeated Busalmeh of the seas. Perhaps Mahjamal and the man who had lit up the nights of the world were one and the same. Who knows? Sometimes a human being comes to the land somewhere and at a particular time, and his guardian comes somewhere else and at a different time, in order to make the world happy. Tears would well up in Zayer Ahmad's eyes when he saw the lamps at the side of the asphalted roads. He would stare at the light of those lamps until late at night and thank the sky and the sea.

Despite all this, Maryam had to read Khatun's letters to her and write the answers under the light of a lantern. In one of her despondent days, Khatun sat beside Maryam by the sea and talked about a worker who was from Tabriz and worked for the Oil Company nearby. Mesmerized by Khatun's story, Maryam listened to her, and told her whatever she could think of and began reading and writing the letters. Later on, however, Khatun lost her wits, and waiting for letters from Tabriz, she would run after pieces of paper brought by the wind; and she would not even recognize Maryam, and cursed herself. If Maryam had not made up the contents of the letters of the worker from Tabriz that she read for her, and had told her that he had a wife and he had to go to Tabriz where his children were waiting for him, and she had instead not told Khatun about the burning love, emotions, and promises of a wedding rather than what he actually said, then Khatun would be able to recognize her and she would not have lost her wits. But during those days, Khatun was already old. Time had passed. And from the way Maryam's grandfather, Zayer Ahmad, in the final days of his life sighed because time did not revolve around itself like the earth but went straight forward, Maryam knew that time was more stubborn than her mother, Kheyju, that it would never return, and that that lonely, madness-afflicted woman in Jofreh would never become young and sane again.

Dr. Najafi, who had settled in Dr. Adeli's former practice, eventually, by sending three or four patients to Zayer Ahmad, took the first step toward establishing a friendship between them. Zayer Ahmad, who had a shooting pain in his heart during those days and whose long white fingers trembled, sent a message to the doctor:

"I am finished, Doctor."

In early spring, Dr. Najafi arrived in the village carrying a small briefcase. He sat beside Zayer Ahmad's bed and examined him. "It was a mild heart attack," the doctor said. The medicine that the doctor prescribed was "rest and quiet." Dr. Najafi, who had been a classmate of Dr. Adeli and who came to see Zayer Ahmad two or three times a week, in order not to cause him any anxiety, never told him what had happened to that exiled colonel of the military, Dr. Adeli, and about how the military prosecutor had once again examined his file and summoned Dr. Adeli to the capital city to have him put in jail. Before he was summoned to the capital city, Dr. Adeli had written a number of letters to Dr. Najafi about Zayer Ahmad and the people of Jofreh. Nevertheless, when Dr. Najafi sat and listened to Zayer Ahmad, he was stunned by his strange, simple world. In his letters, the exiled colonel had not been able to accurately describe the mentality and outlook of Zayer Ahmad. Amazed by Zayer's curious and lively mind, Dr. Najafi would inform him of the scientific news of the world and witness his eyes lighting up from excitement regarding human abilities.

The last report of the doctor to Zayer Ahmad was about a man who had been able to replace a defective heart with a healthy one. Smiling, Dr. Najafi had called it a heart transplant. The doctor showed a picture of that professor to Zayer Ahmad and the people of the village. With astonishment, Zayer Ahmad touched the photograph. Next to Mahjamal, he was the most handsome man Zayer Ahmad had seen in his life.

Kheyju took the photograph of that professor and stuck it on the wall of the room with five sashed windows, so that every day under some pretext she could show it to the children: he was a man who regularly washed himself in the water of the sea and, unlike Hamayel who runs away from water and smells like muck, all his attention was focused on the world; unlike Shamayel whose heart was not tied to anyone or any place other than a deer whose ribs were sticking out, he would listen to his mother; unlike Bahador, he would not paint so much, and for that matter, painting a woman with blue eyes and no legs; and unlike Maryam, who never helps her mother and instead constantly writes poems in her notebook and reads poems.

Becoming a professor was not a simple thing, and Hamayel, who would get dizzy from all that her mother said, once and for all took the photograph off the wall, held it in her hand, and sat in front of a goat that had grown thin waiting for grass. With its tiny teeth and lips pressed together, the goat ate the photograph and set everyone's mind at ease.

Dr. Najafi came back once again. Zayer Ahmad did not feel well. The doctor gave him no news about the scientific world and listened to the complaints of Zayer Ahmad, who thought the village was hiding something from him.

For two weeks now, without letting their men interfere in their work, the women of the village every day were destroying the guardrails that were placed around a vast area on the other side of the Shrine of Sire Ashk. The guardrails were replaced again at night by workers who were putting a fence around the land, and the women did not know on whose order they were doing so.

Two weeks earlier, Khatun's mother had gone to the Shrine of Sire Ashk to light the lantern, and during the night, she had seen the workers installing guardrails around the land next to the sea. She had been frightened, and thinking they were the jinn of the land who come every sunset by the sea to wash themselves, she had invoked the name of God, but they had not disappeared. That night, Khatun's mother came to Zayer Ahmad's house to tell him about it; but Kheyju had not allowed anything about the calamity that was about to befall the village to reach Zayer Ahmad's ears.

Azar was explaining to the people of the village what the word *plage* meant. Having sewn bathing suits for all the children during the night, Azar took out her two-piece bathing suit from the suitcase that she had packed many years earlier for traveling abroad. She sighed, showed it to the women of the village, and told them that a *plage* was for proper people to lie down on its sand after swimming in the sea to get their bodies *bronze*, and in order to convince the women of the village that a *plage* was a good thing and that all the advanced people in the world were *bronze*, she resorted to describing what she meant in a thousand ways, until finally, tired and helpless, she pointed to their sun-burned faces and showed them what she meant by *bronze*.

How half-witted does one have to be to lie down stark naked on the sand next to the sea for hours and burn the skin of her body and face? The pictures that Azar took out from the bottom of her suitcase and showed to the women of the village made it worse. The efforts of the teacher of the village, who was talking about all sorts of *plage*s in the world until cockcrow, did not get anywhere, and they took an oath together that as long as their bodies were alive on the land of Jofreh, they would not allow such a place to be built.

Hopeless and helpless, Azar placed her things in her suitcase and told Kheyju that the village of Jofreh would never prosper, and that she herself would not waste her life more than she already had to tell anyone about the advancements of the world.

Eventually, Hamayel, who was afraid that all the women who go to the *plage* would get pregnant from the water of the sea, told Zayer Ahmad about the imminent disgrace. With his ailing body, at nighttime, Zayer Ahmad went to the Shrine of Sire Ashk and saw the guardrails with his own eyes.

"This stuff has to be removed!"

After three weeks, during which whatever the workers built was destroyed, hopeless and defeated, they stopped working and set out for the city with their shovels and pickaxes. In the midst of Azar's yelling and her pouting and shouting, the people of the village went back to the village, and no matter how Kheyju tried to make Azar understand that everything that the government had had a hand in had resulted in destruction, she would not listen. The women of the village had to listen to Azar's complaints for a long time, as she was digging into the stories of the village to learn the reason for its people's backwardness: the death of Golpar, the fleeing of Ms. Zari who had brought a sewing machine, the loss of the *plage*, and ignoring the soldiers who had occupied Zayer Ahmad's house and the village during the disappearance of Mahjamal, soldiers who had only come to do their military duty, some of whom were so tall and blond that one would think they were foreigners.

In her complaints, Azar would say that soon, whether from the land or the sea, she would leave not only Jofreh but also the country and go abroad, and from there, she would take as many pictures with bathing suits as the number of ignorant people in the country and send them to men and women to make them understand the meaning of living. Azar talked and talked so much that no one any longer listened to her, except for Hamayel and Shamayel, who were always in her room, because Azar was the only person in the world who believed in freedom and would even allow the deer, like the children, to sit on the straw mat or stick its snout into a cup of milk. With her blue eyes, Hamayel would sit across from Azar and stealthily giggle at her anger and anguish. Azar, who could see the wave of laughter in her eyes, could never figure out what the little girl was scheming. Hamayel's mind was at peace; the *plage* would never be built and no woman's reputation would be ruined.

To the same extent that Azar could not understand the strange world of Hamayel and was confused when she looked into her big laughing eyes, she was comfortable with Shamayel, with the way the little girl petted the deer on its head and face, with her heart that was bothered by nothing but the moaning of the deer, and with the world in which the deer and Shamayel alone existed. Shamayel sat beside Tara quietly and, free of all the problems in the world, listened to Azar. She liked freedom, the same thing that made Azar pay attention to Tara as though it were a human child. For Shamayel, nothing was better than freedom. Freedom made Tara endeared in the eyes of others.

"When there is freedom, all are equal, deer, lions, men, and women."

The world, however, had no intention of calming down. The hand of the company that had driven the people from the upper villages, people who picked up all their possessions and spent their nights and days in their huts around Jofreh waiting impatiently for the oil in the wells to run out, reached Jofreh as well. A week prior to the people being awakened by the noise of cranes, bulldozers, and tractors that had occupied the world, they saw Mahjamal sitting on the dam, his shoulders shaking. Zayer Ahmad, who had never seen Mahjamal cry, stood behind the window bars in disbelief, and together with Bahador, from whose eyes sleep had flown away and the color of whose face during those days had suddenly turned blue, stared at the sea and Mahjamal.

Kheyju, who wanted to convey to the village that what they heard was no more than a delusion, late one night when she came out of the house, quietly walked toward a man whose shoulders were shaking and who was sitting in a halo of blue fog. With the sound of Kheyju's footsteps, he turned his face, and Kheyju saw Mahjamal, whose eyes had become even bluer from sorrow and on whose forehead small and large wrinkles from the bullets had nested. In a world between horror and reality, Kheyju went closer, and to make sure, she placed her hand on the shoulder of Mahjamal, who suddenly, like the mermaids that years and years earlier would disappear in the sea, disappeared.

The truth was as clear as day, like Kheyju's fingertips, which remained blue forever, and the color could not be removed with any chemical, similar to the strange fright of Azar, who would cover her ears at night in frustration so as not to hear the sound of the crying of that fog-engulfed man.

In the morning of the seventh day, the sign that prior to the invasion of tractors on Jofreh had disturbed the sleep and minds of the people of the village suddenly disappeared with the uproar of the road-building machines. Bahador regained his former color, the sound of Mahjamal's weeping vanished, the people were awakened horrified on that same day, and before Zayer Ahmad could figure out what was what, the loaders had leveled the entire area nearly all the way to the graveyard. Had Kheyju and other women with shovels and pickaxes not gone to stop them, no one knows on which truck they would have loaded the bones of the dead and where they would have sent them.

They were leveling the land in order to create green space and build houses, the doors and walls of which had come from abroad, for those who were coming from the other side of the world. The children were not going to cause a disturbance, and the adults, who did not see any good coming from confrontation with the government, for a long time walked around the houses that only had one small door and four wheels, like a car, and their mouths remained open in amazement. Not even Azar had imagined that in the foreign countries people lived in small rooms that had four wheels and could easily move.

Zayer Ahmad was at a loss. Was there a shortage of God's land to the extent that the government would have to turn the lands of Jofreh upside down for those who had come from the other side of the world to, as the deputy to Brigadier-General Senobari had said, modernize?

Bahador accompanied Zayer Ahmad, who could now hardly walk, from this government department to the next. He wrote down what Zayer Ahmad dictated and had the people of the village place their fingerprints on it; and finally, in his last effort, Zayer Ahmad was admitted to the office of Brigadier-General Senobari, where he was told:

"Many of the people of Jofreh are ready to sell their houses."

Zayer Ahmad rushed back to Jofreh, walked all around the village, and found out that the only people who had consented to sell their huts were those who had migrated from other villages. The government was paying good money to those who sold their houses, and many people, tempted by this money, packed up their stuff and ignored Zayer Ahmad, who was urging them not to leave.

The original residents, whose minds were still filled with the memories of the mermaids, remained in the village and did not agree to sell their houses. When Zayer Ahmad objected to the barbed wire that surrounded all the lands around the village, they asked him for his deed. Zayer Ahmad was shocked and astounded, and his astonishment increased when the government people took over the empty houses of Mama Mansur and Captain Ali, and in response to the cries of protest by Zayer Ahmad and the people of the village, they said that the deeds were in the names of those who had either died or had left that place. In his insanity, Zayer Gholam and a few young men, looking for Mansur, left to go to those small dark houses. There, no one knew anyone by the name of Mansur, and Taji, the woman who had pilfered all that Mansur possessed, had died two years earlier and was replaced by Kanizu, a tall thin woman with hazel eyes, who attracted the men of the city and the villages near and far to that place.

Hopeless, Zayer Gholam and the young men from the village went back, and it was around the same time that the workers who had houses near Jofreh left that place, Khatun became mad forever, and Maryam, despite all her efforts and the stories she told her, could not restore her wits.

Wednesday was the day on which Khatun was going around the small empty rooms of the workers in a frenzy. Without worrying about her lost reputation, she wept. Khatun screamed for three days and nights under the blows of the shark tail, but the activities had so speeded up and the world was so filled with all sorts of noises that no one heard the sound of Khatun's screams, no one except Maryam, who was writhing in herself and witnessing that everything was being plundered before her eyes.

Jofreh was rapidly becoming empty; it was returning to the days when no one came to the village from anywhere, and the only problems the people were facing were the wrath of Busalmeh and the crying of the mermaids. The remaining houses and dilapidated huts showed that this time, someone else had taken the village under his dark wrath. The helpless women saw that the talismans had lost their power and their prayers no longer worked. During the same time, when the people of the village would no longer be surprised by any incident, Azar received a sheet of paper and realized that the following year, she was supposed to be teaching in the city. The village did not say anything, as though everyone expected the shutting down of a school the sound of the bell of which at one time had made the world jump up from sleep.

Plundered Zayer Ahmad could see the spark in the eyes of the village losing its brightness. In his loneliness, Zayer Ahmad would recall the days when the blond men in a boat that could go on land and sea came to the village, and he remembered the warning of his first grandchild, who had now grown up to be a tall, broad-shouldered teenager.

How late Zayer Ahmad had understood the meaning of that warning, and how many people he had lost during all that time! Mahjamal, whom no one knew on which corner of the land he came to rest, and Madineh, who when she found out that Colonel Senobari wanted to bring out one of the mermaids from the bottom of the sea and send her to the capital city developed a fever and took out all her talismans to prevent the colonel from achieving his purpose.

Zayer Gholam, having become old, in his insanity, with long hair and a white beard, would cut the barbed wire at night and, with the actions that at one time made Ms. Zari flee, would stand before the government people and open and close the flap of his loincloth, but no one fled from him. Now, even the children of the village laughed at Zayer Gholam and teased him. One day, Kheyju saw the soldiers surrounding Zayer Gholam and laughing hysterically. Zayer Ahmad's sole daughter brought the insanity-stricken old man home, washed his head and face, and made him understand that he should not ruin the reputation of Jofreh, the Jofreh in which Mahjamal had grown up, Mahjamal who was still alive in the stories of the men from Dashti and Tangestan. Upon hearing Mahjamal's name, in his insanity, tears welled up in Zayer Gholam's old eyes, and as if he were the wisest man in the world, he no longer hung around the strangers, that is, until those strange nights when suddenly Jofreh was filled with the jinn who sat on and under the palm trees, the jinn who sat with pressurized kerosene lanterns and played music.

One night, a strange sound resonated in the village, and Zayer Gholam, who as always was in the alleyway, and the young men, who had been sitting on the mound of dirt alongside the village road, came to Zayer Ahmad's house horrified. The women closed the doors and windows, and until morning, they listened to the sound of a jinn that howled like the wind.

For two weeks, no one left Zayer Ahmad's house at night; and, lost and confused, Zayer Ahmad did not know how, despite all the metal and machines, the jinn could come and go in the village. Until late at night, the people would listen to the pitter-patter sound of the feet of the jinn who chased one another in the alleyways, and they trembled in fear. Azar, who was about to give up the ghost, would not even leave the house during the bright daylight. She would sit right there in her room with Hamayel and Shamayel, her lips white from fear, and she prayed that, even if for one day, the jinn would leave the village alone so that she could pack up her belongings, leave this jinn-haunted village, and not even look back.

With her own eyes, Kheyju had seen that the jinn in their strange clothing sat on the palm trees, played music, turned off and turned on the light of the lamps, and sometimes walked around under the palm trees with pressurized kerosene lanterns. Their horrifying laughter reverberated in the village, laughter that could only match that of Busalmeh.

On one of the jinn-haunted nights, in the midst of the fright of others and the endless thinking and imaginings of Zayer Ahmad, Bahador secretly went to the alleyway, came face-to-face with one of the jinn, and the jinn suddenly fled. Bahador, who thought that he had inadvertently invoked God's name, lost and confused, went back to the house and tried to remember if he had invoked the name of God, but he did not get anywhere.

Two nights later, when the jinn climbed the walls of the houses and took what they needed, once again Bahador went to the alleyway with Zayer Gholam and saw one of them coming out of a house with a stack of fishing nets. The jinn did not disappear, even though both of them invoked the name of God a thousand times, and Bahador saw with his own eyes that the jinn took the fishing nets to the house of Mama Mansur, which was the place for the comings and goings of the strangers and which had been confiscated by the government.

No jinn would steal the property of poor people, unless he is a government jinn. The rumor that was spreading in Jofreh more and more, that the village was the residence of the jinn and must be evacuated, lost its hue. No jinn, not even those who know nothing about Mohammad's religion, as long as you do not bother them, would engage in plunder and theft.

One night, the men of the village, with the shark tails that had been hanging on the walls and had remained unused, waited in ambush in the alleyways and attacked the government jinn. It was the day following that night that, fevered and frightened, in the midst of the crying of Hamayel and Shamayel and before the stunned eyes of Maryam, Azar packed up her suitcases and left the village.

When Zayer Ahmad went to the city for the last time and

confronted Brigadier-General Senobari, a deathly cold shot through his body. With a heinous smile on his lips and a choppy voice that uttered the words one or two at a time and looked at those around him and laughed, the general said:

"So, you no longer...believe in the jinn...and the mermaids?"

Zayer Ahmad responded:

"We believe in everything but you."

The general laughed boisterously. It was on the same day that Zayer Ahmad saw Morteza in a bookstore. He had become old and broken; he was selling books. Joyfully, Zayer Ahmad had approached him, but Morteza in response to Zayer Ahmad's smile and words that had the scent of friendship, had pulled back and in an unfamiliar voice had asked:

"How many notebooks would you like, sir?"

Keeping silent, Zayer Ahmad had bought some notebooks for Maryam to write her compositions, which she read to him in the evening. Then, feeling fed up, he left the bookstore.

That night, Zayer Ahmad reached the village exhausted. The smell of oil had made the air of Jofreh heavy. Even the seagulls were flapping their wings sluggishly in the air. But some day, for sure, the oil wells would reach the bottom and Jofreh would be rebuilt. Despondent and tired, Zayer Ahmad went to bed. Worried about a school that had no teacher and children who needed to go to school, soaking wet in sweat, he talked deliriously until morning. His fever went up moment by moment. Dr. Najafi's medicine could not lower the heat that was melting Zayer Ahmad's body.

Zayer Ahmad's large house, in which at one time men and women gathered and talked about mermaids, was filled with the people of the village, people who had stared at the sky at night and were at a loss at the flying of so many stars. In villages near and far, in the villages where they knew Zayer Ahmad, the villagers again and again saw a coffin that was carried on the wings of seagulls. Many men and women, unbeknownst to one another, set out for Jofreh.

They would arrive together at teahouses along the route, and from one another's eyes, they knew that all of them were drawn to the village of Jofreh because of the coffin on the wings of the seagulls.

At sunset on the tenth day, Bahador stood in the courtyard looking at the sky. Seagulls were carrying a coffin toward the horizon. At that very moment, in all the houses of Jofreh, the women and men of Jofreh as well as the children about whose education Zayer Ahmad had been so concerned saw that crystal coffin. Kheyju looked at the sky, bewildered; she saw Zayer Ahmad lying down all stretched out in his long white cloak in that crystal coffin. A moment later, when the seagulls disappeared on the horizon, she rushed anxiously into the room with five sashed windows. In a tired voice, Zayer Ahmad said:

"Help me go to the sea."

In a sea that smelled of tar, Zayer Ahmad performed a full-body ablution and came out with a smile. Until late at night, the people sat around Zayer Ahmad, who was wearing his long white *dishdasha*, and without a sound, he looked at them. He was observing them silently and intently, as though he were seeing them for the first time. His lips were puckered, the wrinkles on his forehead knotted. The movements of the people of the village seemed sluggish to him. Their voices reached his ear with delay, as though they had spoken years earlier, and the words were struggling to reach him from the layers of the green waters. He moved his hand with difficulty. No! He was not on the land, and this weak movement of the hand that can only be slowed down by the strong pressure of the current of water. He was doubtful. He made an effort to rise, and he saw several golden fish swimming around him. A small fish approached him and pecked at the corner of his eye, and he saw starfish, colorful aquatic starfish that expanded and contracted. Where had he heard that old legend? The legend that said that the dead return to the land on Friday eves alone and go to the sea during the course of the week until the time that the village is completely dead, then the water of the sea will be dumped over the village, all the dead will return to their own homes and lives and will live with the thought of their previous lives.

So, had the village died years and years earlier, and was everyone at the depths of the green waters, preoccupied with his own imagination? So, is this Kheyju who is covering him with a bedding wrap and pushing away the children from around her only alive in his imagination? He struggled to call out, "Kheyju..."

But his sole daughter seemed not to hear his voice. The pressure of the water would not let him hear the voice of anyone easily. The voice had to push aside many particles of the waters. The voice needed to struggle to reach someone's ear.

Ding-dong...

But the sound of the school bell was still reverberating in his head, was pushing aside the compressed layers of water to reach him... A thousand signs indicated that he was one of the drowned, and a thousand signs, that he was a denizen of the land.

Ding-dong...

Was it the sound of the school bell, or the death toll? He felt a chill. Kheyju was sitting by his head, and those who were left in the village were sitting all around in the room with five sashed windows.

Ding-dong.

Zayer Ahmad's hand rose slowly, grabbed Kheyju's skirt, and his lips moved:

"Don't forget the children's education."

* * *

In the morning, with the arrival of the people of Dashti and Tangestan, Jofreh began the most crowded day in its life. Zayer Ahmad's coffin was passed overhead, and the people, the people of the village, the men from the city who knew him, and even the soldiers who had been forced to occupy his village at one time, in civilian clothes, saw him off up to the graveyard of the village, and the women of the village entrusted Zayer Ahmad Hakim to the soil with their own hands. Zayer Ahmad Hakim was the man who had held them in respect all his life, and despite the fact that he could not read and write, his pride and good will had made him strive to build the village and make it prosper. In her sorrow and her strange mourning dance, with a green shawl over her shoulders, Kheyju sang in the circle of women. Her voice and the voice of the others who sang the refrains went to the end of the offing of the sea:

"Our commander has departed. The entire army is gone."

Madineh rose up from the sea with her fish-like half and, surrounded by mermaids, she reached the edge of the shore. The women struck themselves on their heads and chests; the children, holding the handles of flagellation chain clusters, arrived at the graveyard in orderly lines; and the sound of the cymbals and drums of the men resonated in the village.

After seven days and nights of mourning, Zayer Ahmad Hakim was placed to rest in the soil.

In the course of the following two years, as the village became empty and only Khatun remained, along with the pieces of paper that she gathered around her, numerous incidents befell Jofreh. The sound of the music and singing that came from the prefabricated houses became louder day by day, to the point that no one could hear the sound of the sea waves any longer. Every morning, the servants of the prefabricated houses passed the barbed wire fences with baskets full of empty bottles, and from the dam, dumped the empty whisky bottles over the dam into the sea, the sea in which Bubuni had disappeared with its waves and Madineh had gone to the mermaids with her fish-like half.

The condition of the sea was strange. Its gray muddy color, the small lazy waves that moved slowly and spread on the sand, the dead fish, large and small, that came from the sea, and the clusters of seaweed smeared with tar that had turned the color of the sand black all were indicative of the surrender of a sea the waves of which at one time had reached the stars. The sea moaned, as if an old rebel who placed his Brno rifle on the ground and was coming down the slope of the mountain slowly and sluggishly. A gray fog was standing still on the sea. And it was unclear whether it was the smoke of the ever-bubbling hookahs of the people of the village or the smoke from the distant smokestacks that moaned day and night and brought sorrow to the people's hearts.

The children no longer played on the shore. Occasionally, if a child was not cautious and felt like going to the sea, he would come back crying with his feet smeared with tar and cut by the shards of glass. Despite all this, the people had stayed in Jofreh to gather every Friday eve at the tomb of Zayer Ahmad and, in the custom of the days of old when they circled around Zayer Ahmad in the room with five sashed windows or on the top of the water cistern, to sit around his grave, smoke hookahs, and chat. On Friday eves, they stayed in the graveyard until late, and if that old legend—which said that on other nights the dead go to the sea and become companions of the drowned, or move around in the depths of the green waters as small and large fish—were to leave their memories, it was quite likely that the people would gather there on all the nights of the week and would give the sorrow of their hearts to the smoke of the hookahs.

Searching for the blue color of the sea and tired of the gray fog, Bahador became sick. He was bedridden for three months, and during all that time, with the paper and pencils that Kheyju brought for him from the city, he would made a sketch of a woman who was blue, her long hair spread on the background of the paper, her eyes a strange blue color, which was reminiscent of Mahjamal's eyes in Kheyju's mind, and with long thin fingers. All these sketches would remain unfinished once they reached the woman's legs. For the woman's legs, Bahador was looking for something, he did not know what; and Kheyju, who was worried about a teenager whose blond mustache had grown, thinking that a young girl somewhere in the city had made Bahador have a crush on her, bombarded her teenager with questions, and when she heard his tedious disjointed answers, she resorted to her talismans. She tied together iron figurines and placed them under fire for forty days and nights in order for the woman who was drawn on the papers to find her legs and come to Bahador. Despite all this, the talismans seemed to have lost their power. Even though Bahador got out of bed, he remained gaunt and scrawny, until one day when they were already living in the city, he came home with a passport that he had obtained, and smiling, he said:

"I will be leaving in four days."

Based on their habits of years earlier, the patients still came. Kheyju would wash their wounds and treat their trachoma with blue lapis lazuli; and this time, the children now gathered around her to hear stories about Mahjamal and Zayer Ahmad: Mahjamal was alive; the bullets had merely wounded him; they had frequently heard the sound of his revolver from the Dizashkan mountain pass; and women still left goatskins full of water, mirrors, and bread along his route. The children, entangled in the nightly stories of the patients, and Kheyju, in the exhausting daily work, would forget one another. Occasionally, a woman in her last month of pregnancy would go into labor and Kheyju would go to her. Sometimes some people, distressed from the smell of oil, would pack up to leave, and Kheyju would remind them of their shared memories and make them change their minds. Registering the children of the village, going from this school to the next, which would not agree to admit the students under the pretext that they lived far away, and begging and pleading, which she had to do despite her wishes in order to ensure that the children would not be left without schooling and make Zayer Ahmad's soul tremble in the grave, had made Kheyju so oblivious to her own home that she noticed too late that Zayer Gholam had collapsed in the corner of the water cistern, and Maryam was putting drops of water into his mouth with an eye dropper. In his strange deliriums, Zayer Gholam talked about the eleven young men who wanted to leave the village one night and cross the border in Mansur's big boat to the other side of the waters.

Maryam, who was constantly putting soaking wet cloths on Zayer Gholam's hands and feet, and while a lump was pressing in her throat, figured out the root cause of Zayer Gholam's insanity. As she lowered her head to hear Zayer Gholam's final words, she was thinking about a man who had been able to escape and disappear in the dark.

One day when from the smell of oil and tar the air became so heavy that the seagulls were falling down from the sky and, flapping their wings on the ground, would die, Zayer Gholam passed away. In the midst of the commotion of the deaths of the seagulls and of Zayer Gholam and of the sheep whose bellies would swell up and burst, no one heard the yelling of Shamayel, who with her small hands was grabbing the bottom of the clothes of this and that person to find a solution about Tara, the deer, whose eyes smelled of death.

There was a sad spark in Tara's eyes, like the final flickering of a lantern. Shamayel's little kisses on the corner of the eye of Tara, who was bewildered by this chaotic world, would not do any good. The cry of pain that resonated in those black eyes and the dumbfounded expression on Tara's face made Shamayel a wanderer to other cities and countries. Finally, at sunset one autumn day, Tara, the deer whose ribs were sticking out from pain and whose legs had become so thin that they could not hold its body, died. As the men of the village were dragging Tara to submerse it in the sea, no one heard the cries of Shamayel, cries in silence that extended from Jofreh to the southern fronts of the war, when times had changed. Not even Maryam heard the cries of Shamayel, Maryam who was fated to read Shamayel's letters from the southern fronts and who had gone to one of the battalions of the south to receive her black chador and a few things she had had.

Shamayel, who, searching for the drowned eyes of Tara, wandered all her life, finally one night when the battalion was preparing for operations, broke her camera, and bewildered about the games of the time, wrote a letter to Maryam, which was no more than a few lines:

"Here is the end of wandering, and everything is as clear as day. Tara's eyes are duplicated in the mirror before me. Maryam, you have no idea of the tumult in my heart."

After Tara's death, dizziness brought the people to their knees. It was as though that mysterious heavy smell that had blanketed the village was merely intended to empty Jofreh. The humans on the other side of the barbed wire were busy building the world. On the top of the rooms, some wires on pitchforks were sticking out in the air, and the children in the village swore that through the cracks of the doors, they had seen people on a black box who played music and danced.

Eventually, the sad gray color of the sea, its lazy lethargic waves, the loss of the seagulls over the Jofreh Sea, the tar that had reached the top of the dam, and that heavy smell forced the people to sell their houses to Brigadier-General Senobari and leave the village. Kheyju was the last person to surrender to the times. She boarded up the doors and windows, and hoping to return to Jofreh someday, she bought a small house in the city.

When the pickup truck that was carrying Mahjamal's family passed the village road, Maryam saw Khatun with a crumbled sheet of paper in her hand, pleading with an imaginary person to read the letter to her. Maryam turned her face away and stared at the corner of the pickup truck. In her sorrowful silence, Shamayel had a lump in her throat, and a sparkle of joy shone in Hamayel's eyes. Bahador was looking at the gray sea, which had been green at one time and from which Mahjamal had once risen.

FIRST BOOK

Jofreh, Bushehr, 1988
Second re-writing: Nevada Desert, August 2012
Starbucks, Henderson, January 2013

MAIN CHARACTERS OF THE VILLAGE OF JOFREH

Bahador: son of Mahjamal and Kheyju
Bubuni: childless wife of Captain Ali
Captain Ali: husband of Bubuni
Golpar: daughter of Setareh
Hamayel: daughter of Mahjamal and Kheyju and twin sister of Shamayel
Kheyju: daughter of Zayer Ahmad and Madineh
Madineh: wife of Zayer Ahmad and mother of Kheyju
Mahjamal: husband of Kheyju
Mama Mansur: mother of Mansur
Mansur: only surviving son of Mama Mansur and husband of Nabati
Maryam: daughter of Mahjamal and Kheyju
Nabati: daughter of Zayer Gholam and wife of Mansur
Setareh: a young widow and the mother of Golpar
Shamayel: daughter of Mahjamal and Kheyju and twin sister of Hamayel
Zayer Ahmad Hakim: husband of Madineh and father of Kheyju
Zayer Gholam: father of Nabati

Made in the USA
Thornton, CO
08/22/22 06:36:44